Also by R.W Peake

Marching with Caesar®- Birth of the 10ᵗʰ

Marching with Caesar-Conquest of Gaul

Marching with Caesar-Civil War

Marching with Caesar-Antony and Cleopatra, Parts I & II

Marching With Caesar-Rise of Augustus

Marching With Caesar-Last Campaign

Marching With Caesar-Rebellion

Caesar Triumphant

D1600950

R.W. Peake

Marching With Caesar®
A New Era

Volume Nine

By R.W. Peake

R.W. Peake

For Sandy

The First Person Who Told Me, "You Should Write A Book"

Foreword

In moving forward with *Marching With Caesar®-A New Era*, I am going back in a sense, returning to the first-person style of account that began with the story of Titus Pullus in *Marching With Caesar®-Conquest of Gaul*. This is part of my long-term plan, to create a "record" of accounts, written by the men who did the actual work of expanding and defending what by this point has become the Roman Empire.

In doing so, I am still working with a paucity of historical record, in this period of time that could be classified as the middle of the reign of Augustus, during what has been named "The Pax Romana". But "peace" is a relative term; there was just less fighting going on than what had been the norm for many years. One thing I tried to keep in mind when I was researching this period, although in this story it spans just one campaign season, was that nasty outbreaks of peace weren't always welcomed by Romans. At least, upper-class Romans intent on climbing the ladder, who needed a war and the rewards it would bring to them. And those who were being groomed for a world where Augustus no longer ruled needed to be seasoned and gain experience in command and all that went with leadership of the most powerful nation in the known world.

Consequently, we have the campaigns of Nero Claudius Drusus, and much like *Marching With Caesar®-Rebellion*, there are not exactly a plethora of original source materials that I could use to provide much detail. Cassius Dio, of course, was the primary source, but I want to say that I found the book *Eager for Glory-The Untold Story of Drusus the Elder, Conqueror of Germania* by Lindsay Powell to be especially helpful.

When I began this story, I viewed Drusus as merely a means to an end, in essence a stopgap character who would help me tell this next part of the MWC saga. However, as I learned more about Drusus the Elder, the more intrigued I became. Next to Germanicus, I find him the most compelling "What If?" figure in Roman history. What would have happened if the more popular, more likeable brother had lived instead of Tiberius? Would he have become embittered and cruel like his brother? Would he allow a Sejanus to institute a rule of terror? Would we have had a Caligula? Or a Nero? Who knows?

What we do know of what would turn out to be Drusus' final campaign was that he was in command of the 14th and 16th Legions; at least that is what is believed at this time. Therefore, my inclusion of the 8th, which was stationed in Pannonia at the time, is of my own invention, and is done only for the purposes of the story. For that I beg the indulgence of the readers.

Another challenge with this story was in creating a new character that reflects someone whose personality is their own, but has been shaped by the giant that was the first Titus Pullus. I want who I call Titus II to be his own man, but at the same time I want the reader to be reminded of Titus II's "Avus", the character who is the foundation of this entire saga. Only you readers will determine whether or not I accomplished that goal.

Although I normally do not care for stories that are more focused on political intrigue, as I delve more deeply into this time period it has become clear to me that one of the unforeseen consequences of the Augustan reforms that allowed men of the equestrian and higher orders to purchase a posting in the Centurionate was putting men into leadership spots that may not have been qualified to command troops in combat. Going farther, I would submit that by allowing posts to essentially go to the highest bidder, Augustus would attract a certain type of man, one who was not above cutting a corner here and there in order to fulfill his ambition. In short, the kind of political maneuvering and backstabbing that was a commonplace occurrence in the Forum of Rome seems to have come to roost in the ranks of the Legions as well. While it is a truth that whenever humans congregate to work towards some common purpose there will always be some form of political intercourse, figuratively and literally, oftentimes it seems that there comes a point where the mission of the organization takes a back seat to the backroom wrangling and maneuvering of individuals who are seeking to improve their own position.

No organization is immune to that, but there is a fine line where the effectiveness of the organization is compromised because the people within lose sight of what the overall mission is, if they ever took ownership of the mission in the first place, and concern themselves with their own personal goals. We see it today, in our elected representatives, in our judicial system, our education system, and it plagued the Legions of Rome as well, proving there much truth in the adage that there is nothing new under the sun.

As always, my thanks goes to my editor Beth Lynne for reining in my impulses for long paragraphs, and to Marina Shipova for producing yet another excellent cover. And, of course, my most heartfelt thanks goes to you readers. I hope you take young Titus into your hearts in the same way you did his Avus, and enjoy following this next generation of the iron men of the Legions as much as I do writing about them!

Semper Fidelis,
R.W. Peake
July 26, 2014

Preface

By these words, you will know me. I am Titus Porcinianus Pullus and, as my father was, and my adoptive grandfather, Titus Pullus of blessed memory as well, I am a man of the Legions of Rome, and this is my story.

Before I begin, I feel it is important to relate the motivation and purpose of my narrative. In doing so, I am continuing a tradition started by Titus Pullus, one of the most famous men from the ranks the Legions of Rome have ever produced. I would even go so far to say that only Dentatus ranks as greatest in the line of iron men, but while my adoptive grandfather never became Consul, even now, a bit more than twenty years after his death, I hear his name uttered around the Legion stoves and fires on a regular basis as older Legionaries regale their younger counterparts with tales of his exploits. I will often stop and listen, and I will say that, sometimes, the stories being told are even true!

One key difference between my account and my grandfather's, who I even now think of by the name I first knew him, my beloved Avus, is that I have made the decision not to wait to start telling what I hope will be just one more chapter in an unbroken line of accounts that extend into the future, started by my Avus and carried on by my descendants. I want this for two reasons; one selfish and one that, perhaps, is a bit nobler. The first reason is based on that of my Avus' desire, to leave a record to pass on to his descendants, so that they would know him and all that he accomplished. And his achievements are prodigious, although the one that was most important to him has turned out to be temporary, which I will explain later. However, the second reason is not quite as selfish. As my Avus learned very early in his life, when he marched for a man who is now revered as a god in Divus Julius, what is written about and remembered by members of all the classes of Rome are the exploits of the men of Caesar's class. Men like my Avus, my father, and me, along with all the comrades we march with and who have fallen, receive barely a mention in any of the annals and accounts. If one were to read all but the account of Divus Julius, when he was known as Gaius Julius Caesar, readers unfamiliar with Rome would come away with the impression that the generals accomplished all they did singlehandedly, with no help from us men of the lower classes, and our swords. Only Caesar, in his account of the campaign in Gaul and in what is now known as the Second, or sometimes Caesarian Civil War, made any mention of the bravery, fortitude, and sacrifice of the Legions.

As for me, I am now in my thirtieth year, and am a thirteen-year veteran of the Legions. I hold the rank of Tertius Pilus Posterior, the commander of the Second Century, Third Cohort in the First Legion. I have been in the Centurionate for four years, which makes me young to be in one of the Cohorts of the first line. But like my Avus and my father, I have been blessed with certain...gifts; gifts that have enabled me to make a name for myself, and not just because of my bloodline. In fact, as I was warned by my father when I made the decision to embark on a career in the Legions, in some ways, the name I carry has been an impediment to my advancement.

Fortunately, I inherited more than just my name. My father, like my Avus, is much taller than average, but where my father has a lean build, although he is nonetheless very strong, deceptively so, I have his height, but I have the same breadth across the chest and shoulders as my Avus. In fact, both my father and mother, who are still alive, claim that I might be even a bit more muscular than my Avus, something that I find hard to believe. I remember him well, despite the fact that the last time I saw him I was a little more than six years old. In fact, while I love and respect my father dearly, I say with no hesitation that Titus Pullus was, and is, the most formative figure in my life. And a huge part of that impact came not from my actual interaction with him, but in the record he left behind.

10

Chapter One

I still remember the day very clearly, as if it happened yesterday and not fourteen years ago. Of course, every boy remembers the day he dons the *toga virilis*, but mine was made even more memorable because, in many ways, it put the last pieces of a puzzle together; a puzzle that had tormented me for some six years before that. Although I was born and lived the first ten years of my life in Siscia, which is now the capital of the Roman province of Pannonia, the place I think of as home, even to this day, is Arelate. It was where my Avus moved after his retirement as Camp Prefect of the Army of Pannonia, purchasing a villa just a block from the forum of what is now almost a small city on the Rhodanus River. When he died in his sleep, he not only named my father, his only nephew, his heir, he also formally adopted him as his son. Although I was still very young and had only a dim understanding of such matters, what I knew was that this was very, very important to my parents, particularly my mother, Iras. This was due to the fact that Titus Pullus had managed to achieve his lifelong ambition, and had secured his elevation to the equestrian order. By naming my father as his heir, not only my father, now Gaius Porcinianus Pullus, but I, my brother, and two sisters became equestrians, as would our children. At least so both my parents believed. And yet, here I am, a man of the ranks who started out as a *Tirone*, just like every other of my comrades. By rights, under the reforms of Augustus, at least, as an equestrian, I would have been able to purchase a posting in the Centurionate, but I have no regrets that this is not the case and that I had to start at the bottom, just as my father and my Avus. Not about that anyway, but that is for later. It was on the day I donned the *toga virilis* that I learned the full story of why this is so, at least as far I have been able to piece together, between what I already knew and what I learned once I became considered a man by Roman law.

As was my custom, I had risen at dawn. Normally, I must confess that rousing me was usually a chore; even now, I do value my sleep. Not on this day, however, and again, as was my habit, after breaking my fast, I went out to the now-scarred set of stakes, where I spent a third of a watch working on my forms with the *rudis*, the wooden sword we use for training. And, as always, my father was there to supervise, comment, and correct whatever mistakes I made, although by this point, it was rare that he made any remarks. At least, not about my handling of the *rudis*. Even now, when I close my eyes, I can see him standing there, leaning on the one crutch that he used to help him get around, compensating for the leg he lost while serving as Quartus Pilus Prior of the 8th Legion.

Once I was done, he gave me the curt nod that I knew signaled his satisfaction, then said, "Get cleaned up. Then come to the study."

Naturally, I did as he commanded, but while he had given me the same command on other days, I knew this one was different, so I took extra care and time in bathing and grooming. One of the conveniences of my Avus' villa is that it has a smaller version of a bath in a small building next to the main one. It has the *caldarium* and *tepidarium*; the only thing it lacks is the *frigidarium*.

Thus refreshed and invigorated, I made my way to the room that I had first visited when I was ten years old, after my Avus had died and my family, minus my father, who was on campaign, made the journey from Siscia to see what had been left to our family. That trip, and all that transpired during and because of it, still ranks as one of the most important periods of my life, so I suppose it was fitting that I was meeting my father there. Even then, six years later, I still associated the study with my Avus and not my father, despite the fact that as soon as we moved in, he had taken it as his own. In truth, for the first couple of months after we moved he could barely be pried out of there, but that was because he was coming to terms with the end of his career in the Legions and the loss of his leg, in his own way. He had done so, although I can say with honesty and much sadness that my father was never the same after he lost his leg, although I think it is understandable.

When I knocked and was bade entrance, I was somewhat surprised to see not only my father seated there, but my mother as well, because she very, very rarely entered this room. Frankly, I was more surprised to see her than I was to see the third person there, and it pleased me a great deal that both my parents understood how important it was to me that this man was present. Next to my Avus and my father, my Avus' former slave and scribe Diocles is, or was, the most important person in my life in shaping the man I have become. And it is not just because he was my tutor, turning me from a boy barely interested in writing his own name into the voracious reader I have become today. Diocles also served as a reminder of one of the more important lessons of my life, that it is an unwise man who judges another based on such superficial things as his appearance, what he does for a living, or how many men he has killed. Even when I was ten, I was an inch taller than this slightly built Greek, who I had known all my life and barely registered as a man worthy of knowing. I am somewhat ashamed to say that before my trip to Arelate and return to Siscia, I viewed Diocles in the same light as I did all the various slaves and servants attached to my parents' and Avus' households. They were there to serve me and my family, and there was little else of value that they could teach me, or so I thought. I thank the gods that I was disabused of that stupidity early on; I see many men, not just of my class, but particularly of the upper classes, who still feel as I did when I was a child. I suppose that it has always been so; even those on the next to lowest rung on the ladder of our society make themselves feel better by sneering at those one rung down. So it

13

goes all the way up the ladder to the patricians, who have many more rungs to look down upon. But even among the patricians, there are yet more rungs; poorer patricians at the bottom being sneered at behind the hands of those with more money, or more exalted bloodlines.

Seeing the three of them standing there, despite knowing this was not only an important, but happy occasion, I could feel my heart thudding heavily in my chest. Their expressions were hard to read; at least, my father's and Diocles' were. My mother's eyes were shining, and that more than anything shook my own composure because my mother is not prone to tears. In her own way, she is made of as hard an iron as my father, or any of the men of the Legions, for that matter. But I suppose seeing her firstborn son taking this step into manhood was sufficiently emotional that now she stood, trying to keep her tears from falling. Nevertheless, she was smiling at me broadly. My father, on the other hand, was not. He was not frowning exactly, and I could see that he was proud, but there was an expression of gravity on his face that gave me a hint that perhaps there would be more to this encounter than just donning the snow-white toga he was now holding in his hands.

"Titus." My father's voice sounded huskier than normal, although it had lost the raspy quality that, as I would learn myself, comes from frequently bellowing commands. "Today's the day you don the *toga virilis*. It's an auspicious day in many ways, and not just because it's your birthday." He paused to take a breath and, while I kept my gaze on him, I saw out of the corner of my eye my mother shooting him a sharp look. Despite the fact he never took his own eyes away from mine, I saw him give a slight nod, and it reminded me of something I and my siblings had learned long, long before, that my parents seemed to be able to communicate with each other without saying a word. I took his nod to mean that he understood whatever message she was sending him and, with his next words, seemed to confirm my guess. "But your mother and I have also decided that it's time to give you…access to something else that is part of your birthright."

I must admit I was quite confused. Until, that is, my father lifted a hand and indicated what, to anyone else, looked like nothing more than a square, wooden box. However, I knew the purpose of this box, and if I thought my heart had been beating strongly before, it was now positively leaping out of my chest. For a horrifying moment, I felt myself start to totter, but somehow, I managed to maintain my equilibrium and not shame myself and my parents by fainting. It might seem strange that I would get so excited about a battered wooden box; it was not a big box, just large enough to contain something about the size of a scroll. Or, a set of scrolls, perhaps twenty in all.

"However," my father's voice cut through my haze of growing excitement, "these scrolls will remain here, in this study. They are not to be taken from this room, for any reason. Do you understand?"

I indicated that I did, but it was only then that I realized he had chosen his words carefully, and there was one in particular that I found troubling.

"You said 'access'." I surprised myself because my voice sounded much stronger than I felt. "What does that mean exactly?"

My father is not quick to anger, nor is he excessively harsh. But in the intervening time since he had lost his leg, he had become much sterner than he had been previously, so I admit I felt a bit of trepidation when I asked this. Instead of getting irritated, I saw him, and Diocles, still standing to the side, give a small smile.

"Good," he replied softly. "You caught that." Lifting his head, he continued in a tone that I had learned to recognize was a command, one that he was issuing as paterfamilias. "It means that these scrolls still belong to me. They are still my property, and will only pass into your hands on my death. And then, only

15

with the understanding that they be kept safe and secure, and that only you or your own heir, and his after that, be allowed to read them."

I must admit that at the time I did not quite understand the need for such strict security. But I had not read the scrolls yet. Once I did, I understood completely.

Frankly, I do not remember much more about that day, mainly because my mind was completely occupied with the thought of reading that first scroll. However, one other memory that stands out is when I was given something else that I still carry with me to this day. As anyone who is Roman and reading this undoubtedly knows, when a Roman boy becomes a man, he takes the *bulla*, the amulet to ward off evil we all wear, starting a week after our birth, from around his neck where it has been hanging. It is very common that the *bulla* is replaced by something else; in the houses of the upper classes, it is usually something related to their line, a symbol, or artifact that has been passed down. In my case, while it has no intrinsic value – it's not made of gold, nor encrusted with gems – I treasure and value it no less than if it were. In fact, even if I were offered something a thousand times its value to wear in its place, I would not even consider it. As I write this, I am holding it with my free hand, and it has been pointed out to me that I often do as much when I am deep in thought or troubled. Not much to look at; it is simply a metal disk, with some writing inscribed on it, with a hole drilled in it by which a leather thong can suspend it around my neck. It was Diocles who pressed this into my hand, and although I knew this was coming – he had in fact showed me this disk when I was ten – I was still overcome with emotion. The disk is one that is issued to all men of the ranks of the Legions who complete an enlistment and serves as proof to all that they have marched under the standard. The one in question, as you probably have guessed, belonged to my Avus, and was inscribed with, of course, his name, the Legion in which he

16

served, and, in fact, was the Primus Pilus of, the famed 10th Equestris, which no longer exists. And in his case, his final rank, or office, comprised the rest of the inscription. As I mentioned, my Avus had retired as Camp Prefect, a post that, when compared to the entire history of Rome, is still a fairly new position that had been used from time to time, but was made permanent during the reforms wrought by Augustus. After performing the small ceremony that accompanies this ritual – we Romans have a ceremony for everything it seems – I am somewhat surprised that the act of evacuating our bowels does not require some sort of sacrifice to the gods, my parents, and Diocles left me alone, in my Avus' study, with the scrolls.

"Don't try to read them all at once," my father admonished me, putting his hand on my shoulder as he prepared to leave. Then, he favored me with a grin, which made this occasion all the more special because it was a fairly rare occurrence after he lost his leg that he smiled at all. "But I know you'll try. I don't think I slept for two days."

As usual, my father was right.

While I think of Arelate as my home, and even now is where my parents still live, along with the youngest of my four surviving brothers and sisters, Siscia still figures prominently in not only my past, but my present. That was where I traveled, a year after my sixteenth birthday, to enlist in the Legions, in the year of the Consulship of Nero Claudius Drusus and T. Quinctius Crispinus. While it is true that there were cities that were closer where I could have enlisted, my father, demonstrating his usual good sense, insisted that I make the extra effort to travel to the place where I had spent my first ten years, and where my father had served so long and so well, before the vile act of treachery by his Primus Pilus cost him his leg. Traveling with me was a bag of coin, part of the contents meant for the *Conquisitore*, the man in charge of recruitment for the Army of Pannonia. This portion of my hoard was to ensure that I landed in my father's old Legion, the 8th. In case you are not aware, what my father and I were doing is not uncommon; in fact, a man can now secure a position straight into the Centurionate, provided he has the means to purchase a post. However, while my father could certainly afford to do so, there were, and are circumstances that prevented this as a possibility for me, and later for my younger brother Sextus, who also chose to enter the Legions. Fortunately, by the time I had departed, I had read the entirety of my Avus' account of his life, so I not only knew what the circumstances are, I understood that this was the right, and in fact, the only course for me to take. Being completely honest, I was not that upset. Because of the regard in which I hold my father and my Avus, both of whom started out as *Tirones*, that was the path that I was determined to follow as well.

What, or more accurately, who was not traveling with me was a source of sadness, as I was forced to leave behind my most faithful friend, going back all the way to my childhood. However, unlike most Romans of means, this friend was not a slave who had been charged with my care since I could remember. In fact, this friend was not human, or at least, was not in the form of a human. But even now, I have never had a companion and confidante who I trust and love more than I did my beautiful Ocelus, the massive gray stallion I had inherited from my Avus. Ocelus had been a gift to my Avus upon his retirement as Primus Pilus and taking the post of Camp Prefect, and had served him well until his retirement, a service for which my entire family is thankful. But he is, or was, more than a mount to me; my earliest and fondest memories of my childhood involve Ocelus, and I, even now, can recall my Avus carrying me to feed him what had become his daily treat of an apple. Once I could walk, it was a ritual I performed every day, at least whenever my Avus and he were not out performing their duties. Being honest, I am finding this difficult to write because I can feel the tears starting to form, certainly not very dignified for a Centurion of Rome! But as faithfully and well as Ocelus served his original master, his service to me was no less important. In fact, Ocelus saved not just my Avus' life, but mine, when I was ten years old and my family, minus my father, was attacked by Latobici rebels as we were returning to Siscia from Arelate a few months after my Avus' death.

Through a combination of circumstances, out of our small party composed of my mother, two sisters, brother, Diocles, and the woman who would become his wife, Birgit, and our two bodyguards Gallus and Libo, I was the one sent to ride for help, which I managed to do. I was not unscathed; as Ocelus and I were swimming across the Sava River I was struck from behind by an arrow, fired by one of the Latobici rebels. And it was only because of my mighty, strong Ocelus that I managed to evade capture and a certain death, since I had killed one of their own in my escape, as he carried me into a heavily wooded area on a ridge riddled with caves. After that, Ocelus and I had a bond that I was told was at least as strong, if not stronger than the one formed with his first master, my Avus. Both Diocles and the Armenian slave assigned by my Avus to Ocelus' care, an expert horseman in his own right, asserted that this was the case. I suppose they were telling the truth and would be in a position to know, since they had close contact with my Avus and the gray stallion.

Sadly, while Ocelus still lived when I departed from Arelate, he was in no shape for a long journey. Less than a year after my departure, I received a letter from my father informing me that my magnificent champion finally breathed his last, dying peacefully, much as my Avus had. And I can think of no two souls who deserved to die that way more than my Avus and Ocelus. Even now, a little more than thirteen years after he died, I find it painful to think about him, and I catch myself looking at the horses of other men and measuring them against Ocelus. And they are all wanting, at least to my eyes.

19

My money did what it was supposed to, as I was assigned to the 8th Legion. More specifically, I was assigned to the First Century, Fourth Cohort of the 8th. This is noteworthy because this was the Century and Cohort that my father led, as the Quartus Pilus Prior. Two days after I arrived in Siscia, and the day after I took the oath as a *probatio*, I was met at the gate of the camp by the Optio of the First Century. Once I got close enough to see who it was, I could not help a smile from crossing my face, recognizing the man.

"What are you smiling at, you big oaf?" the Optio growled at me, giving me the first glimmering that perhaps my reception was not going to be what I thought it would be.

"Nothing, Optio." I at least managed to remember to address him by his rank. Thinking that this surly greeting was some sort of formality, an external sign that he did not know who I was, I then said, "*Salve,* Aulus Galens, I…"

Before I could say another word, he lashed out with his fist, catching me full in the stomach and I was completely unprepared for the blow. My next memory was me looking up at him as he stood over me, hands on hips, staring down with what can only be described as a fierce scowl on his face.

"Shut your mouth, *Probatio,*" he growled. "Nobody gave you leave to talk."

Now, there is no denying that I was in some pain, but what I remember most vividly was how bewildered I was. Did he not recognize me? How could that be? I wondered. While it was true the last time I had seen Aulus Galens he had been a *Gregarius*, he had been one of the men who sometimes took me around the camp, showing me things and telling me stories about my father.

Oblivious to my internal confusion, he ordered, "Get on your feet, oaf. We have a lot to do today."

I pulled myself to my feet and automatically assumed the position of *intente*, a posture I had learned almost as soon as I could walk. He examined me for a moment, looking me up and down.

"I've seen worse," he grunted.

Without waiting, he turned on his heel and beckoned me to follow him. Grabbing the small bundle of personal items I was allowed to bring with me, I hurried to follow him. We had gone a few paces when he looked over his shoulder at me and grinned.

"Welcome to the 8th, Titus."

My next meeting was with the Quartus Pilus Prior, and I will say that it was with some trepidation that I entered the outer office of the quarters of the Pilus Prior. This was a room with which I was very familiar; it would be impossible for me to calculate the number of watches I spent in my father's quarters in the camp. Galens entered first, jerking his thumb at me as I followed him inside.

"We have a new *probatio* to enter into the rolls. It looks like the *conquisitores* are getting more desperate all the time if they're taking a big ox like this one."

Because of my height, I could see who Galens was addressing, although I already knew who it was, by title if not by name. The slave assigned as the chief clerk of the Legion sits at that desk, but the face looking up at me was also known to me.

"Titus!" Lysander, who had been my father's clerk as well, smiled up at me. "By the gods, you've grown! You're taller than your father already! And you're as big as your uncle. Er," he hastily corrected, "your grandfather, I mean."

"Yes, yes," Galens said impatiently. "We're all happy to see the youngster. But we've got work to do if he's going to be worthy of the Fourth!" Beckoning to me, he continued, "Give him your records, boy."

I hurriedly stepped forward, handing Lysander the scroll that contained my information, along with my signature under the oath that all men must take when becoming a *probatio*. Then, there would be another oath that changed my status from *probatio* to *tirone*. As I understood it, this is a holdover from the days when a *dilectus* was held to raise a Legion and had to do so by traveling the province in which it was being raised. I learned from reading my Avus' account that it usually took a matter of time, sometimes weeks, before a *dilectus* would reach the training ground, making an oath necessary to instill in men the understanding that there were consequences if they were to have a change of heart and slip away one night. But once a man is actually ready to train, there is another oath for *Tirones* to take. The major difference is the range of punishments that can be administered for violation of the rules and, once the training begins, there are vastly more rules that must be remembered. In the past, it was either the Primus Pilus or the Legate himself who administered the oath for *Tirones*, or *Tiros*, which is the more common term used. When, that is, you are not being referred to in some other, more vile manner. But with the reforms of Augustus, among the many small details that were changed along with the huge ones with which most are familiar, it devolved onto the Pilus Prior of the Cohort into which the *tirone* is enrolling to administer the oath. That, or at least so I assumed, was why I was there. This was one of the few assumptions I made in the first days of my training that I got right.

"The Pilus Prior will see you now," Lysander announced after he had taken my records into the second office that serves as the private office of the Pilus Prior, as well as his quarters whenever he is in the camp.

In my father's case, that was not very often, since he had a family, meaning that most nights, he came to our apartment in town. While this was also true for the current Pilus Prior, I knew that his reasons for spending nights away from camp had nothing to do with a family.

Determined not to make the same mistake twice, I entered the Pilus Prior's office without a smile. Marching to the desk, I stopped at what I knew was the proper distance from it, and rendered what I was sure was a perfect, parade-ground salute.

"*Probatio* Titus Porcinianus Pullus, reporting as ordered, sir."

I cannot tell you how proud I was of myself for remembering to append the proper title to myself, since I had yet to take the *Tiro*'s oath. The Pilus Prior, on the other hand, did not seem to be nearly as impressed. Leaning back in his chair, he gave me a coolly appraising stare.

Finally, he said, "Didn't anyone teach you that *probationes* aren't allowed to salute their superiors yet? That's only for *Tirones.*"

As hard as I tried, I could feel my mouth twist into a grimace of chagrin and disappointment.

"And now we're making faces?" The Pilus Prior shook his head sadly, and said, "I don't know who taught you about the Legions, but I should have a talk with him."

Without thinking, which I have been told is a bad habit of mine that both of my parents had admonished me about before I left, I replied, "My father would like that very much. In fact, he wants to know why you haven't written lately. Sir," I added hastily, feeling the blood rush to my face.

The moment I said it, I inwardly cringed, and with Galens behind me, I mentally prepared myself for a blow between the shoulder blades.

Instead, the Pilus Prior threw his head back and laughed, then stood to offer his hand.

"You're right," Gnaeus Corvinus told me. "I'm terrible about writing. I promise I'll send him something tomorrow. I should at least let him know you've arrived here and are about to start training."

Gnaeus Corvinus, the Quartus Pilus Prior, had been the Quartus Hastatus Prior, Centurion in command of the Fifth Century under my father. More times than I can count, I had heard from my father and others that they are as unalike as it is possible for two men to be in many ways. While my father was a devoted family man, at least as devoted as it is possible for a Centurion of Rome to be, Gnaeus Corvinus never met a whore he did not want to bed. While my father was abstemious in his imbibing of wine, rarely a day went by where Corvinus did not partake and, as my father told me, and Corvinus cheerfully admitted once our relationship became friendlier, he was often hung over at morning formations. Still, despite their differences, my father counted Gnaeus Corvinus as his closest, and more importantly, most trusted friend.

"By the gods, you're huge," he began, once he had bade me sit down. "You're not quite as tall as your Avus, but you're every bit as broad in the shoulders. If not a bit broader."

I had, in fact, heard this before, although it was, and still is impossible for me to imagine that this was so. My mental image of my Avus is such that I cannot fathom the idea that I would be larger than he was, in any way.

"Are you as strong as you look?" This came from Galens, who was also there for what I would learn was a very unusual occasion.

I could only answer with a shrug because, back then, I really had no way of knowing. What I did know was that I had started doing strengthening exercises at an even earlier age than my Avus had, when the *lanista* of the *ludus* in Arelate, which turned out to be secretly owned by my family, had prescribed them for me.

"Of course he is, Galens," Corvinus retorted, then turned to me. "What I want to know is, have you killed anyone else since the last time I saw you?"

Despite the fact that I had been expecting this somewhat, I still flinched as if someone had prodded an open wound with a knife, which was true in some ways. However, Corvinus was not speaking anything less than the truth. I do not know exactly, but I am fairly sure that not many ten year-old boys have killed two full-grown men.

"No," I replied quietly, hoping with my tone that I imparted the message that I had no wish to discuss this.

Corvinus eyed me, his face betraying nothing, but then he gave a small nod, which I took as a sign that he understood this was not something I wanted to talk about.

"Well," he gave me a smile that, while friendly, seemed to hold some other meaning only he and Galens knew about. "When your father wrote me and asked me for a favor, I was more than happy to comply, and not just because the gods know I owe him."

"No more than he owes you," I interrupted, again without thinking. "Once I got older, he told me of the many times you've saved his life."

If Corvinus was irritated that I had cut him off, he did not seem to be. He just shrugged.

"No more than he did mine. That's what we do in the Legions. And I will say that, unlike most of the *Tiros* we get, you probably know that better than any of them." His expression hardened as he continued, "But that's what I wanted to talk to you about. Or," he amended, "warn you about." He leaned forward to pin me with a steely gaze that, frankly, made me uncomfortable. "Because this is the last time we're going to be having a cozy little chat for some time to come. In a moment, I'm going to give you the oath of the *Tirone* and, once I do, I don't know you. You're going to be just like every other slab of fresh meat that shows up in the ranks of my Century, and like every other slab of fresh meat, you're going to be tenderized before we decide whether or not you're worthy to march with the men who've already proven themselves. But," only then did he lean back in his chair, "the truth is, I'm going to expect more out of you than I do other *Tiros*."

He paused, and I sensed he was waiting for something from me, so I considered what he had just said.

"Because of who my father is?"

"That's part of it." He nodded. "But not all of it. I know you don't want to talk about it, but the facts are the facts. You're going to be one of the few *Tiros* who knows what it is to kill a man, and not some other drunk, but a warrior." He shot a glance over at Galens, who was sitting to my side, and I saw the Optio give a small shrug out of the corner of my eye. Evidently, the Pilus Prior took this as some sort of sign, as he continued. "I'm going to tell you something that nobody in the ranks knows. They will in a couple of days, but they better not hear it from you. Do you understand?"

When put that way, I was not sure I wanted him telling me anything, but I also knew that this was a sort of test, and I really had no choice.

"Yes, sir," I answered. "I swear on the black stone I won't say a word."

"The black stone." Galens laughed. "It seems we have a religious boy here, Pilus Prior."

Like all lads of seventeen, I bristled at being called a boy, but I managed to keep my mouth shut.

"We'll see how long that lasts," Corvinus replied dryly. Turning his attention back to the subject, he said, "What do you know of the overall situation as it concerns the Legions?"

I thought for a moment, recalling all that I had heard.

"I know that Drusus is still campaigning on the Rhenus," I answered. "And that, the last I heard, Pannonia is quiet."

Corvinus gave a snorting laugh, but nodded. "While I wouldn't call it quiet, I will say that it's probably as quiet as it's ever going to be. Frankly, that's one of the reasons I'm telling you this because you were born here and grew up here until you were, what was it? Ten?"

I nodded.

"So, yes, Pannonia is quiet. At least, it's considered quiet enough that we're being detached and sent elsewhere. Can you guess where that is?"

It seemed obvious to me, but I did not want to insult my new Pilus Prior, so I pretended to think about it before answering, albeit in the form of a question.

"The Rhenus (Rhine)?"

Corvinus gave me a small smile as he nodded.

"That's right. We're being sent to reinforce Drusus for his last push this year. We're going to be leaving a few days short of a month from now."

I felt a hard lump form in my throat. My expression must have betrayed my dismay because Corvinus smiled again, but it was a grim one.

"As I said, it's a good thing you are who you are. You're going to have to get some of your training on the march. Now," he abruptly stood up, which I took as a sign that I was to do as well, "it's time to take the oath."

It was fortunate that I did so, because the cordial part of my introduction to the First Century, Fourth Cohort was over. Commanding me to raise my hand, I repeated the words of the oath administered to all *Tirones*, the Pilus Prior's voice now as hard and unyielding as the iron in his sword. I think my words were still hanging in the air when Galens' fist once more slammed into my body, this time aimed at my ribs, just above my kidney.

WHAM!

And once more, I was on the floor of Corvinus' office, with both men staring down at me, all hint of friendliness and warmth gone from their faces.

"You better learn to keep your feet better than that," Corvinus said, "if you expect to march with us."

Thankfully, I did learn to stay upright better; that was the last time Galens was ever able to knock me down, although it was not from a lack of effort. I learned very quickly that, if anything, my status and background drew more than their share of attention, in the form of the fists of Galens and the *vitus* of the Pilus Prior. Nothing I did seemed to be right, and when those *Tirones* who were assigned to the Fourth Cohort made some sort of collective mistake, I do not believe I am exaggerating when I say that I was usually the one who bore the brunt of the wrath of the Optios and Centurions. As frustrating as it was, it was made less so, thanks to the knowledge I had garnered from my Avus' scrolls. Because of his size and the fact that he and his best friend Vibius Domitius had sought out a retired Legionary to begin their training for the Legions several years before their enlistment, the treatment I received was much like that my Avus did when he was a *Tiro* in Caesar's 10th Equestris. Perhaps it is what one might call rationalization, but I chose to take my treatment, or mistreatment, as a mark of pride, a sign that the officers of the Cohort recognized that I could take whatever abuse they could mete out.

As I would learn later, this was only partially true. While Galens, Corvinus, and most of the other officers involved in my training did indeed single me out for the reason I suspected, more than one of the others did so because they hated me. Not for what I was, but what I represented in their collective minds. It was an attitude I had first run into when I was still very young. In fact, it was in Arelate where I first experienced the same kind of hostility, when, through a combination of circumstances, I discovered the truth about the ownership of the *ludus* in the town. Using this knowledge as leverage, I prevailed upon the *lanista*, a one-eyed brute named Maximus Vulso, to teach me how to fight. Being frank, I never had any intention of entering the arena, although it is not unknown for free Roman citizens to choose this path. I wanted to learn to fight because, honestly, it is in my blood. My family was in Arelate for a bit less than three months, and I spent a part of every day at the *ludus* for two of those. In the beginning, Vulso had me doing nothing but exercise, but as I imagine both of my parents, and the man who became my tutor, Diocles, will tell you, what I may lack in intelligence, I make up for with stubbornness. And I wheedled, whined, and harried Vulso to allow me to fight a real, live, breathing opponent. I suppose that he finally just got worn down, finally relenting, but I posed a unique problem for him, in many ways. I was, after all, only ten. But I was a very, very big ten-year-old and, thanks to his exercises, as I discovered, I was as strong as many full-grown men, as well as being their size. I have always been larger, and stronger, than my peers, but it was thanks to my Avus, who was exactly the same way as a child, that I like to think that I never used that advantage unfairly. At least, most of the time. But I was also the son of the owner of the *ludus*, although this was a secret that very, very few people knew. However, Vulso was one of those who did, so I can only imagine the quandary he felt as I kept up my pressure to be allowed to face a living, breathing opponent.

29

His solution was brilliant, although it had unforeseen consequences, which I will explain in a moment. Knowing that he could not pit me against any of his other full-grown trainees, no matter how much I might have matched them in brute strength, he instead had me face one who, while closer to my size, was a fully developed man. At least, he was as fully developed as he would get. As you undoubtedly know, dear reader, in order to please the people of Rome who are enthusiasts of the arena, one of the relatively new wrinkles is the addition of what I hear called "novelty acts." In the case of Vulso, he had acquired a dwarf and had been training the dwarf to fight. Because he was a Thracian, and since we Romans never, ever forget those who have been a threat to the eternal city, he was given the name Spartacus in a mocking tribute to the slave who mothers still tell stories about to scare their children. This was my first opponent in a sparring match, and only now can I say without shame that Spartacus thrashed me and did so soundly. Unfortunately for Spartacus, and less so for Vulso, neither of them knew exactly what I was made of, and of all the lives I have taken in the intervening years, I still have much regret about what I did to Spartacus. Up until my match with the dwarf, I had managed to hide my activities at the *ludus* with the collusion of one of the two men my father had hired when we traveled to Arelate. Gallus had marched with my father, not in his Century but his Cohort, and had since retired. In fact, he had been good friends with my first Optio, Galens. Gallus was a fan of the arena, loving to see blood in the sand, and since my mother had given Gallus the task of being my escort as I wandered around Arelate, after I came home with a black eye that, ironically enough, had nothing to do with the *ludus* and was courtesy of a member of the town watch, it was not hard for me to make him an accomplice. Mutually deciding that this was something neither of us felt my mother needed to know, he would take me to the *ludus*, then watch the activities that comprise the routine of a gladiator. The beating Spartacus gave me was so severe that I required stitches to close the gash his *rudis* had inflicted on my head, and I shudder to think what would have happened if I had not been wearing a helmet. Naturally, a wound of this nature was impossible to explain away like the black eye, so my mother not only forbade me to go north of the forum in Arelate, where the *ludus* was located, but she changed my shadow from Gallus to a man called Libo. One day, while riding out west of Arelate, I tricked Libo who, like Gallus, had marched with my father. Unlike Gallus, Libo had actually been in my father's Century, and I knew him from my childhood because he was one of the men, like Galens, who would escort me around the camp. That makes what I did to him even more shabby, but I was thirsting for vengeance and, thanks to Ocelus, who even in his later years was the fastest horse in the area, I drove his own mount away, then galloped back to Arelate to have my vengeance.

The dwarf Spartacus was the first man I ever killed, which is something not many ten-year-olds can claim. But it also marked the first time I ever experienced what I can only describe as a divine…fit, where I lose all conscious thought but am able to fight with a fury and effectiveness over and above my usual prowess. In fact, I would go so far as to claim that it gives me an ability over and above that of other men, and as proof I would merely point to the fact that I am still alive. Even now, some twenty years after the first of these fits, and having experienced them more than a dozen times, I find it impossible to explain. In the case of my fight with Spartacus, what I remember was seeing him standing across from me, both of us surrounded by a living boundary, in the form of a circle of men and a couple of women, composed of full-fledged gladiators, trainees, and the women slaves who Vulso bought to serve their needs. But it was not just the first occasion of this divine madness that I experienced; it was also the first time I learned that, contrary to what I had believed, men of my class did not view me as if I was one of them. While I remember little of the actual fight that afterward saw me standing there, chest heaving, with a bloody *rudis* in my hand and a dead Spartacus at my feet when I finally came to my senses, I vividly recall the wave of hostility that emanated from every man there. Even now, I can close my eyes and I see the hostile stares, hear the muttered oaths and curses as these men watched me approach the dwarf. It was extremely confusing to me for, in my mind, because of my father's status as a member of the Head Count, and my mother's beginning as a slave in the court of Cleopatra, I was one of them. That day, I learned they did not view me in the same light. They knew that I was somehow connected to the owner of the *ludus*, which in turn meant that they belonged to me, and while, as far as I know, Vulso never revealed the connection, they somehow understood that I was nothing like them. This marked the first, but far from the last time I would experience this kind of hostility, something that I never fully understood until I finally read my Avus' account. The truth is that, for lack of a better way to describe it, my Avus Titus Pullus was responsible for putting me in the position in which I found myself.

Now that I was a *Tirone*, I ran into this same kind of hostility, mainly from a fortunately small number of Optios of the Fourth Cohort. To them, I was a pampered, spoiled rich boy; the fact that I was standing in the ranks as a *Tiro* and, consequently, was a sign that I was not what they thought, was ignored. Instead, they took it as a sign from the gods that they had been provided a target for their wrath at the unfairness and injustice of their own plight.

This is probably the best point to expand on what likely appears to be a mystery to you, dear reader, which is what exactly I am. For while it is true that, according to the census performed by the Censor of Rome, I am still a member of the Head Count, my actual circumstances are far, far different. Although I had known, in a very superficial way, that my Avus was an extraordinary man, it was not until I donned the *toga virilis* and, between my father's explanation and reading my Avus' account of his life, that I understood just how remarkable a man he was. He had been born as poor as I suppose it is possible to be, on a farm just outside of Astigi, in the province of Baetica. Due to either a gift from the gods or a freak of nature, depending on whom one asked, my namesake Titus Pomponius Pullus was born much, much larger than is normal for a Roman. So large was he that his mother died in childbirth, for which his father never forgave him. I only met my grandmother Valeria once, when my father took me to visit the farm where my father had grown up, but it was from her that I learned the circumstances of my Avus' childhood and, as wonderful and loving as my parents were, his father Lucius was as opposite to them as it is possible to be. My natural-born Avia was very old by the time I met her. At least she seemed that way to me, although as I have learned, to anyone eleven or twelve years old, someone in their sixties appears older than the gods. But my Avia was, in truth, very old; my father said that she was close to seventy years old when we went to visit. This was perhaps a year after we moved to Arelate, so I was around eleven, and my father and siblings traveled there with the express purpose of bringing my Avia back to Arelate, where she could live out her days in peace. The only problem was that she refused to come back with us; perhaps my stubbornness goes back even further than I thought! Nevertheless, it was from her I learned the specifics of my Avus' childhood, one from which was born his burning ambition. One thing my Avia impressed upon me was that the hatred my Avus' father held for him was returned tenfold, not just from my Avus, but from all of his children. Despite my youth, it was easy to see that hatred and contempt on the wrinkled face of my Avia who, despite her age, was still in many ways a beautiful woman. In fact, between my mother and my Avia, I have great hope for my as-yet unborn daughter, or daughters.

The goal of which I speak was my Avus' ambition to elevate the status of his family from the lowly Head Count into the class of Equestrians. Everything my Avus did was mindful of that desire and, as I learned, he attained it. When he retired as Camp

Prefect of the Army of Pannonia, in accordance with the bargain he struck with our beloved leader, the divine Augustus, Titus Pomponius Pullus, son of a drunken farmer, was elevated to the Equestrian order, with a personage no less than Augustus himself as his sponsor. When my Avus retired to Arelate, thanks to a combination of factors, starting with the fact that he enlisted in the Legions under the auspices of Divus Julius, when he was Praetor of Hispania, in the year of the Consulship of Publius Servius Vatia and Appius Claudius Pulcher, and marched for him in Gaul and, during both the First and Second Civil Wars, my Avus was an extraordinarily wealthy man. Unlike most of his comrades, and the men that I march with today, he did not drink, gamble, or whore to excess because he was always mindful of his larger goal. As you undoubtedly know, dear reader, it takes a fortune of 400,000 sesterces to be elevated to the Equestrian order and, by the time my Avus retired, he had much, much more than that. While he would have no doubt accrued the requisite amount on his own, the reason that he had enough money to purchase his way not just into the Equestrian order, but into the Senate, was due to Diocles. As I would come to learn, this man, diminutive in size but a lion in the stature of his heart and devotion to my family, had managed my Avus' affairs so well that he could have purchased a seat in the Senate if he so desired. My Avus did not; in fact, he could barely stand being in the presence of other Equestrians and, through Diocles, I learned that often was the time when my Avus would turn away a man of his own order, or even one wearing the iron ring of the Senate from his door, in favor of a bedraggled, dirty beggar who could prove that he had once been under the standard. More than once over the years, I have wondered how much of this attitude of Titus Pullus played into the events that transpired after his death, although I have no regrets. Whatever the cause, within a few weeks of his passing, my parents learned that all that my Avus had worked for – securing not just his place in the Equestrian order, but even more importantly to him, a place for his heirs – was for naught. The divine Augustus, in his infinite wisdom, informed my father that information had come to light that disqualified my Avus' heirs from membership in the order. It is a mark of his mercy and kindness that my Avus' name was allowed to remain on the rolls of the Equestrian order, but none of his heirs, nor theirs, meaning me, would be allowed that honor. Thus was the cause for my own circumstances, but although Augustus, because of this information, confiscated a large portion of my Avus' fortune, his knowledge was not quite as extensive as most people think. As a result, as my father often jokes, my family is probably among the richest members of the Head Count in history. However, we do not flaunt this wealth, for I have little doubt that in the intervening time between when I am writing this and my Avus' death, Augustus learned of his error. But since my parents are not the type of people to hold large parties where they serve such expensive delicacies as larks' tongues, I believe it is safe to say that we have no fear from Augustus. At least, that is my most fervent hope.

No matter what my background was, the life of a *Tirone* in the Legions of Rome is a harsh one. And given that our training period in the camp was reduced to two days short of a month before we departed for the Rhenus, this meant that the group of *Tiros* of which I was a part were subjected to even harsher treatment. Ever since the reforms of Augustus, the practice of allowing a Legion to be whittled down, man by man, is a thing of the past. Now, if a Century falls below a certain level, the *conquisitores* round up men, supposedly qualified, to fill those holes. I was the only *Tiro* assigned to the First Century, a fact of which I was reminded on a daily basis. Overall, the Fourth Cohort had taken on a total of fifteen *Tiros* in order to get the Cohort up to the proper strength, scattered through all six Centuries. I suppose that this is the appropriate time to introduce some of the *Tiros* with whom I actually developed a relationship during that month. Decimus Quadratus, Aulus Titius, Lucius Curso, Marcus Sergius, and Vibius Tuditanus were all about my age, which I suppose had much to do with our bonding together, and we spent most of our days either being marched about the forum of the camp, or at the stakes.

The duty of those men responsible for training us was rotated among mostly the Optios of the Centuries into which we would be added, although sometimes, the Centurions of those Centuries would be present. Watch after watch, we either worked on our marching, accompanied by the lash of the *vitus* on the part of the Centurions, or the fists of the Optios, since Augustus' reforms had barred Optios from carrying the twisted vine stick that is the sign of command. Frankly, I preferred the *vitus* to the fist because the blow is spread more evenly across the body. Up and down the forum we marched, very quickly learning the command *Repitate*, as we never seemed able to impress our officers with our ability. This was the one area in which my skill and experience was roughly equal to that of my fellow *Tiros*; as often as I had watched my father march men around, it is not quite the same as actually doing the marching.

Within a few days, we at least looked like Legionaries when we moved from one place to another, although our officers were not reticent about reminding us that we were nowhere near being Gregarii. It was a week after our training began before we were brought to the stakes set up outside the walls of the camp. That first day, Galens was in charge of our training, and he ordered each of us to face a stake. As unfamiliar as learning to march had been for me, it was the exact opposite facing the scarred wooden post. Naturally, we had brought our *rudii*, attached to our belts with a leather thong instead of being in a scabbard, since it did not fit.

"Draw your *rudii*," Galens commanded.

As I did so, I prepared myself for another beating or some form of chastisement, sure that Galens would notice that I was gripping my *rudis* differently. He did notice, but his reaction was the last thing I expected.

Seeing how I was holding the *rudis*, his eyes narrowed, then he called to me, "Come here, Pullus."

Walking over to him, I kept my eye on his hands, which were dangling down at his side. Noticing my gaze, he just gave a harsh chuckle, but shook his head.

"All you *cunni* gather round Pullus and me."

Naturally, the others did as he commanded, which made me even more nervous.

"Lift your arm up so that they can see," Galens told me, and I did as commanded. Pointing to where my hand was wrapped around the handle of the *rudis*, he continued, "See how he's holding the sword? With the fingers wrapped over the thumb and not under it? Anyone know what this grip is called?"

Of course, I did, very well. In fact, I not only knew what it was called, but I knew why it was called such. However, when I opened my mouth, Galens shook his head at me.

"Not you, Pullus. I know you know. Anyone else know?"

For a moment, nobody spoke, then as I remember, it was Marcus Sergius, one of the other *Tiros* with whom I had become friendly, who offered, "I believe it's called the...Vincian grip?"

"Close," Galens told him. "It's called the Vinician grip. And it's the way we hold our sword in the Fourth Cohort. Everyone do it now. Hold them up high so I can see you do it."

Although everyone did as they were commanded, more than one man had hands that were a bit smaller than normal, making the grip difficult for them.

To those men, Galens said, "Tonight, I want you to shave the handles down a bit so that your hand fits better. You'll do the same for your sword, once it's issued to you. Now, Pullus," he commanded, "get in front of that stake."

I did as he commanded, then, using me to demonstrate, Galens showed the others what are called the forms that are part of the arsenal of the Legions, starting with what is called the first position. This marked the first time that I was singled out, but not for punishment of some sort.

In fact, once I was through, Galens gave me what for him was high praise, saying, "I've seen worse."

For the rest of that day, my fellow *Tiros* and I worked on the stakes and, for the first time since my arrival, I felt comfortable doing something I knew how to do.

I suppose I should not have been surprised that the attitude of some of the Optios who hated me as a rich boy was adopted by some of my fellow *Tiros*. But as I found out the night of our first time at the stakes, not just the Optios felt that way.

"So, did you learn all those moves from your private tutor?"

I was sitting with the *Tiros* with whom I had become friendly, eating our evening meal in the communal mess hall next to the *quaestorium* before we retired to our respective section huts. Although we spent the day training together, when it was time to sleep, we retired to the huts of the tent sections that we would be part of when our training was complete. At first, I did not realize that the words were aimed at me, intent only on soaking up every bit of olive oil with my last hunk of bread. Even now, I eat a prodigious amount, but back then, as a teenager, it was impossible to fill me up, and I was always hungry. I became aware that the low chatter that was a feature of our meals together had stopped, and I glanced up to see that all eyes were on me, as if expecting an answer. Sitting up straight, I looked up to see another *Tiro,* his name Lucius Curso, standing across the table from me, staring down with hard eyes.

"What was that?" I asked, because the truth was I had not really been paying attention.

Curso gave a laugh, but it held not a hint of friendliness in it.

"What was that?" he mimicked, and I felt the first prickling of anger. "I asked you who taught a rich boy like you to handle a sword? And why would you need to?"

Putting the last crust of bread down on my plate, I straightened up and pushed the bench back from the table a bit, which was difficult because of the men sitting on either side of me, but I managed.

"Who told you I was rich?" I asked carefully, never taking my eyes off Curso.

Actually, I had been expecting something like this to happen, and I had also chosen Curso as one of the two or three most likely to start trouble. However, what did surprise me was that he had somehow guessed, or worse, had heard something that led him to believe I was better off than he and the rest of my new comrades were. Curso was older than most of us, with a scarred, battered face that proclaimed his enjoyment of a good brawl. He was several inches shorter than I was, but my guess was that, while I outweighed him, it was not by much. More than anything, I knew he was the kind of man who wanted to show everyone that he was the toughest of any group and, because of my size, I was the obvious target. I have no doubt he was also encouraged by my youth.

"Oh, a little bird," he said cheerfully, then he leaned forward to put his fists on the table as he stared down at me. "I know all about you, boy," he said softly, his upper lip curling into a sneer. "You may be big, but I've whipped men just as big and a lot tougher than you. And," he bent a little closer and made a sniffing sound, "I can smell the softness on you. You're just a pampered, soft little boy who wants to play soldier, and you better stay out of my way if you know what's...."

He did not say anything else, mainly because I suddenly reached up with both hands, clasping them around his head and, while I did not use my full strength, knowing that would kill him, I nevertheless exerted enough force to slam his forehead down onto the wooden table. There was a loud, hollow thud as the wood and his skull met, and his lower body immediately collapsed onto the bench on the opposite side of the table, as his torso lay slumped onto the table. The noise caused the other men in the mess to turn around, but all they saw was what looked like a man so tired he had decided to lie down and take a sudden nap. Without waiting for the inevitable questions, I stood up as I stuffed the last piece of bread into my mouth.

In between swallows, I told the other *Tiros,* who were staring up at me in open astonishment, "When he wakes up, tell him that I'm the grandson of *the* Titus Pullus of the 10th Equestris, and he's the one who taught me how to fight." I turned to leave, then thought to add, "And tell him if he tries me again, he'll have more than a headache."

When we assembled for training the next day, Curso was missing from the ranks, yet when one of the other *Tiros* asked the Optio in charge of our training that day, from the Fifth Century, as I recall, he only said, "Curso took a bad fall when he was on the way to the latrines last night. He'll be in the hospital for a couple of days."

I could not be sure, but it seemed as if the Optio shot a glance in my direction, although since I was at *intente* and staring straight ahead, I could not be sure. The personal clashes of *Tiros* aside, our training continued and, thanks to what I had read from my Avus' account and what my father told me, I had a distinct advantage because I knew that everything happened in cycles of a week. Where it became complicated in our case was that we only had a bit more than two weeks at that point before we were marching to join with Drusus. One thing working in our favor was that we *Tiros* were joining a veteran Legion, every man around us knowing how to perform the various duties of the Gregarii. Although we knew how to march in formation now, we had yet to make a marching camp, but as the veterans were always happy to point out, we would get to learn in what they insisted was the best manner possible.

"There's no better way to learn how to dig a ditch than after you've done a good, hard thirty-mile march," was how Servius Metellus, one of the veterans of my permanent section told me, favoring me with a smile that was notable because he was missing three of his bottom teeth.

Despite my suspicion that he was not telling me for my education, but for his amusement, I was compelled to ask, "Is that how you learned?"

Giving me a look of horror, he shook his head and exclaimed, "By the gods, no! I doubt I would have survived if I had to spend all day eating dust, then bend my back to dig a ditch that early on!" Apparently, my face reflected my dismay, which was undoubtedly his goal because he burst out laughing, then gave me a hard punch on my shoulder. "Cheer up, boy! A lad your size should be just fine!"

As I drifted asleep that night, I just hoped that was true.

"How can you fight holding your sword like that?"

It was the morning of our second day at the stakes, and we were waiting to be marched out to them to begin the day. We had learned that we had a short period of time before we were expected to be in formation in the morning, and I found I was quickly surrounded by most of the other *Tiros*. Happy to show off a bit and anxious to win, if not the friendship, then at least the gratitude of my fellow *Tiros*, understanding that I was likely to be facing Curso again at some point, I pulled my *rudis* from its thong and held it aloft so everyone could see.

"It does take some getting used to," I admitted, then thought for a moment as I tried to come up with something that might help. Then, remembering something, I said, "There's an exercise you can do that will make your hand really strong. My father

41

showed it to me. He learned it from my grandfather," I continued with what I believed was understandable pride. "You thrust your hand into a bucket of sand with your fingers out like this." I held up my left hand, my fingers spread wide. "Then," I demonstrated by curling my fingers into a fist, "you do this."

"How many times?" If I remember, it was Aulus Titius who asked the question.

"I started at a hundred," I told him.

More than one of the other muttered a curse or groaned, and I decided against telling them that I had worked my way up to five hundred.

"Why do they call it the…what was it?"

"The Vinician grip," I answered, and I will admit I was more than happy to show off how much I knew about this. "It's named for Aulus Vinicius."

"Who? Never heard of him."

"He was the weapons instructor of the First Century, Second Cohort of the 10th, under Gaius Crastinus," I explained.

"Gaius Crastinus?" Titius asked. "You mean *the* Gaius Crastinus? The one who died at Pharsalus?"

"That's him," I confirmed.

"*Gerrae,*" exclaimed Marcus Sergius. "Now you're telling tales!"

I turned to look at Sergius with a cool gaze, and I must say I was happy to see him blanch; what I had done to Curso was barely a day old.

"Why do you say that?" I asked him quietly.

"Because you said this Vinicius was in Crastinus' Century," he protested, "in the Second Cohort. Everyone knows Gaius Crastinus was the Primus Pilus!"

"Shut up, idiot," Titius cut in, giving Sergius a shove. "Do you think a man starts out in the Centurionate as Primus Pilus?" he scoffed. "They have to work their way up the ranks."

"Oh," Sergius said, suddenly interested in the dirt.

While I normally would have been inclined to make more of an issue of him insinuating I was lying, I already had Curso to worry about.

"Thank you, Titius," I said instead. "Anyway, you're right. When the 10th was formed by Divus Julius, Crastinus was the Secundus Pilus Prior, and Vinicius was his Optio. He's the one who invented this way of holding the sword. Then, when my grandfather took over as the weapons instructor of the Century, he began teaching the same way. Then," I shrugged, "as he worked his way up the ranks, he made every Gregarius under his command learn to hold the sword that way. That included my father. He's the one who taught me."

This seemed to satisfy everyone, and when one of us spied the Optio, Galens again, coming our way, we immediately began shuffling into our respective spots.

As we did, Sergius asked, "You said your grandfather took over as weapons instructor?"

I told him that was the case.

"Well, what happened to this Vinicius?"

For an instant, I thought of saying I did not know, but dismissed it. I am not sure why, but I felt I owed the truth not just to my fellow *Tiros*, but to the shade of Aulus Vinicius, wherever he is.

"He was doused in boiling pitch during the 10th's first campaign in Hispania when they were assaulting some town wall," I said just loudly enough for everyone to hear. "My grandfather watched him burn to death."

Curso rejoined our group two days after our encounter in the mess, still sporting a large, yellow bruise on his forehead and glaring poisonous hatred in my direction.

As we were standing in what had become our places in the formation of *Tiros* where we waited for whoever was going to train us that day, the *Tiro* who was to my left, Vibius Tuditanus his name, whispered, "I'd watch my back if I were you. I heard Curso telling some of the bunch he hangs around with that he's going to get even."

Although this did not surprise me, I thanked Tuditanus nonetheless. I had grown to like Tuditanus quite a bit and, despite the fact he was going to be assigned to the Third Century, I wanted to maintain a friendly relationship with him. Because of my size, I was destined to be on the outside file on the far right of the formation; in this case, we were part of the last rank. Tuditanus was about three inches shorter than I was, but he was not particularly muscular. He had wiry red hair and very pale skin that would never tan, but while he did not have my advantages in coming from a line of Legionaries, he had adapted very quickly to the strict regimen and discipline. When I asked him about it, he had just shrugged and said something vague about his father being strict. Sensing he had no real desire to discuss it, I did not press, which my father had advised as the best course before I departed Arelate.

"Men join for a number of reasons," he had counseled, "and all men have secrets. The Legions are the one place where a man can keep those reasons and his past private. Don't ever try to pry into a man's past because you might not like what you hear."

In the case of Tuditanus, I found it hard to believe that he would take offense, although I did as my father suggested. But while I had, and still have, a volcanic temper, and when I was seventeen, was very quick to take offense at any slight, real or imagined, Tuditanus had an easygoing, pleasant disposition that made him impossible to dislike. He had very quickly become one of the most popular *Tiros*, often serving as intermediary and peacemaker between those who quarreled about one thing or another. It probably will not surprise you to learn, dear reader, that I availed myself of Tuditanus' skills as a mediator probably more than any other *Tiro*. Now that time has passed, I can say that I bear responsibility for a fair number of the conflicts in which I found myself with the others, and I would also say that when one gathers together a group of young men, all eager to prove themselves in the harsh world of the Legions, such conflicts are inevitable, through no real fault of any individual. That being said, I cannot lie; it did not take much to offend me, and I never, ever backed down, even when the wise course would have been to walk away.

The week before we left, it was determined that we had learned just enough where we could be paired off in sparring sessions, and I had been looking forward to this a great deal. I will also admit that I was influenced once more by my Avus, specifically by his account of his own sparring with the man who was his nemesis in his Century, Spurius Didius. Almost as quickly as Curso had confronted me, I had associated him with Spurius Didius; I was always looking for parallels between my own story and that of my Avus. I suppose, in many ways, I still am.

However, the gods deemed it to be otherwise; we were never paired together, but as I learned later, this was no accident. Nevertheless, we went at each other, protected by extra padding and the wicker faceguards that were made standard in the Augustan reforms, with a great deal of enthusiasm and varying levels of skill. I know how boastful it sounds, but I am simply stating the truth when I say that I was never seriously challenged by any of my fellow *Tiros*; it was not until I faced off with veterans that I met men who were my equal. Again, I felt that I was simply following along in the footsteps of my Avus, but unlike him, I always reminded myself that this sparring was meaningless, and that until we faced battle, only then would I know if I was truly as good as I thought I was. At times, I shudder to think what my fate might have been if I had not been fortunate enough to read and, more importantly, absorb the story of my Avus' career. One episode in particular stuck in my mind during my training, and that was how he almost met his end in his first battle. Like me, because of the early training he and his best friend Vibius had undergone with Cyclops, the nickname of a former Legionary who fought for Sertorius, he had earned the attention and praise of Gaius Crastinus. In fact, before the campaign even started, men had begun wagering on how many kills my Avus would make in his first battle. Seduced by this praise, when he was selected by Crastinus to follow his Pilus Prior as the second man up the ladder during their first assault, he almost got himself killed because, in his excitement, he forgot probably the most important and basic step of drawing his sword. I kept this in mind throughout not just the training, but my first campaign; in this way, I can say that the *numen* of my Avus was watching out for me.

There was one thing for which I was not prepared; a change that had occurred in the intervening years between my father's retirement from the Legions and when I showed up in Siscia. Once I was old and strong enough, my father had me train wearing the *lorica hamata,* the mail shirt that the men of the Legions have worn for centuries. However, when I was issued all the equipment of a Legionary of Rome, what I was handed as my armor bore no resemblance to the mail armor with which I was so familiar.

Seeing my confusion, the *Immune* responsible for dispensing our gear laughed, but it was not in a mocking way, and he told me, "Ah, I see someone hasn't heard about the new armor."

Holding it up, I tried to make sense of it and, as I was about to learn, the one drawback of this new armor is in putting it on, at least the first few times until one both figures it out and adjusts

46

it to fit the body properly. That day, what I was holding up did not look like anything resembling armor, but was instead a series of overlapping, curved iron plates that was held together by a series of straps and buckles.

"That," the *Immune* said proudly, "is the *lorica segmentata*. All new *Tiros* are being issued a set."

"How does it work?" I asked, still bewildered and trying to determine exactly how these plates were supposed to protect me.

"Your Optio will show you," the *Immune* had said before moving on to the next piece of my inventory.

However, when I approached Galens with the new *lorica*, he only looked at it with horror and shook his head, exclaiming, "I don't know anything about that piece of *cac*."

That was when I learned that this new piece of equipment was viewed with nothing but suspicion by the veterans. Which, I must say, should not be surprising, and it was a distrust I shared. It turned out that the man who helped me decipher the mystery of the *segmentata* was the Sergeant of the section to which I was permanently assigned. Appius Asinius was his name, a thin, wiry man from Umbria originally, but who had joined the Legions in Siscia. He was on his first enlistment and was in his late twenties and, while he had allowed the others to have the fun that all veterans have with *Tiros*, he had never participated. Like most everyone else, he was a few inches shorter than I was, but he had something which, at the time at least, I envied and coveted for my own, and that was a prominent battle scar in the form of a long, pinkish-white line that ran down the outside of his right forearm from elbow to wrist. More importantly, at least for my needs at that moment, he was familiar with the *segmentata* because when he had taken his old mail shirt to the armorer to be repaired, they had kept it and given him the new armor. This was how the *segmentata* was introduced to the rankers, at least in my Legion: as the old armor needed to be repaired, instead it was replaced. Asinius was the only veteran in my section, and one of the half-dozen in my Century, who had the new armor. That night, he showed me how the system of buckles and straps work and, in fact, can be used to adjust the fit so that it is like a second skin. Not in my case, as we learned, at least not at first. We quickly discovered that my chest is simply too large for the *segmentata* as it is normally made, the curvature of the plates needing to be shallower to accommodate my larger torso. The first time we tried it, the best fit we could achieve was such that there was a gap much wider than my hand between the plates, running down the center of my chest.

"Well, that's not good," Asinius muttered. "It would take one of those Germans all of one breath to put one of their spears right there." As he spoke, he punched me hard in the chest in the gap between the plates.

To say that I was dismayed would be an understatement.

"What am I supposed to do?" I asked Asinius, hoping that his answer would be that I could wear the old armor.

I can freely admit now that my desire to revert back to the old *lorica* was based more on my realization that, for the most part, those of us who were *Tiros* would be easy to spot in the ranks and, although I knew I carried that status, I felt that I was more than that. Not a full-fledged Gregarius, perhaps, but certainly no raw *Tiro*. My hope lasted all of the time it took him to shake his head.

"You're going to have to pay for a set that's big enough for you."

"I can't afford that," I gasped.

Asinius did not immediately respond; instead, he just regarded me with a raised eyebrow for several heartbeats.

"Really?" he finally asked quietly. "That's too bad, because I'll tell you now that the orders have come down that no *Tiros* are going to be wearing the *hamata*. Apparently, Augustus wants this new armor adopted as quickly as possible." He gave a shrug that indicated it was not his concern. "But, if you can't afford it, you can't afford it."

Neither of us spoke for a few heartbeats, then I finally muttered, "Fine. Who do I need to talk to in order to get this made?"

He gave me the name of a man in Siscia, and it was actually a name with which I was familiar, having been an armorer *Immune* before his retirement.

"But how do I do that?" I asked Asinius. "You know I can't leave the camp."

"I'll take care of it," he assured me. "You'll have the armor by the end of the week. Just give me the money."

That is when I informed him that I did not actually have the coin, but gave him the name of another man in town.

"Go to him," I told Asinius. I rummaged around in my pack and found one of the tablets that my mother had packed in a not very subtle hint for me to remember to write. Scribbling a quick note, I signed it, then handed Asinius the tablet. "Give him this, and he'll give you what you need."

Asinius shot me a grin then.

"How do you know I'm not going to ask him for more than it will actually cost?"

Although I thought he was joking, I remained serious. "Because I trust you. We're going to be fighting and killing together."

He regarded me for a long moment, gave me a thoughtful nod, then clapped me on the shoulder. "You're absolutely right. And I'll take care of it."

Asinius was good to his word; by the end of that week, I had a *segmentata* that fit me perfectly and, once I finally got it adjusted properly, I immediately felt more comfortable. The only thing I needed to worry about after that was how well it stood up to an enemy blade.

I must admit that I worried that Asinius would waste no time letting the rest of my section mates know that a lowly *Tiro* like me actually had an account with the man in Siscia who was known to be a plutocrat, but my fears were in vain. He never mentioned it to the others and, in fact, it would not be until some time had passed before I finally let my tentmates know what they had suspected. Before I left for Siscia, my father and I had the most violent quarrel we ever had, over my refusal to take a sum of money with me to deposit in Siscia.

"I don't want to be treated any differently," I had told him. "And how many *Tiros* are going to show up with that much money?"

"None," he agreed, but he was unmoved. "But whether you like it or not, you *are* different, not only because of who you are, but your size, strength, and skill. And you need to listen to what I'm telling you." He had grabbed my arm and, as strong as I am, I still winced from the crush of his grip. "The army is going to charge you for all manner of things, which is fine. But at some point, you're going to need some coin, and there are men in the ranks who will appear to be your friend and will 'loan' you the money. You do *not* want to owe men like that, Titus." He shook his head to emphasize his point. "No, you're depositing this money with Papernius as soon as you get there."

Seeing that he was not going to be swayed, I relented, although I was not completely done. "But a thousand sesterces?" I asked him. "Isn't that a little…much?"

My father shrugged and said, "Better to have too much than not enough. Just as long as you don't go doing something to draw attention to yourself."

"You mean like buying wine and whores for my Century?" I grinned at him, knowing this would get a reaction.

He looked at me in alarm, then saw I was joking, and gave a kind of snorting laugh.

"Yes, like that. Don't even joke like that. You're likely to give me an apoplectic fit," he grumbled.

Although a thousand sesterces, when measured against the un-confiscated portion of my Avus' fortune, was just a drop in the amphora, it still represented more than a year's pay to a Gregarius. I was young, but I was wise enough to know that there were men in the ranks who would have gladly cut my throat if they thought I was carrying that sum on my person. That was why I was extremely happy to rid myself of all but a handful of coin when I got to Siscia. My newly forged *segmentata* arrived just in time for our sparring sessions, and I quickly discovered that contrary to what one might think, it actually allowed for more supple movement than the old armor. It was lighter, but the way the plates overlap with each other allows your torso to move more easily from side to side; the only area where it does not compare favorably with mail is in twisting movements. Although I personally did not have problems with that kind of movement, I will say that it takes a bit more effort to twist the body. Best of all, at least as far as the armorers are concerned, if a plate is damaged, it is just a matter of unbuckling that plate and replacing it. Of course, once I became aware of this, I started worrying about what would happen if we were out on campaign and I needed to have plates replaced. I brought this up with Asinius, who agreed it was something that needed to be discussed with the armorers. When I returned to our hut the night I brought it up, he had welcome news.

"As long as they have the original plate, they can heat the replacement plate and curve it to match yours," he assured me. "But," he warned, "they're not going to do it for free. So you better bring enough coin along in case you need to pay them."

I was not particularly happy about this, but understood there was not much I could do about it.

In our sparring sessions, I performed about as well as I expected and I was the only undefeated one among the *Tiros*. Although I was proud of this, I also behaved differently than my Avus did, and I did so as a direct result of reading his story. Like him, I could not help being bigger and stronger, and I will not deny that I was, and am, proud of that fact. However, after reading of some of the troubles my Avus, by his own admission, brought on himself with his need to leave absolutely no doubt that he was superior to his comrades in every way, I decided on a different approach. Not once did I exert myself fully against my sparring partner and, although I always emerged victorious, I made no attempt to humiliate or embarrass others. Thankfully so; as I mentioned before, I was never matched against Curso because I know myself well enough to understand that no private vow I made would have stopped me from beating him as badly as I could get away with. Unfortunately for my fellow *Tiros* who were paired against me, while I did not go to the extent my Avus did, I still saw, and see, no reason not to use the gifts that the gods have given me. The fact that these gifts left my opponents with more than their share of bumps and bruises only reinforced the fact that I was not to be trifled with, and I will say that even Curso gave me a wide berth after that, preferring instead to do his talking about me outside of my earshot. Naturally, I heard this talk, albeit relayed after being passed through many mouths, but I chose to ignore it rather than confront Curso. Unlike my Avus, it was enough for me that he was refusing to say any of these things to my face or within my hearing.

I do not want to give the impression that matters went all my way. After I had gone undefeated against the *Tiros*, on what turned out to be our last day of sparring, one or more of the officers involved in our training decided that I needed to be taken down a notch because when my name was called to step into the area designated for our mock combat, waiting for me was not another *Tiro*. Instead, it was the Optio of the Fourth Century, a stocky, hard-looking man named Servius Pinna. Seeing him standing there got my heart beating even faster than it normally did before I sparred another *Tiro,* both because of the fact he was an Optio and from all that I had heard about this man. While he was not in the same league as my Avus, he still had a formidable reputation as a fierce fighter and a great man with a sword. He stared across the open space at me, and I noticed that he was not wearing the wicker faceguard, nor was he wearing the arm padding that we are required to wear. Even with this protection, men are taken to the hospital tent quite frequently with broken bones, and I had been responsible for two of these cases with my fellow *Tiros*. Fortunately, neither of the *Tiros* were injured so severely that they could not continue their training and were dismissed; that would have upset me quite a bit. However, seeing Pinna showing such disdain for me by foregoing the normal precautions ignited in me a flicker of anger that I felt deep inside me. I remember thinking, with some grim amusement, that while I might not come out as the victor, I would make sure that Pinna had cause to regret his decision.

I did not win my bout with Pinna, but neither did I lose. At least, according to all but a small handful of men who were witness to our contest. However, those who did not see it the way the majority did were the men who mattered, consisting of the Optios of the Century, who served as the arbiters of winners and losers whenever we sparred. Nevertheless, my fellow *Tiros,* along with a number of the veteran Gregarii of the Cohort who either had no duty or had managed to sneak away, were not shy about voicing their opinions, in the form of a chorus of boos and whistles when Galens who, being the Optio of the First Century, served as chief judge, announced their decision that Pinna had won. Even at that moment, I knew that the majority of those making a disturbance were not doing so because of any feeling towards me, but that there was money riding on the decision. Frankly, I was too tired and hurt too much to be angry about any possible injustice. Even with the padding, when Tuditanus helped pull them off my arms, there were several large, red welts covering my arms and, that night, when I finally removed my tunic, my torso was a close match to my arms. Surprisingly enough, my pride was not as lacerated as I thought it might have been, and as I am sure at least some of the Optios wanted. I can now say with no shame that Pinna was better than I was that day, but the gap was not nearly as wide as he and his fellow Optios would have liked, and I took some satisfaction in the fact that he was as bruised as I was, perhaps even more so because of his decision. That was probably why I was as satisfied as I was afterward because, by appearances alone, he looked like he had taken the worse beating. It also marked a change with the Optios over the last ten days of our training period before we began our preparations to march to join Drusus. They no longer singled me out as often and, while my fellow *Tiros* did not care for it all that much, I was more than happy that the treatment I had been receiving was being shared more equally.

"Why did you have to almost beat him?" was how Tuditanus put it to me one day, grumbling under his breath after he had been cuffed about the head and shoulders for an error we had committed as a group for which I normally bore the brunt.

"Now you know how it feels." I was not sympathetic in the least.

"Yes, but you're big as an ox. And you were born for this, not like some of us," he argued, but I was unmoved.

"Bah," I told him cheerfully. "It'll just make you tougher for when we face those smelly Germans for the first time."

As soon as I said it, I regretted speaking about the danger that was looming ahead of us, and Tuditanus turned even paler underneath his freckled skin.

"Why'd you remind me?" he muttered.

I said nothing more; in truth, as soon as I said it, I felt a flutter in my own chest at the thought of what lay ahead for us. In fairness, I was not the only one talking about our immediate future. It was the predominant topic of conversation, not only among the *Tiros,* but when I would return to my section hut every night, invariably, the men of my section would be discussing the upcoming march and sharing all the tidbits that they had heard. This marked my first, but far from my last, experience with what I have learned is the lifeblood of the Legions, and that is gossip. I doubt that it would surprise anyone to know that, especially in the days preceding a move to either start or join a campaign, the predominant topic is focused on what we could expect in the coming days and weeks. Next to talking about our betters, both socially and up the chain of command, rankers are obsessed with finding out all that they can about an upcoming operation and, most specifically, about the enemy that we will be facing. I doubt that the conversation I am about to relate is from one conversation, but is most likely an amalgam of many talks that were taking place in my section hut in the days before we left Siscia. However, I remember this exchange as one conversation, although I doubt that it occurred this way. As I said, I do not have the memory of my Avus.

As I recall it, it was a few days after my sparring match with Pinna, and Asinius was applying a salve that he swore by to one of the worst of the bruises on my chest, which had turned a yellowish-purple in color. I was sitting on one of the benches that lined the single table in the center of our quarters, and he sat across from me, dabbing the foul-smelling concoction onto my chest. Every member of my section was there, as I recall it, either lounging on their bunks or sitting on the opposite bench on the other side of the table.

I believe it was Numerius Poplicola, the second-youngest Gregarius next to me, who was sitting on his bunk and asked, "Have any of you fought these bastards before?"

There was no need for Poplicola to elaborate on the identity of who he was asking about, and I freely admit that I made no pretense that I was not keenly interested in what anyone else had to say. Nobody spoke for several heartbeats, and I had just started to believe that Poplicola's question would go unanswered, when Lucius Bassus finally spoke.

"I have." He was lying on his bunk, staring up at the ceiling, since he had the top bunk.

I glanced over at him, as did Poplicola and, frankly, most of my comrades as well. The only one who seemed uninterested was Asinius, but as I learned, it was because he had already heard what Bassus had to say. Where Poplicola and I were the youngest, Bassus was the opposite. Deeply tanned, with enough wrinkles that his face looked like a raisin, he was in his early forties and as tough as old boot leather. Normally the quietest of our section, he was at the far end of our rank from me, at what is called the "little end." Because of my busy training schedule, I had had little chance to get to know much about any of the men I would be fighting with, but what I did know of Bassus was that, while he was a veteran on his second enlistment, he came from another Legion, I believe it was from the 17th, that is stationed on the Rhenus. I never learned the specifics, but there was some mystery surrounding his transfer from the 17th, and I subsequently heard whispers of a dispute between Bassus and his Optio, the cause of the disagreement supposedly a woman, and the Optio took care of his competition by arranging for his transfer.

Seemingly oblivious to the sudden silence, Bassus did not seem disposed to elaborate for several heartbeats, and I saw Poplicola opening his mouth when the older man finally said, "They're big bastards, I'll give them that." Turning his head on his pillow, he nodded in my direction. "Most of them are Pullus' size. And they make a lot of noise. I mean, a *lot*," he emphasized. "They're so loud, it's almost impossible to hear yourself think and it is impossible to hear anything but the *cornu*. You damn well can't hear the Centurion's whistle." He paused, as if collecting his thoughts. "Oh, and they smell. I mean they put out a stench you can't believe until you're up close to them, but I think that's on purpose. I heard something once about how they think bathing's for women, not warriors."

I had heard that as well and I could see that the rest of my comrades were growing impatient because Bassus was telling things they already knew.

"Yes, we know all that." This came from Manius Tubero, who was one of the men playing at dice on the other side of the table. He and his opponent, I believe it was Spurius Dento, had paused in their game, and I believe Tubero was just eager to resume. "But how do they fight?"

"Like demons," Bassus replied quietly. Giving a slight shake of his head, he continued, "At least, that's the only way I can describe it. They come swarming at you, every one of them howling like mad dogs, and they move *fast*. They've learned that their only chance to beat us is to break our formation, so they have warriors who throw themselves at you. But they're aiming for your shield more than you, so they can knock it down out of the way for the *cunnus* who's following right behind."

He paused again as we digested this, the hut completely quiet as we all waited for what came next.

"Most of them carry spears, but they have a fair number of bastards who carry swords," Bassus said. "The ones that do are their nobles, or at least that's what we were told. But the ones you have to worry about aren't the spear carriers or sword wielders, it's those bastards that carry an axe." Even from where I sat, I could see a shudder go through Bassus' prone body. "Most of them are double bladed and, when they swing them about, if you don't keep your head about you, you'll lose it." He gave a harsh chuckle at his own wit, but I for one was not disposed to join in, although some of the others did.

When Bassus said no more, after a moment's silence, Poplicola, who had started the whole conversation, asked, "What tribe were you fighting? That makes a difference, doesn't it? Some are worse than others?"

"It does," Bassus agreed. "To a point. And yes, there are tribes that are wilder than others. The ones we were fighting that day were the Marcomanni. My Century was manning an outpost on the Rhenus, and a warband of about three hundred of the bastards managed to cross the river during the night. They attacked at dawn and used the mists that come off the river most mornings as cover to get close. I was one of the lucky ones who happened to be standing guard. One moment it's quiet, the next it sounds like Hades has suddenly freed all of the demons and *numeni* from their cages, and they come swarming up to the ditch."

"Didn't you have scorpions?" one of my comrades asked. I do not remember who it was.

"We did." Bassus gave another laugh that held no humor. "But they were pointing in the wrong direction. The *cunni* went sneaking around so they could hit the wall farthest from the river. Oh, we got them moved, but by the time we did, it didn't make much difference. They had already crossed the ditch and were climbing the walls." He fell silent again and, as I would come to learn all too well, it was because the memories of that day still haunted him. "We had our hands full, I'll say that," he resumed. "They actually got over the wall and into the camp for a bit. We had to fight them among the tents, but only the gods know how we managed it. We kept them from getting to the gate and opening it. A lot of good men died that day," he finished quietly.

With that last statement, he made it clear that he was finished and, soon enough, we all resumed what we had been doing. While I cannot speak for the others, I suspect that their thoughts were similar to mine. Of all the things Bassus said, the one that was lodged in my mind was not the specifics, but the identity of the tribe we would be facing.

It was not until the day before we left Siscia that I learned of the presence of one of my childhood friends, also marching in the ranks of the Fourth Cohort. Gnaeus Figulus was in the Third Century, and I just happened to spot him in the ranks as they marched by. Despite the flurry of activity as everyone hurried about performing their last-moment duties or were scrambling to replace some broken or lost piece of gear, I managed to sneak away from my Century street just after the evening meal and hurried two streets over to the Third Century's area. Fortunately, I spied him outside his hut, where he and another Gregarius were seated, applying the coat of wax we use on our shields to make them more water resistant as well as giving the fresh paint job a gleaming finish. His back was to me, but I immediately knew it was he by virtue of the pair of ears that stuck out from his head almost perpendicularly. Our other friend, Quintus Pacuvius, and, being honest, I as well had never tired of making jokes at Figulus' expense about his ears, but he bore it well and gave as good as he got.

"It's good to see that those Germans will never be able to sneak up on us with you and your ears," I told his back.

Whirling around with the rag he was using to apply the wax still in his hand, his fair features flushed a dark red, his eyes narrowed as he was ready to make an issue of my words. He stopped short, and his expression changed, first from a wary puzzlement, then to recognition.

"Titus?" he gasped. "Titus Porcinus?" Before I could answer, he dropped the rag and stepped towards me, holding out his arm and saying, "Of course it's you! Nobody else is your size!"

I took his arm, but then, by common consent, we hugged each other as brothers, kissing each other on the cheek, both of us laughing with delight at this reunion.

Only then did I think to correct him. "And it's Titus Porcinianus Pullus now, not just Titus Porcinus."

His expression faltered for a moment, and I felt badly as he uttered an apology.

"By the gods, I'd forgotten about that," he told me, the words coming out in a rush. "Forgive me, Master *Pullus*." He gave me a mock bow, which I answered with a shove, both of us laughing.

"When did you join up?" I asked him.

"Two years ago," he told me, and it reminded me that he was indeed two years older than I was, despite the fact that I towered over him as I had all of our lives. "What about you?"

"Almost a month ago," I answered, a bit grudgingly.

"Ha!" He gave a short, barking laugh, which I had forgotten was another trait of his that we often teased him about. "So you're still a *Tiro!* That means I outrank you!" Suddenly, his expression changed, and he pointed to the discarded rag. "*Tiro!* Pick that up!"

For a moment, I did not move, unsure whether he was serious. I could see his companion, still seated on the stool, his own work forgotten, grinning over Figulus' shoulder at me, clearly enjoying my sudden discomfort. Figulus' smile had disappeared, and he stood, pointing at the rag. Finally, I stepped to the rag and bent over to pick it up then, since that was all he had told me, I stiffened to *intente*.

"Ha ha!" Figulus' stern demeanor dissolved in a fit of delighted laughter. "I finally got you to do something I told you to do! I've been waiting years for that!"

His companion joined in, and the two of them were soon so consumed in mirth that tears were streaming down their faces. I, on the other hand, was furious, at least at first. But when I felt the sudden bolt of anger, and not just of the kind that I experienced when I stubbed my toe, or was somehow thwarted in something, but the kind that I had only experienced once in my life before this moment, that scared me so badly that it immediately disappeared. I was still standing at *intente*, but I could feel a rush of sweat rolling down my chest and back as my mind raced through all that this meant. I do not know how long this state lasted, but it could not have been very long because Figulus and his comrade were still laughing when I finally joined in.

"You should have seen your face," Figulus hooted, pointing at me. "You looked like you swallowed a turd!"

By this point, I had sufficiently recovered myself that I could see the humor and had begun laughing as well.

"That's the only way you could get me to do anything, by outranking me," I said, shaking my head, absurdly pleased that I had made Figulus laugh so hard.

"I have to take my advantage wherever I can find it," he shot back. "Gods know I've never been able to beat you in anything else."

This mollified my wounded sense of pride at being mocked in front of a stranger, and we spent the next few moments catching up on our respective families, as well as our mutual friends, one in particular.

"So where's Quintus?" I asked Figulus. "Is he still in town?"

"That *mentula*," Figulus scoffed. "He's still here. But he's an apprentice to a smith in town."

Quintus Pacuvius was the other of my two closest childhood friends, and the three of us had been inseparable during my time in Siscia. Like me, he was the son of a Centurion, and his father had been under the command of mine in the Fourth Cohort. He was the oldest of the three of us by a year, so he had been allowed to accompany the army on campaign. It had been an action against the Varciani, one of the native tribes of Pannonia who had, and still have, a bad habit of forgetting they are under Roman rule now. Pacuvius had gone to serve as his father's body servant, which is fairly common for boys who have reached their teen years and whose fathers are under the standard. I had good cause to remember that campaign because, as momentous as it had been for my friend Quintus, it was no less so for me, if for completely different reasons. As far as Pacuvius was concerned, the end result of all that he had experienced and seen was his decision that life in the army was not for him, which was why Figulus was showing the attitude he was towards our friend.

"Well," I replied, "I think it's better that he recognized he wasn't cut out for it and not join than enlisting and then having his nerve fail him at a moment when it counts."

"Bah," Figulus scoffed. "He's a girl. He knew what he was getting into before he ever left on that campaign. He's just scared."

Of course he's scared, I thought to myself. I was about to remonstrate with Figulus and remind him that both Quintus and I had seen things that gave him good cause to feel as he did, but then I stopped myself. I recalled that there had always been a bit of bad blood between Figulus and Pacuvius, and it is only now that I am able to recognize its cause, which was me. Both of them wanted to be considered my best friend; these are some of the things that come with being the biggest and strongest because I am certain that was the reason for their feelings towards me. It certainly was not because of my status; back in my childhood, I had no real status, and neither did my father.

"Why don't you come in and have a cup?" Figulus' invitation broke into my thoughts. "I can finish this up in a bit."

Frankly, I was not tempted to accept, both because I realized that my absence was probably being noticed, and I needed some time with my own thoughts. Naturally, I used the first reason as my excuse, and once more we clasped arms and, despite the uneasy feelings that had been stirred up by my visit, I was happy that I had made it. We parted with the mutual promise that somewhere along the march we could do more catching up with each other, and then I headed back to my Century street. Despite knowing that I needed to return to my duties, I took the long way, needing the extra time to think.

What had happened with Figulus had scared me badly, both for the fact it came from such a trivial matter, and because I knew where the road led if I had not quelled that coil of rage. Although it had been more than seven years, the memory of the first and, to that point, the only time I had experienced what had been described to me as a fit, albeit divinely inspired, was still vivid. But the results of that fit was what woke me at night, the memory of a blood-spattered, battered corpse of a dwarf that had been named Spartacus lying at my feet. But as I learned the hard way, a man who is fully grown, no matter what his size, is still stronger than a boy who is the same size and, the first time we faced each other, he thrashed me soundly, inflicting that large gash that required sutures, along with several bruises. However, more than the physical pain was the humiliation from our bout occurring in front of all the other trainees and gladiators in the *ludus*, and I can still hear their mocking laughter now, twenty years later. From that moment, I resolved to exact vengeance on the dwarf. It was just two days before we were to leave Arelate and return to Siscia that I gave Libo the slip while on our daily ride to return to the *ludus*. Once there, I enticed Vulso by putting up my most prized possession, my wonderful Ocelus, as a wager, in a bid to face Spartacus again. And while I was prepared for our contest, what I was completely unprepared for was the level of hostility exhibited by the spectators, all of it aimed at me. As I said, it was an important lesson for me because of my mistaken belief that they viewed me as the same as they were. All they knew was that I was free, and somehow connected to the faceless owner of the *ludus*, which by extension meant that I represented their master. The hatred was so palpable it frightened me, at first. Then, as I stood waiting for Spartacus to make his way through the people that formed the living boundary of the ring in which we would face each other, something happened. The fear turned into an anger, but of a type and power that I had never experienced before, as within me a terrible rage grew to the point that, when Spartacus appeared, I was told I had launched myself at him with the velocity of a scorpion bolt. And now, all these years later, I can only recall disjointed bits and pieces of our actual fight, mainly just the vision of his battered, broken body, with his skull cracked open, pouring its contents onto the sand. When Figulus had played his trick on me, that was the same kind of rage I felt boiling up inside me, but what gave me pause more than it actually occurring was the fact that, somehow, I was able to stop it before it came bursting forth. In the immediate aftermath of my killing of Spartacus, I had been told, first by Diocles, then by my father, that my Avus had experienced similar fits, but it was not until I read his scrolls that I learned he had never been able to control them, or predict when they would strike. All he knew was that it came to him in moments when he and his comrades were in the greatest danger and kept them alive. That day with Figulus gave me the first glimmering that I might have some way to stop these fits at the very least, if not control them.

Chapter Two

Two parts of a watch before dawn, I was roused by a kick to my bunk, opening my eyes to see Asinius staring down at me.

"Get up, *Tiro*," he ordered. "It's time to get ready to march."

I was surprised that I had managed to fall asleep at all, but obviously, I had. After I rolled out of my bunk, I performed my last-moment checks of all that I would be carrying on my *furca*, including my portion of the uncooked rations that we would be carrying for the first five days of the march. In truth, I was carrying more than just my portion, but frankly, I was neither surprised nor did I mind all that much that this was so. From the first day I arrived in Siscia, I knew that I had a very large pair of *caligae* to fill; to whom much is given, much is expected and, therefore, I was, if not happy, then willing to do more than my share. Very quickly, we fell in on our Century street, the gloom only broken by the guttering torches that are placed at the corners and midway down each street. Assuming my place in the formation, it was with a quiet sense of pride that I realized that, like my Avus and my father, I was the last man to the right, although I was in the rear rank. Only if I proved to be inept at the actual fighting would I have to relinquish my spot, since the outside man is the only one not protected by a comrade's shield. As strange as it may sound, on this morning two days shy of a month after I had taken the oath of *tirone*, I was part of the full Century formation for only the third time. And it would be the first time I ever participated in a march on the open road and, truthfully, I was more nervous about this than the prospect of facing battle, at least at that moment. We had been told it would take at least two weeks to reach the point where we were supposed to join with Drusus and his Legions.

Pilus Prior Corvinus strode up after Galens had formed us up and, after a brief inspection, gave the command to march to the forum, where we would form up with the rest of the Legion. By the time the entire Legion, along with the baggage train, had been assembled and was ready to march out the gate, dawn was just breaking. Because it was just our Legion, there was no real fanfare or any kind of commotion when a Legate, or even a Tribune is marching at our head. It would just be the Primus Pilus, Publius Canidius his name, more commonly known as Urso because he was covered in coarse, black hair and, while he was average height, he had what looked like a chickpea barrel for a chest. So muscular was he that his arms actually stuck out at a slight angle. I had yet to meet him, at least as a *Tiro*; the fact is that I knew him quite well, for he had been the Quartus Pilus Posterior, my father's second in command. Had it really been seven years, I wondered, as I saw him striding across the forum to take his place at the head of the First Cohort and the Legion. Although I was still a child the last time I saw him, I was aware that his relationship with my father was incredibly complex. My father had never spoken openly about what happened the day he lost his leg, other than to say that Urso had saved his life. Although I knew their association had been very strained before that event because my father was sure that Urso had been undermining his authority, since Urso believed he should have been Pilus Prior instead, saving my father's life had understandably improved matters between them. Nevertheless, while my father had told me more than once that Urso was an honorable man, there was a reserve there when my father spoke of him that told me almost as much as his words. What I knew, even as a child, was that in the aftermath of the action in which my father was wounded, Publius Canidius had suddenly been promoted. This was to be expected, given the nature of my father's wound; what was completely unexpected and unusual was the fact that he was promoted all the way to the post of Primus Pilus. Again, this was something my father never spoke about, but before we left Siscia permanently, while he was still recuperating from the loss of his leg, I remember hearing the talk in the streets of Siscia, wherever members of Legionaries' families congregated, that Urso's appointment had been payment for some great service he rendered to one of the upper classes. When I first heard this talk, I quite naturally assumed that it could only have been the divine Augustus who was so pleased with whatever it was that he had done. It was only a day or two later that I learned my assumption was erroneous, at least according to the prevalent gossip on the streets of Siscia. In fact, it had been Tiberius, whose military career was launched on a campaign against the Rhaeti in which my father and the 8th participated, who supposedly had given this prize to Urso. I was, and still am, naturally curious, but no matter how much I pressed my father or worked it into a conversation by what I was sure were clever means, he never said a word to me about what he knew about the veracity of this tale. Actually, he did say something, when he finally lost his temper with my constant pestering of him about it.

"You don't need to know everything!" he had thundered at me, which, while it was more frequent after his amputation, was still not a common occurrence. "In fact, there are some things you're better off not knowing anything about, and this is one of them! Never ask me again," he had finished and, while he was no longer yelling, I recognized his tone as one that signified he meant what he said.

Nor did I ask him again, but I suppose it was natural that this was what was in my mind as I watched Urso take his place at the head of the column.

"Urso hasn't changed much," I commented to the man next to me, Asinius, who would be the man I would be protecting with my shield during my time in this spot in the formation of the First Century.

While I was still looking ahead, I sensed him giving me a sharp look.

"You better not ever let him hear you call him 'Urso'," he warned me.

I looked at him in some surprise.

"Why?" I asked. "That's what he's been called since I've known him, which is all of my life."

"He doesn't go by that anymore, and I've seen him stripe a Gregarius who he caught using that nickname."

"How long has he been like that?" I wondered aloud.

"How long do you think?" Asinius laughed. "Since he became Primus Pilus. Now, you call him Primus Pilus Canidius if you know what's good for you." Suddenly, Asinius' voice dropped to just above a whisper, making it hard to hear him over the muffled conversations that were taking place up and down the ranks since we had been released from *intente* in preparation to begin the march. "Porcinus, I know you've been around the ranks a long time, but things have changed. A lot," he added ominously, "since you've been gone. If I were you, I wouldn't count on your knowledge of how things used to be. Or who your father was." He hesitated for a moment, as if weighing what he was going to say next. "In fact, it may actually work against you, being Gaius Porcinus' boy. Or," he added, "Titus Pullus' grandson."

At this, I turned my head to stare him fully in the eyes, looking for any hint or sign that might tell me what his motivation was for telling me this. Although it was still not fully light, it was bright enough that I could see him clearly and I could not see in his expression any hint of guile or dissembling there.

"Thank you for warning me," I told Asinius, who just gave me a shrug in reply. Then, I do not know what moved me, but I said, "Since it looks like I'm fucked either way I go, I'm going to ask that you call me by my real name, not my old one."

Asinius shot me a look that appeared to be a combination of amusement and irritation.

"Whatever you say...*Pullus*." He made no attempt to disguise the bow of his head as anything but a mocking one. "But don't say I didn't warn you."

It no longer shames me to say that the next ten days were the most physically demanding of my life. As fit as I was when it came to fighting, I had not turned a spade of dirt, nor had I cut any turf in my young life before that first night on the march. My Cohort was selected to dig a part of the ditch that surrounds and protects every encampment of the Roman army when it is on the march. The one small blessing, or at least so I was reminded of this on a regular basis by my veteran comrades, was that we had not been required to wear our armor, but it was small comfort to one exhausted, dirty teenage boy at the end of that first day. Not surprisingly, the second day was harder than the first, as my body rebelled against the demands I was placing on it. One consolation that I did take was when I spotted my fellow *Tiros*, scattered throughout the Centuries of the Cohort, all of whom looked at least as bad as I felt, I was sure. Poor Tuditanus in particular was having a rough go of it because the sun shone brightly for the entire day, turning his skin a deep red, a shade that it would stay for the entirety of the campaign season.

Now that I look back on it, I realize that I, in fact, did have something in my favor, over and above being bigger and stronger. Ironically enough, it was the territory through which we were marching that actually helped distract me from my misery, although I cannot say that it was without a certain cost, in the form of a troubled mind and unpleasant memories. The route Urso had chosen for us was along the Via Postumia, which I had foregone on my way to Siscia to enlist, for a number of reasons. One of them was the cause of my distraction. Marching anywhere gives a man time to think about all manner of things, and I cannot calculate with any accuracy the number of watches

I have whiled away the time as my body moved automatically along with my comrades, and this first march was no exception. But, unlike other marches, the road that we were traveling and the surrounding countryside carried deep meaning for me because it was over this very same road I was traveling with my family when an event occurred that, even now, twenty years later, ranks as one of the most frightening of my life.

I was with my entire family, with the exception of my father who was on campaign, returning from Arelate in the months after the death of my Avus. I was bringing Ocelus back to what I thought of as his proper home while the rest of my family, composed of my brother Sextus and sisters Valeria and Miriam, the latter of whom was still suckling, rode in a wagon loaded down with our combined baggage and necessities. We were just a bit more than a day's travel away from Siscia when a band of Latobici, one of the tribes of Pannonia, ambushed us. It was only through the selfless sacrifice of the bodyguard Tiberius Libo that my family was able to retreat to the temporary safety of an abandoned farmhouse. The surviving bodyguard, Quintus Gallus, my family, Diocles, and the woman who would become his wife, Birgit, along with the slave who had cared for Ocelus in Arelate, an Armenian named Simeon, defended the farmhouse from the raiders while they waited for help from the army in Siscia. And I was the one chosen, or actually, who chose himself, to be the person of our party to go and bring aid back. I was ten years old – a big ten years old, it is true – but it was not me that I was counting on to rescue my family. That job fell to Ocelus, and my magnificent horse was equal to the trial, carrying me right through the attacking Latobici. Despite the fact that I was wounded in the shoulder by an arrow fired by one of the rebels, the scar of which I carry to this day and still the only wound I have ever received to my back, Ocelus and I evaded capture for a night before running into a cavalry patrol the next morning. Ocelus and I spent the previous cold, dark, and shivering night in a cave while I tried to care for my wound the best way I could. And although matters turned out well for my family – the Roman cavalry hurried to the farmhouse, where they were retrieved unharmed but shaken – it was still an event that I did not like to think about much. Now, as we marched past and I spotted landmarks, like the ridge on the other side of the Sava (Savus) River where I had hidden, I had no choice but to think about my ordeal. I saw the spot at the river where I crossed it, holding onto Ocelus, who, to be fair, did all of the swimming and, while it was probably my imagination, I nonetheless felt an ache underneath my left shoulder blade as I recalled the arrow that struck me. Not surprisingly, I was unhorsed, and I would have drowned if it had not been for Ocelus, who grabbed me by the arm with his big yellow teeth and pulled me out of the deeper water. More than the physical wound and its aftereffect was the feeling of helplessness and despair that crowded into my every thought in the days between my contact with the cavalry and the safe return of my family. That feeling, more than any other memory, threatened to overwhelm me as, oblivious to the internal torment of a *Tirone*, the 8th Legion marched past. From my point of view, I was just quiet during this stretch of the march; I would answer to anything that Asinius said, but I did not participate in any of the conversations that are conducted during a march all up and down the ranks. However, I was disabused of my belief that my silence was unnoticed the second night of the march, when I had my second audience with my Pilus Prior.

I was sitting at what would become my normal spot around the fire outside of our tent, still more in the mood to listen, albeit half-heartedly, than talk, when Asinius called us to *intente*. I jumped up, as did the others, and saw that Pilus Prior Corvinus had appeared, standing before our tent, holding his *vitus* behind his back as he stood there.

"What dark and dirty lessons in debauchery are you trying to teach our young *Tiro*?" He asked this of the group and, as I am sure was his goal, evoked a laugh, even from me.

"Only what we learned from you, Pilus Prior," Asinius replied cheerfully, and this, in turn, drew a laugh from Corvinus.

"Well, at least you learned from the best," Corvinus quipped. Then, he turned to me and pointed with his *vitus*. "Porc...Pullus," he corrected himself, "come with me."

Without waiting to see if he was obeyed, he turned heel and began walking away, moving quickly enough that I had to trot a few paces to catch up. I was still incredibly stiff, sore, and tired, but I was also determined not to show it in front of Corvinus.

When I drew abreast, he shot me a sidelong glance, then asked, "How are you holding up on the march so far?"

"Fine, sir," I lied. "It's been hard, but nothing I can't do."

In answer, he gave me a grunt that told me nothing, and we continued to walk in silence for a few more paces before he spoke again.

"So, how does it feel to see this part of the world again?"

His question caught me completely by surprise, which I am sure was his intention.

"S-sir?" I do not normally stutter, but I was sufficiently rattled and I tried to stall for time. "I'm not sure what you mean."

"I think you do," he replied quietly, but without sounding angry about my attempt to gain time. "I know I remember it, like it was yesterday. I can only imagine that it's the same for you."

"It is," I finally said, reluctantly perhaps. "But yes, sir, it does feel...strange, I suppose is the best word, to be marching past this spot."

"I can see why," Corvinus agreed. He had stopped, and only then did I notice that he had walked us to the edge of the cleared area around the *praetorium*, the forum, so that we were separated from prying ears. "After all, not many children can claim that they killed their first man, somewhere right around here."

I automatically opened my mouth to correct and remind him that the Latobici I had stabbed was in fact the second man I had killed, after Spartacus, but I quickly realized that, in all likelihood, my father had not told Corvinus about this. It was true that the Pilus Prior was my father's closest friend, but even men who are as brothers keep secrets from each other.

Instead, I said, "We passed the spot about a third of a watch before we made camp."

"Ah." Corvinus nodded his head. "Near that farmhouse?"

"Yes, sir," I confirmed.

It was, in fact, the same farmhouse, hastily abandoned by the occupants when the Latobici started their uprising, where my family had sheltered. It was occupied when we marched past that day; I have no idea whether it was the original settlers or not, but I was somewhat bothered that it was in a state of habitation, if the gods must know. I felt, with no real reason, that it should have remained empty, as a sort of shrine to an event that had had such a huge impact on my life. Such is the hubris of the young, I suppose.

"I remember how worried your father was after Silva's troopers brought you in," he commented. "And there we were, supposedly preparing to go back out on the march again." He shook his head. "I'd never seen your father like that."

"Neither had I," I told him honestly. "But I was just as worried because I might not have gotten to help in time to save them."

He turned to look at me then, regarding me with an expression that I could not easily read.

"Well," he finally said abruptly. "You did, and that's all that really matters. I know it was a lot of responsibility and pressure

73

for someone as young as you were, but you're your father's son and Titus Pullus' grandson, through and through."

"What happened to my father?" I suddenly blurted out and, in truth, I do not know who was more surprised that I had asked the question that had been burrowing its way into my brain for seven years by that point.

Following the look of surprise on Corvinus' face was one I would describe as a wary caution, but he did respond.

"What do you mean what happened to him? You know perfectly well what happened to him," he said evenly, but I was not going to be put off without pursuing this further.

"Yes, I know he lost his leg." I tried to keep the impatience from my tone, still remembering the lesson of my first day's introduction to the Pilus Prior. "But how did it happen?"

"Didn't he tell you?" he asked, then gave a shrug. "He fell."

"I'd never known my father to make a false step in his life," I replied calmly, although I could feel my heart thudding in my chest, understanding that I was pushing the boundaries of our relationship. "I'd never seen him trip, or fall. Not once. He wasn't clumsy."

"There's a first time for everything," Corvinus shot back, his tone turning sharp. "And you know everything there is to know. Or," he paused, and there was no mistaking the warning in his voice, "need to know."

I immediately saw there was no pursuing this line of questioning and, at a loss, I fell back on our training and drew myself to *intente*. Seeing the change in my posture, Corvinus' lips thinned, but he did not say anything more than, "You can return to your area, *Tiro*."

I saluted him and did as he told me, more confused than a few moments before.

Fortunately, by the beginning of the second full week, I was sufficiently inured to the toil and effort that is the lot of the Gregarius on campaign. What I was lacking was in any training related to fighting as a unit with the other men of my Century; it was also something beyond my control, so I did my best to put it out of my mind. The march continued without incident, and it served to knock the flab off men who had been in garrison for some time, while little by little, as my Cohort was rotated through the series of duties required for making a camp, my fellow *Tiros* and I learned each job. We universally loathed digging the ditch; only marginally less did we hate the job of packing the spoil to create the rampart. In my case, I tried to follow my Avus' example, looking at it as an opportunity to show off my superior strength, but while we were of a similar size, he had grown up on a farm and was used to such labors already. In my case, I just could not muster the enthusiasm required to dig faster or carry more dirt in my wicker basket than the others. I suppose that it was a result of my upbringing and, although I know my parents, particularly my mother, had the best of intentions in doing so, they had instilled in me that there were some tasks that were beneath me.

In my mother's case, it came from two causes; she had been born a slave, and not just any slave. She was part of the court of Cleopatra VII, the same Cleopatra who perished by her own hand after her and her husband Marcus Antonius' plot to take over Rome was foiled by the divine Augustus, back when he was still known as Gaius Octavianus Caesar. I suppose I should take pride in the fact that I have royal blood in my veins because my maternal grandfather was none other than Ptolemy XII, while my maternal grandmother was one of the palace slaves, making Cleopatra and my mother half-sisters, not that this fact meant anything to the woman who would become Pharaoh. But because my mother was born a slave, she was fiercely determined that her children would never have to perform the kinds of jobs that are normally performed by the slaves in our society. However, I can see how one would think that she should have understood that, should I follow my father, and his father before him, I would find myself as I did, with a shovel and turf cutter, bending my back like the meanest slave in the Empire. It is a natural assumption to make, but it leads to the second reason my mother never allowed me to perform this kind of work because she was sure that I would not join the Legions, or if I did, it would be straight into the Centurionate. Her belief was not groundless, bur unfortunately for my mother's hopes and ambitions, the gods, and Augustus, deemed otherwise, which was why I found myself at the end of a day's march with some implement in my hand, paying the price for my relatively soft upbringing. The one part of our duties that I did enjoy was chopping down trees that would become part of the towers or other pieces that are an integral part of the Roman camp. I could make the chips fly, as we like to say in the Legions, and I enjoyed the feeling of power and the rhythm of swinging the axe, but while I did, I tried not to think of a similar weapon in the hands of the men we were about to face.

There is one event on our march that I believe illustrates the lot of the Gregarius very well, and that was how, somewhere along the way, there was a change that then became the topic of conversation around the fires for the remainder of the march. When we departed Siscia, we had been informed, albeit by way of the informal network of slaves and freedmen who act as the clerks of the army, that we would be marching against the Marcomanni. As we drew ever nearer to where we were to meet with Drusus, more and more time was spent talking about our prospective enemy, so perhaps one can imagine the shock when, seemingly out of nowhere, the word being whispered changed. Suddenly, we were not going to be facing the Marcomanni first, but the Chatti, yet another tribe whose reputation was, if anything, fiercer than the Marcomanni. The first hint of this change only became clear to us in hindsight, when we changed our westward march to a more northerly direction. In doing so, we passed through country that, while I was not personally familiar with it, many of my more veteran comrades were, although I did know something about the region. We were marching through the heart of Rhaetia where, during the summer my family and I traveled to Arelate, my father was participating in a campaign against the Rhaeti, who had risen up in rebellion. As I had learned, that campaign was noteworthy because it had marked the beginning of the military career of both Tiberius Claudius Nero and the man to whom we were marching to join, his brother Drusus. My father had spoken often about that campaign, marking as it did the penultimate time he would march under the standard, but as I was about to learn, there was one incident of which he had never spoken and, once I learned the particulars, it was easy to see why.

After our northward turn, we entered much more mountainous terrain and, in doing so, we left the relative comfort and security of a Roman road and followed what was more than a goat track, but was just wide enough to accommodate our wagons. Making it even more difficult was the road tilting upward, cutting our conversations shorter as we struggled for breath. Although the area was inhabited, it was in the form of small settlements, but when we approached one of them that was the largest of those that we marched through, a marked change fell over my comrades in the ranks as they became even quieter. Because there was no way to march around this town, we had to march through it and, as always, our presence drew a crowd of spectators lining the road. However, unlike all the other times, the men of the 8th did not exchange in the banter and good-natured catcalls and taunts that, under normal circumstances, livened up the day's march and gave us something to talk about afterward. The citizens of the town began cheering as they always did, but fairly quickly, when there was no return on our part, they fell silent and, fairly quickly, the only sound was the tromping of our hobnail soles on the hard-packed dirt. But it was as we marched through the small forum of the town, when I saw almost every man around me look in one direction and, in fact, at one spot, that I realized there was something significant taking place of which I was unaware. I could not work up the nerve to ask Asinius directly about the cause of this behavior.

Instead, I began by asking, "Do you know the name of this town?"

"Yes," Asinius replied tersely.

His eyes had returned to the front, to stare at the back of the man in the rank ahead of us, and it took a moment for me to recognize that he was not going to say anything more.

Inwardly heaving a sigh, I pressed, "And what's it called?"

"Veldidena." (Innsbruck)

That gave me a start because I had heard of this town, but it had been under mysterious circumstances. It had been while my father was recovering from his amputation, and he had finally begun to receive visitors in the week before we left Siscia for good. The first visitor he had received was my Pilus Prior, Corvinus, and, although I had been banished from the room, I can now cheerfully confess that I spent that time with my ear pressed against the door of the room. Unfortunately, they spoke in such low tones that it was impossible for me to learn much, but I distinctly recalled hearing my father mention the name of the town through which we had just marched.

"What happened here?" I asked Asinius.

He did not immediately answer; instead, he just turned to give me a stare that was somewhat troubling in its intensity. Finally, he seemed to come to some conclusion.

"I suppose you might as well know," he said, shrugging.

As inured as I thought I was to the kind of barbarity that war brings out in men, having heard what I believed at the time were the goriest stories that Legionaries could tell, I learned that I had been sadly mistaken. Although I cannot in good conscience describe what Asinius told me in any detail, what I learned was that, during their pursuit of the Rhaeti on the way to the place now called Brigantium (Bergenz), the 8th had closed to within a matter of two or three watches behind the fleeing rebels. It was not close enough to stop them from exacting a terrible price on the inhabitants of Veldidena – in particular, those horribly unfortunate women who were carrying children. The Rhaeti savages chose to make a statement by their treatment of these poor souls, and the lengths they went to in order to let Rome know their intentions were so vile that seven years later, as we marched through the town, it still had an effect on my comrades who had been here before and been forced to witness the butchery of the born and unborn alike. Asinius went on to tell me that Drusus had commanded the entire army to march past the scene of this atrocity, and my Sergeant was adamant in his belief that in doing so, he instilled in the men such a sense of outrage and resolve to have their vengeance on the Rhaeti that was instrumental in their defeat when they were brought to battle on the shores of the great lake where Brigantium is now located. When Asinius was finished, I at least understood why my father had mentioned it to Corvinus, especially when he informed me that it had in fact been the Fourth Cohort who were the first to stumble upon the scene of the slaughter. That gave me much food for thought for the rest of that day, at the very least.

After learning that we were not facing the Marcomanni, but the Chatti, it made sense that we changed our destination. Now we were marching to Mogontiacum (Mainz), a place I had never heard of before because, at that time, it was only three years old. It had been founded by Drusus, during the beginning of his campaign against the Germans, and served as his forward base and supply depot. As is natural and to be expected, especially when it is founded by one with the power and connections of Drusus, Mogontiacum had become a raw but thriving town, as all manner of people were drawn to the place by the lure of Roman silver. Located along a stretch of land where the Rhenus changes from its north/south axis to a westerly direction for a distance of about twenty miles, it is situated where the Moenus (Main) and Rhenus meet. Our arrival was met without any fanfare or ceremony, although there was an informal reception from the small army of whores who had relocated to the town. Unsurprisingly, for the first time on our march, my comrades showed high spirits and enthusiasm at the sight of a row of women on each side of the muddy road into the town, baring their breasts and nether parts as we went marching by. I suppose I could say that I kept my eyes straight ahead, but that would be a lie, and I was as avid as any of my comrades in my appreciation of the wares on display. The camp where Drusus and the rest of the army were waiting had been turned into a permanent installation, although at that point, the walls were still made of wood. We were just happy, especially we *Tiros,* that we would not have to do any digging or chopping, and we were directed to the section of the camp designated for our use. Like all such encampments, whenever possible, we occupy the same part of the camp no matter where it is, although when combining several Legions that have not marched together, there are times where two Legions are accustomed to occupying one particular space. Luckily, our area was in the exact same spot as at Siscia, which made it easy to find when, as many Gregarii did, they came back to camp stumbling drunk. We were given only enough time to deposit our gear in our huts, then were called to the forum, where Urso informed us that we would be given the liberty of the town for the night. It was hard to hear the rest of what he said over the cheers, but what I caught was that he expected us to be here no longer than a week before the consolidation, then we would be crossing the Rhenus. Despite being happy to be given the liberty of the town, I was still somewhat preoccupied by what lay before us in a week, but I quickly forgot that as I went with my section into Mogontiacum. Since we only had one free night, most of my veteran comrades were determined to see just how drunk they could get and, despite my best intentions to the contrary, I am afraid that I followed suit. Although it was not the first time I drank to excess; my most notable dance with Bacchus to that point had been with Quintus Gallus, the surviving bodyguard that became more or less permanently attached to the household of my father after his service during the Latobici attack. Shortly before I left to enlist in Siscia he had insisted, with the silent blessing of my father, who made me swear a vow that I never let my mother know it was with his consent, to teach me how to debauch myself in a manner befitting a Legionary of Rome.

"I wouldn't have any of my former comrades in the 8th say that Quintus Gallus didn't teach you everything you need to know," he had told me with a grin that was missing several teeth. "Besides, if you do end up in the Fourth under Corvinus, he isn't going to trust you until he sees you puking in a gutter somewhere."

While I had gotten gloriously drunk in Arelate, it was a shade compared to what happened on our one free night in Mogontiacum, of which I remember only bits and pieces. What I do remember is that we started out at a place that, despite its relative youth, looked so dilapidated I had to be shoved in the doorway by one of my section mates. I believe it was Tubero.

"You're not one of us until you have to go through drills hung over," was how Asinius had put it to me and, like any good Sergeant, he led the way into what would be the first of several stops.

As I recall, the place was called something like Bacchus' Delight, although over the years, I have been in so many places with that name, it is just as likely that this was not the name of the place. But it had tables, chairs, and, most importantly, what they called wine and, once more, I was reminded that my circumstances were not the same as my new comrades. My father was not a big drinker, almost always cutting it at least in half with water, but when he did drink it unwatered, it was of a sufficient quality and vintage that it did not bring tears to one's eyes like the swill I was forced to choke down that night.

Just before we left the camp, we had been informed by Pilus Prior Corvinus that we would spend the next day training as Centuries for the first time, in an attempt to integrate the fifteen of us new *Tiros* into the Cohort.

"It's not much, but it's the best we can do under the circumstances," was how he explained it to us.

Naturally, my mind was more absorbed with the prospect of the next day's training, at least at first. By the third or fourth cup of unwatered wine, however, not only did I no longer worry about the next day, I noticed that the wine no longer burned my throat, much. Somewhere during that night, at what I believe was our third or fourth stop, we ran into some Gregarii of one of the other two Legions that we would be marching with, the 14th. As I would come to learn, men from two Legions meeting generally turn out in one of two ways; either they become new comrades in arms, great fellows with whom sharing a cup is a wonderful occasion, or you find yourself rolling about on the floor as your opponent is chewing on your ear, while you are trying to gouge his eyes out. Fortunately for all concerned, especially the tavern owner who looked very much like a man waiting for a sentence in the courts to be announced, this first night turned out to be of the former type. Knowing what I do now, I believe it was due to the recognition that within a week we were going to be facing one of the fiercest tribes of Germans that found us arm in arm with men of the 14th, singing marching songs and united in our loathing of all officers. Our Legate, however, was another story.

"This will be the fourth season we've marched with Drusus," was how one Gregarius put it, a man with a livid pink scar across the bridge of his nose and down his left cheek, telling me that he had acquired it the previous season. "And all I can tell you boys is that you're lucky it's him that's leading us against those *cunni*."

"We know," Asinius agreed, and I saw that by unspoken consent he was the one of us who was going to do the most

82

talking. "We marched with him against the Rhaeti. He was green as grass then, but even then, we could see he had his wits about him."

"Well, now he's got his wits and he's had a lot of experience," the other man countered. "Like I said, you're lucky." He jabbed a finger at Asinius and, suddenly, the other chatter around the two tables we had commandeered grew quiet.

I was watching Asinius, but I could see out of the corner of my vision Tubero subtly shift his weight in his chair, preparing to pounce, and, despite my inebriation, I felt my heart quicken with excitement. If the truth was known, I was hoping that fists would start flying; what better way to prove myself to my comrades, besides actual battle, than wading into a brawl?

But Asinius was our spokesman for a reason because, without visibly taking offense, he lifted his cup and said loudly, "To Drusus! May his luck continue with us as we face the Chatti scum!"

"To Drusus!"

It was a bit ragged, but it was heartfelt, and the hostility in the air immediately dissolved as the men from the 14th joined in the toast. Now that it was clear that there would be no fighting amongst ourselves, Asinius steered the conversation towards what was a safer topic, and that was the coming campaign.

"You've marched with Drusus against the Germans before, then?"

"All three years before this," the scarred Gregarius said proudly.

"Have you faced the Chatti before?"

The man's proud grin seemed to falter a bit, but he answered readily enough.

"No," he admitted. "We haven't."

"What do you know about them?" Asinius asked.

"That they're bloodthirsty bastards," another man of the 14th blurted out and, when I blearily peered over at him, I saw that he did not look much older than I did.

"What would you know about it?" the scarred man scoffed. "This is your first campaign! You're green as grass!"

The other man blushed, but he said stoutly, "That doesn't mean I haven't heard things! You know that's all everyone's been talking about for the last two weeks!"

"True enough," the scarred Gregarius granted. "So, Glaxus, tell them what you've heard."

Suddenly, this Glaxus did not look as comfortable, but seeing all eyes on him, he plunged ahead, knowing that the honor of the 14th was as much at stake as his own.

"You can tell their warriors because once they've killed a man, they shave their beard and plait their hair," he began.

"That's good to know," Asinius said, and I had become acquainted enough with him to know he was taking care to sound as if this was new to us, despite the fact that we had heard this before. "Anything else?"

"Well, they are supposed to drink the blood of the warriors they kill," Glaxus replied and, seeing he had our complete attention, he really warmed to the subject. "And they take the heads and strap them to the saddles of their horses. At least," he amended, "their nobles do."

"So they have a lot of cavalry then?" I believe it was Poplicola who asked this.

Before Glaxus could answer, the scarred Gregarius cut in.

"No, they don't," he said firmly, shooting a glance at Glaxus in what I took to be a silent rebuke. "In fact, they're mostly infantry. That's one of the things that makes them different from the other tribes we've faced."

"Do you know anything about the country we're heading into?" Asinius asked.

Now the scarred Gregarius was the one who looked, if not worried, uncomfortable enough that I could see it through my haze of inebriation.

"The Hercynius Saltus is what I heard the likes of Drusus call it. Apparently, some knob like Aristotle or one of them one pasty Greeks named it that. But that's not what the locals call it."

"What do they call it?" As shocked as the others appeared to be, I was no less so since I was the one who blurted out the question.

The scarred Gregarius did not seem to notice the reactions of my comrades, locking eyes with me.

"The Black Forest," he said more quietly than before.

It was the name that jarred a memory in me and, through the wine, I tried desperately to remember where I had heard that term before.

Suddenly, I asked, "Does anyone know where the bridge that Caesar built is from here?"

The scarred Gregarius' head jerked in surprise, but his eyes narrowed as he thought about it.

"In fact," he said, "I overheard the Primus Pilus of our Legion telling my Hastatus Posterior that it's maybe a day's hard march north of here."

I thought hard, trying to put several pieces together and, since it was made more difficult by the wine in my blood, during the ensuing brief silence, Tubero spoke up, asking, "So why do they call it the Black Forest?"

Without thinking how it would be perceived by older, more experienced men than me, I was the one who blurted out the answer.

"Because the trees are so thick that the light never shines all the way down to the forest floor," I said quickly, drunkenly proud of myself that it was I, the youngest one there, who supplied the answer. "The undergrowth is so thick that men have to chop a path through it and, when an army like ours marches through it, they have to chop trees down to clear enough room for us to pass."

"Now how by Pluto's thorny cock do you know that?" Tubero demanded. If the tone of his voice did not inform me, when I looked across the table at him, I could see that he was truly angry. "And who the fuck are you to say a word anyway, *Tiro?*"

"Remember who his father is," Asinius interjected quietly, but Tubero was too angry, too drunk or both to take heed to his Sergeant's words.

"I don't give a brass *obol* who his father is," Tubero shot back, his words slurred as he continued to glare at me. "And his father never marched across the Rhenus, so how would his fucking father know anything about it?"

I do not remember the heartbeats of time immediately afterward, but from what I was told, I had leaped across the table more quickly than Asinius or Scrofa, who was on my other side, could stop me. My next conscious memory was of being on top of Tubero, who I had apparently knocked from his chair, and one of my knees pinned him to the ground.

"Don't ever disrespect my father again." I said this quietly, but I was pleased to see him blanch, even as he struggled to get out from under my weight.

"I didn't mean anything by it." Tubero's voice always had a whiny quality to it, but it was more so on this occasion. "I...I...was just talking about you."

A pair of hands grabbed my shoulders, and I tensed, ready to make an issue of it, but I looked up to see Asinius staring down at me, his eyes as hard and unyielding as his voice.

"Get off him. Now," he commanded. When I hesitated for a fraction, he did not. Yanking hard on the back of my tunic, he half-dragged, half-lifted me off Tubero, who went scrambling to his feet.

I was vaguely aware that we had drawn the interest and attention of the other patrons of the place, while the owner had stepped from around the counter where he served up trays of his swill, holding what looked like an axe stave. Suddenly, I was more sheepish than angry, and I allowed Asinius to shove me back down in my chair, then go to speak quietly to Tubero for a moment. Then he brought Tubero back to the table with him.

"Stand up," he ordered me, which I did.

"Now, you're going to apologize to Tubero for attacking him," he told me, but when I opened my mouth to argue, he just gave me a look that stopped the protest from coming out.

Turning to Tubero, I offered my arm and mumbled, "I'm sorry I jumped on you."

Asinius turned to Tubero and told him, "Now you're going to apologize for being careless with your mouth so that it sounded like you were being disrespectful Pilus Prior Porcinus."

Pullus, I thought, but did not say anything.

Apparently, Tubero and I had something in common because it looked very much like he was going to refuse as well, but although Asinius was turned away from me, he apparently gave him the same look because Tubero extended his arm as well, while he mumbled his own apology.

"Now, the two of you sit down. You're interrupting our drinking," Asinius seated himself, as did Tubero and I, both of us staring into our cups.

"So how *do* you know about this Black Forest?"

I looked up to see that it was the scarred Gregarius who asked the question, and I opened my mouth to blurt out that I had read my Avus' account of his time with Caesar. Fortunately, I stopped myself, settling for giving a half-truth.

"My grandfather told me about it," I said. "He marched with Caesar when he crossed the Rhenus."

"What Legion was your grandfather in?" This came from one of the other men of the 14th at the far end of the table who had been silent to this point.

"10th Equestris," I answered him, not bothering to try and hide my pride.

Despite the fact that it had been disbanded in favor of the 10th Legion that had marched for Augustus, the Legion formed by Divus Julius in Hispania some fifty years before was, and is still, the most famous and respected Legion in the Roman army. Even in my inebriated and humbled state I could see that the men of the 14th were impressed.

Then I felt a nudge in the ribs from Asinius, who whispered in my ear, "Tell them everything."

I do not know why, but I was reluctant to do so, but after another prod, I added, "And my grandfather was Titus Pullus, Primus Pilus of the 10th."

I remember very little of the evening after that, other than I did not pay for another drink.

The next day was even worse than I had feared. It started with me puking up my breakfast almost as soon as I had downed it. My head was pounding the entire day, but somehow, I not only survived the day's training, I apparently did not make a fool of myself. Pilus Prior Corvinus worked us through several different maneuvers, spending the most time on what is the most critical one, moving from a marching column into a line of battle. Over and over we practiced this, first as a Century, then as a Cohort, outside the camp where there was enough room. All around us, the other Cohorts of the 8th were doing the same, as we learned the day before that the 14th and 16th had been waiting in Mogontiacum through the entire winter and had long since integrated their batch of replacements. While we trained, they continued their own preparations to leave, making the camp a bustle of activity. Somehow, I do not really know how, I survived the day of training, despite the fact that I only felt marginally better at the end of the day than I did at the start.

"Looks like our *Tiro* doesn't have a good head for wine," Servius Metellus said with a grin when he saw me bent over at the waist, retching up food and liquid that had long since left the area, a fact that my stomach did not seem to accept.

All I could do was look at him in misery, which only heightened his enjoyment. Slapping me on the back, he laughed long and loud.

But then he whispered, "About Tubero. Don't worry about him. He always talks too much when he's drunk. And with every cup, he's a bigger and bigger warrior." He gave me a wink. "Too bad we're not allowed to go into battle drunk because when he's sober, he's not quite the Achilles he is when he's in his cups."

"That's good to know," was all I could think to say.

"Oh, he's a good enough man," Metellus said hastily, "but just keep that in mind if the fighting gets as tough as it's supposed to."

With those sobering words, he left me in my misery. It was not until the next morning that I felt even a semblance of my normal self, but even then, I was still queasy. Fortunately, there was so much to do that I did not have time to dwell on it. I was given the task of carrying pieces of our artillery to the *quaestorium*, where the armorers are located, to have them checked for cracks, along with the replacement of frayed torsion ropes. Other men were drawing barrels of water, while still others were involved with the slaughtering of the herd of pigs that were waiting and designated for our use. Everywhere one looks there is motion, and it was when I was walking back and forth carrying the artillery that I saw Drusus for the first time. Being accurate, I should say it was the first time I saw him in Mogontiacum; I had seen him once before, in Siscia, when he and his brother Tiberius had led the Legions in Siscia on a campaign to crush yet another rebellion of one of the Pannonian tribes, the Varciani. This was the campaign that ended my father's career and, defying my father's orders to the contrary, I was there at the camp gates, along with my brother Sextus and sister Valeria, all of us sitting on my Ocelus, which was the way that I wriggled out of his command not to walk with the Legions, which had become something of a tradition. Waiting for the command group to go by, that was when I saw Drusus and Tiberius, both of them wearing their best armor. Of the two, it was easy to pick out Drusus because he is, or was a handsome man, with an open and friendly demeanor that made him popular with his troops. Seeing him there in Mogontiacum, what met my eyes was a man in his prime; that softness of features that I know now I had as well that marks the teenager was long gone. The planes of his cheeks were taut, almost hollow, all spare fat gone from them, while his jawline was firm and definite. Even so, there was an air about him, and I swore I saw the glimmer of a smile on his face as he strode, along with his Legates, towards the *praetorium*. Fortunately, he was far enough away that I did not have to stop what I was doing, drop my cargo, and render a salute, but I would have done so without any rancor. He was an upper class Roman, it is true, but he was a man made for the Legions and, knowing what I know now, fourteen years later, I realize how lucky I was with my first general.

Precisely one week after we arrived in Mogontiacum, we departed through the gates, the 14th being given the place of honor at the head in recognition of their long association with our general. The 8th was marching drag, my first such occasion with an army this size, and, although the Fourth had certainly taken its place as the rearmost Cohort on the march from Siscia, a single Legion on the march is far different from an army of three Legions going on campaign, with the baggage train. One difference was that, while the wagons of the baggage train were in front of us, a large proportion of them were empty. Pilus Prior Corvinus had informed us that we were marching to a spot on the other side of the Rhenus, in territory that Drusus had conquered and was being held by several Cohorts of auxiliaries. Specifically, we were going to an advance base that was held by auxiliaries and where Drusus had sent those consumables that could be considered dry goods that can be stored for extended periods of time. Barrels of chickpeas and wheat had been sent ahead, but when I asked why, nobody seemed to know why.

Asinius guessed, "I think he wants to have a base on this side of the Rhenus in the event that we get cut off for some reason."

"But we're taking all the supplies there, or most of them anyway," Metellus pointed out.

Asinius could only shrug at this, knowing Metellus was correct. As it would turn out, they were both right, at least partially so. Drusus wanted this forward base in place because, as we would find out, he had grand ambitions for this campaign. While it was true we were emptying the three warehouses, Drusus had already given orders to transfer more of the consumable goods to this base to replace the loss. He planned on using this as his supply base as he led us into the Black Forest because he was intent on penetrating deeper than any army of Rome ever had. We reached the depot on the second day, where it was situated on a rise that, while relatively low, still gave it a commanding view of the surrounding countryside. To the north, stretching east in more than a quarter turn, there was a thin, dark green line that the veterans of Germania told us marked the boundary of the Black Forest. On the third day after we left Mogontiacum, with our larder barrels filled to the brim, we began marching in the direction of the Black Forest, heading almost exactly northeast.

There was little said and no fanfare when we reached the edge of the Black Forest, but as inexperienced as I was, it was easy to see the mood among my comrades change. Following a narrow, twin-rutted track, the 8th was the Legion leading the way that day and, by the time we had gone no more than a hundred paces into the forest proper, a gloom that is very difficult to describe settled over us. Although it is true that the cause of the darkened conditions was because of the thick, interwoven canopy of trees above us blocking out the sun, it was more than that. Along with the visible darkness, there was a subsequent dampening of our spirits, making what little conversation there was among us become desultory, consisting of short, one- or two-word queries and responses. Being on the outside of the formation, and because of my status as a new *Tiro*, I hope I can be forgiven my own case of nerves. Drusus had given the command that day to wear our full armor and to uncover our shields, the latter being the most potent sign to a ranker that the commander expects contact. I had become accustomed to the *segmentata*, but I was still having troubles adjusting to the new-style helmet. While it had the reinforced strip of metal above the brow of the helmet and the hinged ear pieces, there had been an extension of the neckpiece in the back, which the veterans of Germania were happy to point out was due to the proliferation of axes wielded by the Germans. Although I was certainly happy to have more protection for my neck, it did make sudden movements of the head problematic, as the back of the helmet tended to catch one of the plates when I whipped my head about. And my head was certainly moving about quite a bit as I nervously scanned the undergrowth that crowded right up to the edge of the track. Ferns, small shrubs, and seedling trees were so thick that I often could not see the ground underneath and I became accustomed to the feeling of the fronds and leaves brushing my hip as we marched by.

"And to think, this is the good part," I heard Asinius mutter. "It won't be long before we run out of this...whatever it is. It's no road."

Thank you so much for pointing that out, I thought sourly, but said nothing, keeping my eyes fixed to the right. As is standard, the Primus Pilus had sent out sections on either side of our direction of travel, two per Century, and I was just thankful that we had not been selected, although I knew our time was coming. While the standard is to be at least a hundred paces and even further out, this is impossible in places like the Black Forest, so the security elements were just fifty paces away. Even with this shortened distance, I only caught the occasional glimpse of them through the trees and underbrush, and just the thought of being out there, so close, yet feeling completely isolated, made my heart pound. Naturally, our normal pace could not be maintained; I had heard veterans familiar with this part of the world claim that a good day's march would see fifteen miles covered, while ten was more common. As I would come to learn, that first day in the Forest was the fastest we would travel during that campaign. And despite our anticipation, our first day in the Forest was uneventful.

I do not want to paint a picture that the Forest is entirely unbroken and impenetrable; there are clearings, some natural, but most made by the native tribes, where the inhabitants scratched out a living of sorts with subsistence farming. It was in one of these clearings that we made camp the first night, and my Cohort was part of the guard for the night. This night marked the first of what I would come to learn was a series of unusual happenings. Not knowing any better, as I stood on the rampart with Poplicola as my companion, the two of us naturally gravitating toward each other since it was the first campaign for both of us, I had never seen such complete darkness as I peered into the forest. The woods began less than ten paces from the ditch, all the room that the clearing allowed, making us all, veteran and *Tiro* alike, extremely nervous. It would not take much effort for a force of Chatti to sneak up to the very edge of their concealment, then dash the ten paces across to the ditch. If they brought hurdles and ladders, there would be precious little time to employ our javelins, meaning that matters would go straight to the sword instead. The one salubrious effect this had on the two of us was that there was no danger of us falling asleep, which is usually one of the biggest threats of sentry duty. Even if we were so inclined, despite the overall situation, the sudden howling of first one, quickly followed by another, then another what we were sure were wolves ensured that we would stay alert. There is something about the howl of a wolf that triggers a reaction in men, and I am not immune to that, as I felt what I was sure was every hair on my body suddenly stand up straight. Next to me, Poplicola let out a little gasp of fright, but while I might normally have teased him about it, I was not so inclined because I was no less so, particularly because it sounded very much like at least one of the wolves was directly in front of us, just inside the edge of the sheltering forest. If that had been all that happened, it would have been enough to keep us alert, but within less than thirty heartbeats, the trio of wolves across from us were joined by first one, then another of what we were sure were packs of wolves. Very quickly, it sounded as if we were surrounded, the ghastly howling creating such a ruckus that I heard men behind me who should have been asleep in their tents come out and call to some of us on the wall, asking what we saw. Because of the enveloping darkness, there was not much we could say, and the howling continued for at least a third of a watch, sufficiently unsettling all of us that sleep was next to impossible. Just before we were relieved, as I walked my part of the post Poplicola and I had been assigned, I passed by one of the torches that line the camp rampart. I suppose that it was because of that extra light that, as I stared into the darkness, I caught a glimpse of not one, but at least three sets of luminous, green eyes, unblinkingly watching me as I passed. Even with all my self-confidence in my strength and ability, I suddenly had a flash of what might be called insight, fighting what I can only describe as the same feeling that a deer or elk must experience when it becomes aware that it has drawn the attention of the wolves. Although I was able to shake it off fairly quickly, it was an unsettling feeling, knowing that those eyes were measuring me not as a man, but as prey, coolly calculating their best method and plan for taking me down to fill their bellies. Despite my fatigue, sleep did not come easily, as every time I closed my eyes, I saw those staring, stalking eyes.

As predicted, our progress slowed even more on the third day of our ingress into the Black Forest, as that small track finally petered out, ending in yet another clearing. This one still contained the ruins of several of what pass for buildings in this part of the world, but was otherwise deserted. Judging from the way the tendrils of ferns and shrubs were entwined among the bare bones of the buildings, this settlement had been abandoned for more than just one season. Since this was the first time for any of us, with the exception of Bassus, to be in this part of the world, we relied on him to tell us what he knew and, according to him, this had been a settlement cleared out by Drusus and the Legions two years before.

"This is as far into the Black Forest that we got," he told us. "And this ends the easy part of the march," he added grimly.

He was correct. Drusus wasted no time, designating two Cohorts from the lead Legion that day, the 16th as I recall, to begin chopping a path through the forest on the eastern side of the clearing, which was our direction of travel in our pursuit of the Chatti. Not only were trees cut down, but in a swath wide enough for our wagons to pass; any trunks that would obstruct the path were either sawed flush to the ground, or if for whatever reason this was not possible, the trunks were ripped from the ground and the hole filled in. Naturally, this meant that we spent a good deal of time standing, facing outward, watching and waiting for any possible threat. To this point in the campaign, our mounted scouts had only reported signs of what was assumed to be Chatti movement, in the form of tracks, and not in any numbers sufficient to cause alarm. That did not make us any less wary, and we would be happy when we finally began moving again, although it was only for a mile before we were stopped once more. Two fresh Cohorts exchanged places with the first two, with the same task as the first, clearing a path for the army a mile at a time. As I would come to learn, the way it is done is that one Cohort works in the immediate path of the army, while the second marches out no more than a quarter mile ahead. Then, leapfrogging each other, they clear about a mile of track. Meanwhile, a heavily armed scouting party ranged a short distance ahead, navigating around the many obstacles that the *exploratores* deemed to be too difficult to overcome in a short period of time. These obstacles were usually stretches of marsh or bogs, of which there are numbers beyond counting in the Black Forest. What made matters even more difficult was that, while the *exploratores* did their best, there are patches of ground that, to the eye, look the same as what one is standing on; it is only when one suddenly finds themselves calf-deep in a sticky, stinking, slimy mud that is extremely difficult to wash off that one realizes he is no longer on firm ground. Once this accidental discovery is made, all progress stops, while the boundaries of this hidden danger are determined, and the decision is made whether it can be navigated through, or another path must be found. What I found particularly loathsome about this when it happened to me the first time was that the moment one's foot plunges into the muck, it releases many thousands of small, flying vermin that apparently use this mud as their abode. They are very small, meaning that before one is aware, you have sucked them up your nose and into your mouth, causing a fit of coughing, choking, and cursing. What is even worse is that, once released, they apparently decide to follow their victim wherever he goes, creating a walking cloud that swarms about the head in particular, making more ingestion or inhalation of the little bastards inevitable. All in all, it was a miserable situation, and I was fated to have this happen not once or twice, but no less than four separate times.

With our progress down to ten miles a day, every one that passed where there was no contact with the Chatti served to increase the tension in much the same way a musician tuning his harp will twist the knob, pulling the string tighter and tighter. And if he makes one twist too many, the string can no longer bear the strain and snaps. In many ways, that was what happened to Drusus' army; after a week of plodding progress, with no sight of the Chatti, I know now it was inevitable that there was a slight relaxation. I do not say this to fault anyone, from Drusus down to the lowest *Tiro* like me, because it is just part of human nature that it is impossible to maintain a high state of vigilance, day in and day out, without letup. Our string had snapped, and the gods apparently decreed that the price would be paid for the laxity of the army by the 8th.

It was our fate to be the leading Legion the day the Chatti attacked, and my Cohort was one of the two designated to clear a path. Five Centuries, including mine, were doing the actual work, while the Sixth Century was designated as security, split in two with the Hastatus Posterior with half the Century on one side, the Optio with the other half on the opposite side. Both halves were spread out in a line, with perhaps fifteen paces between each Gregarius; their job was to provide us with early warning of an attack and not to hold off any assault, which would have been next to impossible because of their spacing. Fortunately, we were in full armor, and I had worn the *segmentata* enough now to appreciate the relative freedom of movement when compared to the *hamata*, mainly because it was lighter, but also due to the design of the overlapping plates. And despite the discomfort, Corvinus had insisted that we wear our helmets as well. That was a piece of equipment I was still getting accustomed to, but I am glad I was wearing it. I vividly recall what I was doing; I had just finished chopping down one of the trees in our path, although I do not remember what kind it was, and was watching it fall. Apparently, so were some of the men who were supposed to be watching elsewhere, their attention

97

drawn to the sight of the tree, which was quite large, toppling to the ground. Moving slowly at first, it gained speed quickly, ripping down branches of neighboring trees while emitting a groaning sound that, despite myself, I found unsettling because it sounded almost human to me, just before slamming into the ground with tremendous force, crushing all life underneath its massive weight, plant or otherwise. A tree falling makes quite a disturbance, and I believe that whoever was leading this Chatti band timed it perfectly. Even as the sound of the tree crashing down was still in the air, there was a sharp shout, but as it turned out, just like my comrades, I thought it had something to do with the tree. Bits of debris, dust, dirt, and assorted jagged splinters of branches were still tumbling through the air when a second cry sounded, but it was not until there was a short but shrill scream that I would come to learn all too well, did any of us have a hint that something was happening that was not involved with our work.

"To arms! We're under attack!"

I do not honestly know in which order my ears picked up the signs that we were in danger, the shouted order or the roar of what to my inexperienced ear sounded like the voices of a thousand demons, screeching their rage, but it was still at least one heartbeat before I moved and, when I did, it was because of a hard shove from behind.

"Get to your fucking shield and javelins now." Without turning, I recognized the voice of Asinius and I saw him out of the corner of my eye as I finally began moving, pulling alongside me as we both dashed to where the shields of my section were stacked together.

Just like with anything having to do with a Legion of Rome, nothing is random; my shield was leaned against the one of the man to my left, that being Asinius, while the rest of our shields were arranged in such a manner. Despite the circumstances, we managed to separate our shields with a minimum of fumbling, as well as retrieving our two javelins; mine stuck in the dirt next to my shield, his in the same manner. Very quickly, we were at least fully armed, but I still had not seen anything other than my fellow Gregarii dashing about, and I whirled about in a desperate attempt to get a sense of where this attack was coming from, cursing the difficulty caused by that back flap of my helmet. Even as I did this, there was the first of a series of calls by *cornu*, making matters even more confused, because although they were blasting the same series of notes, each *cornicen* was doing it for his respective Century. This was my first battle, and I have since seen and been in many, but this one still ranks as one of the most confused and chaotic in which I ever fought. It was not until I had turned fully about that I saw the threat, and I was just in time to see what looked like a solid greenish-brown wave composed not of water, but flesh, iron, and fury, chop down the line of men from the Sixth Century as if they were not even there. The sight of these attackers, all of whom looked to be at least my size, many bare-chested, with plaited hair and flowing mustaches, rooted me to my spot. Dressed in the *bracae* that we Romans have since adopted when operating in northern climes, waving an assortment of spears, swords, and axes over their large oval and rectangular shields, they were advancing at a dead run. Despite all the training, the fact that I had read my Avus' account of combat in the Legions, and having already shed blood and brought death to men, I am ashamed to say that I froze. My feet seemed to be firmly attached to the ground, as if I had in fact grown roots, and all I could do was watch what I was sure was a thousand Chatti warriors, all aiming directly at me.

I can say now, with only a small amount of shame, that the only way I survived my first battle was because of Appius Asinius and his actions. As I stood there, my mouth open, completely immobile, I was yanked, figuratively and literally, into action when Asinius grabbed my arm and gave a vicious pull.

"Come with me, you stupid bastard," he had to shout to be heard over the rapidly growing roar, but despite my weight, he pulled on my arm strongly enough that the only way I could keep my balance was to move my feet back underneath me.

Fortunately, that seemed to break whatever spell I was under because I turned and followed him, at a dead run, away from the onrushing Chatti. Although the urge just to keep running was very strong, that was not what Asinius was doing.

Close on his heels, over Asinius' shoulder, I saw lines of men wearing our uniform lining themselves up, facing us and the Chatti. Pilus Prior Corvinus had managed to grab his *signifer*, a lanky Umbrian named Vibius Sempronius, and had him run to the spot where he was now standing. Being the *signifer* of the First Century meant that the other five *signiferi* used him as their point of reference, and I was barely aware of a similar stream of men dressed like me, sprinting the same way and in the same direction. Galens was not in his usual spot at the rear, but was standing a few paces in our direction from the front rank, and I saw him waving his arm at us, urging us on.

"Hurry up, you slow bastards," he roared. "They're right behind you!"

I do not know how, but I managed to refrain from looking over my shoulder, and I would like to think that somewhere in the recesses of my mind was the knowledge gleaned from my father, or from my Avus, that to do so would spell inevitable doom. As it was, Galens, apparently seeing that we would make it to the temporary safety of the formation, turned and ran in between two files of the front rank, the men moving their shields aside to give him room. A fraction of a moment later, they did the same for us, and Asinius and I made our way to our spots in the rear rank. It was not an instant too soon because, before we had turned about and gotten into position, I heard an enormously loud crashing sound as the Chatti warriors slammed full speed into our front rank. I did not even have a chance to grab the harness of the man in front of me when he came shuddering two

100

full steps backward from the shock of the impact, relayed from one Legionary to another, all the way to the back of the formation. Rather than using my hand and arm, I found myself putting my shoulder into the man's back, my own heels digging into the soft earth of the forest. Only then did I glance over and see that Asinius and the rest of my section were doing the same. After the initial onslaught we got stabilized, and I was able to take my more normal position, all while standing on my toes to peer up to the front rank. What greeted my eyes was a fury of sights; snarling faces peering over shields, strings of spittle acting as a strange complement to the flowing mustaches, arms rising and falling as the hands they were attached to thrust or hacked at my comrades, depending on the weapon. My initial impression was that most of these men seemed to favor the heavy spear, but very quickly, I saw a flash of grayish-silver and, despite the speed with which it was moving, I somehow was able to identify one of the axes we had heard so much about. But more than anything, it was the noise that threatened to overwhelm me; a combination of sounds, some of them caused when a weapon struck a shield, others when a weapon struck flesh, all of them horrifically loud and blood-curdling, especially the shouts and screams of men who were struck down. In situations such as these, it is impossible to accurately record time, but it could not have been more than a dozen or so heartbeats before the first Roman came crawling back to the rear after being struck down. I say crawling, but that is only partially true, as most of his locomotion came from a man leaning down, grabbing him by whatever he could grab, and roughly dragging him further backward, where the next man repeated the action, until the wounded man was behind the rear rank. I did not want to, but I could not stop myself from glancing over at the first man, and I immediately wished I had not. While relatively superficial, wounds to the face have a particular ghastliness to them, and this man – I could not immediately recognize him – had suffered what I assumed was an axe blow because his cheek was actually hanging outward, hiding his jaw. What I could see

101

clearly were his teeth, while he sat with his legs splayed out in front of him, obviously in shock because he made no attempt to stop the bleeding.

While Asinius saw it as well, he did not hesitate like I did, bellowing "*Medici!*" over and over.

Finally, there was movement, and until the figure detached himself from the group of noncombatants that had been huddling in terror behind our formation, I did not know they were there. But he came running, then quickly dropped to his knees and, with a gentleness that was at odd juxtaposition to everything else that was going on, he began examining the man's wounds.

"Keep your eyes to the fucking front," Asinius growled. "You need to keep watch on what's going on."

It was only a matter of a few heartbeats after that Corvinus blew on his bone whistle for the first time, sounding the signal for a relief of the men of the front line. There was a flurry of motion and a sharp spike in the noise at the front, then men began streaming back, turning their bodies sideways so they could pass in the space between each file. The Gregarius of the front rank of my file was, naturally, a veteran, and supposedly the best man with a sword in not just the Century, but the Cohort. His name was Gaius Maxentius and, as he came staggering back, I felt a stab of alarm at the sight of blood all over the front of his armor, the old-style *hamata*. He saw me staring at him and glanced down at his front.

"It's not mine," he shouted with what I suppose was a laugh as he passed by me.

An instant later, I felt him grab my harness, and this simple act actually helped settle my nerves. Another man came stumbling back, this man clutching his forearm, where blood was shooting out like a geyser with every beat of his heart.

"If he doesn't tie that off, he's a dead man," I heard Maxentius say behind me, but this time, I did not pay attention to what was going on behind me.

Shifting once, then another time, the closer I got to the front, the more my field of vision began to narrow as I tried my best to shut out the sounds and sights. Even so, my eye picked up odd moments and details that I can see even today. A Chatti warrior with a high, conical helmet adorned by the wings of what I assumed was a raven, who was not wielding a sword, spear, or axe, but what looked to me like a giant hammer, which he used to batter down the shield of the Roman across from him is one such memory. There was another scream that was even more piercing than the noise already generated by the combatants, accompanied by a sharp, cracking sound that I would learn was the sound of a shield being splintered. Then the whistle blasted, and I was now the second in line, as the relieved Gregarius pushed past me, babbling incoherently about losing a bet. I began the process of preparing myself to go into battle for the first time, and I was, frankly, scared out of my mind. But then, I felt a shudder run through the body of my comrade in front of me and, when I close my eyes, I can still see the point of a Chatti war spear suddenly burst through the man's body, dripping blood and bits of gore, barely missing my arm.

The first German I ever killed was my height, but with hair the color of summer wheat, and I was aided by my now-dead comrade; his name was Aulus Gemonius, as I recall, in whose body the German's spear was lodged. Apparently, the German's spear had passed through the spine of Gemonius, and when the German tried to withdraw the weapon, it caught in the bone. Not for long, but it was enough for me to take a step forward and to my left and, in a continuation of my movement, make a hard thrust with my sword, aiming for the German's throat. By moving to my left and his right, the only defense he could have offered was by deflecting my blade with his spear, but he was still yanking it, trying to dislodge it from Gemonius, who had sagged to his knees, his head slumped forward and bobbing in obscene rhythm with every jerk of the spear. It was true that the German's throat was at the outer edge of the reach of my sword, at least if I made sure to keep my feet directly underneath me and not lean over too far, which I did. But the throat is one of the softest targets on the body, second only to the one below the waist that is not only soft, but which men hold more dearly than any other body part. Perhaps two inches of the point of my blade that punched into his throat just below his jaw was more than enough to kill him. There was a burst of bright red as I withdrew my blade and brought it back to the first position, while at the same time, the German stopped trying to recover his spear and, dropping his shield, brought both hands to his throat in a vain attempt to stem the flow of blood. With Gemonius no longer held up by the pressure of the spear, he toppled sideways, away from me, but although I had avenged him, I had no time to admire my victory.

"Move into his spot, you fucking idiot," I heard a voice snarl, and I dimly identified it as Maxentius, but I did not hesitate this time.

Making a hopping step to the right, I realigned myself in front of Maxentius, barely in time to meet the onrush of another German who had savagely shoved the yellow-haired man aside as he tottered on his feet for another heartbeat before collapsing backward. I had read in my Avus' scrolls that there is a part of a man's mind that somehow seems to stay detached from the furious spectacle of a battle, observing things that seem impossible to notice, especially given everything else that is going on. That seemed incredible to me, although I believed, and still do, every word of my Avus' account of battles, especially after what I experienced in that fraction of time that affirmed his claim because I vividly remember taking note of the fact that when the yellow-haired Chatti collapsed, instead of falling to the ground, he fell onto what I saw were two layers of men who had already been struck down. That was all the time I had, at that moment, although later that night, this would be the most vivid memory of that day, because the German taking his place was even then launching a powerful, horizontal slicing blow with his weapon. In that instant, the weapon was moving so fast in my direction that my mind could not identify it, but for the first time, I directly benefited from the hundreds of watches of practice that I had undergone since I was ten years old, as my left arm dropped my shield into position to take whatever blow was coming, before I gave any conscious thought about the need to do so. It was only when there was a resounding cracking sound, and the shield in my hand jerked violently, sending the shock of the blow traveling all the way up my arm and into my body, that I saw as it caromed away that the weapon was an axe.

Even as this registered, the Chatti warrior, who was as dark as the first man had been golden, used the recoil of his axe bouncing off my shield, allowing the head of the axe to hurtle back towards him. But then, instead of stopping the weapon, he raised his right arm so that, in the same motion, the axe passed over his head. Then, in a smooth arc, he continued the revolution of the axe so that in less than the blink of an eye, the axe was heading back toward me, but from the opposite side this time, where my only protection was my sword...and my armor. Because of my training, I had returned my sword arm to what we call the first position, where the arm is parallel to the ground, and the hand is pulled several inches behind your waist. While in the offense, the first position thrust is a devastatingly effective attack, not least because of where the point is aimed at that spot I mentioned below the waist, in the defense it is of less value. This is due to the fact that, unless your enemy is aiming a blow at your leg, trying to cripple you, the only direction that you can use your blade to deflect their weapon is upward, towards your torso and, even worse, throat and head. Nevertheless, a bad defense is better than none at all, and again, as if my arm had a mind of its own, it shot up and out, in a sweeping arc that met the onrushing axe, blade to head, creating a tiny shower of sparks.

Unfortunately, my deflection was only partially successful; still, it did rob the Chatti's blow of much of its force, but the momentum he had created with this swing was still too strong to stop completely. I had managed to deflect the axe from its original target, low on my right side, I suppose in an attempt to disembowel me, since that has such a dramatic effect, not just on the victim but on his comrades by his side and, instead, it slammed into my side, just under my armpit. I felt my breath leave me in an explosive gasp, but the pain of the blow was such that I barely noticed; I believe it was only my sheer bulk that allowed me to absorb the blow and take just a staggering step to the side instead of losing my feet. This was also the first, but would be far from the last time that I also learned that, despite the suspicions of the armor by my veteran comrades, which before this moment I shared, it must be said, the *segmentata* proved itself to be at least the equal of the *hamata*. When I thought about it later, trying to piece the battle together from the jumble of splintered memories and fragments of recollection, and was later proven out, I concluded that in the smooth surface of the plates of the *segmentata* lay the key to my survival from what should have been a devastating blow, even counting my deflection. The old *hamata*, made of small links of iron riveted together, provides a level of protection, it is true, but it also is a rough surface, upon which another object, like a sword, or axe blade, is likely to catch. Conversely, the smooth, curved surface of the *segmentata* practically requires a blow that is exactly perpendicular in order to penetrate. That was not what happened here and, despite the fact I lost my breath and was staggered, the axe bounced off and once more rebounded back towards the Chatti. I cannot say whether what happened next was a lucky guess, or was the first sign that perhaps the blood of my Avus carried with it more than my size, but since I am still alive and standing, I like to think it is the latter.

Shaken as I was, it suddenly seemed that time slowed down because I had the time to see the arc of the axe and realize that this German was about to repeat his tactic, except in the opposite direction from his last swing, duplicating his original one. Essentially, he would be repeating his first attack, and the one thing I remember most vividly as I began moving was the thought that I had either read, or been told, that no truly great warrior repeats the same attack twice in a row. Even as the axe was circling back around his head; I am sure if it had just been the two of us, I would have been able to hear the whistling sound it made as it sliced through the air, I was making my own move. Crossing over so that I was putting my left foot forward again, my shield was already moving up to meet the axe, as simultaneously my sword was thrusting up and out in its own vicious arc. Because he had knocked me a step to the left, the point of my sword was coming from an awkward angle for him to bring his shield across his body to block, so his move was too late. At the exact same instant his axe chopped down onto my shield, the point of my sword was punching through his own knee-length chain mail, entering his body right under his breast bone. I had been looking at the center of the German's body, guiding my sword to where it wanted to go, but I lifted my eyes in time to see his own widen in shock, and I was blasted with his breath, smelling strangely of onions and an odor that I would later come to learn was from mead, the fermented honey drink favored by the Germanic tribes. The only sound he made was a low moan, then dropped both axe and shield to reach down, but I had already withdrawn my blade. Taking a staggering step backward, he impeded the advance of one of his comrades, for which I was thankful, but just as I moved back into my original and correct spot and dropped my hips, there was the blast of a whistle. Instead of attacking with my sword, as the next Chatti came within reach, I punched out with my shield. He moved just quickly enough to bring his own to bear, so that we met metal boss to metal boss, making a sharp clanging sound, but he was the one who staggered backward, which was exactly what I was supposed to do. Before he could recover, I took a quick step to the left, seeing Maxentius move into the spot I had just vacated. I was not sure what to expect, but I had at least hoped for a quick "Well done" on my first two kills as a Legionary, but as I turned sideways to shuffle to the back, I was in for a bit of a rude surprise.

"Stupid fucking *Tiro*," Maxentius snarled at me as I stepped away. "You didn't twist the blade and finish this fucker like you were supposed to! Now I have to do it!"

I did not get the opportunity to redeem myself in that battle; before I reached the front again, the Chatti attack had been stopped cold and, as quickly as they appeared, they faded back into the forest in the same direction from which they had come. What they left behind was a sight, with sounds that, as often as I have witnessed and been part of since, I still hate more than any other. The aftermath of a fight, even when it is a total victory, is a gruesome scene, and what I learned that day was that it is one thing to see and cause the violent death of an individual, like with Spartacus. When it is on the scale of my first battle with the Legions, it is so much more horrific a sight that it is impossible to compare the two. One moment, it is all sound, fury, and motion; then, almost before the mind can comprehend, it seems as if it has fallen completely silent, where the only sound you hear is your own harsh breathing. It is only after the fighting is over that you realize your vision has been so completely focused on what is taking place in your immediate area that you have quite forgotten that the battle involves more than just you and your comrades. However, as I gained more experience, I learned that this changes as you become, if not accustomed, at least inured to the tumult in your front, and it becomes almost an obsession to a ranker to try and make sense of the larger situation. Slowly, you become aware that it is not as silent as you thought; it is just quieter than it was a moment before, but now you hear the gasping breath of the men around you and the moans of men who have fallen. As I learned that day, this is the only time when there is no difference between men, whether they be Roman, Chatti, or any of our enemies. Suffering from wounds is universal, and the fallen all speak the same tongue, even if the words are different. But it takes no translator to know when a man who does not speak your language is suffering, and it is this sound that I have learned serves as the catalyst to get men moving.

"Galens, get me a butcher's bill!" I heard Pilus Prior Corvinus bellow, and his words pulled me from the almost dreamlike state I had been in.

Although it was true that I had only gone through one rotation, I was nonetheless extremely tired, but I was ashamed to show any sign of it, at least until I saw my veteran comrades like Asinius, stumbling about. It was Asinius who first spoke to me directly.

"Pullus!"

I jumped in surprise and turned to see him staring at me, his face glistening with sweat despite the coolness of the forest.

"I've called your name three times," he said irritably, at least explaining why his tone had been so sharp. "Get your head out of your ass. Turn so I can check and make sure you're not wounded."

I protested that I was fine, but he refused to be put off, insisting that I face him, then make a complete turnabout.

"I told you I was fine," I grumbled.

"I'll believe it when I see it," he shot back.

It was only later that I learned that this was a particular habit of Sergeant Asinius, and was due to a comrade of his who, in the heat and excitement that is still upon a man after battle, insisted that the blood on his lower body was not his, but that of an enemy. Not until Asinius' comrade collapsed and died shortly afterward was it discovered that the blood was in fact his. Ever since then, Asinius scrupulously examined each of us to make sure that he did not repeat the same mistake.

He signaled his satisfaction with a grunt, then turned away to check the rest of my section. I took a step to the side and looked down our rank and, at first, I was afraid my heart would pound out of my chest when I saw that, of the eight files that comprise a section, three of them were empty. However, then I examined the ranks in front of us and I saw the faces of Scrofa, Metellus, and Bassus, prompting me to whisper a prayer of thanks. Scrofa and Bassus were two ranks ahead of me, but Metellus was three spots up, telling me that at least seven of the men of the First Century had fallen, wounded severely enough that they could not continue fighting.

Before I could ponder the deeper meaning of this, I heard Pilus Prior Corvinus call out, "Tenth Section! Up front and take care of these bastards!"

Not surprisingly, I had no idea what Corvinus meant, but Asinius, when I did not move, grabbed me by the arm, not roughly, but in a clear indication that I was to follow him.

"Come on," he said over his shoulder, "now you get to see what the dirty work is all about."

Pushing past my comrades, most of whom had just collapsed onto the ground, panting and pulling out their canteens because Corvinus had given them leave to do so, I trailed Asinius and the others. Reaching the front of where our Century had stopped and fought, I got my first real look at the carnage we had managed to wreak on the Chatti. In truth, it looked something like a wall, coming up to most men's waists, but hitting me in mid-thigh, that had been erected along a line paralleling where our Cohort had formed up to stand and fight. The difference was that this wall was composed of what I at first thought were the corpses of the Germans we had slain, but I was quickly disabused of that when suddenly, there was a spastic, jerking movement in the part of the pile directly in front of me, originating at the bottom. I can laugh about it now, yet in the moment it happened, I gave out an undignified yelp of fright as I jumped back, drawing my sword. What I can also say is that I was not surprised at all when my reaction drew peals of laughter from not just Asinius and the rest of my section, but the men of the first line right behind me.

"Don't worry, Pullus," I heard someone call out, "they won't bite…much."

This drew more laughter and, frankly, I should have been more embarrassed than I was, but I was more pleased that I had just been referred to by my adopted name, something that had been long in coming. Giving what I knew was a sheepish grin over my shoulder, I was still uncertain what we were supposed to do, at least until Asinius informed me by demonstrating.

"I hate this part," he said so quietly I was not sure that I was meant to hear, but there was no hesitation in his movements as he bent over and started examining the Chatti dead.

Dragging a German who was clearly dead off the pile, I saw that underneath the first corpse was another Chatti, except that this man's eyes were not only open, which is not uncommon, they were moving about. It did not take any experience for me to see the fear in them as they looked up at Asinius, nor to see the pleading in them as Asinius drew his *pugio* and, without any hesitation, sliced the man's throat. Bright red blood sprayed up, then there was a gurgling sound as the Chatti vainly tried to draw in breath through a severed windpipe.

"Well, don't just stand there," Asinius said irritably. "You've seen what needs to be done. Get to it!"

I did not reply, but I did as he instructed, and I began examining the pile of bodies that had moments before been snarling, spitting fiends trying to take my life. Since I was working around the spot where my file had been fighting, it meant that as I dragged the limp, freshly dead bodies from the top of the pile, I would run into a familiar face. The fact that it was the first Chatti I found who was still breathing just made it more memorable, as I stared down into a face that was familiar and, as I would learn, would come to haunt my dreams. It was the black-haired Chatti wielding the axe, both hands still pressed on the puncture wound I had inflicted just below his breastbone; obviously, Maxentius had not followed through on his complaint

111

that he would have to finish what I had started, since I had not twisted the blade as we were trained. It was the first time I was confronted with such a graphic example of why we are trained to twist and rip our blade when we recover back to our fighting position, and I am happy to say that it was the last. It is a profoundly disturbing experience, at least it was for me, to face a man you had vanquished but not finished off. Blood was still oozing from around where his hands clutched his torso, and there was more of the same dribbling from his mouth, but there was no mistaking the look of recognition he gave me as I bent over him, *pugio* in hand. His mouth twisted into a bitter grimace at the sight of me looking down, and I know I should have felt nothing but satisfaction at being in the position of the victor, standing over my vanquished foe. Instead, I thought I would throw up and, if the truth must be known, I would rather have been anywhere but where I was at that moment. The hatred and anger I had felt toward this man, when he was trying to kill me, was gone and, despite myself, I felt nothing but pity. Ignoring these feelings, I forced myself to put my *pugio* up to his throat and I was just about to draw it across his throat, when I was stopped by a single word.

"Wait."

I cannot honestly say what it was that surprised me more – the word itself or the fact that it was in my own tongue. But he got his reprieve; my hand froze, and I stared down at him, my heart in my throat.

Somehow, I managed to croak out, "What do you want?"

"What is your name?" he asked me quietly. "I would know the name of the man who sends me to meet with Woden."

Woden is the name of their god that I suppose is the equivalent to Jupiter Optimus Maximus, and I was at least familiar with his name, if nothing else. I know that I did not have to answer this defeated foe, but I did so nevertheless; I like to think that I was paying homage to both my father and, most importantly, my Avus, since he had actually been on this side of the Rhenus.

"My name is Titus Porcinianus Pullus," I told him, quietly enough that the others could not overhear. "My father is Gaius Porcinianus Pullus, formerly Quartus Pilus Prior of the 8th Legion. The Legion," I did not attempt to hide my pride, "and the Cohort you just faced. And lost to."

The Chatti's mouth twisted into a tighter grimace, but it was the despair in his eyes that triggered in me an unexpected feeling of sympathy, so I hurried on.

"I'm also the grandson of Titus Pullus, whose name I bear. He was the Primus Pilus. The First Spear Centurion," I hurried to explain when I saw this meant nothing to him, "of the 10th Legion Equestris. It was the bravest and most favored of the Legions led by Divus Julius…Caesar," I corrected, "when he led them across the Rhenus the first time, forty years ago."

Instantly, I saw the flame of recognition in his eyes, at the name of Caesar and, for the first time, his face showed what little life was left in him.

"Caesar!" he whispered. "He was the greatest of your warriors, was he not?"

"He was," I agreed. "And my grandfather is almost as famous."

"Then do what must be done, Roman," he replied, lifting his chin to show me his throat.

And I did, but without any sense of joy or victory.

It was a somber group sitting around the fire outside of our tent that night, as it always is in the aftermath of a battle where we sustain losses. While I was relieved that the circle of faces was still intact, the knowledge that just one tent away there were men missing filled me with a sadness that, while we all share it, must never be spoken of aloud. I do not know why this is so, but from what I read, it was the same way with my Avus forty years before, so I assume it has always been the case. We had all cleaned ourselves up, at least as much as can be done in the field without the pools, but our section slave had rubbed us with oil and scraped us, as well as giving us a vigorous rubdown, so that I was refreshed in body, if not in spirit. I had also received another happy surprise when I followed the example of the others and cleaned my armor. Unlike the *hamata*, which must be vigorously scrubbed with a stiff brush in order to get the blood, yours or your enemy's, out from between the links, the *segmentata* with its smooth surfaces requires much less effort. Being as inexperienced as I was, I went to Asinius to show him the slight dent in the plate that protects the area directly under the armpit, asking him if it needed to be replaced. He only gave it a brief glance, then, in partial response, he lifted his own and pointed to a spot.

"See that?" he asked, and I assured him that I did.

He was referring to a deep indentation that was in almost the identical place, just on his left side rather than his right.

"I've had that since last year," he explained.

I must have shown some sort of embarrassment or chagrin that I had come to him because he went on to say, "I had the same question you did, except I had to go to the armorer to find out. They gave me an earful about wasting their time with such a trivial dent." He gave a rueful laugh, apparently at the memory of it. "But they did at least explain to me that the only time these plates need to be replaced is if they've been pierced. Although," he laughed again, "I would imagine that if one of them is pierced, you're going to have more on your mind than getting your armor repaired."

I joined laughing with him, but although I had learned what I came for, I still stood there, and the truth of it is, I do not know why. At least I did not at that moment. Seeing me still unmoving, shifting from one foot to the other, a habit I am told that I have when I am in doubt or in uncomfortable circumstances, Asinius regarded me with a raised eyebrow.

"Well? Is there something else?"

Again, my conscious mind did not know that there was, until I blurted out, "I just wanted to apologize for moving so slowly when the attack first began." I dropped my eyes, unwilling to return his gaze as I finished, "I was just..."

"Scared *cac*less," Asinius replied quietly, but his voice held no censure.

In answer, I just nodded my head, too ashamed to say anything else.

"Do you know what I did in my first battle?" he asked, still in the same quiet tone. I shook my head, and he went on, "I pissed myself. All the boys could smell it."

Only then did I look directly at him, regarding him carefully, but I saw nothing in his face that would indicate he was lying. He returned my stare calmly, with a small smile on his face.

"Really?"

"Yes, really," he assured me. "And I moved even slower than you did. My Optio had to put his foot up my ass to get me into line." He gave an abrupt chuckle at the memory. "I wanted to be anywhere else but where I was."

I considered his words carefully, but when I opened my mouth to thank him, he cut me off.

"Now, go finish getting your gear cleaned up. I'm going to want to look at it in a bit."

Returning to my spot, I felt much better.

After Asinius inspected our armor and weapons, and we ate the evening meal, it is a tradition on the night after a battle that the men are released to wander the camp and go to the other Centuries and Cohorts of the Legions that faced battle that day in order to check on other comrades and, many times, relatives. In my case, I wanted to check on those fellow *Tiros* with whom I'd grown close during our month of training, but I headed to the Third Century first, looking for Gnaeus Figulus. I did not see him seated outside his tent and I stopped in my tracks, trying to decide whether or not I wanted to continue and ask about him. Deciding being directly informed would be better than hearing about it secondhand, I walked up to the Gregarius who had been with him the previous time I had visited. But before I could open my mouth to ask, there was a flurry of movement out of the corner of my eye, and I turned to see that it was, in fact, Figulus, who had thrown back the tent flap and stepped back outside.

"By the gods," I gasped, not bothering to hide my relief, "it's good to see you."

"And you." Figulus strode over, and we clasped arms, then hugged each other.

We examined each other, pleased that we were essentially unmarked, although Figulus had what was already a large bruise on his left forearm.

I pointed to it and asked, "How did you get that?"

He shrugged and, with a laugh, said, "I have no idea. I just noticed it a little while ago myself." Looking up at me, he asked, "And what about you? Did you get your sword wet?"

Although the gods know that this would change, on the occasion of killing my first two men as a Legionary, I did not feel like boasting, or discussing it.

Nevertheless, I replied, "Two. One had a spear; he killed Gemonius of the ninth section. He couldn't get it pulled out of poor Gemonius' body in time. The other," I looked away, "I took

116

him out of the fight, but I forgot to twist the blade and finish him off."

Figulus searched my face, but he immediately understood. "You're in the last section, right?" When I nodded, he finished softly, "And you're always the lucky bastards who get to finish off those *cunni* who haven't had the good sense to die already."

I only nodded in response.

"I know how you feel, Titus." He patted my arm awkwardly. "I've had to do that myself and, gods know, it wasn't my first battle, or the first man I had killed. And if you're like me, it was harder than I thought."

"It was," I said, staring anywhere but in his direction. "By the time I got to him, I wasn't really mad anymore." Despite the subject and my intentions, I could not help laughing. "In fact, I couldn't really remember why I had wanted to kill him. But," I felt like this was important, "I did what I was ordered to do."

"And that's all you can do," Figulus replied. "They can order us to do all manner of things, but they can't tell us how to feel about it."

There was nothing much to be said then, so we parted, and I continued my search. Tuditanus was also in the Third Century, but in a different section than Figulus, so I only had to walk two tents down. Unlike Figulus, Tuditanus was sitting there, easy to spot because the light from the fire danced off his red hair, making it seem alight itself. He was seated facing away from me, watching a conversation between one of his comrades, also seated, with another Gregarius who, like me, had come by to check on a friend, or at least so I assumed since he was standing like I was.

"You're lucky we have to wear helmets. With hair like that, you'd make a German very proud to have that head hanging from his saddle."

117

Tuditanus stood and turned about in one motion, his face lighting up in a smile as he saw that it was me, and we went through a repeat of my meeting with Figulus. However, Tuditanus had a bandage covering his right arm, from just below the shoulder to the elbow.

"What happened with that?" I asked, not needing to point it out.

One thing about Tuditanus was that, with skin as pale as his, when he got embarrassed or flustered, it was impossible for him to hide it because the blood rushing to his face turned him a bright pink.

"I was slow on one of my recoveries," he confessed.

"*Gerrae!*" I exclaimed. "Tuditanus, how many times did you get smacked because of that?"

"A lot," he admitted sheepishly. He gave a slight grimace as he moved his arm about. "But I promise that I won't forget again."

"You better not." I was only partly jesting. "Because next time, it might be the whole arm."

"I know," he assured me.

Suddenly, I had a thought.

"If we get the time, I'd be happy to work with you on that," I offered.

His face was just returning to normal, but the blood came rushing back, except this time, I could see that he was pleased.

"Really?" he asked. "You'd be willing to do that?"

"Of course," I assured him. "But it will cost you."

His smile faltered.

"How much?" His tone was, if not suspicious, at least wary. "Because I'm sending money home."

"Not money," I promised. "And I don't know exactly what, but I'll think of something you can do for me. Like," I gave him a grin, "shoveling *cac* in case I ever get put on punishment detail."

"Deal." He gave me his own smile and his hand.

With that, I left, looking for the rest of the *Tiros* with whom I had become friendly.

Unfortunately, the news was not all good. One of the *Tiros* I considered a friend, Marcus Sergius, had been in the Sixth Century and had been in the half of the Century standing watch on the side from which the Chatti attacked.

"He never had a chance," was how one of his section mates, a veteran Gregarius who had a bandage encasing his entire upper leg from hip to knee, put it. "Those bastards were able to get close up because those fucking colors they wear blend into the forest so well. It was like," he paused for a moment before continuing, "they just…appeared out of nowhere. Like *numeni*." He spat on the ground in the old sign to ward off evil. "Anyway, Sergius barely had time to get his sword up before he was gutted."

For a moment, I stood there, not sure what to do or say. Despite my inexperience, I knew that there was nothing I could offer that would be any comfort to Sergius' comrades, particularly since there were only four men sitting outside the tent. Therefore, I did not even try, and the Sixth being the last Century, I returned to my own tent just in time for the *bucina* call to retire.

It is traditional on a day after a battle that the Legions of Rome do not march that day, and the next day was no exception. Because of the losses, particularly in the Sixth Century, the day was spent in preparing those comrades of ours who had fallen for their trip to the afterlife. I cannot remember who said it, but when they commented that at least there was more than enough wood for the pyres, they were speaking nothing but the truth. Our camp had been made on the spot, and the other two Legions were forced into duty to clear an area large enough for a camp to be made, with a sufficient space around the perimeter so that, should any Chatti decide to do so, they would be unable to use the cover of the forest to get up next to the ditch surrounding the camp. Columns of smoke rose in the air as the souls of our fallen were cleansed in the flames of the pyre, released from the flesh that imprisons all of us. But as somber as the day was, as I learned on the night after the battle, men of the Legions do not linger in a state of darkness and despair very long. And while it may seem hard-hearted, it is just a recognition of the harsh realities of our lives; if we were to remain melancholy after we lost friends and comrades, our lot would be so joyless that it would not be long before we all opened our veins. That is why, except in the case of monumental battles, or catastrophic losses, we do not devote more than a full day to mourning. I do not want to give the impression that men who have lost very close friends, or the close comrade who is the holder of their will, put away their sorrows along with the rest of us, but they do their grieving in private. Consequently, the second night found us sitting around the fire, this time relating the more humorous moments that, as I also came to learn, are at least as prevalent, and important, as the horrible ones. It had been my turn to fetch the water that would be used for the evening meal and, when I walked up, I heard just the tail end of something Asinius was saying.

"He was standing there like a big fucking lump of clay," he was telling the others, each of them chuckling as they worked on their respective tasks. "But his mouth was hanging open so wide that if those *cunni* had been throwing javelins, he could have caught one of them with his teeth!"

This brought more laughter, and I felt my face flushing red, knowing that they were talking about me.

"Eyo, Pullus," Dento called out. "Asinius was just telling us you were already posing for the statue they're going to make of you one day! A bit early for that, don't you think?"

Now everyone was roaring, but while I normally did not like being the butt of anyone's jests, instead, this time, I felt a burst of warmth in my chest, as I recognized that I had passed some sort of test, and this was my comrades' way of showing their acceptance of my presence in their ranks.

"What are you talking about, Dento?" Bassus was the one who spoke up; Dento stood next to Bassus in our formation. "I distinctly remember smelling *cac* when those bastards showed up!"

"It wasn't from me!" Dento protested. "I've never lost my bowels once in a fight!"

Immediately, the others began hooting and shouting, and Dento started blushing furiously.

"You can't hold the first time a man goes into battle against him!" he exclaimed.

"Then why are you fucking with Pullus about the fact that he froze?" Bassus hooted, pointing at Dento's expression of wounded indignation. "At least he put paid to two of those *cunni*."

"Even if he didn't finish that second bastard off." I had just set down my buckets and I whirled about at the sound of this voice, since it was not normally one heard around our fire.

It was Maxentius; I do not know if he had come to our tent specifically, or just been walking by and heard that I was the topic of conversation. He was standing there, arms folded, regarding us with a mixture of amusement and what looked to me like contempt, although I would learn that he viewed almost everyone else in the Century the same way.

"Neither did you." I had not planned on saying it, but there was something in Maxentius' tone I did not like. "So at least I was the one to finish him."

It was pleasing to me that my retort was met with a chorus of cheers and mocking laughter, but I had kept my eyes on Maxentius, who looked anything but pleased at my response. Standing on the opposite side of the circle of my comrades, he stared at me, his mouth in a thin line, and I could see he was truly angry.

"You have a big mouth, *Tiro*," he said quietly, but his words were not lost amid the chatter of my friends. "I know you think you're good with a sword, but you need to remember who you're talking to. I am Gaius Maxentius, and I've seen the death of more men than you can possibly imagine."

Suddenly, the noise stopped and, although I kept my eyes on Maxentius, I could feel the gaze of every one of the men of my section.

"That's true," I replied, and I was happy to hear that my voice sounded cool, almost bored, despite the fact that I could feel my heart hammering against my ribs. "But I'm just getting started. Haven't you been in the Legions for, what, twenty years? That's quite a head start."

"You need to be careful, *Tiro*," Maxentius shot back.

"So do you."

I was not the one to say this, and I do not know who was more surprised, Maxentius or me. Asinius stood up from his spot and walked over to face Maxentius.

"I know you like being thought of as the best man with a sword in this Century," I heard Asinius say quietly. "But I've seen Pullus. You may be better right now, but I'm willing to bet that it's not going to last that long."

If Asinius had slapped the man, I do not think that Maxentius could have looked more shocked, but he recovered quickly.

Looking over Asinius' shoulder at me, he said loudly, "Any time you get tired of hiding behind his shield, you come look me up."

I cannot accurately describe the weight of the pressure I felt, as all eyes turned back to me. Despite my own anxiety, I understood that more than my pride was at stake here; the honor of my section was being challenged as well.

"Whenever we get the time, I'll be sure to find you," I told him, speaking in a tone that was much bolder than how I actually felt.

Asinius continued standing in front of Maxentius and, while I could only see Maxentius' expression, I am sure that Asinius' was no less unyielding. Then Maxentius turned away, muttering something under his breath that I did not hear. After ensuring that he was walking away, only then did Asinius turn around, greeted by cheers and salutes by the others. My Sergeant just looked embarrassed, and he walked over to me.

"All I know is you better beat that *cunnus*," he said, and although it was with a smile, I knew he was serious.

With Maxentius gone, the rest of the evening passed more sociably, as each of us told stories about the other, going from one to the other until I was the only one left who had not aimed at one of my comrades. I did not realize that at first because I was staring into the fire, lost in thoughts of Maxentius, but I became aware of a silence that lasted more than a heartbeat. Looking up, I saw seven other pairs of eyes looking at me expectantly, and I felt the blood rushing to my face yet again as I thought furiously of something that I had noticed about one of my comrades. The truth was that I had been so absorbed in my own problems that I did not really take the time to notice what others were doing.

"I forgot my own name," I finally blurted out. "Asinius kept calling me and I didn't remember my new name."

Eyes turned to Asinius, and he confirmed what I said, remarking blandly, "It's true. I called the big ox a half-dozen times and he just stood there, staring up at the birds."

"Ha!" Tubero hooted, pointing at me. "You've been so quick to remind us about your name, and then you forgot it yourself?"

I did not particularly care for the fact that it was Tubero who had spoken, but I was pleased that my attempt at self-deprecation had gone over well, as the rest of my section roared with laughter.

With our tasks done, and our ration of wine consumed for the night, one by one, we went to our tent, knowing that the morning would begin early, with the shouts of Galens and Corvinus rousing us to resume the march.

Chapter Three

The attack by the Chatti, although it had cost the Fourth Cohort dearly, particularly the Sixth Century, had been even more costly to the Chatti, who left more than a thousand of their number behind. Despite this good news, veterans of the previous campaigns were quick to remind us that this was just a drop in a huge bucket of blood, that the Chatti were one of the strongest and largest tribes of the Germans. When we resumed our march the next morning, instead of two Cohorts to clear the way, Drusus commanded four, although two still did the work. The other two were posted as security, one on each flank, and it was in this manner that the army continued its push, deeper into the Black Forest. No matter how hard I may try, there is no way for me accurately convey the scale and majesty of the Black Forest. In fact, it is one of the few times that, despite how vivid a picture men who had seen it wanted to paint, emphasizing the feeling of isolation and all-consuming nature of the darkness for those of us consigned to the forest floor, none of them could do it justice. Imagine entering a tunnel where the far end is not visible, but not just for a moment as you continue your progress, but for days, then weeks on end. That was the nature of our march, and I cannot lie when I say that what small comfort I took came from the fact that not just *Tiros* felt the suffocating pressure of that damnable place. The entire army was on edge, and matters were not helped by the fact that the rumor began circulating that the wolves we heard howling every single night, in fact came from the same source as what we had heard on our first night.

"It's the same damn pack that's stalking us," Tubero insisted one night.

Of all of us, Tubero could be counted on as the one most likely to repeat the direst of the prophecies and rumors that hover about an army like a swarm of gnats. Over time, I observed that

125

he seemed to pay special attention to the most lurid of the gossip, particularly if it concerned our fate.

Oblivious to my internal musing, he continued, "I've got a friend in the 14th, in the Second, and he's heard the camp priests talking about what this all means. They're saying that it's a sign that either this whole campaign is cursed, or just one man in the army is."

"So if it's just one man, out of all of us, then that's not much to worry about, is it?" Poplicola pointed out.

I saw Asinius open his mouth to say something, but Tubero beat him to it.

"Depends on who it is," he muttered. Then, casting a quick glance over his shoulder, he hunched forward and kept his voice low as he said, "But my friend says the camp priests are afraid that it's Drusus who's the one man who's cursed. And if he is that one man, well, we're all fucked then, aren't we?"

From where I sat, I could see Asinius' features darken, and he thinned his lips down so much it looked like a slice of a razor had opened up a bloodless slit across his lower face. I had learned that this was the surest sign that he would explode, which, at the very least, would mean a lashing with his tongue, if not his fists or feet. But I was surprised when his tone was pitched to match that of Tubero.

"You need to stop paying attention to the gossip and more attention to your own affairs, Tubero," he said quietly, pointing to the harness in Tubero's hands, which he had ostensibly been mending, although from what I saw, he had not made any progress whatsoever because he had been too busy talking. "That harness isn't going to fix itself, and if it breaks again on the march tomorrow like it did today, and you have to drop out, you and I are going to have...problems."

Now it was Tubero's turn to flush and he protested, "I'm going to have it fixed, Asinius! Besides, I was just talking. There's no rules against that, at least not on our free time."

In that, Tubero was technically correct, but Asinius was not going to be put off the scent by that reminder.

"But there are rules about spreading rumors that will make the men more worried than they already are," Asinius pointed out, which was also true. "And I'm pretty sure that you don't want me reporting to Galens that you're doing something that you've already been warned about once."

I sat up, watching Tubero closely; this was something I had not heard before, but I could see that the others had, as they all shot glances at him, with a variety of expressions. Fortunately for Tubero, the warning from Asinius that night was enough to stop him, at least for a bit. But the rumors about the wolves, and who their true prey was, persisted and, from where I sat, they did not need Tubero's help in being spread and taking root.

Despite these dire signs, we continued hacking and chopping a path through the forest. Over the years, I have often tried to occupy myself by trying to calculate exactly how many trees were chopped down on that campaign. When it came our turn again to clear the way, I kept track of how many trees just my Century was responsible for downing. Very quickly, I realized that I had to restrict my count to trees of a certain size; if I tried to count the seedlings, the young trees and the variety of tree that is barely more than a shrub, I would have quickly expended my knowledge of numbers. Consequently, I only counted trees that were large enough that it took at least two arms to surround the trunk, with no more than the length of a hand's overlap. During our day of clearing, just my Century cut down sixty trees of this circumference and larger for every section we were designated to clear; my very loose estimate of the smaller variety would be in the hundreds, and I did not even attempt to calculate the undergrowth that was ripped out by the root. Considering that my Cohort was responsible for a half-mile of clearing at a time, and we generally cleared at least four of these sections before we were replaced, my closest estimate of how many trees removed numbers around seven hundred trees for every mile we traveled. It did not take long before I recalled a passage in my Avus' account, during his own foray into this land, as he wondered if there would not be some sort of reckoning with whatever gods of the Germans who watched over the Black Forest for all the trees that perished at the hands of the Legions of Rome. Although I kept these thoughts to myself, until now at least, I will say that there were others who were speaking such concerns aloud, and it was not Tubero who uttered them. It seemed with every passing day, the mood of the army grew darker. Then, a week after we were attacked, the Chatti struck again.

This time, their attack was not on the working party, but the baggage train. Under circumstances such as what we were experiencing, with our slow progress, the baggage train was not positioned last, with just a Cohort trailing behind, as is usual. Instead, it is positioned in front of an entire Legion, so that with an army of three Legions like ours, it is roughly two-thirds of the way back from the vanguard. Additionally, Drusus had commanded a full Cohort to march next to the baggage train, three Centuries on each side, spaced with about two hundred paces between them. And while, unlike my Avus who had severed all ties with the gods, and my father who is at best only partially religious, I cannot help thinking that there was some reason the gods decreed that this day the Fourth Cohort would have drawn the straw to be escorting the baggage train. Over the rumble of the wagons, the tromping of our hobnails, and the low hum of our conversations, the air was split by a roar that, this time at least, I immediately identified.

"We're under attack!"

I do not know who shouted this, but it had come from the far side of the baggage train, where the even-numbered Centuries were marching. Nevertheless, I whipped my head to the right in the direction of the forest, cursing once more when the longer back flap of my helmet snagged on my shield still strapped to my back, but I dropped my chin an inch or so and was able to turn to view the woods. This time, not only did it not take me long to see that the Chatti were attacking both sides, I did not hesitate in shouting a warning, although my voice was just one of a few dozen men who had seen the onrushing Germans at the same time.

"About turn! Wheel right at the double! Hurry, you bastards! Hurry!"

Corvinus' voice sounded like a whip crack, and he had not hesitated more than a heartbeat, instantly assessing the situation and understanding the best course. This was an unconventional order because, in turning ourselves about, then having the marching formation swing to the right, Corvinus, in essence, reversed us. Whereas I normally was in the last rank on the far right, this time I was in the front rank, on the far left. I did not have the time, nor the experience to appreciate the brilliance that Corvinus, in the amount of time it takes to draw a breath, had comprehended the quickest and best way to meet this attack. And in many ways, he did me a favor, although I know that helping settle the nerves of a *Tiro* in only his second battle was not part of his calculations. If he had ordered us to make a left wheel turning movement, we certainly could have done it, but not without collapsing our spacing because the distance between us and the wagons of the baggage train was such that there was no room to do so without us crashing into each other. The salutary effect it had on me was that I did not experience any pre-battle nerves, if only because I had just enough time to unsling my shield and set myself for the oncoming Chatti. I was lucky in one respect; all I had to do was essentially make a turn to the right and bring my shield up, since I was the base of the pivot. When Drusus gave the orders to chop a path, he specified that it had to be wide enough that the best among us with a javelin could not hurl one from his spot in the column into the trees. However, it was not much wider than that, perhaps a pace or two beyond a javelin's throw, meaning that when the Chatti were spotted, just a half-dozen paces into the shelter of the forest, we only had the time it took for a running man or, in this case, hundreds of them, to cover the forty paces. In other words, we had no time to deploy our javelins.

"Draw swords! Get ready, boys!"

"Jupiter Optimus Maximus, protect this Legion….."

That was all I heard of the Legionary prayer before it was drowned out by howling, cursing madmen. Although I had enough time to bring my shield up tight to my body and drop my right leg back to brace for the impact, that was all I could manage before a pair of warriors, side by side, both of them with spears and shields came to end me.

SLAM!

One of them, couching his spear much like a rider would with a lance, threw his whole body weight into a thrust, aimed right at my shield. Despite being braced and, even with my bulk, I felt myself rocked backward, my right leg sliding a bit before I felt the oddly comforting push of a hand grasping my harness.

"That's as far back as you go." The voice was not instantly familiar, but a corner of my mind reminded me that it was the man who had marched to the left of Gemonius and had been moved over.

I did not have time to give any sign that I had heard because, just as the point of the first Chatti's spear embedded itself in my shield, with perhaps two inches of the point suddenly appearing on the inside of it, the second Chatti was launching an overhand thrust. As inexperienced as I might have been, I instantly recognized that these two were acting in concert because I felt a tremendous downward pressure on my shield as the first Chatti used the shaft of his spear to try and pull it down in order to open up a target for the second German. It was a good tactic, and I can only imagine how well it would have worked if I had not been as strong as I was. But although they had clearly planned this attack, when my shield did not budge, it meant that the second thrust simply struck my shield as well, this one high and to the

130

right. In fact, it was more of a glancing blow, as the point of his spear skittered off the curved surface of the shield, flashing past and over my right shoulder. This was the first instant I acted offensively, and I did not waste the slight opportunity that I had been given. The thrust of the second Chatti had not gone as he had envisioned, and I can only assume that the momentum of his attack was the cause of his body essentially following in the direction of his spear. It was not much, but he had to take a stumbling step to his left and, in doing so, for the briefest of instants, I could see his upper body because he had been forced to move his shield just enough for my purposes. My arm shot forward in a simple, straightforward thrust, but as I think back on it, this was the first time I actually had an idea of my own strength because although I did not twist my hips in the manner in which we are trained, just the strength of my arm was enough to punch through his mail and penetrate several inches at a spot just below his right armpit. Once more, I did not twist my blade, but that was deliberate because, even as I launched my own attack, the first Chatti had given a hard yank on his spear. While I retained my grip on my shield, the Chatti was a strong man in his own right, and I was unable to keep the shield perfectly vertical and next to my body. That gave another Chatti who, without a downward glance at his fallen comrade, hurdled the second Chatti's corpse while raising his weapon, a long Gallic sword and, in the same motion, brought it down in an overhead blow. I believe he was aiming for my sword arm, since it had been extended outside and beyond the protection of my shield when he began his attack. Fortunately for me, the manner most favored by the Germans as an offensive move, particularly with a sword, starts well above the head and, while devastating if it lands, takes what in combat seems to be a full watch actually to do so. Consequently, by the time this third German's blade came whistling down into the space occupied by my arm an eyeblink before, the only damage he inflicted was to the ground, when almost a foot of his blade buried itself in the soft dirt. This German was not armed with a shield, making him extremely vulnerable to a counter-thrust of my own, since my arm was pulled back in the first position and ready. Luckily for him, at least in this instant, I was more concerned with the intention of the Chatti who had originated this assault now that he had recovered his spear.

As the swordsman cursed and jerked his blade out of the dirt, the first Chatti, with a deft toss of the spear, changed his grip from an underhand to overhand grip, then, with what was essentially the same motion, made a hard thrust, aiming for the spot just above my shield, where only my eyes were showing between the rim and my helmet. Even now, I am not sure why I did not bring my shield up; I was certainly not experienced enough to have seen this maneuver before, but it was good that I did not. It was a feint, and again in one smooth motion, the Chatti had altered the direction of his attack, now thrusting from a slight angle aimed at my lower left side. Because I had not gone for his feint, I did not have to move my shield other than to turn my wrist to change the orientation so that instead of hitting the shield square as he had with his first thrust, it struck a glancing blow, then bounced off. That gave me an opportunity, and I did not waste it. I did not answer with my sword; we Romans are trained to use our shield as an offensive weapon as well as for defense, and that was how I used it now. Taking just a slight step forward, I shot my left hand out as if I were throwing a punch. The fact that my shield was attached to my hand not only extended my reach thanks to the large metal boss in the center that protects our hand, but it increased the damaging power of it greatly. With his spear arm fully extended, he tried to bring his shield across his body to block mine, but he was too late, and the force of the metal boss slamming into his cheekbone with terrific force shivered all the way up my arm and into my shoulder. If I had not heard it, even over the noise of battle, I would have known I crushed his cheek by the feeling of it collapsing under my shield. His muffled scream had not even died out before I had recovered, perhaps not as quickly as if I had just thrown a punch with my fist, but fairly close to it. That was enough time for me to move my shield back into position by twisting my body, just in time to meet the second swing of the sword by the Chatti swordsman. Something I first learned when I read my Avus' account, and is being reinforced now as I write this, is how difficult it is to portray events accurately in such a way that it makes the reader keep in mind how quickly all of these things are taking place. Despite how it may seem as I describe them, I would doubt that more than a dozen heartbeats had elapsed from the instant the first Chatti's spear slammed into my shield. But, as I had gotten a glimpse of in the first battle, and was seeing demonstrated even more vividly in this one, was how slowly my enemies seemed to move. It was almost as if we were going through a rehearsal for one of those mock duels that are performed on stage that people love so much, and such was the case as my shield moved to meet the downward stroke of my foe's sword. I had seen the Chatti with the crushed face take a staggering step in the opposite direction, but as I turned to face the swordsman, I sensed the movement that indicated yet another German was rushing to take his place. Because the swordsman had no shield, he had to rely on either the fury of his attack, or his skill in using his blade to deflect my own thrust and, as I quickly determined now that I had weathered his second attack, his skill in trying to parry my own thrust was almost pathetic in nature. I suspect that much of it was due to the length of his sword, but more than anything, I believe that his hubris was the cause of him only partially deflecting the point of my sword. Instead of hitting him in his gut as I intended, his desperate, sweeping move with his sword just meant that instead of my original target, my blade thrust into his upper chest. The extra resistance caused by the hard bone of his breast meant that I was unable to make a kill with just my arm, but the instant I felt the extra resistance, I gave a savage twist of my hips, using the weight and power of my lower body to punch through both mail and bone. This time, I did twist the blade, which is even harder to do than penetrating, and I heard a low-pitched half-grunt, half-growl that I can only assume came from me. I was rewarded by the sight of the swordsman's eyes almost comically opening wide as he gave a moan that quickly started gurgling as

133

blood came dribbling out of his mouth. Before he even fell, I was returning my attention back to whoever it was that had taken the place of the Chatti with the crushed face, but before I could even begin to engage this man, somewhat surprisingly with a full beard, wielding an axe and hefting a kite-shaped shield, there was the blast from Corvinus' whistle, signaling the relief.

"Knock that *cunnus* off his feet," I heard the man behind me urge.

This was the first time I remember not feeling overwhelmed in a fight, where I was not merely reacting and doing my best to stay alive, so it was with some confidence that I tried to do as he said. The bearded Chatti was the first German who did not appear to be out of his mind with a killing rage, just throwing himself at me. Immediately after the whistle sounded, instead of pressing his attack, I saw his eyes dart to the three men at my feet, then take a step back. A feeling of fierce delight surged through me at what I saw as his recognition of me as a formidable foe, and I was about to ignore the whistle and take a step forward in order to demonstrate to him that he was correct in his judgment. That was when, for the first but certainly not the last time while I was under the standard, what I can only describe as a moment where my Avus stepped in occurred, stopping me from making a mistake that might have cost me my life.

I have had thirteen years from the occasion of that moment against the Chatti until now, when I am writing this down, to come up with another explanation for what happened that day. However, try as I might, I have never been able to ascribe what took place as anything other than my Avus, Titus Pullus, somehow intervening and keeping me from doing something stupid. Although I cannot say with any certainty that I would have lost my life, it is extremely likely. Now, my Avus did not suddenly appear to me, standing in between me and the bearded Chatti with the axe. Instead, what I experienced was inside my head, but in the form of what I suppose could be called a story, one that I had read just a year before. Except rather than recall the words and seeing them in my mind's eye, as I have every other time I remember something I have read, I heard a voice, reciting the words that I read, as clearly as if the reader and I were sitting in a quiet room, and his was the only voice raised. Compounding my shock, and what caused me to heed the words being spoken, was the identity of the voice speaking the words of this story. Perhaps you have a suspicion by now and, if you do, I will confirm that it was the voice of my Avus that I heard, but more than that, it was what he was saying, which was a verbatim retelling of a part of his account that I read. Like with me, it had been his first campaign when he had been faced with an almost identical situation. Unlike me, he had in fact ignored the whistle sounding the relief because his opponent had recognized him as a brash youth, full of pride in himself and his ability with a sword, and done exactly what this Chatti had done and taken a step backward. Just as I had been tempted to do, my Avus took this as a recognition of his ability, not as an understanding of his inexperience and overconfidence. It had almost gotten him killed; this was what he read, aloud in my head, just as I was about to take that same step forward. Instead, since I did not have to push my foe backward, I took a step to the side, although I did manage to do that wrong. Forgetting that we were reversed, I took my customary step to the left, which would have been the proper thing to do, since it gives the man being relieved the protection from the file of men of which he is a part. Unfortunately, when I took that step to the left this time, I was essentially standing there by myself, but while I immediately realized my error, instead of trying moving over to squeeze past my comrades, I just backpedaled, my shield up, until I felt a hand grab at my harness.

"Get back in line, idiot." I do not know why, but I was surprised to hear Galens' voice.

"Yes, Optio," I replied sheepishly, remembering that he was in his accustomed spot at the left rear of the formation, and I was actually the one out of place.

Dropping behind Maxentius, who had been in the last rank, I saw him looking at me with undisguised hostility but, panting and still feeling the quivering nerves that come with combat, I managed to keep my mouth shut. Maxentius, on the other hand, was not so disposed.

"So how many kills did the great swordsman make?" he asked, his tone mocking and lacerating my pride, despite knowing that was his intent.

"I didn't keep count," I said, but not until after I had taken a drink from my canteen.

I do not know whether it was my answer, or my delay in doing so that angered him; my suspicion is that anything I said would have yielded the same result.

"Probably because you didn't make any," he snapped. "Just stood up there waving your sword about hoping you'd kill these *cunni* by making them catch cold."

"Shut your mouth, Maxentius," Galens growled. "I may be here in the back, but I can see that he put paid to at least two of these bastards. That's not a bad shift by anyone's standard."

"Bah," Maxentius spat, "you can take up for him if you want…"

I do not know if he intended to say something else because, just then, there was a shout from about midway through the formation, and we all turned to see one of our comrades come crawling back before collapsing on the ground. His face was covered in blood, so I did not recognize him, but Galens wasted no time, moving at a trot to check on the fallen Legionary.

"That's the second time you've been saved by someone else." Maxentius turned his head just enough so that I would be the only one to hear him amid the noise. "I can't wait to see what happens when you don't have anyone to hide behind."

It is true that I was a *Tiro* still and, technically, Maxentius, who was a Gregarius, although he was not *Immunes*, outranked me. What is also true is that I inherited more than my size from my Avus, and it was this second gift that caused me to not do the smart thing and keep my mouth shut.

"By the time I'm through with you," I only had to lean forward a bit and lower myself to his level so my mouth was next to his ear, "you're going to be the one who's looking for someone to hide behind."

Not surprisingly, Maxentius whirled around and, for a moment, I thought he would come after me, despite the fact that just a few paces away from us were men who would not care about our squabble and who wanted to kill the both of us. I braced myself, but then the whistle blew again, which seemed to break the hold his anger had on him.

Turning back about as we made our shuffling step forward, I heard him mutter, "We'll settle this later."

His anger might have been cooled by the blast of Corvinus' whistle, but mine was not. In fact, as we continued through the rotation and I neared the front again, my rage was steadily building. Staring at Maxentius' back, I was finding it hard to concentrate on what was about to come, and I experienced for the first time something that I would come to learn was extremely valuable. One of the most difficult things about a battle, other than the obvious hazard of having your head lopped off or your guts spilled onto the ground, is keeping one's concentration when bombarded with so much noise. It is a relatively simple matter to block out the things that are happening in front of the eyes, especially in a Roman Legion, and you are in the back of the formation. By keeping your eyes averted and on the back of the man in front of you, it is possible to exclude the horror that the eyes perceive. The sound is another matter, but as I waited my turn, staring at Maxentius' back and seething with a growing rage, it was with some surprise that I found I did not notice the noise at all. There was one exception; the blast of Corvinus' whistle sounding the relief penetrated, but I believe that I was aware of it only because, at the same time, we would take a shuffling step forward. Besides that, the silence seemed to envelop me completely, while at the same time, I felt what had started out as a white-hot anger turn into something else, something colder and more focused. For some reason, when whatever it was inside me changed, it made me break out into a sweat that instantly soaked my tunic, spreading all the way to my padded undershirt, although I would only learn this when I removed it later and found it sopping wet as well. For the entire time since I had taken place behind Maxentius and we had our words, my rage had been aimed at him as my mind ran through all the things that I wanted to do to him. Yet, when I was perhaps the third man back from the front rank, and I could see more of the fighting just two men away from me now, what happened next is impossible to describe.

In the space of a few heartbeats, I transferred the focus of my killing rage from Maxentius, to the snarling menace just paces away from me. Before, the target of this killing rage, this fit, had been indiscriminate, so that whoever stood before me was going to be the object of my rage. This was the first time that I saw that I could shift this monster inside me, that I had some sort of control over the beast that, frankly, I had worried about ever since it first appeared when I was ten, against Spartacus. Another salutary effect that came from the silent cocoon I seemed to have drawn around me was that it allowed me to think more clearly and observe. And it was because of this and, thanks to the reversal of the formation, that I was able to watch Maxentius work with his sword, something that normally never would have happened. Even as I held firmly onto the back of his harness, my eyes and concentration were solely on him and his movements. And in that period of time, no more than perhaps a hundred heartbeats of time before I heard the blast of a whistle, I had seen what I needed.

In fact, when Maxentius pushed away the Chatti he was facing, then stepped aside, as he backed up between the files, he muttered, "That's how it's done, boy," I made no answer, except with a small smile as I took his place.

When I performed my second rotation, it was as if I was a different man than the one who had faced the first onslaught just a few moments before. By this point, there were perhaps a half-dozen bodies littering the ground in front of me and the man to my right, and at the edge of my field of vision, I sensed a backward movement, but lower down next to the ground, which was at least one wounded Chatti crawling away. Immediately in front of me was the warrior Maxentius had shoved backwards, now recovered and throwing himself at me. Armed with a spear, he did not wear mail, but a cuirass of boiled leather, and his shield had clearly seen better days, and it was this that I noticed as he made his first thrust. I had once tried to describe to my father what happened during one of my fits, and the example I used is the way honey flows on a cold day, compared to the way it flows when it is warm. As slowly as it seemed the first men I faced were moving, it had been much faster than the thrust of the spear that came at me now. It seemed to be coming at me at such a leisurely pace that I barely glanced at it as my shield easily blocked the blow. While this one hit squarely, just like the first one that punctured my shield, the force behind this Chatti's thrust was such that I could barely see the tip of the point poking through. His body was not my first target; I had examined his shield and I could clearly see at least one crack, running horizontally across his shield, just above the boss. I made no attempt to get past his shield with my thrust, instead making it the focus of my attack and, even as my arm was moving, I knew that this would be a brutally powerful blow, making sure to twist my hips at the last instant as I did. There was a resounding crack and, suddenly, the top half of his shield detached from the rest of it and went flipping over and over, back in my direction, but above even my head, landing somewhere behind me, where I heard a curse as I suppose it struck one of my comrades. Suddenly deprived of half his defensive weapon, the warrior, who was probably not much more experienced than I was, stood motionless for a moment, the spear in his hand seemingly forgotten. He was already dead, although it would be an instant before he learned of it himself, by way of the point of my blade slicing into his throat, just beneath his mouth, still hanging open in shock. Truthfully, I had stopped paying attention to him, already looking past him to the Chatti who would replace him, even as he dropped to his knees, ruined shield and spear forgotten as he clutched in vain at his throat. I felt a flicker of surprise because it was a face I recognized, despite the circumstances.

Although it is possible that the bearded Chatti with the axe had been dispatched and was lying near the bottom of the pile of bodies in front of my part of the formation and the man coming toward me was his twin, the grim smile that split his features as he approached disabused me of that thought. Now that I had a second chance to examine him, as he began performing a movement that, in my limited experience, I had never seen before, actually swinging his axe in some sort of pattern in front of him, I saw him more clearly and was able to take in details that I had missed before. He was not as young as I had thought him at first; there were liberal streaks of gray in his hair, which had been hard to spot since his hair was pulled tight against his skull. His beard was jet black, but there were what looked like small bones plaited into them. He was also almost exactly my height, but he was wearing what looked like a bearskin cloak fastened around his neck, although about halfway down, I saw a glimpse of what I assumed to be a gold chain that drew it back away from his body and behind him to keep it from hindering his movements. He wore a helmet that rode higher on his head than what I had seen before, a higher conical shape that made him appear even taller and, on top of that, was adorned what I can only believe was the skull of the bear, of which his cape had been an integral part. With the cloak pulled back, his arms were bare of sleeves, with the exception of several gold rings on each arm, which I had learned were similar to our *phalarae*, awards for bravery given to them by their chieftain, and there was what looked like a matching gold torq hanging from his neck. I had noticed that his kite-shaped shield was sheathed in copper, but it was only this second time that I noticed the series of patterns that had been etched into its surface, patterns which were the twin of the series of tattoos that ran down the length of both arms and his neck. But it was the Chatti's eyes, or more specifically, the expression in them, that I can still see today when I sit back from my desk and close my eyes. And although he did not yet know it, it was the look in them that sealed his fate, and brought me the first share of attention by men outside my Century. They were regarding me with what I took to be a look, and am sure was made of equal parts amusement and contempt, that told me he had taken my measure that told him I posed no challenge to him whatsoever. It was somewhat difficult to see his face clearly because by this point, perhaps three or four heartbeats after he had stepped forward to take the place of the Chatti I had just dispatched, his axe was moving in a blur of motion in front of him, weaving back and forth in a pattern that I found impossible to decipher, which I am sure was his intent, despite my heightened vision and slower sense of time. However, my eyes never left his face, never once giving him any sign or sense that I was trying to pick up the movement of his axe in an attempt to discern from where and when his first attack would come. Then, I saw a subtle change in his expression; his mouth, hard to see already because of the beard, virtually disappeared and the corner of his eyes suddenly turned down. His axe somehow seemed to behave in an impossible manner, suddenly changing not just the direction but the angle that it had been traveling less than eyeblink before, slashing down at me from a height high above both our heads and to my left. The prudent course was straightforward; my left arm, holding the shield, would lift it while at the same time I would rotate my wrist, bringing up the shield and almost parallel to the ground, but with the bottom tilted outward, in order to allow my shield absorb the blow across its entire width and breadth, rather than trying to deflect the blade by only partially blocking the force.

I did not do the prudent thing. Instead, I performed what I suppose could best be described as a hop forward, in order to keep my stance essentially the same, except for being a step closer. Meanwhile, I did not raise my shield at all, but kept it in front of me in preparation for what I had planned. Looking back, the move I made is not one that I would perform now, having seen all that I have when it comes to the strength and reliability of the *segmentata*. Yet the hubris and what I can only say is the self-confidence of youth that, thanks to the gods, proved to be justified, prompted me to take that hop forward and allow the blow of the axe to fall onto the piece of armor that curves over our shoulder. Because of my move, the most dangerous part of the axe, its blade, whistled past me so closely that I felt the blast of air on the left side of my face while at the same time the stout handle slammed down onto my shoulder. Despite accepting the idea that this would be painful, I was only partially prepared for the sudden and sharp stab of agony that started at my shoulder, causing me to expel a rush of air that I imagine was part groan, part curse. Unfortunately, what was worse than the immediate pain was its transitory nature, shooting down the length of my left arm in what I can only describe as a lightning bolt that left my hand tingling and numb at the same time. For a horrifying instant, I thought I would lose my grip on my shield, which would have been catastrophic, as one might imagine. Somehow, I managed to retain my grip, extremely crucial because this was going to be my first weapon and, despite the numbness, now that I was inside the arc of the Chatti's axe, I was not going to waste the opportunity. Putting all of my weight behind it, I ignored the pain as I punched with my shield, the boss aimed for the middle of the Chatti's face, determined to wipe that smug look off it.

His eyes had widened in what I am sure was surprise, but while he brought his own shield up in front of him, he was only partially successful in blocking my blow. There was a tremendous crashing sound, and again, I felt the impact all the way up my arm into my shoulder, which was still in considerable pain, but my blow inflicted its own type of agony, as the boss of my shield caromed off the edge of his upraised shield, then struck the Chatti a glancing blow, just above the rim of his helmet. It was not a killing strike, nor did it inflict serious damage, except this time when he made a backward step, it was not to lure me out, but to give him a moment to clear his head, which he shook in a manner that I would describe as being akin to the bear he was wearing. However, I was in no mood to give him any chance and, despite knowing I was violating orders, I tore myself away from the grasp of my comrade in the second rank.

"Pullus, you fucking idiot!"

I heard, but did not make any indication that I did, instead stalking forward almost into the midst of the Chatti. To my immediate right, I sensed movement and, using the corner of my vision, without moving my head, I made a thrust straight out from my body. I felt the point of my blade make contact, although the best that I could tell was that it was in the facial area of the Chatti who had thought he was about to make an easy kill, drawing his spear back and dropping his shield. I did feel a crunching sensation travel up my arm, followed by a gurgling cry and the detached part of my mind made the assumption that my sword had actually entered into his mouth, knocking out his teeth and driving the shattered remnants back and through his throat. Being honest, I did not learn this was indeed the case until later, when I was told what happened by Asinius, who had been the one battling with this Chatti. My eyes never left the bearded Chatti, but I believe it was my presence, pressing him as I was, that rattled him because, while he unleashed another blow with his axe, it was much slower than his first. My shoulder was settling into more of an ache, but my hand was still numb, and although I blocked this one easily enough, it actually came closer to knocking my shield from my grasp than the first blow. As my shield was doing its work, my right arm was moving, this time aiming low and, as I expected, despite his muddled state, he dropped his shield to block the blow. Between the angle of his attack, which forced me to move my shield slightly to the left of my center, and the angle of my own thrust, which I had aimed so that it was coming from roughly the same direction as his but from the opposite side, for a brief instant, we both stood there, arms apart, leaving our entire bodies from head to toe vulnerable, exactly what I wanted. Taking yet another step forward, as I did, I violently whipped my head at the Chatti, aiming the reinforced iron strip of my helmet for the center of his nose. Stars of a million colors exploded in front of my eyes and, for a brief instant, although my eyes were open, I could not see, but my ears informed me that I had accomplished my goal, by way of a sickening cracking sound, followed by a shriek of such animal ferocity I was surprised to find later that my ears were not bleeding.

The Chatti staggered back once more, except this time, I did not pursue him, mainly because my vision was still clearing, but through the haze, I saw him drop his shield to clutch his face and, through his fingers, blood was pouring out. Seeing me unoccupied, and I imagine my appearance gave this warrior the belief that I was vulnerable, I sensed a rush of movement, again from my right, this time turning my head to see a Chatti, pigtails flying and a vicious smile pulling his lips from his teeth in a snarl, even as he was swinging his long sword down. It was a smart and well-timed attack, and I imagine it would have worked, even on me, if I had not been in the state that I was in because my right arm was already moving upward. Our blades met, sparks leaping from the point of contact, but the strength behind my parry was such that it was his blade that bounced off, its trajectory altered, while mine continued as if it had not been impeded at all, making an arc to my right. When my blade was at the end of its own trajectory, with what I am sure looked like the same motion and no more than a flick of my wrist, I swept the blade so that it made almost a perfect circle, the tip whipping back towards me, barely slowing down as it sliced through the throat of this attacker. Before the man fell, my attention returned to the bearded Chatti, who was bending down to retrieve his shield. I could have ended him right then, with a simple thrust down through the back of his neck, and I imagine that, if he had known what his remaining time on the earth would be like, he would have been happy for me to do so.

Since it is so difficult for me to judge time accurately in these moments, when I seem to be the only thing moving at what I consider a normal speed, it would be impossible for me to say how much time had passed since I returned to the front rank. But just as the bearded Chatti picked up his shield, I heard the blast of Corvinus' whistle, signaling my time at the front had come to an end, meaning that perhaps a hundred heartbeats' time had passed. As I said, I heard the whistle...but I did not move. Nor did I care, although I will admit that in a corner of my mind what I suppose is the rational part of all of us that is the watchman over our well-being and fortune was screaming at me, reminding me that, no matter who I was, or who I was related to, I was still a *Tiro*, and the Legions do not tolerate disobedience for any reason. Frankly, I did not care at that moment, which was the one symptom of this condition, divinely inspired or otherwise, over which I do not seem to have any control. As coldly calculating as I might have been, which from everything I had experienced before, and what I had read of my Avus' account was something new to me and he had never been able to achieve, there was still a recklessness that seemed to have a hold over me that, when that whistle blew, compelled me to stand there.

"Pullus! Pullus! The fucking whistle blew! Move your ass! Now!"

Even over the din, I recognized Asinius' voice, but I was not about to turn to address him because the bearded Chatti,

145

blood streaming down his face, had begun his approach. And because I had jerked myself free of the hold my comrade in the second rank had, there was no way for anyone to remove me. Just as the bearded Chatti began moving his axe in that stupid pattern again, there was another flurry of movement from my right and also from behind the Chatti as another warrior stepped forward to his right, with a second to my left, both of them approaching along with the bearded man. That was when I experienced my first stab of doubt; as confident as I was, I recognized that three men attacking at once would be difficult for me to overcome, no matter what my state. Despite that, I made no move backward.

"Pullus! By the gods, you're going to get your fat ass back here, or you're going to be scourged!"

It was Asinius again, and I felt a twinge because, like me, he had not removed himself from the front rank, but for an entirely different reason.

"Don't make it two of us," I called out loudly, but without turning my head, keeping my eyes fixed to my front, as the three Chatti faced me.

Salvation came from an unlikely source, as the bearded Chatti seemed to realize that his two comrades were intent on helping. Although I had no way of knowing the words themselves, his intent was clear as he snarled something in that guttural, harsh tongue of theirs, and gestured toward me. The man to his left started to argue, but without taking his eyes off me, the bearded Chatti made a hard swipe with his shield, catching his comrade and, I assume, his underling, completely unaware, knocking him backward. Even as he did so, he was leaping forward, his axe suddenly coming at me from waist level, in a horizontal swing designed to disembowel. It was a canny move, but again, it seemed to come so slowly that I had the time to decide how to answer it. Instead of blocking with my shield, I pulled my left arm back so that the shield was hard against my body, which would mean that even if the shield absorbed the blow, I would be staggered, but I also leaned backward at the same time. Because of that move, the axe went slicing by, although I felt a nudge against my shield as the top of the axe grazed it, but it did not alter the Chatti's swing in a material way. For an instant, his arm was extended, the axe now to my right, and I wasted no time, but while I could have taken his hand without much effort, I chose instead to inflict a long, slicing cut all the way up his forearm. The Chatti's breath burst out of him with a hissing sound, although he did not cry out, nor did he drop the axe, although by the time he returned back to his ready position, his arm was dripping blood.

"That looks like it hurts," I called out, only vaguely aware that all other movement in our immediately surrounding area had ceased.

"Fuck you, Roman."

I admit that I was surprised when he answered, in heavily accented but recognizable Latin. The words were followed by a roar as he leapt forward with an agility and speed that was impressive, and this was the first time I was caught flat-footed and by surprise. Even as he moved forward, he did something else that startled me, dropping his shield, then producing from behind his back yet another axe which, in one smooth motion, he brought forward in a blow originating from just above the shoulder, coming down at an angle. His right hand was also moving and, for the next three or four heartbeats, he was a flurry of violent motion, swinging both axes at me in what might have appeared as random blows, although I am sure he had some design. During that interval, I was unable to launch my own offensive move, concentrating only on blocking or parrying the flurry of blows. Only one landed, at least partially, the tip of his left-hand axe slicing a gash in my forearm, although it was not nearly as long or deep as the one that I had inflicted. My biggest concern was that, after perhaps a half-dozen blows landed on my shield, the last one was accompanied by a cracking, splintering sound, and I could feel a sudden instability in the shield.

I could not divert my attention away from the Chatti, his eyes down to mere slits, while for the first time, his mouth was plainly visible as he snarled what I imagine were either curses or supplication to his gods for strength. All I was fairly certain of was that my shield would not last much longer under the rain of blows, and that had more to do with altering my plan to torment this man more than the idea I would be punished. Finally, he was forced to pause, and I wasted not another heartbeat. There is a position, called the fifth position that, although we train with it, is not used very often because it is somewhat awkward and difficult to perform, and involves a motion that is counter to every other thrust or slash that we are trained to do. In one motion, I went into what is best described as a crouch, while my blade made a wide, sweeping arc, where my arm was extended so that about half of the blade went beyond the Chatti's body. Then I brought the sword back in my direction, as if I was recovering from a miss, except that his left leg was between my sword and me. I felt the blade bite deeply into his leg, just above the knee, but despite putting all of my strength into it, when I felt the blade hit his thigh bone, I was unable to cut through it. Nevertheless, it was enough to cripple the German, and he let out a shriek of such unimaginable agony that it made the hairs on my body stand up. As I raised myself from my crouch, he collapsed to his left, his leg now spurting blood and unable to support him. He caught himself from falling prone with his left hand, dropping the axe as he did so, his eyes rolling back in his head from the pain. Consequently, he did not see the thrust that I made into the base of his throat, my blade driving deeply into his body because of the angle. Through my sword, I felt a strong spasm as his body fought the inevitable, as for an instant, I was the only thing keeping him semi-erect. My gaze was not on the bearded Chatti, but on the two men who had been flanking him, and I was relieved to see that, for the moment anyway, I seemed to have been forgotten. Quickly, I withdrew my blade and took a step back towards the safety of my comrades, my sword now covered in blood. Risking a quick glance over my shoulder, I took a step to the right so that I was between the files, then began moving backward. Only then did I start regaining a slight awareness of the world outside that small space in which I had been fighting and I sensed that although there was still a swirl of motion off down the length of my Century, and the Centuries beyond, the movement in front of them was actually reversing in direction. That drew my attention and I saw the beginning of the Chatti retreat, starting with the pack of warriors immediately behind those men still fighting, as they turned on their heel and without giving any warning to their comrades still engaged, at least one that I could discern, they began fleeing the field. The only thing I can liken it to is an avalanche, where a few rocks and clumps of dirt trigger a wider reaction. From my point of view, I had moved no more than three rows deep into the formation when, with howls of sorrow and despair, the Chatti began to flee. Within a heartbeat, the *cornu* sounded the command that launched us in pursuit, and my comrades around me answered with their own roar. Without hesitation, on both sides of me there was motion as the First Century went off in pursuit, but I stayed there, immobile. Although my plan was to wait for the formation to pass, then attach myself to the back of my file, when I began to do so, I was grabbed by Galens, who had stopped to stand next to me. There was no hint of warmth or regard in his gaze as he stared up at me coldly.

"No." He did not yell the word, which was actually more unsettling. "You're not going anywhere. You're on a fucking charge. You stand right here and you'll wait until I return. If I find you moved from this spot, I swear by all the gods, I'll make you regret it. Do you understand me?"

"Yes, Optio," I replied automatically, drawing myself to *intente,* made more difficult because I had not yet sheathed my still-dripping sword. "I understand and will obey."

For some reason, he looked surprised, as if he was expecting me to argue. So he gave me a curt nod, then turned and ran off in pursuit of the rest of the Century, leaving me to wonder about how much trouble I was in.

From my vantage point, I was able to watch the Fourth Cohort chase the Chatti into the woods, but it was not long before a series of *cornu* notes sounded the call to halt the pursuit. While it was unlikely, there was a possibility that this attack had been designed to lure a Cohort out into the deeper woods, but Corvinus was too experienced to take such chances. During the time I stood there, despite feeling somewhat ridiculous, I maintained the position of *intente*, although I did take the time to reach down and pick up a discarded neckerchief that was already bloody, making me wonder to whom it belonged. Finding a clear spot of cloth, I tried wiping my blade down so I could sheathe it, but quickly discovered there was more blood on the blade than clean cloth. My sword was literally caked with blood from the point to the hilt, but despite not cleaning it, I reluctantly sheathed it. Although it was not yet from experience my father had instructed me, and I had been reminded during our training that leaving blood on a blade pits it and, if left too long, it could weaken the blade itself and make it more prone to rust. Why this is so is a mystery; I asked my father at the time he informed me of this, but he could only repeat what he had heard, and that I have heard since. There is some property in the blood that acts as a corrosive to iron, but nobody knows what it is.

As I waited, I also took the time to look down the length of what had become the battlefield. The baggage train was untouched, but peeking in between the wagons, over on the other side, I could see a scene almost identical to the one on mine. One could mark where the front rank of our Cohort fought by the bodies, some lying side by side, some in small heaps, like where I had been standing. Non-combatants, the slaves who worked as the *medici*, along with those Legion slaves who normally were assigned to a section and worked as stretcher bearers and labor in the aftermath of a battle, were moving all up and down the line. Because all of the Cohort had taken off in pursuit, I could see all the way down to where the Sixth Century had been located. In the space between where I was standing and there, along with the bodies of what I could clearly see were Chatti, there were bodies wearing the same uniform as mine. However, even as I watched, I saw men lying prone on ground that had become churned up from all the hobnailed soles scrambling for traction, make some sort of movement that indicated that they were still alive, at least at that moment. Moving between each of these men were the *medici*, and although most of them who knelt down by a body would then turn and shout for a pair of stretcher bearers, more than once I saw a *medicus* suddenly bow his head, then stand and go to another fallen Roman. I am not sure why, but I had refused to look nearer to me, in the area of my own Century, putting that off to last, until finally I had to drop my gaze and actually examine where, moments before, we had been fighting so furiously. I felt a tightening in my stomach at the sight of more than a half-dozen bodies, although I was partially relieved to see two of them sitting up.

There was one man, lying still on the ground, but with his face turned away from me that triggered in me a sense of unease, both because I had just seen the *medicus* assigned to our Century kneel for a moment, then leave him, and because there was something familiar in the man's shape. I had begun to recognize how to tell the difference between a man who is seriously wounded and one who is dead; there is what I can only describe as a relaxed shapelessness to the latter, and I ascribe this to the fact that the man's soul had departed. The Roman I was examining now had that shapeless form, and my eye had gathered enough information to start forming an idea of who it was, causing me to struggle between the order I had been given to remain there or to go see if my fears were correct. How literal had Galens' order been, I wondered? But just as I began to turn and walk over to where the man was lying, I was interrupted by the sound of onrushing hooves, coming from my left, where the head of the column was located. Turning about, I saw two riders

151

leading another dozen or so, and my heart sank as I recognized one of the leading men; it was Drusus.

"Why are you standing there, Gregarius, and not with your Century?"

It not actually Drusus who asked this, but the man with him, who I had only seen from afar before, and I knew he was the second in command.

I had dropped my shield to lean against me so that I could render a proper salute at the proper position of *intente*, and I answered with what I hoped was a confident tone, "I was ordered to stay behind by my Optio, sir."

"And who is your Optio?"

"Aulus Galens, First Century, Fourth Cohort, sir."

I did not feel the need to remind him which Legion. The second in command, who I was examining out of the corner of my vision, was much older than Drusus, with iron gray hair, but not in the style that has become popular, wearing it close-cropped instead. His face was seamed, and although I could easily see he was of the upper classes, he had a no-nonsense air about him that I would learn was a sign that he was a military man through and through. Meanwhile, during our exchange, Drusus had remained silent, choosing instead to survey the battlefield, his face revealing nothing.

"Where's your Century and Cohort now?"

Since I had not been given leave to recover from my position of *intente*, I did not feel it would be wise to point, so the best I could do was nod my head in the direction of the forest. Even then, I could see the brush shaking and I spotted at least one standard bobbing along as the Cohort returned.

"Pilus Prior Corvinus sounded the call to pursue, sir. They're in the forest over there."

That animated Drusus, who nudged his horse and moved in the direction of the forest line, stopping roughly at the spot where our front line had been.

"I hope he doesn't take them too far into that mess," the second in command commented. "It could be a trap."

"It could," Drusus agreed, speaking for the first time as he pointed. "But I can see them returning now."

The second man said nothing, just gave a grunt, but he continued staring at me in a way that was making me uncomfortable. I felt that he was trying to place me and I saw him open his mouth to say something, but Drusus beat him to it.

"Well, well," he said, for the first time sounding pleased. "It looks like one Gregarius has earned himself a nice reward."

He turned towards Drusus, and whatever he was about to ask was forgotten. He asked, "Why is that, sir?"

In answer, Drusus pointed down to a clump of bodies and, when he did so and I risked a glance at where he was pointing, I felt my heart beginning to pound heavily, my mouth suddenly going dry. Even from where I stood, I could see he was pointing down to where the bearded Chatti was lying, on his side, but with his face turned up to the sky.

"Because I recognize this man," Drusus replied. "He's a sub-chief of the Chatti and is one of their warband leaders. He came to a meeting I held two years ago during a truce." He paused for a moment, then continued, "If I remember, his name is, or was," he corrected, "Vergorix, I believe."

Then he turned to me and asked quietly, "Did you happen to see who slew this man, Gregarius?"

I felt not just Drusus, but the eyes of the second boring down into me, but when I opened my mouth, it took two tries before my answer came out.

"I did. Sir," I added hastily, yet as nervous as I was, I know the pride in my voice was clear to hear.

Drusus gave a sudden start, causing his horse to take a nervous step, and he turned his mount so that he was facing me directly. Now his face was cold.

"Really?" he asked, and made no attempt to hide his skepticism. "You did? By yourself? Or did you have assistance?"

"On my own, sir."

I felt the first flickering of anger at the doubt written on the Legate's face. My mental state was not helped when I heard the second give a snort that sounded to me as if it was laced with contempt.

"Not likely." He shook his head. "Look at him, sir. He's wearing the *segmentata*, and look how young he is. My guess is that he's one of the *Tiros* we took on right before we left. That means it's doubtful, at best. Oh," he amended, making it sound as if he were conferring a favor upon me. "Maybe he distracted this Vergorix while one of the veterans put paid to him, but kill an experienced warrior like him?"

"Is that true?" Drusus asked me, his tone quiet, but his gaze still piercing me. For a moment, I was confused; he must have seen it on my face because he added, "I mean that you're a *Tiro*? One of those that joined just before we left Serdica?"

"That's true, sir," I replied. Then, before he or the second could say anything else, I added, "But I swear on the name of my grandfather and my family name that I killed that man, on my own and in single combat."

"Well," the second exclaimed with a mocking laugh, "if you're willing to swear on the name of your grandfather and family name, then by all means it must be true! So, who is this grandfather of yours, boy? Would we know his name?"

It was difficult for me to stifle the smile because, by his tone, he made it clear that he was not expecting to hear a name familiar to him. Although I cannot say that the sense of pride and triumph I felt at that moment was more than when I saw the bearded Chatti fall at my feet, it was close.

"His name," I replied, raising my voice so there would be no mistake, "was Titus Pullus."

The gasp of shock and surprise that I heard coming from my left where the second was sitting his horse was sweet music, but my eyes stayed on Drusus, and only the sight of his jaw dropping was better.

"That's why I thought I recognized you!" This came from the second. "When we rode up, I swore you looked familiar!"

While this was nice to hear, I was more concerned with Drusus' reaction, and he again nudged his horse so that he drew abreast of me, staring down. Not far down, which I could see was not lost on him.

"You mean your grandfather was Titus Pullus, the Primus Pilus of the Equestrians? And one of the first Camp Prefects?"

"Yes, sir." I made no attempt to hide the pride I felt in my answer.

He said nothing for a moment, but his frown was somewhat unsettling, and his eyes narrowed as if he were trying to recall something.

"From what I remembered about him, he didn't have any children," Drusus finally said.

"My full name is Titus Porcinianus Pullus," I said, giving him the answer for which he was searching.

"Ah." He nodded, and it appeared to please him that his memory was correct. "You, or your father," he corrected, "was adopted by him, true?"

"Yes, sir."

"And your father was," his eyes narrowed again, then he snapped his fingers, "your father was a Pilus Prior, as I recall. In fact," this seemed to amuse him a bit, "if I remember, he was the Quartus Pilus Prior of this Legion!"

"Yes, sir," I answered yet again.

Now he gave a short laugh and slapped his thigh, clearly delighted for whatever reason at this connection. But then I saw what I can only describe as a shadow cross his face.

"Ah," he said softly. "I remember it all now. The 8th was my first command. We were marching against the Rhaeti." He paused for a moment, and I could see that his thoughts had turned to a more melancholy frame. "I made many mistakes in that campaign. Did your father tell you that I got the Primus Pilus of the 8th killed? Vettus?"

My blood seemed to freeze, yet my mind was racing. What was the answer he was looking for, I wondered. Of course my father had mentioned it; in fact, he brought it up often and, when he did, it was always as an example of what happens when an overeager but inexperienced noble has the command over a Legion, or even worse, a full army. However, my father held no animosity towards Drusus; that much I know and, in fact, had spoken highly of him and Tiberius.

"He might have mentioned it," I said cautiously, "but never with any rancor or bitterness."

"He's a better man than I am," he replied thoughtfully, his gaze now elsewhere. Shaking his head as if to drive this train of thought away, he asked, "As I recall, your father lost his leg when my brother was in command of the 8th later that year. Is that right?"

Now it was my turn to be sad, but I confirmed that this was indeed the case.

"Is your father well now?" he asked, and I assured him that he was.

"Well, now that we've established your bloodline, I can see how it's possible that you are the one who slayed Vergorix."

I tried to keep my shoulders from sagging in relief, but it was short-lived feeling.

"However, that doesn't explain why you're standing here while your Century is still fighting." His tone was still soft and even, but all warmth had left his face.

Over the rump of his horse, I could see that Corvinus and the rest of my Century was about two hundred paces away, meaning I had a decision to make, quickly.

"Because I disobeyed orders, sir." My voice was strong, without any tremor, but that was the only part of me that was not shaking.

As I expected, Drusus' face darkened and his eyes narrowed.

"Explain yourself."

"While I was facing Vergorix, I had driven him backward, and I moved forward to keep pressing…."

"Wait," he interrupted, "you left your spot in the line?"

"Yes, sir."

Although it was by a mere fraction, I sensed him relax a bit.

"Well, that is technically a violation of the regulations, but if you were pressing your advantage, it's understandable. So that's why you were ordered to stay behind?"

"No, sir," I admitted.

"What then?" he snapped. "What else did you do?"

"When Pilus Prior Corvinus blew his whistle for relief, I continued to engage with the German," I told him, feeling the cold lump of fear growing in my stomach.

"So you disobeyed an order *and* a regulation." I had not thought it possible, but Drusus' tone was even colder.

"Yes, sir."

He opened his mouth, but the sound of the Century crashing to a halt, just on the other side of him, stopped him. Turning, he regarded the assembled men for a moment.

"Wait here," he commanded.

Although I know it was not, it felt like I stood there, with my Century aligned in front of me, for at least a full watch, while Drusus led Pilus Prior Corvinus off a short distance. He had maneuvered his mount so that Corvinus was screened from my view, and Drusus' back was turned to me, although I could hear the soft buzz of their conversation, there was no way to hear what was being said. Once or twice, Drusus glanced back in my direction, and once I saw him point to where Vergorix's corpse was lying. That was the only time I got a glimpse of Corvinus, when he leaned so that he could look past Drusus' horse to where the Legate was pointing. Immediately after that exchange, I heard Corvinus shout, and I saw Galens move from his spot in the rear of the formation to come trotting up. Because Corvinus was Pilus Prior and he had not had a chance to do so, the rest of the Cohort was standing in a long line and, given that I was the only man standing erect who was not clearly wounded, or busy doing something, I do not think I was far wrong in feeling that every eye was on me. The worst part was that almost directly across from me was Maxentius, now that the Century had been returned to its proper formation and, even fifty paces away, there was no way to miss the malicious grin he was giving me, sure that some sort of official misfortune was about to befall me. Frankly, although I hated to admit it, I at least agreed with what I am sure was his opinion. Despite the fact that I had believed I had stumbled onto the key to harness the power of this affliction of rage that my Avus had passed down to me, my pride and belief in myself had put me in a position where my career was about to be harmed, probably irreparably, before it ever really got started. Ignoring Maxentius, I kept my gaze directly ahead, but I was watching intently out of the corner of my eye the continuing exchange between Drusus, my Centurion, and now my Optio. Finally, Drusus straightened in the saddle, said something that I could tell was a command and, an instant later, both Corvinus and Galens came marching from behind the screen of Drusus and his horse. At the same time, Drusus turned his horse and trotted back to where his second in command and bodyguard were waiting.

Pulling alongside his second, Drusus was facing in the opposite direction, and I could only tell that he was speaking. Then, the second stiffened, and I saw his mouth open in what I assume was going to be some sort of protest, but then Drusus made a single gesture, a chopping motion with his hand. With obvious reluctance, the second shut his mouth, while Drusus then circled his mount around so that they were again facing in the same direction. Even as Drusus did so, I heard Corvinus' voice ring out, and just the First Century marched in my direction, before Corvinus gave the command to halt, just at what was the far edge of the battlefield, where the last of the Chatti bodies were laying. Galens, while my Century was moving, went trotting over to the Second, who had remained motionless. A moment later, I heard a series of shouts, then the formation consisting of the other five Centuries broke, and men began sprinting in the direction of the baggage train. I did not understand at first what was happening, but when I saw men stopping suddenly to either drop to their knees or bend over the first of the Chatti bodies, I realized they had been released to do the thing that many men live for while marching under the standard, looting the corpses that they have created. Drusus gave another command, and one of the mounted men behind him, part of his bodyguard, slid off his horse and strode over to the Legate. Giving him brief instructions, the bodyguard saluted and walked over to where Vergorix was lying. Bending over, the bodyguard quickly and efficiently stripped the gold rings off the arms of Vergorix, and I was struck by how limply each limb fell away. But when he was unfastening the gold torq from around the Chatti's neck, something happened that threatened to mar the moment, when even from where I stood, I heard a sudden loud moan, originating from just behind the bodyguard, followed by an arm thrusting up from the pile of bodies. A howl of alarm issued from the bodyguard, and I was sure I had never seen someone leap as high in the air and, despite being at *intente*, my comrades in the First, Corvinus included, roared with laughter. I, on the other hand, was too worried to do anything other than continue to stand there, although I do recall a small chuckle escaping my lips. Fortunately, both Drusus and the second found it as amusing, the second pointing at the now red-faced bodyguard who, when returning to the ground from his leap, landed awkwardly and stumbled a couple of paces before recovering himself. The arm, still hovering in the air, appeared to be attached to a Chatti who was pinned underneath the corpse of one of the men I had killed, and it beckoned weakly.

"I think he wants you to join him, Valerius," Drusus called in a loud voice that I knew was meant to be heard in the rear rank, my normal spot.

"I'd rather not, sir," Valerius seemed to at last see the humor of it, although I feel fairly certain it was at least partially forced jollity on his part. "In fact, if I might, I'd like to put the bastard out of his misery."

Drusus' smile faded a bit, but he gave a nod. Valerius, one hand full with the arm rings and torq, drew his blade, and stood over the Chatti for a moment. There was a low murmur of words between them, then Valerius' blade flashed down in a blur of grayish silver, and I heard the choked, gurgling last cry of the Chatti. Valerius sheathed his sword, the point still bloody, then marched over to Drusus and, with a great show, handed the rings and torq to Drusus, who took them with the same show of ceremony. Then, Drusus nudged his horse, walking it across my front until he was now directly in front of my Century.

Without turning his head, he called out, "Gregarius Titus Porcinianus Pullus, attend to your Legate!"

I have been blessed by the gods to be singled out on many occasions since that day, but never did I do so with as much trepidation and fear as I felt over the several paces it took me to do as ordered. Nor can I say I did it particularly smoothly; the truth was, I had no idea where exactly the command of attending a Legate fell in the manual of drill, so I was not sure where I was supposed to stand. Thankfully, Drusus seemed to understand my cause for hesitation, as I slowed when I came alongside him and his mount, so with his free hand, he pointed to a spot directly in front of him and bit to his right. As I moved into the position he required, I noticed his horse, a stallion of pure white, but with eyes of black obsidian, watch me move across his nose, and I remembered that there are some horses that find that movement across the nose distracting. Drusus' horse was a fine mount, but I had taken the time to examine him thoroughly, and he was not a shade of Ocelus in my eyes. I came to *intente,* facing Drusus, with my Century behind me, awaiting my fate, and I was certain that as close as I was to the Legate, he could see my *segmentata* bouncing with the beating of my heart.

Staring down at me, he opened his mouth, but his eyes never left mine as he called out, "Today, the Fourth Cohort fought magnificently! Pilus Prior Corvinus," now he turned to where Corvinus was standing, off to Drusus' left, "I apologize for being tardy in my arrival, but I am happy to see that you and your men had no need of my help. In fact," he made a gesture over his shoulder with his left hand, sweeping it across the expanse of ground littered with Chatti bodies, "it looks like you have been so thorough that we are unlikely to see these bastards for several days!"

This prompted a cheer from the Century, but I was a bit surprised when I heard sounds of the same coming from the opposite direction, and I risked glance to my left to see that a fair number of men from the other Centuries had paused in their stripping and looting of the bodies to watch what was taking place. I did not know it then, but what was happening was fairly unusual.

"But they will be back," Drusus continued, once the cheers died away. "Make no mistake. And that is why we will need men like the one you see standing before you today." He was still looking down at me as he continued. "It has come to my attention, and has been verified by his Pilus Prior, and his Optio that, young though he may be, Gregarius Titus Pullus is already a formidable Legionary, and I have proof!"

He thrust his right hand in the air, the rays of sun that managed to penetrate the cover making the gold wink and glitter.

"These are the torq and armbands of a Chatti sub-chieftain named Vergorix! I have met Vergorix, and I know that he was a formidable warrior of his people. Yet there he lies," Drusus pointed back to the corpse, "killed by a Roman! A Roman who, by regulation, is still considered a *tirone*! But this is no ordinary *Tiro*, as I am sure all of you know! In case he has been too modest to mention it," blood rushed to my face when I heard a number of snickers ripple through the formation, prompting an amused smile to cross Drusus' lips, "he is the grandson of none other than Titus Pullus, perhaps one of the greatest men to march under the standard in the history of Rome!"

The blood that had been slowly returning back to its normal circulation came rushing back into my face, but this time, it was in pleasure at the sound of the cheers, issued by not just my Century, but the other members of the Cohort, more of whom had come to gather around.

"But he is also the son of Gaius Porcinianus Pullus, who was Pilus Prior of this very Cohort!"

Now the cheers became even louder and, for a horrified moment, I was sure that I would completely lose my composure at this show of affection and regard for my father. Not lost on me, and what pleased me the most was that the cheers, while loud for my Avus, were even more so for my father, and I believe that neither of them would have been displeased to hear this.

"He is proof that blood will tell! That men bred to a certain profession, or station, will rise to the occasion! In his slaying of Vergorix, I declare that Titus Pullus is no longer a mere *tirone*, but is a full-fledged Gregarius!"

There was no way that I could pretend that I did not hear that, as enthusiastic as my comrades had been at the mention of my Avus and my father, their reaction to this news was decidedly more muted, and I knew that it was not just Maxentius who would be less than thrilled. I had heard the muttering around the fire when I walked by, and Figulus had informed me that it was not confined just to my Century. Still, it stung, I cannot lie. At least, I thought it stung, but Drusus was not through.

"However," I do not know whether it was the word itself, or a change in tone that gave me the barest of warnings that something was coming my way that I would not like. "I have also been informed that, as valiantly and with as much skill as he showed in slaying a warrior like Vergorix, Gregarius Pullus also disobeyed not just a regulation, breaking free of the hold his comrade in the second rank to move ahead of the formation, he also disobeyed an order, in the form of refusing to respond to the call to relief!"

During the time we had been standing there, although it was not nearly as riotously noisy as the fight itself, there had been the sounds that are common after a battle, most notably a low, droning hum of those men lying on the field still alive and suffering. And although little by little, as the other Centuries went about the business of the Legions after a battle, not just looting and stripping the bodies, but administering a quick slice across the throat, the level of noise had been steadily dropping, it was still audible. Yet, at that moment, I was sure that even the wounded stopped their moaning, intent on hearing what would come next. Adding to my distress was a sudden weakness in my legs, as for a horrifying instant, I thought I would faint. For a period that I still believe lasted at least a third of a watch, Drusus said nothing, but still stared down at me, all hint of warmth or approbation gone.

Then, just as I was sure I would topple over, he continued, "But it is an unwise and unjust commander who would punish a man for showing such zeal and bravery that he is willing to risk a punishment that, while just, is terrible, for disobeying an order. Gregarius Pullus," he asked severely, "do you know what the punishment for an act such as the one you committed is? Do you know what it is within my right to do to you?"

I felt my mouth open, but my mouth had gone so dry that I had to swallow twice before I answered, "Death, sir?"

For the truth is, I did not know; I had not yet been versed in the regulations to that degree at that point. All we *Tiros* had been taught were the regulations of which we were most likely to run afoul, like being late for watch and the like.

"That is one punishment, yes," Drusus replied, his jaw still set in a hard line, "although it is up to the Legate. At a *minimum*," he emphasized, "I can order you to be flogged, with the scourge, to the count of ten lashes!"

Despite my best intention to the contrary, I felt a gasping breath escape my lips as now I turned my head to look him in the face, my expression, I suppose, was one of supplication. Our eyes locked, and he was silent for just a pause, then I saw just the tiniest quirks at one corner of his mouth.

"But as I said," he continued again, "what sort of example would a Legate set if he delivered such a harsh punishment to a Gregarius for violating an order because he is so eager to fight? What would that do to the fighting spirit of this Legion, if they saw one of their own punished in such a manner as a flogging because he had slain a chief of the Chatti?" He shook his head, exaggerating the motion because, as I was sure he was aware of the attention of so many others, he wanted more than just our Century to see it. "No, I, Nero Claudius Drusus, Legate of the Army of the Rhenus, and was born into the same class of Romans that the first man to command the great Titus Pullus, Divus Julius himself, do not punish, but reward men like this young giant here!"

I am under no illusion that the roar of approval that emanated not just from my comrades in my Century, but the others, had anything to do with me and my fate. No, it had everything to do with the knowledge that Drusus was not going to punish men for initiative, and that if they showed the same kind of desire to wade into our enemies that I had shown, a reward awaited them. The simple truth is that it could have been Tuditanus, or one of the other *Tiros* standing there, and they would have been as lusty in their cheers.

Waiting for the shouts to die down, Drusus once more thrust the gold accoutrements stripped from Vergorix aloft, and said, "Therefore, I award to Gregarius Pullus the spoils of his victory, in the form of the five gold arm rings and gold torq that, up until a short time ago, adorned one of our enemies and proclaimed his prowess at war among his people. Now, it will be the property of a Roman!" Quite frankly, I was too stunned and confused at that point to do more than stand there mutely as once more the men around me showed their appreciation, but Drusus was not through yet. "And I hereby decree that, whenever and wherever the Legions gather in a formation for purposes other than war, he is to wear one gold arm ring, as a sign of not only my appreciation for his services to Rome, but to serve as an example of what can be attained by men of all ranks when they march for me!"

Then, with a great show, he hopped off his horse, the white prancing nervously, as Drusus beckoned to Pilus Prior Corvinus. He appeared from my right and joined Drusus, standing to his left as Drusus faced me. The men were still cheering as, with great ceremony, Drusus handed me each piece of gold, including the golden chain Vergorix had used to pin his bearskin cape back, and leaving the torq to last. I had barely noticed it during the fight, but as I took it in my hands, I could not suppress a gasp as I felt the weight.

"That is very valuable, Pullus." Drusus' voice was pitched so that just the three of us could hear.

I was now standing with both hands out, palms up and full of gold, but I tried my best to look dignified and was staring at the imaginary spot above Drusus' head, which was not hard since he was a head shorter than I was. But while I was undeniably thrilled, mostly at the knowledge I was not going to be flogged, since what it meant to have so much gold had yet to hit me, I was also aware of Corvinus staring at me coldly. His face showed no emotion that I could see, so I was trying to find some sign of what awaited me in my immediate future by studying his expression as much as possible out of the corner of my eye. That was why it took a moment for what Drusus said to register.

"But you did disobey orders," he continued, "so while I'm allowing you to keep the arm rings and that chain, the torq you will give to your Pilus Prior." Once the words sunk in, I was more confused than unhappy, but then Drusus turned to Corvinus. "Corvinus, you will either get what you can for it from one of the shopkeepers with the army, or have it melted down, whichever yields the most, and that is going to be split between the men of your Century."

Turning back to me, Drusus finished by saying, "You are dismissed, Pullus. Go back to your spot in the Century. And remember this," I believe he made a point to look me directly in the eye as he finished, despite having to look up to do it, "if you disobey orders again, for no matter what reason, you will be punished. Severely. Is that understood?"

I assured him that it was, then shifting everything to one hand, I rendered a salute, which both Drusus and Corvinus returned. Corvinus was also dismissed, so we walked side by side to the respective parts of our formation.

"You and I," he said out of the corner of his mouth, "are going to have a talk later."

Somehow, his tone of voice did not make me feel any better.

Whatever joy I might have felt at being singled out was tempered, not only by what Drusus had said, but when my suspicions about the identity of one of the dead in our Century was confirmed. It had been Poplicola, the only Gregarius close to my age and experience, an axe blade cutting so deeply into his body that there was a gaping slash wound from his left shoulder down to his belt.

"He was always bad with a shield," was how Servius Metellus put it, who stood to Poplicola's left. "He blocked a bastard that was trying to gut me, but he moved his shield too far outside his body and it left him open. He couldn't recover in time to save himself."

Metellus said this with tears in his eyes as we sat around the fire that night, after we had prepared Poplicola's corpse for its journey. I had resolved to myself that this was one night where my voice would not be heard and, in fact, I was doing my best to make myself as small and unnoticed as I could, something that did not come naturally and was not easy to accomplish, considering my size. Tubero was next to say something about our comrade, each man of our section expected to contribute something they remembered about Poplicola. This is as much of a tradition as our practice of cremation when we lose a comrade, and I was dreading when it came my turn, not because I had nothing to say, but I was still unsure about my own status now among my comrades. One by one, each of the surviving men of the Tenth Section, First Century of the Fourth Cohort spoke a few words, making a circle around the fire. As I had observed early on, we tended to sit in the exact same order around the fire as we stood in formation, and there was an empty seat third from the left across from me. Asinius was sitting next to me to my right, and he had yet to speak a word, outside of orders, to me, which also worried me greatly. Then it was Asinius' turn, but he had just opened his mouth when we heard someone approach from behind the two of us; when I looked at my comrades facing me across the fire and saw they had come to *intente*, he and I copied them.

"Pullus." It was Pilus Prior Corvinus, standing just behind me and Asinius.

I turned about, and although it was not technically required, since he was just wearing his tunic like us and carrying his *vitus*, I decided to play it safe and rendered a salute nonetheless. He only nodded in response, making me feel slightly ridiculous, and I heard a couple of my comrades snickering behind my back. He gave no indication that he heard, instead just motioning to me to follow as he turned about and began walking away.

"Bring your trophies with you," he called over his shoulder, meaning I had to scramble into the tent, grab them from my pack, then run to catch up to him.

I believe this was his intent, so that when I did reach his side, I was panting a bit. He did not speak, but in the torchlight, I saw him shoot a glance at me, looking me up and down.

He gave a grunt, then said, "I suppose that will have to do."

And he continued walking. When he approached the spot on our Century street where his tent and the Cohort headquarters were located, instead of turning and entering his tent, he continued walking. If he is trying to confuse me, I thought, then he is doing a magnificent job of it. We continued on, and for a moment after making a turn onto the Via Praetoria, I was sure that he was taking me to see Drusus, and my mind began grappling with the import of that. Had that display he put on in front of my Century been all for show? Was I actually being brought before him to hear that he was, in fact, going to punish me? Thankfully, before I could dwell on that horrible idea any longer, he walked past the forum, continuing in the direction of the Via Principalis Dextra, the right-hand side gate. That put into my head the thought that he was going to take me outside the camp gates to administer an unofficial punishment, although that did not seem likely to me, if only because we were in the middle of the Black Forest and surrounded by hostile Germans. Only now can I admit that the other thought that crowded its way into my fevered mind was the belief that Corvinus would not be so foolish to do something like that because, when all was said and done, I was much larger and much stronger than he was.

Immediately following that was the voice in my head that said, "Unless he has help. Like Maxentius and Galens and a couple others."

Thankfully, I could not dwell on that because Corvinus made what would be the final turn, rounding the corner of the last street next to the wall, whereupon he strode to the largest tent there. It was the only tent larger than that of a Pilus Prior, at least for men of the ranks, and he walked up to the flap, then rapped on the piece of wood dangling from the center pole that is used for what he was doing, announcing that there were visitors outside. Immediately, the flap was thrust aside and, by the guttering light of the oil lamp, I could just make out the face of the slave I knew was the chief clerk of the 8th Legion.

"Come in, Pilus Prior," the slave, his name was Crito, said to Corvinus while looking over at me, "the Primus Pilus is expecting you."

Publius Canidius, Primus Pilus of the 8th, had once been called by another name, Urso, because his entire body was covered in coarse black hair so that, coupled with his barrel chest that was so large his arms stuck out at angles from his body, he did resemble a bear. He had also been the Quartus Pilus Posterior under my father. His rise through the ranks had been nothing short of spectacular, since he went from the command of the Second Century of the Fourth Cohort straight to the post of Primus Pilus. This had happened in the immediate aftermath of the campaign against the Varciani, when my father had been injured and subsequently lost his leg. To go to the post of Primus Pilus without serving as a Pilus Prior was unusual, to put it mildly and, being a child of the Legions, I had been as curious as any ranker about the circumstances of Urso's rise. Yet, as close as my father and I were, and still are, this is a topic, the only one, he refused to discuss, and that holds true to this day.

The most he would say was, "He's a good Centurion, one of the best I've served with, and Corvinus has said he's been a first-rate Primus Pilus, as good as Vettus. Not," he added, "in the same league as your Avus. Or even Macrinus."

Aulus Honorius Macrinus had been the Primus Pilus of the 8th when I was a young child and, when my Avus stepped down from his post as Camp Prefect, he had taken over the role, serving the ten years and retiring not long before I enlisted. As to Urso, that was all my father would say about the man. Until, that is, the day I left Arelate for Siscia.

"Titus." He was seated at our table in the kitchen, watching me devour some honey-smeared bread. "About Urso," he said, which was enough to cause me to stop chewing and start listening.

But then he did not say anything, staring off into space.

"Yes? What about Urso?"

My words seemed to startle him, and although I cannot swear to it, his expression looked very much like he was surprised to hear me utter his name, as if he had not done so himself just a moment before.

Finally, he said, "As I told you, he's a good Centurion. He's hard, very hard, and he plays no favorites. Ever."

He looked me in the eye, as if imparting some message, and I did think I had an idea what it was he was trying not to say aloud.

"So I shouldn't expect him to make sure I never pull latrine duty," I said jokingly.

My father snorted, something that I had learned was now his version of a laugh, and I remember that I was struck with sadness at that moment at the table because it had been so long since I had seen him really laugh.

"Not likely," he agreed, but he paused again, then continued, "In fact, I want you to be prepared for the opposite. Even to the point where, if you're in some sort of difficulty, don't be surprised if he's harder on you than you deserve." He gave a shrug, but broke away from my gaze to look away as he muttered, "And don't ask me any more than that."

I did not, but that was certainly in the front of my mind as, on shaky legs, I followed Corvinus and Crito to the partition that cuts the tent of a Centurion in half. The front half serves as Century, Cohort, or Legion office, while the rear is his private quarters. Crito motioned us to wait, then pushed through the partition, but Corvinus' body blocked my view. I heard a quick burst of mumbled conversation, then Crito returned.

"You may enter," he announced with a bit of smugness, I thought.

Just as Corvinus entered, he called over his shoulder, "Watch your step."

That confused me further, although it did cause me to look down, and I saw why he had warned me. I took a step up onto a wooden floor, perhaps two inches thick. Although I had heard that some Centurions, usually at least Pili Priores or Primi Pili indulged in such luxuries, this was the first time I had seen it. My immediate thought was worry that we would track mud onto his nice wooden floor, but directly in front of his desk was a battered, filthy carpet that was obviously used for that very purpose. Any other examination was cut short by Corvinus, when he squared himself at his desk and, with an impatient gesture, indicated I should stand next to him. I did remember to shift my loot to my left hand, but in doing so, I lost my grip on the torq, which landed on the dirty carpet next to me with a dull thud.

"Pilus Prior Corvinus and Gregarius Pullus reporting as ordered, Primus Pilus," Corvinus was saying just as the torq fell to the ground, catching him in the middle of his announcement.

Despite being at *intente,* I could not keep a grimace of embarrassment from my face, but Urso did not seem to notice.

After returning our salutes, he leaned back in his chair, only saying, "That sounded heavy."

Since he did not actually issue what I considered an order, I stood there.

"Pick it up!" Corvinus snapped and, as I hurried to bend over to retrieve it, I heard him mutter, "Idiot."

The blood was in my face when I resumed my previous posture, but I was determined my face would not betray me again. Nothing was said for a moment as I felt Urso's eyes examine me, while my own gaze remained fixed on a spot on the wall above him.

"You're grown since the last time I saw you," he finally said. "It's been what, five years?"

"Seven," I answered, remembering to add, "sir."

Urso gave a small laugh.

"This is what you have to look forward to when you get old, Pullus. Your memory goes to *cac.*"

Corvinus chuckled, and I felt obliged to join in, although I did not find his jest that amusing.

"Gods know you were almost as tall as I was, even then. You remember him, Corvinus? How he was always underfoot? Always curious about everything we did?"

"That I do, Pilus Prior," Corvinus said with a smile.

I cannot say why, exactly, but I was growing more uneasy instead of less, which I am sure was Urso's intent, to get me to relax. There was nothing in the banter that hinted there was an undercurrent there, but as I think back, I believe that what my father did not say about Urso prepared me for what was coming more than what he did.

"In fact," Urso said, still with the same light tone, but when I risked a glance down at him, our eyes met and they were not friendly. At all. "You could say he was a bit of a snoop. Isn't that true, Corvinus?"

I sensed Corvinus tense, but his tone matched that of Urso's as he replied, "No more than most boys his age. No more than I was, Primus Pilus. Or I imagine as you were."

Although my gaze had returned to the wall, I saw Urso's head turn to regard my Pilus Prior, and could see at the edge of my vision that there was no warmth in his expression.

"So you say, Corvinus," he said finally. "Boys will be boys, neh?"

Nothing more was said for a moment, then Urso suddenly sat forward and slapped a hand on his desk. Which, as he wanted, made me jump. That seemed to restore his good humor, so I suppose it was worth it.

"Be that as it may, enough reminiscing about old times. Although I do want to ask, how is your father?"

"He's doing well, sir."

I was determined to say no more than I absolutely had to at this point, convinced that he would try and use my words against me.

Seeing nothing more was forthcoming, he pressed, "And, has he come to terms with the loss of his leg?"

My stomach began churning, but I responded in kind, telling him, "As much as a man like him can, I suppose, sir. He gets around quite well now. And he helped me train for the Legions."

"And as I heard today, he obviously trained you well," Urso replied. "Of course, I'd expect nothing less from a man trained by Titus Pullus." Urso paused, the silence causing me to glance down again. This time, he seemed to be looking at a spot in between Corvinus and me, but far, far behind us. "Your grandfather was the best man with a sword that I've ever seen," he continued, quietly now, with the same faraway look in his eyes. "Even today, I don't think anyone can match him." Suddenly, his gaze sharpened, and he looked directly at me, but I was not prepared for what he was about to say. "Do you remember Volusenus? The Secundus Pilus Prior?"

I did indeed; I had hated him with a passion as a child because I knew he did not like my father. But for reasons I do not understand, my father seemed fond of Volusenus, and I was extremely surprised when about two years before I enlisted, he showed up at our villa in Arelate, wearing a patch to cover the eye he had lost on the same campaign that claimed my father's leg. I had not seen my father that happy in some time, and I was allowed to stay up late one night to watch them get uproariously drunk and swap tales, as if there had never been an unkind word between them.

Oblivious to my own internal musing, Urso continued, "Well, this was before your time, I think. Or you might have been a babe in arms. Anyway, Volusenus took up a challenge that your grandfather issued when he assumed the post of Camp Prefect, to face him in a trial with the sword. He offered a bounty of a hundred sesterces, I believe, and a week free of all duty, for anyone who could best him. And Volusenus was very, very good with a sword."

"I remember that," Corvinus spoke up, giving a small chuckle. "I didn't see it firsthand, but I saw Volusenus afterward."

Corvinus' interjection seemed to irritate Urso more than please him at being corroborated.

"Yes," he continued, with a glance at Corvinus that I could not interpret, "but what's less well known is who the primary instigator was in getting Volusenus to challenge Pullus." He had returned his gaze to me as he began, but when he finished, he looked at Corvinus.

Who seemed to receive and understand the message, as he gasped, "You? You were the one that put him up to it?"

Urso gave a small smile, but suddenly, he did not seem so interested in looking in our direction, staring down at his desk instead.

"I wasn't the only one," he admitted. "But I certainly was the most insistent. More importantly, I was there to watch it." He shook his head at the memory. "I have never seen someone beaten that badly, or that quickly. Volusenus never had a chance. I thought your grandfather was going to kill him, *rudis* and wearing full protection or not."

Not only did I know this story, for the first time, I felt like I had something I could contribute because the night Volusenus and my father stayed up, the subject had come up.

"It was after his wife Miriam died," I blurted out, clearly surprising Urso, and I could feel Corvinus' eyes turned towards me. "My father said that he grieved for a long time after she died. In fact, he said my Av... grandfather was never really the same after that."

"That makes sense," Urso commented.

"Did your father tell you how she died?"

I turned in some surprise to Corvinus, who had asked the question, and he had a curiously intent look on his face as he waited on my answer.

"In childbirth, I think."

Corvinus nodded, but went on to say, "Yes, that's the bare bones of it. But she died because the baby of Titus Pullus was too large, and she bled to death."

I know now that, in his way, Corvinus was trying to warn me what might await me, or more accurately, any woman who bore my children. But I was seventeen, and there is rarely enough brain in a teenager's head to stop something from going in one ear and right out the other. That was a lesson I had to learn the hard way, but that is for later, if I ever choose to speak of it.

"So, when I read Corvinus' report, and after talking to him and ... some other men who were in a position to see you in action against this German," Urso interrupted, "that was what came to mind. Your grandfather and his skill with a sword. And clearly, you've inherited more than his size and strength. Although," he regarded me thoughtfully, "sitting here now, I think you may actually be bigger across the shoulders and chest than he was. Maybe not quite as tall."

I had heard this often, but I felt compelled to point out, "I'm six feet four, just like he was. As far as being broader than he is," I shrugged, "I've heard that. But I doubt I'll ever be as strong as he was."

"Only time will tell," Urso said. "You're young yet. You may grow even more."

Without any warning, he shot up from his chair, put both hands on his desk to support him as he leaned over and roared, "BUT IF YOU EVER DISOBEY AN ORDER AGAIN, I WILL FLAY YOU AND PUT YOUR SKIN ON MY TENT POLE FOR THE LEGION TO SEE!"

I freely admit that, at that moment I was terrified beyond belief, at least as scared as I had been when I was ten and was being chased by the Latobici when I was trying to save my family. Only Corvinus was unchanged, standing impassively next to me; I imagine that, if he had not been warned, he knew Urso well enough to guess what was coming.

As quickly as it came, the rage seemed to leave Urso, which to anyone else would probably have been the most unsettling thing of all. But if anything, his behavior reassured me because it told me that this was mostly artifice. It did not occur to me that anyone else would ever be able to turn their rage on and off as easily as flipping a coin from one side to the other.

"I don't care how many Germans you kill, or how important they are," he spoke in his former tone. "I will tolerate no disobedience in my Legion. Is that understood?"

"Y-yes, sir." I stammered.

"Good." He dropped back into his seat, then indicated the gold pieces in my hand. "So let's see what you won today."

I put the pieces on his desk and, using his stylus, he spread them apart, then, using the tip, picked up each ring, then the chain. The torq he had to pick up with his hands and, as he turned it over and examined it closely, gave a low whistle.

"This is some of the finest work I've seen." He glanced at Corvinus, who nodded in agreement. "In fact, it would be a shame to melt this down. You do know it's customary for the Pilus Prior and Primus Pilus to take a cut of the loot, don't you?"

Ah, I thought. Here we have the real reason for me being brought before him. And while it was true that it was a reason, it turned out not to be the only one. However, I could only deal with one problem at a time, especially since this was the only one of which I was aware, although that would change shortly.

"Yes, sir."

I made the decision then and there if I was going to get squeezed, I did not have to make it easy for either of them.

Seeing I was going to add no more, Urso gave a grunt that I took to be irritation, and continued, "Yes, well, normally, it would be straightforward and we would each take a tenth part. But your case is more...complicated."

Although I had a suspicion why, I was going to continue to play my part to the hilt, as we say.

Feigning confusion, I asked, "Sir? Why's that?"

Urso paused, searching my face, but there is enough of what my mother calls my father's innocent fresh face in me that I suppose he found me believable.

"Because our Legate, Nero Claudius Drusus," there was something in the way he said the name I did not care for, but he continued, "awarded these spoils to you. Although," he glanced over at Corvinus, "as your Pilus Prior informed me, the Legate did specify that the torq be either melted down, or if you could get a better price for it whole, which I think you can because of the quality, and then shared with the entire Century. Is that your understanding as well?"

"Yes, sir."

"Well, that's all well and good for the rankers, but what about your Centurions? Are they supposed to be ignored? It certainly seems that way to me, that our Legate is more concerned with the feelings of the Gregarii than the men who control the Legions!"

I do not know exactly who sucked in a breath, me or Corvinus, but suddenly, I was wishing the ground beneath the wood floor would open up and swallow me. Urso either ignored or was oblivious to our reactions, staring at me beneath the two pieces of fur that were his eyebrows.

"You're in a difficult spot, Pullus. Because of a nobleman's thoughtless generosity, you're in a position where you're going to have to ignore a few hundred years of custom."

"But why?" I asked, truly bewildered now.

"Because let's just say that Drusus sees you wandering around one day, and he asks you how you enjoyed drinking and whoring with all your gold. What will you say?"

I was beginning to get a glimpse of where I thought he wanted me to head, but I was still not completely sure.

"That while I kept some for myself, I didn't feel right about not following a few hundred years of custom, so I gave my Pilus Prior and Primus Pilus a portion of it?"

I posed it as a question, but Urso's reaction told me I had answered correctly. Giving a booming laugh, he slapped the desk, looking over at Corvinus triumphantly.

"Didn't I tell you, Corvinus? The boy is not only strong as Hercules, he's smart! Like his father!" Turning to me, he favored me for the first time with a full smile, and I saw that he was missing several teeth, not unusual for a man his age. "I'm glad that's settled!"

While I was not particularly happy, neither was I that upset; there is much to be said for the security provided by the knowledge that your family is rich. And since I did not, nor do I now have extravagant or expensive tastes, I did not need to worry about the loss. Sensing that was the end of our interview, I thought that was the case when Urso nodded to Corvinus.

"That will be all," he said, but when we both made to take a step back from his desk, then turn about to exit, he waved at me. "Pullus, I want you to stay."

I saw what I can only describe as a look of alarm and unease cross Corvinus' face, but he said nothing, just shooting me a glance that seemed to carry a warning as he left. But as I was about to find out, nothing could have prepared me for what was to come.

I took the long way back to my Century area, needing the time to think about all that had occurred because, as eventful as the day had been, in many ways what happened that night had an impact that lasted long after the gold was spent. Since we would be staying in place the next day to conduct the burial rituals for our fallen, the *bucina* had not sounded the call to retire, and it would not. Although nobody has explained why this is so, my guess is that in its own way, that entity that we rankers refer to as "The Army," usually in connection with some injustice done to us, was giving us the time to grieve and to visit with friends and kin. That was why there was still a great deal of activity, as men came and went from one part of the camp to the next, some of them weaving, the flagon or skin of wine in their hand giving the lie to why this was so. I very well could have been as unsteady, albeit for a totally different reason, if my gait matched the spinning in my head. By the time I returned to my tent, perhaps a sixth part of watch after I left Urso's tent, only Asinius was sitting outside. But if I was expecting to retire, he quickly disabused me of that idea.

"The Pilus Prior wants to see you immediately." He did not even glance up from the fire. Suppressing a sigh, I turned to head to Corvinus' tent, but he called out, "You need to stop at the Optio's tent first and get him as well."

Galens was clearly waiting for me because I did not even have to knock, and he came out without a word, his face giving nothing away. We walked the few paces to the Pilus Prior's tent in complete silence and, just like with Galen, Lysander had been waiting and opened the flap.

"Go right in," he said quietly. "He's expecting you."

We entered to a scene that had become familiar; this time, it was Corvinus sitting at his desk, and Galens and I presenting ourselves, but then Corvinus waved Galens to a stool that was next to and slightly behind Corvinus' desk. The impression I took from that was he was resuming a seat that he had just vacated a few moments before, although I had no way of determining if this was the case.

"Where's the torq?" Corvinus pointed to my left hand, where I was still carrying what I had been awarded.

At least, I was carrying all that I had left, which consisted now of nothing but five golden arm rings.

"Primus Pilus Canidius said that he knew someone who would get us the best price for it, and he would take care of it and give you the money."

There was no mistaking the look that Corvinus and Galens exchanged, but when Galens muttered, "Greedy bastard," Corvinus did not hesitate.

"*Silete!* You should know better, Galens!"

"Did I do something wrong?" I asked. "Was I not supposed to give it to him?"

"No, Pullus," he sighed. "You didn't do anything wrong. At least about this. There's nothing else you could have done differently." Looking at me carefully for a moment, he went on, "It's just that our Primus Pilus has a bad habit of…forgetting to split proceeds with the rest of us."

"You mean he's done this before?" I gasped.

My clear naivety prompted a bitter laugh from the other two men.

"You could say that," Corvinus granted. "So what did he take outright as his?" Before I could answer, he said, "Wait. Let me guess. The gold chain."

I suppose I could have pointed out that the answer was obvious, since I was holding neither torq nor chain, but thought better of it. Instead, I just nodded.

"No big surprise there." Corvinus shook his head.

Hoping to offer some sort of solace, I held out the rest of the rings, except for the one I was supposed to wear.

"Sir, do you want the rest of these?"

Corvinus looked at me sharply, as did Galens, and they exchanged a glance.

"Why would you be willing to part with that much money?" Corvinus asked.

I did not answer, thinking that considering to whom I was speaking and his relationship with my father, the answer should be obvious. And, after a couple of heartbeats, I saw his face dawn with the realization.

"Ah," he said softly. "That's right. I forgot; you don't need the money."

Galens started nodding his head, understanding as well, and the pair exchanged a glance again. Shrugging, Corvinus started to lean forward, then stopped himself.

"While I appreciate the gesture, Pullus, I want to make sure that you understand this won't win you special favors or treatment."

A flicker of anger made my stomach flutter, but I kept my tone even as I replied, "Nor is it expected, Pilus Prior. And even if it did, I wouldn't accept it. That's not how I was raised," I finished softly.

"That's true," Corvinus conceded, then took four of the rings from my hand. "Thank you, Pullus."

Then, he sat back again, and his expression changed again; frankly, I was growing weary of feeling like I was in waters where the current changed so much and so quickly. Not that I could do anything about it.

"But that's actually not why I called you here," he informed me. "I want to know what the Primus Pilus wanted from you."

Despite suspecting this was the case, there was another flutter in my stomach to accompany the anger, and that was anxiety. Urso had, in fact, been very explicit about this, and had given me a story to tell Corvinus that he thought would serve to explain. But when I opened my mouth to utter the words, Corvinus stopped me with a wave of a hand.

"Wait," he sighed wearily. "Unless I don't know him as well as I think, I'm sure that he gave you some sort of story to tell either Galens or me if we asked." He fixed me with a stare. "True?"

"I…I don't know what you mean, sir."

I tried to look confused, but Corvinus was not fooled in the slightest.

"I take that as a yes," he replied. Glancing over at Galens, I saw the Optio give him a shrug. Turning back to me, Corvinus continued, "Let's do it this way. I'm going to tell you what I think he told you. You don't have to say anything. Unless you want to." Without waiting for me to answer, he said, "He wants you to keep your ears open and listen to what the men of the Century are saying, particularly about what they think about Drusus. More importantly, he wants to know what we," he indicated Galens and himself, "say about Drusus. Now, you may have asked what he wanted you to listen for specifically, but my guess is that if you did, his answer was 'Anything and everything.' But more than anything, he wants you to listen for talk about Augustus. And Tiberius. Maybe even Tiberius is the most important one." Sitting back, he regarded me, but said nothing.

I have been told I am not a good liar, and I suppose this must be true because I am fairly certain that Corvinus got his answer just by my face. After a moment, he nodded slightly.

"That's what I thought."

183

"So what am I supposed to do?" I had not planned on asking, but I felt it was appropriate, and the misery in my voice was genuine. "He's the Primus Pilus."

"Yes, he is," Corvinus agreed. "Frankly, Pullus, you're in a tough spot. What do you know about the day your father lost his leg?"

If his goal had been to catch me off guard, he did so superbly.

"That there was a fire, and he would have burned to death if he hadn't been saved by Urso," I told him.

Which was true, but that was really the extent of my knowledge at that time.

"That's true, as far as it goes," Corvinus agreed. "But the real story is a bit more complicated than that, and the truth is, I don't know the entire story myself because your father was...evasive about the matter."

The flare of anger that had been simmering in my gut now burst into a full flame, like when a piece of fat drops into the fire and, before I had any conscious thought, I snapped, "My father doesn't lie, Pilus Prior. And any man who calls him a liar to my face is going to have problems he really doesn't want. No matter who he is. Or his rank."

Oh, I was a hothead, that is true, and, as I write the words that I spoke then, I wince at my carelessness. Galens jumped to his feet and I braced for him to come at me, but Corvinus waved a hand at him to sit back down, which the Optio did, clearly reluctant. I had known Aulus Galens most of my life; I had tumbled around underfoot like a puppy, but while I respected the man, I was unafraid of him, at least in this sense. Corvinus was a different matter, but my anger was such that it overrode any sense of caution. Fortunately for all three of us, Corvinus did not seem to take any offense at all.

"Pullus," he sighed. "I'm not saying your father was lying. But no matter how angry it makes you, he did keep things to himself about that day. So, settle down."

He pierced me with a hard stare that, even in my state, I saw was as much of a warning as I was going to get. Mollified, I swallowed down the rage and gave him a nod that I understood.

Seeing that I was not disposed to anything more, he went on, "And let me say that I know that he withheld the rest of the story, not just from me, but from you and everyone he cared about, for the best of reasons, to protect all of us."

Now I was feeling a bit foolish, which I suppose I deserved.

"I suppose you remember Quintus Barbatus?" Corvinus asked, and I am sure he knew the answer.

Since Corvinus was not one of the Pili Priores that had a wooden floor, I gave my answer when I spat on the ground next to me.

"I remember him," was all I said, thinking my gesture conveyed everything that needed to be said about the man who had been the Primus Pilus before Urso.

Corvinus gave a small laugh at my gesture.

"I see that you do, quite well. So you know he hated your father, correct?"

I nodded.

"Well, although I don't know for sure, from what I've put together, Barbatus had something to do with what happened to your father."

For a moment, I did not take his meaning, but his gaze never wavered, watching me as I worked it out for myself.

"You mean," I gasped, "that he's the one who hurt my father?"

Now Corvinus nodded, but then he gave a shrug as he added, "Again, that's my belief. I asked your father for the details, but he claimed he didn't remember anything until Urso was standing there."

This I knew, and no matter the reason Urso did it, I would be grateful to him for saving my father from what would have been a horrible death, since the forest into which they had chased the Varciani to finish them off had been erroneously set afire by someone with one of the other Legions involved in the operation. Many men had burned to death and, while most of them were Varciani, there had been Romans who perished as well, and my father, with his mangled leg, would have been one of them if Urso had not shown up.

"But you also know that Barbatus was found dead, from a stab wound to the back?"

I did, in fact, know that and I said as much.

"Do you remember where they said he was found? I mean, after the fire burned itself out?"

I thought for a moment, then said, "It was down at the bottom of some gully or something as I remember. They said that was why they knew he had been killed before the fire because, for whatever reason, the fire didn't go down into that gully."

"Correct," Corvinus agreed. "And do you remember where Urso found your father?"

I thought for a moment, and I suppose this was the instant I began to get an idea of what was coming.

"Down in a gully," I said slowly. "But I remember hearing that the ground in that forest was riddled with them."

"It was," Corvinus admitted. "But I just find it…odd that both your father and Barbatus were in a gully. And I also find it interesting that when they found Barbatus, he was by himself, with a single thrust to his back. That's unusual, for a Primus Pilus to be isolated like that."

"That's true," I agreed. "But I imagine it's happened before."

"Yes, I'm sure it has. But that's not the only thing. I had a chance to see his body, and I saw the wound. It wasn't a slash, but a single thrust, with a wider blade."

I did not see any meaning in what he was telling me, but I quickly learned.

"Pannonians, like the Varciani, use the Gallic sword, that long bastard where they try to lop off your head. The problem is that for thrusting, it's a *cac* weapon." He shook his head, "No, that thrust was from a Roman sword."

"Are you saying that my father killed Barbatus?" I gasped.

"No." His tone was adamant. "What I think happened is that Barbatus somehow caught your father unaware and pushed him down into that gully. But when he saw that your father was still alive, he went down to finish him. Before he could, Urso showed up and stopped him, the only way. And the best way," Corvinus finished emphatically. "Because the only thing Quintus Barbatus was a first-grade in being was a *cunnus*. He wasn't fit to lead a Century of Suburan whores."

He paused as I digested this, wondering if this night could get any stranger.

"Now, the question, at least to me, is why Urso did it," he continued. "I suppose you remember that he and your father weren't on the best of terms."

"I remember," I assured him. "But couldn't it be that Urso saved my father because it was the right thing to do?"

"It could be," Corvinus granted. "But I know Urso as well, and maybe even better than your father. We were *Tiros* in the same *dilectus,* in case you didn't know. And while we weren't in the same Century, we were in the same Cohort. So I've known Urso for a long time, and I can tell you that I've never met anyone with his ambition. Except," he added as an afterthought, "your grandfather, perhaps. Although I only knew him at the end of his career. But I remember the stories." He shook his head and finished. "No, the one thing I know about Urso is that he never does anything without an eye towards his larger goals. Which makes me believe that his killing of Barbatus, while the right thing, wasn't done because it was right, except in the sense that it suited his larger purpose."

I considered what Corvinus said, but I was not convinced. Then, he added the last piece of his reasoning.

"And the last thing you should know was that Barbatus had been sent to replace Vettus with orders to spy on our new Legate from his post in the Praetorian Guard. During our operation against the Varciani, something occurred that involved your father, through no fault of his own. But the circumstances were such that, depending on how it was reported, they could have been used to put the Legate into a position that made him vulnerable to Barbatus, who had engineered the whole incident that he was then using to squeeze the Legate with the man Barbatus worked for."

For the first time, Corvinus looked away from me, pausing in what I looked at as time to allow me to work everything out. And I did, or at least I believe I did. However, that is all I wish to reveal about what I believe. Nevertheless, I left Corvinus' tent with at least the understanding that, despite my father's best attempt to keep me out of danger, through a combination of circumstances, I had found myself embroiled in the middle of a very dangerous game that seems to be the chief pastime of the members of the upper classes of Rome, using men like me and Urso. Ultimately what mattered was that, for the foreseeable future, I was supposed to spy for Urso. If that was not bad enough, my Pilus Prior and Optio knew that was the case, and although I did not think they would do it on purpose, I could easily imagine that, during off duty time, while drinking and carousing, the spirit of Bacchus would loosen tongues. Never far from my thoughts, even before that night, was the fact that Galens and Maxentius were good friends. I did not want to imagine what my lot would be if this became known to my comrades in my Century. It was this frame of mind that made it difficult for me to sleep, on what was easily the most eventful day of my life to that point.

Chapter Four

The trials and triumphs of a *Tiro* aside, the army of Drusus continued its progress through the interminable expanse of the Black Forest. And while my Cohort managed to avoid it, that did not mean the Chatti were not busy, and I believe with all my heart that their constant harassment played a role in what was to come. Knowing what I know now, I think that if we had just been forced to cope with the sense of isolation and the feeling of being stranded in a strange and foreign land, the army probably would have been all right. Day after day, we chopped our way deeper and deeper into a country that, according to some of the veterans who had been salted into our ranks from the East, was as remote and invariable as the deserts of Syria. What I learned on this, my first campaign, is that no matter how strange and alluring a new territory is to see and march through the first time, after a matter of a few days, when what lies before your eyes remains exactly the same, it becomes not just monotonous, but dangerous to the concentration. There seems to be something in a man that requires variety for him to maintain a proper frame of mind, and an unending diet of sameness will start to wear on even the strongest constitution. And, as I learned in subsequent campaigns, this is already a problem, stemming from seeing the same faces, sleeping with the same men, and even pitching one's tent in the same spot, in every single marching camp, which looks exactly the same as the previous one. Tempers start to fray, and although, as I discovered as my career advanced, it is normal that quarrels that had been just verbal before start to erupt into something more. What would turn out to be the last campaign conducted by Nero Claudius Drusus was marred by even more strife than usual. That is why it should come as no surprise to anyone acquainted with some of the stories associated with Drusus' campaign, in the year of the Consulship of the man himself, along with Titus Quinctilis Crispinus Sulpicianus, that they are so dire and fraught with portent. This always seems to be the case when looking back; only then do events that are occurring at the moment make sense as part of a larger pattern. I will say that this was one time that, even as events were occurring, there were men who assigned them evil omens, and it should come as no surprise that it was the same men who were the most eager and vociferous in spreading word around the camp. We had one such man in our very own section.

"Did you hear about...?"

The moment Tubero uttered these words, I had to stifle a groan and I could see that I was not alone; Asinius mouthed a silent curse, while Dento grimaced in distaste as well. However, despite our reaction, I could see that the others – Bassus, Metellus, and Scrofa – were listening eagerly.

Oblivious to those of us who did not care to hear, Tubero went on, "Those two boys that one of my friends in the 14th saw, riding through camp? In the middle of the night?"

My overall lack of interest in hearing such things aside, I freely confess that got my attention.

"What? Two boys? Who told you that nonsense?" Bassus scoffed.

"It's true," Tubero insisted. "I heard it straight from my friend! He was on guard duty that night, at the *praetorium*! He saw with his very own eyes two boys, both of them riding horses, go trotting by, nice as you please!"

"And he didn't stop them?" Asinius made no attempt to hide his skepticism.

Even with the firelight, I saw Tubero flush.

"I asked him the same thing," he admitted. "But he said that he was so surprised, and they passed by so quickly that he just stood there and watched."

"And did anyone else see these mysterious boys?" Asinius pressed. "Or was it just your friend?"

"No, it wasn't just him," Tubero protested, but I saw his eyes dart around and he saw what I did, that he was losing his audience. "In fact, when I asked him the same thing, he called to two that were there, and they swore they saw the same thing."

"Did they report it?"

Tubero shook his head.

"No," he admitted, "but only because they knew that if they said they had seen what they saw, the commander of the guard would want to see the proof. And since they didn't stop them, they didn't have any. And none of them wanted a flogging, no matter how strange it was."

There was a silence as each of us digested his explanation and, being frank, I could see the sense of what Tubero said. In fact, if I had been in their shoes, I could not say I would not do the same.

"All right," Asinius sighed, evidently reaching the same conclusion that I did. "So what do these mysterious boys riding through the camp mean?"

Now, Tubero was clearly pleased, given what he took as a sign that, if not accepted, it was at least considered plausible by our most cynical section member.

"Well, we were talking about that," he began, but before he got any farther, Metellus interjected.

"I bet you were," and it was in such a tone that it caused the rest of us to burst into laughter, which Tubero clearly did not appreciate.

"Have you had your fun?" he grumbled. "Do you want to hear what we've come up with or not?"

"By all means, go ahead." Asinius made a mock bow from his seated position, sweeping a hand in Tubero's direction in an extravagant gesture. "You have the floor, and we apologize for our levity."

Tubero was not the smartest among us, but he knew when he was being teased and he scowled at Asinius, yet did as Asinius directed.

"As I was saying," he continued, "what we all noticed was that they were riding down the Via Praetoria, in the direction of the Porta Decumana." He paused for a moment, making it clear he saw this as significant.

"So? What does it matter which direction they were traveling?"

"What do we use the Porta Decumana for?" Tubero asked.

"A lot of things," Bassus answered, clearly not seeing the significance.

I, on the other hand, thought I had an idea, but given all that had transpired after the last battle with the Chatti, now a week past, I had been the most silent of the section in voicing an opinion about anything.

"Yes," Tubero acknowledged. "But there's one thing that I'm talking about." Seeing nobody was willing to venture a guess, he supplied his own answer. "The Porta Decumana is the gate we use for funerals, isn't it?"

Although I was pleased with myself that I had guessed where he was headed, I still was not sure of his final destination, so I listened as intently as the others.

"But I still don't see what that has to do with two boys riding horses," Bassus spoke up, finally.

"Don't think of them as just two boys," Tubero replied. "What could they represent?"

Asinius seemed to be fighting with himself, much as I was, not wanting to encourage Tubero, but curious about where this was headed.

193

I believe that was what prompted him to say, "Let me guess. You think it represents Drusus and...Tiberius?" he guessed.

"Exactly." Tubero slapped his leg, clearly pleased. "Those two boys aren't really boys at all. They're the shades of Drusus and Tiberius as they was when they were boys. Doesn't everyone say they was close as Romulus and Remus?"

"I'm not sure where you learned about them, but my Tata taught me that Romulus murdered Remus," Asinius commented dryly, and again we laughed aloud.

Tubero was not pleased, but he insisted, "I'm talking about when they were boys. Like these two shades."

"Yes," Asinius admitted grudgingly. "That's true." Sighing, he continued, "So you're saying that these two shades, representing Tiberius and Drusus, are going to die? Is that what you and the other bright sparks in the fire came up with?"

"Not necessarily both of them." Tubero's tone turned stubborn. "But given everything else that's been happening, and we're stuck in the middle of this fucking forest and are going deeper into it every day, who knows what spirits we're angering?"

Again, that was something that could not be argued, at least as far as it went. We were, in fact, so deep into the Black Forest that it was being said we had reached a point that no Roman, certainly no Roman army, had ever penetrated. Despite our skepticism, speaking for myself, I retired that night more troubled than what had become my normal state.

If that had been all, it would have been enough, but as we continued north along the Visurgis (Weser) River, while we were relieved that we finally passed through the lands of the Chatti, we then entered into the lands of the Suebi, the most warlike tribe of the Germans. Yet, for reasons that we rankers were never told, but did not argue, Drusus chose not to seek battle with them, and the Suebi seemed content to do the same. While this was something of a welcome development, it also added to the tension, as day after day, we hacked out our path, expecting the air to be split by more than the sound of axes, as the Suebi came roaring out of the surrounding underbrush. It was not until we heard through our sources in the *praetorium* that we were just a matter of two or three days from reaching the northern border of Suebi land that we began to think that perhaps we would not be looking at them across our shields. And yet, it was a Suebi who did what so many others had tried and failed to achieve, bringing Drusus low, but not with a spear or weapon of any kind. What made this even stranger was that his downfall was in the form of a Suebi woman, although the fact that she had inflicted damage that would prove mortal would not be known for more than six weeks.

The only aspect of what I am about to relate that seems to be agreed on by everyone involved is that it occurred the night before we were to cross a river that intersected the Visurgis and marked the northern boundary of Suebi lands. On the other side were the Cherusci, and our advance scouts had already brought back signs of large groups of tracks that seemed to be converging at a point somewhere north of us, intersecting our line of march. As it happened, my Century had guard duty that evening, on the Porta Praetoria, the main gate of our camps, and the one by which anyone attempting entrance must approach if they do not want to be filled with holes without any questions asked.

"Two riders approaching!"

It was Dento who called out from his spot on the rampart directly next to the gate, spotting the pair entering the cleared area. Corvinus, the commander of the guard Cohort, had gone to inspect the other Centuries, leaving Galens in charge. He trotted up the ramp to stand next to Dento; I was perhaps a dozen paces away, also on the rampart, trying not to fall asleep, although this development did wonders for bringing me to a state of full alertness. Not only was this unusual, the fact that the pair were clearly not only German, but Suebi, made clear by the knot of hair that was tied to the side of the head of one of the riders, ensured that we were all paying close attention. Although night was approaching, the light was still good, making it easy to see that as they approached, one of the riders was carrying a white flag. I say this was unusual; it was certainly not unheard of, but what made this even more worthy for gossip around the fires later was the fact that the other rider, who was not holding the flag, was a woman.

"That's far enough!" Galens called this out in Latin; my initial thought was wondering how likely this barbarian would understand him, and I hefted one of my javelins in preparation for an order I was sure would be coming.

But the pair immediately came to a halt and both of them held their arms out so we could see they carried no weapons.

"We come in peace, Roman," the man shouted back.

That was when it occurred to me, with some chagrin, that the likelihood of a Suebi chieftain sending a man under a white flag who was unable to speak our tongue was small, in the extreme.

Fortunately, unlike me, Galens appeared to expect the Suebi speaking Latin and, without hesitation, he replied, "Very well. What do you want?"

In answer, the Suebi turned to the woman, and she was the one who spoke. I was somewhat pleased to see that this did surprise Galens at least as much as it did me and the others.

"My name is Ute, of the Suebi," she called out in a strong voice that, while pitched low, was still clearly feminine, and her Latin was much better than that of her companion. "I come bearing information for your Legate, Nero Claudius Drusus, that is of vital importance."

196

Galens seemed to consider this for a moment before he responded. "All right. Let me know what it is, and I will relay it to the Legate."

She clearly expected this because her own reply was immediate.

"No! What I have to say I must say to him, and him alone! It is for his ears only, and not for any of his minions!"

Now, I do not know if, her command of Latin aside, she had a deep enough understanding of it that she knew what a slur this was, but after all that transpired, I have no doubt she did. I saw Galens' face turn dark, but he did not immediately reply for a moment as he glared down at the pair. For a moment, I thought he might give us the order to hurl javelins at them, although he had stopped them at the very edge of our range. Except for me; I have a very strong arm and, while far, it was well within my range.

Instead, he snapped, "Wait there. Don't move."

He turned to Dento, and I heard him mutter something. It was clear what it was by Dento's response; after rendering a quick salute, he spun and went sprinting down the ramp in the direction of the *praetorium*. There was nothing said after that, but it gave me a chance to examine the pair of Suebi more closely, the woman in particular. Her hair was a thick mane of auburn and, despite its tousled nature, I could see it gleaming in the last light of the day. Her face was almost gaunt, with high cheekbones and a strong chin, but her lips were very full and the upper one was shaped like a Scythian bow. One corner of her mouth curled up and, even from where I stood, it was easy to read her expression of arrogant disdain for the danger in which she had placed herself. No matter what the circumstances were, she was a striking woman, and I felt a stirring below my waist at this first sight of a woman in weeks, since Drusus had forbidden the presence of camp followers on this campaign. Truthfully, there had not been much resistance to this, and Bassus had informed us this was due to something that had happened during Drusus' first foray across the Rhenus, although he refused to go into detail. Even sitting on a horse, clad in the normal Suebi garb of skins and tanned leather, I could see that she had curves in all the places a man appreciates on a woman. However, what I noticed more than anything was her size; even on a horse, I could tell she was taller than average. My examination was disturbed by the sound of pounding feet, and I turned to see Dento sprinting back to the gate.

Stopping in front of Galens, it took him a moment to regain his breath enough to gasp, "The Legate says to let her in. Just her, and bring her to him immediately." Galens' face darkened again, clearly not liking the order, but he turned to obey nonetheless. Dento thought to add, "Oh, and he said to search her thoroughly before you bring her to him."

That seemed to cheer Galens a bit, and he relayed Drusus' instructions. Now it was the turn of the Suebi man not to like what he heard, and there ensued a brief argument between the two that, even if we could have heard it clearly, we would not have understood, since it was in their native tongue. His opinion did not seem to matter all that much because, after a brief exchange, she made a short, chopping motion with her hand, cutting him off.

I heard someone chuckle, and Galens muttered, "I'd knock the bitch out if she did that in front of someone else."

"They ain't Roman," Dento replied, prompting a look of scorn from our Optio.

"Oh, really?" he asked sarcastically. "What gave that away, idiot? The fact they're dressed like savages, or they're speaking gibberish?"

"Both," Dento said helpfully, reminding me that he was not the brightest of the section, clearly not recognizing the fact he was being mocked.

Or perhaps he did, and was exacting his own revenge on the Optio. By then, the disagreement was over, and the Suebi woman kicked her horse forward, leaving her companion to glare at her back. I had the fleeting thought that he might try and stop her and I tightened my grip on my javelin, but all he did was send her looks that, if they had been weapons, would have left her dead in the dirt. Unmindful of him, and with her head held high, showing no fear, she only stopped when Galens ordered her to dismount, just outside the gate. That was the first, and only, time she hesitated, clearly not liking the idea of being afoot.

Seeing her pause, Galens, still on the rampart looking down, told her coldly, "The only way you're getting in this camp is on foot, woman."

She glared up at the Optio, and I heard her mutter something under her breath. I imagine it was not a blessing on Galens' ancestors. Nevertheless, she slid with a practiced ease from the back of her horse, which I had been examining more than the woman at that moment. Although I do not ride nearly as much as I did, I still have an appreciation for horseflesh, and the Suebi are known for the quality of their mounts, on which they supposedly lavish greater care than they do their own children. That rumor seemed to be borne out by the horse from which the Suebi woman had just dismounted, and although it was a mare, its coloring was so similar to that of Ocelus, I experienced an unbidden rush of emotion.

"Pullus! Get over here!"

Startled and horrified in equal measure, I hurriedly blinked my tears away, but I was forced to pause as my vision cleared.

"I said," Galens growled, "get your fat ass over here or I'll bury my foot up it!"

"Yes, Optio," I called out, even as I ran over to him.

He stared me in the face for a moment, a look of puzzlement there.

"Were you…crying?" he asked incredulously.

"No, Optio," I assured him with all the sincerity I could muster. "Something got in my eyes."

In answer, he gave a small grunt that communicated he did not believe me, but he did not have the time to make an issue of it.

"Come with me," he commanded, then strode down the ramp.

Following him, we made our way through the gate, to where the woman was now standing, and that was when I saw that Galens' choice of me as an escort was for a good reason. As we approached, I realized, with a sense of startled unease, that for the first, and so far, the only time, I was staring a woman directly in the eyes without having to lower my gaze. Even for the Suebi, this woman was a giant, but the only solace was that she was as startled as I was at the sight of a "puny" Roman of my size.

"Come with us," Galens ordered, and it puzzled me at first that he did not search her.

However, he was merely waiting until we were inside the camp and out of her companion's sight, a smart move.

"Stop," he ordered, which she did. "Raise your arms," he told her and, for the first time, her expression of amused scorn changed.

"Why?" she asked suspiciously.

"Why do you think, you stupid bitch?" Galens snapped. "You think you're going to see the Legate without being searched?"

"You will not lay a hand on me, Roman," she hissed, and although she was trying to be defiant, I could see that she was as afraid as she was angry.

I was expecting Galens to slap her, or in some other way demonstrate that she was completely within our power, so I was surprised when he merely shrugged.

"Suit yourself," he said, but pointed to the gate. "You can see yourself out of the camp, I'm guessing?"

"But I must speak to Drusus," she insisted.

"The only way that happens is if you're searched. Thoroughly," he added, and this time, it was with a leer that was more in keeping with who I knew the Optio to be.

For a moment, the woman said nothing, her eyes closed as she struggled to make a decision. She did not say anything, but in answer, she raised her arms, her eyes still closed.

"That's more like it." Galens laughed.

His search was as thorough as I expected, and she clearly feared, and if he took a bit longer on some parts of her body, I could tell that she was as unsurprised as I was. Once the ordeal was over, Galens turned about and began walking towards the *praetorium*, indicating with a curt gesture for us to follow. Slightly confused at what I was supposed to do, I chose to walk beside the woman. As we strode towards her meeting with the Legate, I could see her shoot sidelong glances at me, mainly because I was doing the same. I was surprised that, even to my Roman nose, she did not smell as much as the men of her people normally did, although she did not compare to a Roman woman in terms of hygiene.

Finally, she said, "I was surprised to see a Roman who's the size of our people."

"I was surprised to see a woman my size, no matter whose people she belonged to," I replied without thinking.

She gave a snort that I suppose was her version of a laugh.

"Yes," she admitted. "I am larger than the average Suebi woman. There are no Roman women my size?"

She seemed genuinely curious about this, but I assured her, "Not that I've ever seen, or heard about anyway."

"You're not that big for a Suebi," she observed.

"Big enough to kill them," I shot back.

Instead of being angry, she seemed more amused, and I realized that she had been baiting me.

"Have you ever killed a Suebi? A warrior, that is? Women shouldn't count," she added helpfully.

Realizing what she was doing, I managed to stuff the anger down and answered in the same bantering tone, "No. Not yet. I've killed my share of Chatti, though."

"The Chatti," she said scornfully, spitting on the ground, although I noticed she was careful to spit on the ground on the opposite side of where I was walking. "They're all women!"

"You mean like you?" I asked.

This time, her laugh was more than just a snort, and she nodded her head in recognition of my jibe.

"Although I am a Suebi woman," she retorted.

We were drawing near to the *praetorium*, having reached the far end of the forum, but I found myself slowing slightly. If she noticed, she did not make any sign, although she did match my stride. I was silent for a moment, thinking of my next question, and I could see that she was now openly regarding me, clearly curious. Galens had not looked over his shoulder and was pulling farther away.

Finally, I asked her, "Have you ever heard of Vergorix? Of the Chatti?"

She looked startled, but she answered, "Yes, I have heard of him."

"And was he a woman?"

202

Although I had posed it in a half-teasing way, I saw that she took the question seriously.

"No," she said finally. "No, Vergorix was no woman. He was a great warrior. Even if he was Chatti. Why do you ask that, Roman?"

"You know he's dead, don't you?"

She nodded her head, and I do not think her sadness was feigned when she replied, "Yes, we have heard that he fell in battle against you."

Her mouth twisted in a bitter grimace, and I actually hesitated for a moment, but my pride was such that there was no real danger of me remaining silent.

"Well," I told her, making sure to look her directly in the eye as I told her, "I'm the Roman who killed him."

That brought her to an abrupt halt, which I naturally matched, and she stared at me, disbelief on her face.

"You?" she asked incredulously. "You may be large, Roman, but you're just a…"

She did manage to stop herself, but this time, it was my turn to be amused.

"A boy?" I asked gently. "Is that what you were going to say?"

She nodded reluctantly.

"I'm young," I admitted. "But I was born for this. I have the blood of one of the greatest warriors of Rome in my veins, and I've been training to be in the Legions since I was ten years old."

"Oy! What the fuck are you two doing? Having a chat?"

Galens' shout made us resume walking as he stood in the middle of the forum with his hands on his hips, glaring at us.

"So," she asked suddenly, "what did this Vergorix look like? And what weapon did he use?"

I went on to describe him, with his bearskin cloak and helmet with bear skull, along with how he used not just one, but two axes. By the time I was finished, we had reached Galens, who was still clearly irritated.

"What the fuck are you talking about?" he demanded.

"She doesn't believe I killed Vergorix," I told him.

He stared, first at me, then at her.

"How in Hades did *that* come up?"

I shrugged, lying. "I don't remember. But she says that he was a great warrior. For a Chatti," I added, shooting her a glance.

I saw the glimmer of a smile on her face, but she said nothing immediately, and we fell in step with Galens, who began walking alongside us. There was silence for several paces, but as we approached the *praetorium*, she broke it.

"So?" she asked Galens abruptly. "Is it true?"

"Is what true?"

"Did this one," she shrugged in my direction, "really kill Vergorix?"

Galens glanced over at me, then turned his attention on her.

"He did," he confirmed. "I saw it myself. That's why he was awarded all of Vergorix's gold as a reward by the man you're about to meet."

We were now at the *praetorium*, but the woman stopped and turned to look at me. Her expression was, and still is, one that I cannot accurately decipher, but it is one that I believe I will remember for the rest of my days.

"What is your name, Roman?" she asked me. "So that I may tell my people the truth of who slew Vergorix?"

"My name," I told her with obvious pride, "is Titus Porcinianus Pullus."

The Suebi woman was with Drusus so long that we had been relieved from guard duty, midway through the night, so I did not see her, ever again. Not surprisingly, at least to me, the subject of the visit by her was the talk of the entire army, from the moment we woke up, through breaking camp and the resumption of our march.

"I heard," naturally it was Tubero who said this, "that she's a witch and was sent by the Suebi to cast a spell on Drusus."

"You saw her, idiot," Bassus reminded him. "Did she look like a witch to you? She was a giant, sure enough, but she didn't look like any witch!"

"That was her disguise," Tubero insisted. "She cast a spell on us so that we saw what she wanted us to see."

"What I saw," Asinius spoke up from beside me, "was a tasty bit that I'd like to ride."

"She'd buck you off so fast that it wouldn't be worth the ride," Metellus taunted Asinius. Metellus marched on the other side of our Sergeant.

"That'd be half the fun." Asinius grinned. "Breaking a filly like that would be a challenge, no doubt. But it would be well worth it."

"Not if she's a witch," Tubero interjected, and I believe he was determined to take control of the subject. "Pullus walked her to the *praetorium*. Ask him."

"Well, Pullus?" Asinius asked me, eyebrow raised. "He's right that you walked with her. So, what do you say? Was she a witch? Did she cast a spell on you?"

The others laughed, but while I joined in, I admit it was somewhat forced. What I say now I understand has been colored by all that occurred afterward, making it impossible for me to separate my feelings at that moment from what they are today.

What I said was, "No, she didn't cast a spell on me. But she was…different."

"Different how?" Metellus asked, leaning forward so he could ask me past Asinius.

I thought for a moment, trying to decide how much I should say.

"Well," I finally came out with, "she was the tallest woman I've ever seen, Suebi or not."

"Considering you've been that close to maybe a dozen women in your life, and were related to most of them, that's not saying much," Asinius interjected.

Naturally, my comrades thought this was extremely witty, and I felt my face flush, although I had gotten better about not losing my temper when I was the butt of a joke.

"So, man of the world, have you seen one as tall as she is?" I shot back.

"No," Asinius admitted, bringing another round of laughs, and I will say that I felt very clever.

"Anyway," I plowed on, "besides her height, she spoke Latin better than just about any of these barbarians that I've come across."

"I noticed that," Dento agreed. "It was like she's been either speaking it a long time, or she's been around someone who's taught her some of the things that you wouldn't learn on your own."

This surprised me somewhat because it was an astute observation.

"And she wasn't afraid," I finished. "At least," I amended, "that afraid that it was noticeable."

"All I know is that I haven't grabbed a tit that firm in a long time." Galens' voice came from behind us, where he had been

206

marching drag, as is the job of an Optio, informing us that he had been listening to part of our conversation.

"You're the one who took her to see Drusus," Asinius pointed out. "Did you see them actually meet?"

"No," Galens said. "One of the Tribunes snatched her as soon as I brought her in and whisked her off to Drusus' office without so much as a thank you." He spat to show what he thought about Tribunes. "And I didn't stick around to see how long she was there. But I know it was until after we were relieved."

Tubero tried once more to reassert control over the conversation, intent, I suppose, on making sure there was no doubt where he stood on the subject of the Suebi woman.

"It takes a long time to cast spells," he insisted. "Everyone knows that!"

"I don't," Asinius said mildly. "In fact, I would think that it would be important to a witch that she be able to cast spells quickly. Otherwise, she stands a good chance of getting a sword shoved up her ass."

"Not if she casts a spell on her victim first," Tubero argued.

"So she would have to cast a spell to cast a spell?" Bassus scoffed. "That doesn't make any sense at all, Tubero."

This prompted yet more argument, which I will not detail, but this was the tone of not just my section, but through sections, Centuries, and Cohorts throughout the army. This mysterious Suebi woman and what it was she had to tell Drusus at least kept us occupied for much of the ensuing days. I cannot say with any assurance that her visit prompted what happened next, but I do not think it is out of the realm of possibility. As I mentioned, we had been following the course of the Visurgis, but no more than one or perhaps two days after her visit, we changed from our northerly march to one that was directly easterly. If we had continued north, what we had been told was that we would eventually reach the Mare Germanum, the sea where the lands of Germania end. Instead, we were now marching deeper into Germania, and it was not long before we finally heard whispers of what our next objective was.

"The Marcomanni," Corvinus finally confirmed for us one night. "We're going to teach them a thing or two about Roman iron."

He had stopped by our fire on his rounds, but while we were the last stop of his own Century, he was heading to the next Century to give the word to them, and so on. After he left, the rest of our evening was spent speculating on the cause of this change in direction. Not surprisingly, Tubero was sure that he knew the real story.

"The witch," he declared, referring to the Suebi woman, having convinced himself that this was indeed the case. "She's behind this. She's convinced Drusus to leave the Suebi alone and go after the Marcomanni."

Honestly, this was a difficult point over which to argue because Tubero had the rights of it, at least in the sense that we were not going to engage with the Suebi in favor of the Marcomanni. However, it was an open question, at least at that point, whether or not the mysterious Suebi woman was the cause. Whatever the case, we were heading for Marcomanni territory, but what we did not know, or at least those of us in the ranks did not, was that we had marched far north of the Marcomanni. In turning east, Drusus was searching for a landmark, in the form of a river, one that had to that point never been seen by Roman eyes, at least those belonging to the Legions. The Albis (Elba) River was its name, and it was not until we were two days into our eastward movement that someone finally heard whispers of what was taking place. Once more, Corvinus stopped by our fire, and I was trying to suppress my sense of suspicion, telling myself that it was just a coincidence that our Pilus Prior had made a point to stop by our fire every single night, and the fact that he started doing so after our talk. Not that I could blame him much; knowing what I know now and, as a Centurion myself, there is nothing quite so disconcerting as knowing that your superior is spying on you. I imagine that it is better to know this for a fact, as Corvinus did, but only marginally so. Regardless of his true purpose, what he had to tell us was worth whatever discomfort and suspicion one of his Gregarii might have been feeling at his presence.

"Evening, boys," he began in what I had learned was his customary greeting. Squatting down across the fire from us, his tone was casual, but his words, as usual, arrested our undivided attention. "I just thought I'd stop by and see how everyone is doing."

"Same as last night," Asinius replied for us. "Marching, chopping, digging, marching, chopping, digging. The usual."

Corvinus chuckled and paused for a moment, staring down at the ground as he idly scratched his arm, and it seemed to me that he was trying to decide on something.

"Well, I thought you'd all like to know that we're making history. Or," he amended, "are about to make history."

Not surprisingly, this had us all sitting up straight, watching him intently, and it was clear to see he was enjoying keeping us in suspense.

"The reason we've turned east, before we head towards the Marcomanni, which are to the south of us, is for a couple of reasons, although they're both related." Pausing again, he finally continued, "Drusus is marching us towards a river called the Albis, I believe. The reason it's important is that it marks the boundary of Marcomanni lands on the east."

He stopped and surveyed each one of us, allowing us to work out both the immediate and larger meaning of his words. Frankly, I was not inclined to open my mouth, but I had a suspicion that I might know the import of this. However, I was content to let one of the others make a guess, or just ask outright.

Not surprising me in the least, it was Asinius who hit closest to the center of the target.

"We usually come from the west to hit these bastards," he said slowly, and was rewarded with a slight nod from Corvinus.

"Yes," the Pilus Prior acknowledged. "Normally, the Legions have always come from the west into their lands. All their scouts and all their defenses are oriented towards a threat from us coming from the west. At least," he admitted, "that's the hope. But there's more to it than that. When we reach the Albis, it will mark the deepest any army of Rome has gotten into Germania. Even further," he thought to add, "than Divus Julius himself."

I am not sure what reaction he was expecting, but what greeted Corvinus was a distinct show of a lack of enthusiasm for the idea that we were making history.

"So that's what this is about?" Metellus was the one who uttered what I am sure most of us were thinking. "We're stuck in this place that's worse than Pluto's asshole just because our general wants to make even more of a name for himself?" He shook his head, then spat into the fire, and I heard the brief sizzle. "I'm sorry, Pilus Prior, but that doesn't cheer me up. Does it do that for anyone else?"

His question was met by silence, each of us staring into the fire and, while I suppose Corvinus could have taken this for disagreement with Metellus, one glance at our faces gave the lie to that. I shot a glance at him and I saw his face turn a darker shade, the reflection from the flames of the fire creating shadows that made the hard planes of his face appear even starker.

"Metellus, I'm not going to be losing any sleep over whether you, or," he swiveled his head to encompass all of us, "any of you approve of what the Legate is doing. It's not your fucking place to question it and, frankly, I don't care if you carry out your duties with a smile in your face or a song in your heart, or you're scowling and cursing his name. As long as you do it

210

silently. And," he added, unnecessarily in my opinion, "that you do what the fuck you're told, when you're told to do it. Or you and I will have a problem. Is that understood?"

"Yes, Pilus Prior," Metellus responded, refusing to meet Corvinus' gaze.

Corvinus stood to go, clearly still irritated, but before he left, Asinius called to him.

"Pilus Prior," he said, "I don't know about Metellus, but I'd just as soon be smiling and singing when I go about my business. I just have one question."

"What is it?" Corvinus asked, suspicion clearly written on his face, well knowing Asinius' reputation as the Century wit.

"Can I at least pick the song?"

As I am sure Asinius had hoped, the tension of the moment was blown away by the gales of laughter that issued from the Tenth Section of the First Century, and even Corvinus joined in.

Despite the temporary bout of levity, it is hard for me to describe accurately the pall of gloom that hung over the army of Drusus, although I can only recognize that as the case now that I have more experience. Truly, when it was happening, given that this was my first campaign, I saw what was taking place as normal, and my expectation was that every campaign I participated in would be the same. I suppose I should say "provided I survived," but I was still seventeen, and all teenagers are convinced they cannot die, so the idea that I might fall in my first campaign never really occurred to me. Compounding our misery, something that I had not thought possible, at least until it happened, was that, if anything, the forest became thicker, with trees literally standing so close together that one would think that they had been planted in formation. No more than an arm's length between the trunks of trees that, although not huge, were still large enough in circumference that it took perhaps a sixth of an hour to chop down each one. That was bad enough, but the closer we got to the river itself, the lower the ground got, meaning that there were even more sections of swampy, wet ground that we only found when we plunged into them. Even more than what had become normal, the earth itself seemed to conspire against us, holding us back and slowing us up. What had been a solid eight to ten miles per day dropped to perhaps five, but at the end of that day, we were not only tired, we were covered in muck, usually from head to toe, since it was almost impossible to keep one's feet and not fall at some point during the day.

It was during this period that I got another glimpse of Drusus, when I had drawn guard duty around the *praetorium*. The truth is that, at first, I did not recognize the man, only realizing at the last instant that he was in fact the commanding officer, saving me from the mortal embarrassment, and perhaps danger, of stopping and challenging him because I did not recognize him. He had been lean before; now he was gaunt, but it was his demeanor and bearing more than anything that gave me trouble with his identity. Gone was the erect posture of the Legate I had seen before and, in its place, a hunching of the shoulders with his head dropped between them in a manner that bespoke of a terrible burden, or of being occupied with troubling thoughts. Despite his preoccupation, I snapped to *intente*, and, at first, I thought he would not acknowledge it, nor give me even a passing glance. But then, just as he was about to enter the *praetorium*, he seemed to notice me and came to a stop, turning to face me. For a moment, I felt his eyes on me, and I got the distinct feeling that he was trying to place me.

"Eyo, Gregarius Pullus," he finally said, and his voice was filled with a fatigue that matched his outward appearance. Even so, I saw him smiling at me out of the corner of my eye. "Stand at ease, Pullus," he ordered. "We haven't talked since you slew Vergorix."

Now, being completely honest, I did not think of our exchange on that day much of a conversation, but I suppose it was as much of one as a Legate holds with a lowly ranker like I was then. Besides, the truth was that I liked Drusus, and I know that my feeling was colored by the regard that my father held for the man. However, since he had not actually posed a question, I was at a loss as to what was expected from me, so I said nothing, although I complied. For a moment, there was nothing but silence as we regarded each other. Then, he did something unexpected, at least by me, and threw back his head and laughed, hard. At first, I found myself grinning along with him, but he did not stop, and I began growing nervous.

Finally, he stopped and, wiping his eyes, he gasped out, "I don't know why that was so funny. The look on your face, I suppose. But then I realized, I didn't ask you a question, did I?" Then, before I could speak, he answered his own question, "And of course, you're not going to open your mouth unless I ask a question. The ranker's first rule, neh? Don't say anything that might get you in trouble."

"Yes, sir," I agreed, still completely at a loss about what I was supposed to say, other than to agree with him.

"Really, Pullus," he said crossly, although I saw the corners of his mouth turned up as he fought a smile, "we can hardly hold a conversation with just this 'Yes, sir,' 'No, sir' nonsense, can we?"

"I suppose not. Sir," I replied truthfully.

"That's better." He nodded his head. Then, he regarded me for a moment before asking, "So, Pullus. Do you have any brothers?"

"Yes, sir," I replied. "Two, although one's only two years old. My brother Sextus is..." I had to think for a moment, "...thirteen."

"Is he as big as you? I mean," he corrected, "not now, but when you were that age."

213

"No, sir. He's tall, but he's built more like my father than me."

Drusus grunted, telling me nothing.

Then, he asked abruptly, "So where did you get your size? I know that your grandfather was a very large man for a Roman, but I also know he adopted your father, so he's really an … uncle, is it?"

"Yes, sir." I nodded in answer. "He was the brother of my father's mother. Which would make her my grandmother," I added, trying to be helpful.

"Yes, thank you for that, Pullus," he said dryly. "You know how we upper classes aren't very quick about such things."

I felt the blood rush to my face, but he laughed and clapped me on the shoulder.

"Don't worry, Pullus. I'm not a nobleman who'd flog a man because he didn't guard every word out of his mouth." Suddenly, the smile faded, and he repeated, "So do you have any idea why you're as tall as your father and…grandfather? I mean," he hurried on, completely unmindful of me, "I know that your father is his adopted son, but I know that Augustus had the same blood relation to Divus Julius. Augustus was really his nephew, grand-nephew, but all of us in his family refer to Divus Julius as the Princeps' father, so I suppose it's only right to do the same with you and your father. And from everything I've heard, Augustus does favor Divus Julius, despite the fact that he's not a direct descendant."

Now, I know he did not mean it to be insulting, but nevertheless, I felt a flicker of anger at his words, or perhaps it was in the way he waved his hand in what I took to be a dismissive gesture, demonstrating the kind of thoughtlessness that the upper classes often display towards their social inferiors, as if he was bestowing an honor upon me by his recognition that if Roman law worked for his class, it was the same for mine. I felt my jaw tighten as I clenched my teeth, but then I heard a voice in my head, that of my father's, admonishing me that no matter how chummy and kind Drusus appeared to be at that moment, I needed to be cautious.

Completely oblivious to my inner turmoil, Drusus continued, "Why do you think that is, Pullus?" Seeing that I had gotten lost, he repeated, "Why do you suppose you have the same size as the man for whom you're named?"

I considered for a moment, then shrugged. "Honestly, sir, I have no idea. But I remember my Av...Prefect Pullus," I corrected myself, not wanting to give Drusus the name by which I will always remember Titus Pullus, "telling me that it was a gift from the gods and, as such, I shouldn't abuse it."

Drusus considered this for a moment, then nodded thoughtfully.

"Your grandfather was a wise man," he said. "And I would say that extends not just to someone's size, but to other areas as well." We both stood there silently for a moment, then he broke it suddenly, with a question that caught me completely by surprise, which perhaps was his intent. "Do you love your brother?"

I opened my mouth to answer immediately, but I suppose the way he was staring at me, with an intensity that was quite unsettling, actually caused me to pause to consider the question more carefully.

"Yes, I suppose I do," I answered finally, "although I've always considered him something of a pain in my ass...er, rear. Sir."

I am not sure what he had been expecting, but this appeared to please him.

"Do you think he loves you?"

The truth was that, at that point, I had never thought about it, so my reply was even slower in coming.

"I think so," I said. "Or at least, I hope he does."

"It's not easy being a younger brother, Pullus," Drusus replied, reminding me that was, in fact, his status, something that I think all of us tended to forget. "And I know what men think about my brother Tiberius."

I froze, the words on my lips dying before they ever took flight, every word written by my Avus and uttered by my father about the dangers of dealing with the upper classes coming to me. Thankfully, he did not seem to be expecting any kind of response because he continued on.

"And it's true; he's not the most…social of men. And the gods know there are times when I want to shake some sense into him about how he would make things so much better for himself if he would just take that stick out of his…rear." He grinned at me again, and I did not feel it would endanger me to laugh at his subtle jab at my own attempt to avoid being crude. "But he's a good man, and he's my older brother, and I have no desire to be in his boots. It's not fair that men whisper what they do about us, simply because I like people more than Tiberius, so it makes them think that he's not suited for…well, for whatever comes after Augustus."

By this point in the conversation, he was no longer even looking in my direction, instead staring off across the forum. There was no need for him to expand any further; I knew exactly what he was referring to, and it was certainly true that a fair amount of time was spent around our fires arguing and predicting who would step into the role that is currently filled by the divine Augustus. At least, when we were not moaning and complaining about our current circumstances.

Drusus shook his head, only then seeming to return his attention back in my general direction, and there was no mistaking the sadness in his voice when he said, "And neither of us asked for any of this. Speaking for myself, I would be happy to do this," he waved his hand to encompass the entire camp, "for the rest of my days, for however many of them I have left. I hate politics," he finished with a shudder.

Seeing that he was finished, at least for the moment, I was unsure what to say, or do. Consequently, I fell back onto the best and safest weapon in the ranker's arsenal; I did and said nothing. We stood there for a moment before, understanding that I was not about to open my mouth, he gave a soft laugh.

"And here I am boring you with all the troubles of the upper classes. Undoubtedly, you're thinking those are *problems* you'd love to have." I was about to open my mouth to assure him I was thinking no such thing, which was true enough, although it hardly covered the entire range of my feelings on the subject, but then he said something else. "Oh, wait. I forgot that I'm talking to the grandson of Titus Pullus. If anyone knew all the turmoil that comes with being of the nobility, it would be anyone related to him."

"Sir?" While I thought I understood what he was referring to, I was not sure of the intent behind the words. Just as he was aware of my familial connection, I was no less aware of his, so I believe I can be forgiven for suspecting that this was some sort of ploy to draw me out and have me declare my intentions towards addressing the injustice done to my family. "I'm not sure I follow you."

He stared at me intently for a moment, then he said softly, "I think you do, Pullus. But I can understand why you'd be cautious. The gods know you have reason to be, considering all that happened with your grandfather." Heaving a sigh, he said, "In fact, once I learned who you were, I made some inquiries about your...background and situation. I know quite a bit about the story. The question is," now he looked directly up into my eyes, "what do you know?"

I cannot say exactly how much time passed as I tried to decide the best course of action, but youth is nothing if not impulsive and reckless, so I decided at that moment that if this

217

nobleman wanted to know what had been done to my family, I would oblige him. Over the next few moments, I told him what I had learned from the written account of my Avus, from my father, and what I had observed on my own. Once I was finished, he said nothing for a few moments.

Finally, he nodded and said, "That goes with what I know as well. But I also know a couple other things. Namely, I know what happened to your father on the day he was hurt."

The remaining time on guard duty went by quickly, if only because I was so filled with thoughts and emotions, some of them in open conflict with each other. I am just thankful that a band of Suebi or Marcomanni did not choose to infiltrate the camp and get into the *praetorium* because I was in no shape to stop them, or even notice them slinking past me. When we were relieved, I had to fight down the urge to go immediately to seek out the man who was the only one able to either confirm or deny what Drusus had told me. It was midnight, and we were back on the march the next morning, meaning I needed to get what sleep I could, not to mention that the repercussions of disturbing his sleep could have been dire for me. Therefore, I forced myself to go back to my tent, lie down, and try to at least pretend and get some sleep. The moment the *bucina* sounded the call to rise, I leapt up and performed my part of the duties of breaking camp, which we always performed before sitting down to break our fast. I found Galens and lied that I needed to go to the *quaestorium* to draw some replacement leather thongs, which he gave me leave to do, but while I did head in that direction, as soon as I was out of sight, I doubled back to reach my true destination. Approaching his tent, the feelings I was experiencing were akin to those that consumed me before battle, and I suppose that at that moment, it was appropriate.

"I need to see Primus Pilus Canidius," I told his secretary, once I was bade entry into the outer office.

"He's busy right now," Crito informed me, but when I did not budge, he sighed and got up from his own desk. Knocking on the wood, he entered, and there was a muffled exchange, but when Crito reappeared, he had a look on his face that made it seem as if I was going to be refused entry. Fortunately, that was not the case as he said bemusedly, "The Primus Pilus will see you now."

He held open the flap and I entered, then squared myself on Urso's desk, saluting. The Primus Pilus was clearly curious, but he returned my salute, then sat back.

"Is it true?" I blurted out, completely destroying my carefully rehearsed opening statement, composed during the watches of the night that I spent tossing and turning.

"Is what true?"

Urso's tone was mild, but I got the distinct impression that he was not that surprised to see me, nor to be asked that question.

That was what emboldened me to reply, "I think you know what I'm talking about."

For a moment, I thought I had made a serious blunder because his face turned darker, but his voice showed no anger as he admitted, "I do. Or at least I think I do. This is about Barbatus and your father?"

I nodded, and he heaved a sigh.

"I don't suppose you want to tell me who told you?"

Although all that I knew and had learned made me naturally cautious, I had actually thought about this quite a bit, and, sometime in the night, had decided that revealing my source would not do any harm, if only because of his status.

"Drusus told me," and, as I had hoped, I saw that this clearly startled him.

"Drusus," he repeated, as if trying to comprehend how it was possible. "Drusus," he muttered. "How would he know?

Unless…" He did not finish the thought, shaking his head. "Well, however it happened…" He took a deep breath. "Yes, it's true. Barbatus is the man who pushed your father into the gully, then followed him down to finish your father off. I stopped him." He gave a shrug. "That's what happened."

Despite the fact Urso was just confirming what Drusus had told me, my mind still reeled, there being, at least for me, more questions unanswered.

"But, why?" I asked him, just one of the many crowding my brain.

"Why what?" Urso asked, and I felt the flare of anger in my gut, sure that he was being deliberately evasive.

Nevertheless, I managed to stuff it down and ask with a patience I did not feel, "Why did Barbatus want my father dead?"

"Ah," Urso said softly, a small smile playing on his lips. "That *is* a question, isn't it?" He regarded me for a moment, as if trying to decide how forthcoming to be. "Before I answer, I want to know what you know, or think you know."

Understanding that the only way I would get any more answers was by showing him at least one of my dice, I told him, "I know that Augustus was behind blocking the elevation of my father into the Equestrian order, that while my Av…Titus Pullus was made an Equestrian and his name is still on the rolls as one, the status that should have passed to my family because he adopted my father as his son and heir wasn't transferred." By the time I finished the explanation, the anger that I realize now is always just below my surface, waiting to come bursting out like a volcano's eruption because of this very subject, was pushing all the way up into my throat, and I tasted the hot bile of my rage. Looking back, I think this might have been exactly what Urso was trying to accomplish.

"That's the bare bones of it," Urso acknowledged. "Did your father ever tell you where Barbatus came to us from? How he came to be Primus Pilus?"

I thought for a moment, then shook my head.

"From the Praetorian Guard," Urso said, pausing to let me absorb this and what it meant. "And he had never even led a Cohort in the Legions before he was made Primus Pilus. And," he finished, "do you know who's responsible for almost all the appointments into the Centurionate, and especially into the office of Primus Pilus?"

I do not know if his slip with the word "almost" was intentional, but I think it must have been, although I was more absorbed with the larger questions he had just asked.

"Augustus," I replied slowly, as the import of that hit me with the force of a fist to the gut. "You mean," I gasped, "Augustus ordered Barbatus to kill my father?"

I thought there were no more surprises left, but he proved me wrong, shaking his head adamantly.

"No, that is *not* what I'm saying," he said forcefully, and although he did not raise his volume, there was no mistaking the intensity. "I understand why you might think that, but I heard from Barbatus himself, just before he was about to stick a blade into your father's heart, that he was acting on his own. From what I remember, he said that what your grandfather did in elevating himself, or maybe the way he did it, had made his own plans more difficult. Apparently, he had aspirations of his own, but then Pullus had all his troubles with the Tribunal." Urso shrugged once more. "And since your grandfather was already dead, he decided to take it out on your father. Oh," he snapped his fingers, as if suddenly remembering, "and he said that after he killed your father, he was going to finish off the rest of the family Porcinus, and wipe all of you from the face of the earth."

That was the first I heard that and all I can say is that, as soon as I was able, I wrote my father who, reluctantly, agreed that this was indeed the case.

"And you stopped him," I said. "Why?"

For the first time, Urso looked uncomfortable, and I noticed that this was also the first time he refused to meet my gaze as he replied, "Because it was the right thing to do. Barbatus was a horrible leader, and your father was my superior at the time. And," then he did look up, "your father was a great man, in his own way. And a great Centurion. I don't know if he told you, but our relationship in the beginning was…strained." He gave a small laugh at what I knew was his understatement, and I admit I joined in. "But then I saw how competent he was, and how the men, not just in his Century, but in the Cohort, loved and admired him. Most importantly, they respected him, although he wasn't a striper like I was. And," he thought to add, "still am, to a point. But I don't do it nearly as much as I did before your father took over the Fourth."

Nothing was said between us for a moment. Outside, I could hear the sounds of the camp, the way it sounds in the mornings of a movement, and I knew that it would not be long before he had to end this conversation, despite the fact that I still had more questions.

"Now," he interrupted my thoughts, "before we end this chat, I have a question for you."

I braced myself.

"What have you heard the last few days? What's being said in the Fourth Cohort?"

My own situation aside, Drusus' army continued slogging its way until finally, two days after my conversation with Urso, we reached the Albis River, where we stopped and made camp on the western bank, despite the fact it was still early in the day.

This led us to believe that he planned on having us cross the river and, for a brief period of time, I heard men muttering to themselves that they might actually refuse his order to start construction of a bridge. In width and strength of current, the Albis is akin to the Rhenus, meaning that we would be forced to construct a true bridge, and not one made with boats as pontoons because there were none available. This led to a tense evening, until Corvinus came to inform us that we would be breaking camp and continuing the march.

"Where?" I believe Bassus asked, and he was not the only one confused. "Don't tell me we're turning around?" A look of horror crossed his face and his body actually shuddered as he gasped, "By the gods! Please don't tell us we're marching further north!"

There was a ripple among my comrades as each of them muttered something or shifted on their stools, all eyes on Corvinus, whose face gave away nothing.

"Well, Bassus," the Pilus Prior's tone was cool, "if that's what the Legate orders, I won't let it be said that the Fourth did anything that would bring shame to the Legion. Like I've heard other Cohorts are considering refusing the order to march. I don't care what direction it is; if our Primus Pilus orders it, we will obey. Or," his voice remained at the same pitch and volume, but there was no mistaking the menace, "I'll kill the first man who does something to dishonor the Cohort, with my bare hands." He paused, I assume to let the words sink in, then he quickly stood up from where he had been squatting. "But," he finished, his tone much lighter, "as it turns out, you don't need to worry, Bassus. We're marching south, not north. Now," he turned and started walking away, but called over his shoulder, "you girls need to make sure you get to sleep early. We've got a big day ahead of us."

If he heard the mass exhalation of breath as my comrades sighed in relief, he made no sign, but the silence continued even after he was out of sight. As I glanced around the fire, I watched as the expressions of my comrades slowly changed, going from relief to a slowly dawning realization. Only Asinius, sitting next to me as always, seemed to be the only one who understood from the beginning the full import of what Corvinus had said, and he was the one who broke the silence.

"I see you geniuses are just figuring it out." His voice, shattering the quiet, made a couple of the others jump a bit, and I noticed that Tubero was the most startled. "We may not be marching north, but that doesn't mean we're out of the *cac*. There are a few thousand Marcomanni between us and home."

The only good thing I can say about marching along a riverbank is that the vegetation and old-growth trees are not as thick as that to which we had become accustomed. Although we never covered more than fifteen miles in a day, comparatively speaking, it felt as if we were finally making real progress. However, this meant that a showdown with the Marcomanni became more likely with every passing day, a prospect that I saw was displeasing to more than just the men like Tubero; even Asinius seemed on edge at the idea that we were going to be fighting the Marcomanni. That put me in a distinct minority, but in this I plead the ignorance of youth. While I had tasted battle, twice now, and found it to my liking, I would liken my state of mind to the overconfidence of a man who has learned how to dogpaddle and thinks nothing of leaping off a boat into the sea, miles from land, and thinking that he knows how to make it to shore. I will say that I was also helped by my Avus again, in the form of his account of when he was in my position as a Gregarius, marching in Gaul with the 10th Equestris, and they were about to face Ariovistus, a German chieftain. What I remembered was that the reality of the battle against Ariovistus paled in comparison to the fevered imaginings of the rankers, so on the third night of our march along the Albis, I decided to break my self-imposed policy of silence around the fire. All I had to do was wait for the topic of the Marcomanni come up, which as always, Tubero did as soon as he swallowed his last bite of bread.

"I heard," he began, which was his usual method of bringing up whatever topic he had in mind, never admitting that he was the originator of whatever piece of doom he wanted to introduce to the rest of us, "that the Marcomanni make the Suebi look like children playing at war."

Before anyone could comment on this, I took a breath and plunged in.

"This reminds me," I said, drawing more than one look of surprise, "of something I read about, somewhere."

"You *read*?" Tubero scoffed, then shot me a grin that was anything but friendly. "Oh, that's right; I forgot. You're practically nobility!" He made a mock bow in my direction, glancing about as he did so, gauging how his jest was received. On the other hand, I was heartened to see that nobody was laughing, or showing any amusement.

"What did you read, Pullus?" Asinius asked me quietly, ignoring Tubero.

Out of the corner of my eye, I could see Tubero's face flush, but I followed Asinius' lead, replying, "I read that the men of Caesar's army were about to face another German; his name was Ariovistus. And there were a lot of men in the army running around screaming doom and gloom, about how every warrior was bigger than they were, even someone my size, and how they drank the blood of the men they killed. Oh," I acted as if I had just recalled something else, "and supposedly, they had witches that taught the warriors to cast spells that paralyzed their enemies so they couldn't defend themselves."

I paused, and there was a silence for a moment before Bassus broke it, asking, "And? What happened?"

"Well, like I said, there was a lot of running about and men were pulling their hair out and moaning about their impending

225

doom. But then, a group of men from the 10th approached Caesar and told him that even if the rest of the army refused to face Ariovistus that he could count on them. Naturally, when the other Legions heard about this, they were ashamed about their behavior and *they* went to Caesar and promised him that they wouldn't be outdone by the 10th." I shrugged and finished, "And when they faced Ariovistus, they slaughtered the Germans and killed most of Ariovistus' family, and the Germans. At least," I amended, "those Germans never bothered anyone again."

"What happened to this Ario-whatever his name was?" Asinius asked, but when I turned to answer him, I was sure he already knew.

"Oh, he got away," I told him. "In a tiny rowboat, across the Rhenus. But he left his wives and children behind."

Predictably, there were snickers and muttered comments about the shame of a man who would abandon his family.

"Tubero." Asinius turned to our comrade, whose expression had turned sullen; he was not the smartest, but he understood that he had been undermined in his efforts to be the doomsayer. "I can see why you're worried! If this German got away, he's still out there! He might be a leader of the Marcomanni!" He paused for a moment, then shrugged. "Of course, he would be, what?" He turned to me. "About a hundred years old?"

"Something like that," I replied, although I was not sure.

"Well, that means that even Tubero could probably take him," Asinius concluded.

If he said anything more, I did not hear it because of the laughter. As he was prone to do, Tubero did not accept this with good grace, getting up and stomping away to go sulk, the mocking laughter of the rest of us following him.

Asinius turned to me and regarded me for a moment, his eyes giving nothing of his thoughts away, then finally said, "That was a smart thing to do, Pullus."

I shrugged, but inwardly I was pleased at the compliment; Asinius was as stingy with his praise as some men are with their money, treating each coin or compliment like a precious child.

"I'm just tired of hearing all this talk," I told him.

"Where *did* you read that?" Metellus asked me.

I told him, "My grandfather bought a copy of Caesar's account in Gaul. It was what my tutor used to teach me to read."

The moment it came out of my mouth, I was sure that my comrades would not miss a word, and I was rewarded with my faith.

"Tutor?" Bassus exclaimed. "Well, aren't we lucky to have an educated man among us?"

It is difficult to describe in writing, but while the words were very similar to those uttered by Tubero a short while earlier, the tone was completely different, so it was not forced when I joined in the chuckles of the rest of my comrades.

"Someone needs to be able to tell us what all the graffiti says on the walls," Asinius put in.

This brought more laughter, and I breathed a silent sigh of relief, not only because of my attempt to forestall more negative talk by Tubero, but that none of them questioned me further on the origins of the tale I had recounted. Because while it is true that I have read Caesar's account, that is not what I was referring to when I brought it up, but I was loath to mention that my Avus had left any kind of written account behind, not knowing what might happen if it became known. I had been prepared to recount another part of that tale, that, in fact, my Avus had been one of the ten men selected to ride with Caesar on the day he met with Ariovistus, before they faced in battle. It was from this episode that the 10th earned the name the 10th Equestris, and I was, and am very proud of the connection to one of the most famous chapters in the history of the Legions. However, if I had been forced to bring it up, I was prepared to swear on the black stone that I learned of it orally. And although I felt I had done a solid service to my section, and I was gratified that my comrades had essentially taken my side against Tubero, I still felt precariously alone, not knowing who I could trust, although I will say that I had a good idea of who I could not, although the two are not the same.

I take no credit for it, at least all of what happened, but the mood around our fire lightened considerably, mainly because Tubero chose to spend his time elsewhere, probably finding men who had a more willing ear to listen to his prophecies of disaster. Then, a week after we turned south, we were marching and, since we were following the course of the river, we turned more to the west. Fairly quickly into the day, the terrain became more undulating and, while I would not call it hilly, it definitely became more varied. One thing we had learned fairly quickly is that because the forest is so thick in most places, it is impossible to find a vantage point that gives you a view of anything more than perhaps two or three miles in any particular direction. That was why our mounted scouts were so important, but it had become a requirement for them to go out in larger numbers because of the disturbing tendency of smaller five-man patrols to disappear. We had lost perhaps a hundred of our mounted contingent just from being picked off, so Drusus had commanded that nothing smaller than twenty-five-man scouting patrols be sent out. The consequence of this was that there were less of these patrols being sent out; at least, that was what the conjecture was for what was about to happen. It was not until later, after the campaign, when men gather to talk and contribute the bits and pieces of what they know that an idea of the larger situation became known, so I do not want to lay the blame just at the feet of the cavalry.

When we turned westward, it took us closer to a series of ridges that are part of a larger system, so that, in effect, we were marching parallel to this ridge for a distance, with the river still to our left. This created a situation that the Marcomanni could not pass up, where they came swooping down from the high ground of the ridge, with the river effectively to our back. The way we learned of it, marching drag behind the baggage train as it happened, was in the eruption of a roar that could only be produced by thousands of voices raised at full volume. Following an instant behind was the first of what would be several *cornu* calls, starting someplace well up the column, and rippling down the length as each Century and Cohort was alerted that there was an attack. Since we were behind the baggage train, our line of sight was further impeded, but as we scrambled from our marching column into a formation that readied us to defend ourselves, I caught a glimpse of something eerily similar to the first battle, a rolling wave composed of greens and browns, and along the top of the wave was a dull silver-gray, the combination of helmets and weapons of the attacking Marcomanni. Unlike the last battle, where I slew Vergorix, my Cohort was not marching alongside the baggage train; this day, it was actually the Ninth's day for that duty, while half the Legion marched in front of the train and the rest of the Legion was behind it, starting with my Cohort immediately behind. Fairly quickly, we saw that the focus of the Marcomanni attack, unlike that of the Chatti, was not the baggage train, but somewhere farther up the column; Corvinus actually divined its purpose.

"I bet they're trying to reach Drusus," I heard him say as we were finishing getting into position, facing west in the general direction of the high ground.

Because the forest was not as dense, it was a bit easier to see farther, but it took some concentration to discern the beginning of the slope of the ridge, and it was impossible to determine how high it was. More importantly, there was no sign of a horde of Marcomanni pounding down that slope in our direction.

"Looks like we get to sit this one out," I heard down the line, and I recognized Scrofa's voice.

"Thank the gods," Tubero replied.

"Shut up, the both of you," Asinius growled from his spot next to me.

I remained silent, thankful once more for my height so that I could see over everyone else's heads in the event that, for some reason, the Marcomanni had some trick to play and their assault on our line was just delayed. We might not have been engaged, but that was not the case for the other half of the 8th, positioned on the other side of the baggage train. Despite being almost a half-mile long now that each wagon driver had closed the gap to the wagon in front of it, we could still see enough through the trees to at least tell our comrades were engaged, helped by the gentle curve to the right that our column had been making. More telling were the sounds that rolled across the distance and, as inexperienced as I was, I knew enough to determine that the fighting was furious already, very early into the battle. Confirming that belief, Corvinus called Galens to meet him just a few paces away from where I was standing.

"Looks like they're getting it pretty good," he told Galens, both of them staring towards the front of the column.

"Looks like it," Galens agreed. "What do you want to do? Urso hasn't given the order to bring us up."

"No," Corvinus admitted. "At least, not yet."

Turning about, he looked back down the column in the opposite direction of the fighting, frowning as he tried to make up his mind.

"But," he said, finally, "just from the sounds of it, I don't know that he can."

"That's true," Galens granted, but he said nothing else, his eyes on Corvinus.

Finally, the Pilus Prior seemed to make a decision.

"Wait here," he commanded. "I need to talk to the others."

Without waiting, he went trotting back towards the rear of the column, where the other four Cohorts were waiting. Due to the fact that we seldom marched in sequential order, unless we were expecting contact, the composition of the Cohorts marching behind the baggage train meant that Pilus Prior Corvinus was the highest-ranking Centurion behind the baggage train. We stood waiting, in formation, all of us shifting about, some of us drumming fingers on shields, some adjusting bits of gear, while others, like me, could not seem to stop yawning. Although, at that moment, we were still in a formation parallel to the rest of the column and we had moved outward from it by perhaps fifty paces, it would be safe to say that only a few of us were looking towards the ridge, while the rest of us had our attention fixed on what was taking place farther up the column. Again, we could see no details, only a mass of whirling movement, but the sounds that carried to us were clear enough.

"That sounds like a bit of a brawl," Asinius commented, but although his tone was calm, I glanced over and saw the bunching of his jaw muscles as he leaned forward and kept his eyes on the fighting.

Before I could think of anything to say, our attention was drawn away by a shout, and we turned to see Corvinus trotting back. He motioned to Galens, and they had a brief conversation, but I could not hear what was said, not that it mattered, since Corvinus called to us.

"All right," he bellowed. "We're going to swing down on those *cunni's* flanks and roll them up like a carpet. But we're going to have to do it a little differently than normal. We're going to be on the left, and the Cohort is going to execute a wheel maneuver to get us in position."

To that point, he had not said anything extremely alarming or unusual. Other than the fact we were about to go into battle, at least, but he was not through.

"What about the other Cohorts?"

231

I could not tell who asked this because it came from somewhere ahead of me in the middle of the formation, but while Corvinus had every right to punish or chastise the man who asked, he did not seem upset or even begrudge the question.

"We don't have time for the rest of them to get into position." He shook his head. "We're going to lead the way, and the Sixth is going to be behind us, ready to support us or move to hit a weak spot as it develops."

"What about the Ninth?" I heard someone to my left mutter; it sounded like Scrofa.

"If they were going to get stuck in, they would have done it by now," Asinius said scornfully. "But you know they're a bunch of rabbits."

I am somewhat ashamed to say that this was a true characterization of the Ninth, but as I would learn as I climbed through the ranks, there are no Centuries or Cohorts that are filled exclusively with cravens, misfits, cowards, and malingerers. The tone is set at the top, and the Nones Pilus Prior, whose name I will not mention, was the one rabbit in the ranks of the Ninth, and I think it is neither a coincidence nor a crime to say that he was one of those men who purchased his way straight into the Centurionate with enough money to buy a post as Pilus Prior. Fortunately, at least at this point in my career in the army, no matter how much money a man had, they were unable to purchase a posting in the front-line Cohorts, although sadly, this has changed in the last few years.

"Pullus! Pullus! Get up here!"

At first, I did not move, so startled at Corvinus calling my name that I am afraid I froze for a moment.

Then, I felt a hard shove and Asinius snapped, "Get up there, idiot. Don't make the section look bad."

I did so, running to the front of the formation, and Corvinus, clearly impatient, grabbed hold of my armor right under my throat and physically moved me to where Maxentius was standing.

"Maxentius," Corvinus ordered, "go take Pullus' place in the Tenth Section."

Frankly, I was happy that I was not the only one slow to react, as Maxentius just stood, staring at Corvinus in disbelief.

"Pilus Prior?" As much as I hated the man, I knew the tremor in his voice was not one of fear, but bewildered anger. "I don't understand."

"I don't have time for this *cac*," Corvinus snapped. "I gave you an order. I expect you to obey."

"But...but I'm the best man with a sword you've got," Maxentius stammered.

Corvinus released his hold on me to reach out and slap Maxentius, hard, across the face. Fortunately, it was with his open hand.

"Not anymore," Corvinus said coldly, then pointed. "And I don't want just his sword, I want his size. Now, go; move your ass."

It was true there was a battle raging, and I had a multitude of things on my mind, but despite that, I felt a rush of emotions course through me, although not lost on me was that if Maxentius had despised me before, he would probably try to kill me at some point because of this insult. As strange as it is to say, I was actually thankful we were about to go into battle so that I did not have time to dwell on this development. Also, it turned out that it was not just me Corvinus moved; from the Century he had other men closer to my size moved to the front rank, although I knew that this would make no difference to Maxentius. A few heartbeats later, the front rank was to Corvinus' satisfaction, then he trotted out to where he could be seen by the Centuries aligned behind us, along with our *signifer*, who, using his standard, signaled for the Cohort to move into position. I assume he did this without using the *cornu* in order to maximize the surprise, but with an experienced Cohort like the Fourth, there was barely a bobble in the movement as the first three Centuries made a pivot movement, with the First as the base. Once more, it meant that I did not have to move very far, so I got into position quickly and watched as the rest of the Cohort moved into a line. I briefly wondered why Corvinus was aligning us in the double line of Centuries, since that meant our line was not extended as far towards the ridge as it could have been, but quickly dismissed it as something far above my rank. That was a Pilus Prior problem; mine was more immediate and, for what I am sure was the hundredth time, I yawned, while reaching down to check my sword in its scabbard. Corvinus sent the *signifer* back to his spot at the front of our Century, but stayed where he could be seen, more or less centered in the front of the three leading Centuries. Drawing his sword, he swung it down to point in the direction of the fight, and we stepped off. As we drew abreast of the men of the Ninth, I glanced over and saw that none of them would look at us and, while they were standing in formation, nothing in their posture or manner indicated they had a stomach for a battle. I returned my attention back to Corvinus, and we closed on the left flank of the fight.

We were able to close to within javelin range before we saw heads of Marcomanni warriors on the left edge of their battle line and a few rows back turn their heads in our direction. The instant Corvinus saw we were spotted, he stopped us with a shouted command.

"Prepare javelins," he bellowed, and as our arms swept back with our first volley, he trotted back in the direction of our Century.

"Release!"

One reason I believe I am able to fling a javelin farther than most men is because, since we are taught to use our bodies to add our weight behind our throw, my greater bulk works to my advantage. And because this time I was in the front, I could put even more of my weight into it, but it was just one of the almost seventy missiles that went streaking into the air, flying high into the sky before pausing for a fraction of a heartbeat, then turning to plummet down into the packed, heaving mass of Marcomanni. As I returned to my throwing position, I saw the pale oval of faces turned up to the sky, watching and trying to pick out the javelin that was even then hurtling downward as the one most likely to puncture them. Even before the first volley landed, Corvinus was shouting the command for the next volley.

"Prepare!"

A heartbeat passed, which was filled with the clattering, thudding sound of the first volley, and Corvinus' voice was almost drowned out by the shouts, curses, and screams of Marcomanni who had either lost a shield, or perhaps their lives.

Still, there was not an appreciable lag in the second volley and, once more, even as the missiles were still in the air, he bellowed, "Draw swords!"

The sound of our blades being withdrawn from our scabbards competed with the harsh sound of my own breathing as my hand wrapped around my blade in the grip that I had been using since the first day my father began my tutoring at the age of ten. At the same time, I set my shield on the ground to wipe my left hand quickly on my tunic, trying to make sure that all the moisture from my palm was gone.

"All right, boys! Let's put paid to these bastards!" Corvinus turned his back to us, but raised his sword high so that it could be seen by the three Centuries of the first line. It hovered there for perhaps two or three heartbeats, and I sensed the movement of men around me, crouching and bringing their shields up, close to their bodies. I suppose I was sufficiently distracted because when he bellowed, "*Porro!*" I jumped a bit, although thankfully, I did not hesitate this time.

With our own roar in answer, we leaped forward, and I immediately discovered two things in this, my first time in the front rank of a charging attack. The first was that because of my size, when I drew my shield up hard against my shoulder, the lower rim of the shield was in the way of my left leg when I ran. I immediately extended my arm out to my side so that the shield was out of the way, and I remember thinking that I would have to time things perfectly so that just before I reached the Marcomanni, I swung the shield back into position.

The second problem did not become apparent to me until I heard someone behind me and to my left shout, "Pullus! You're out too far ahead!"

In retrospect, I suppose I should have thought about the fact that, my legs being longer and without having a man in front of me to force me to chop my stride, it would be natural for me to outpace my comrades. All I can say is that it was only my third battle, and the first where I was in this position of being in front of an attack. Consequently, I tried to reduce my speed as smoothly as I could, but I was not very successful, although I did think to bring my shield back into the proper position. Perhaps it was not all bad, because my sudden change in speed threw off the Marcomanni directly in my path, causing him to swing his axe in a massive overhand blow designed to split either my shield or me in half, only to bite nothing but the empty space between us. As is natural, he had put his entire body into the blow, prepared for the resistance of wood, iron, or flesh, but when that did not happen, his own momentum caused him to stumble a half-step forward, bent at the waist as he tried to regain his balance. His scream as my sword point thrust into his body, just above the top of his small round shield into the space between his collarbone and top of his shoulder was drowned out by the terrific sound of my comrades to my left and farther away to my right with the Second Century slamming into the Marcomanni. In the short period of time between when we had launched our javelins and at this moment when we collided with what I suppose would be called the left flank of the Marcomanni, a fair number of the warriors arrayed along that edge had turned to face us, so the surprise was not complete. However, even from my limited vantage point, I could see that the Marcomanni who were now alert to this new danger only numbered perhaps three or four deep into the mass of warriors pressing our comrades of the 8th. Just beyond the fourth warrior, because of my height, I could see that the attention of those just beyond this thin line showed no sign of being aware of us. I say this because as I pieced it together later, that is the only reason I can think of for doing what still ranks as perhaps the most idiotic thing I have ever done in battle.

With my first foe dispatched, and now that I had regained my balance and stride, I barely paused as I leaped his body, which was still in the process of toppling to the ground. While I can run faster than most men, at least once I get up to full speed, I cannot leap as far or as high as most of my comrades. I was forced to learn this fact the hard way, losing some money in the process, when we would get bored in winter camp and come up with impromptu games. Because I had yet to learn this, I did not hesitate in leaving my feet, using my momentum to gain what height I could to come crashing down, using my shield to smash into the Marcomanni who had just become part of the front rank, meeting him before he could take a step forward. The force generated by the combination of my bulk and coming from the high ground, so to speak, was such that when my shield met his, despite the fact that he had moved his to successfully block my own blow, he went flying backward, completely leaving his feet to collide with the man behind him. This Marcomanni was either unable or unprepared to catch his comrade, so that both of them lost their feet, tumbling to the ground in a tangled heap of limbs, shields, and weapons. Because we are trained and encouraged to take advantage of every mistake or lapse that we can, I did not hesitate in taking another step forward, thrusting down with most of my strength, once, then twice, at least ending the squirming of my second and third kill in as many heartbeats.

"Pullus! Pullus! Fall back!"

Although I would later claim, with as much wide-eyed sincerity as I could muster, that I did not hear the call of one of my comrades; I believe it was a big, burly veteran, normally in the Third Section, nicknamed Bovinus because he was always chewing on a blade of grass or stick, I think enough time has passed to admit that I did, in fact, hear him. And, the moment he called out, I recognized the danger I was in now that I had penetrated so deeply into the Marcomanni flank. In my defense, I will make the claim that the fault was not all mine because, by rights, the man behind me should have followed me, if only to gain contact and grab my harness. If he had done so, and the man behind him had done the same, make no mistake, I still would have been in peril, just not as much. Nevertheless, instead of keeping my shield up and taking a couple of steps backward, when I saw the warrior I planned on making my fourth kill hesitate as he tried to step over the two corpses still entangled in a final embrace, instead, I pressed ahead. Before I could reach this Marcomanni, I sensed a flash of movement to my right, and either because I was lucky, or the gods had chosen to bestow their favor on me, at least for this fight, I froze in mid-stride. Thrusting itself into my vision, albeit in a blur, came the head of a spear, cutting into the space I would have been in if I had not hesitated.

Turning my head slightly, I saw a Marcomanni that could not have been much older than I was, his face still covered with a light, golden down, his face screwed up in a grimace of hatred and fear. He was not carrying a shield – his only defensive weapon his spear – and he was gripping it so tightly that, in another moment of clarity, I actually saw that his fingers were white as bone. Wearing a cuirass of boiled leather, he was not even wearing a helmet, and his hair was not bound up in the knot of the blooded warrior, but held loosely by something so it would not get in his way. That is the only reason I can think of for what I did. Knocking his spear aside with ease, I unleashed a slicing blow, aimed for his head, and I saw his eyes close in preparation for his death. But with a twist of my wrist, instead of the sharpened edge slicing into his skull, the flat of my blade smashed into the side of his head, dropping him like a slaughtered pig, the boy collapsing so quickly it looked like somehow every one of his bones had suddenly disappeared and no longer supported him. I would never, and I have not so far, do that again, if only because I have seen men who did the same thing snap their blades in half. The real reason, however, is that whatever soft spot I carried as a teenager has long since been obliterated, and if a man stands against me, I will do everything in my power to kill him. I do not know whatever happened to that boy; I do not remember seeing him among the dead or wounded, so perhaps he escaped and is alive today. In that moment, he no longer concerned me, because in the fraction of time that I had responded to this attack, more Marcomanni were turning their attention to this Roman idiot who thought he was invincible and left the security of his formation.

Working much like a pack of wolves, I had been surrounded by enemy warriors and cut off from the rest of my Century, as they formed a circle around me that was just outside the reach of my sword, which I swung first one way, then spinning about, another to keep them at bay.

"Hold on, Pullus! We're coming for you!"

Even through the noise and the shouted taunts and curses of the Marcomanni around me, I recognized the voice of Corvinus. I understand that I should have felt some relief at hearing his words, knowing that he had seen I was in trouble, but it had the opposite effect. Instead, I felt ashamed that I had put myself in a position where I needed help. I believe this was what provided the spark that lit the fire in my belly, but for the first time, I not only allowed the fire to take hold, I accelerated it and fanned the flames. Somehow, I understood that the key to my survival at that moment was to tap into that divine madness of which I spoke earlier, the one that killed Spartacus, and that I had gotten a hint that I could control, with Maxentius. One of the profound fears of my life, since I was ten years old and first experienced this phenomenon was that I could neither control nor predict when it would come, but that day against the Marcomanni was the first of what has been several times where I consciously unleashed the beast that lies within me. Whirling about, I suddenly changed my facing and the direction of my attack, taking a quick step towards the Marcomanni who had been on my shield side, but even as he reacted, I was changing my own focus, shifting back to the man I had originally been facing. Even as I was moving, my mind was fanning the flames of my rage as I thought of all that I had learned about what happened to my father, and the position in which I had found myself through no fault of my own. As I had hoped, seeing me move against one of his comrades, my original target had relaxed his guard, not much, but it was enough for my purposes, as he dropped his shield just a fraction. Honestly, I did not really see the results of my hard, overhand thrust because my head was turning back to the man I had feinted, but I felt the momentary shudder all the way up my arm as the point of my sword came into contact with the warrior, followed instantly by a grating sensation that told me I had hit bone. Simultaneously, I twisted my wrist, both to free it from the bone and to do more damage, and shot my shield out, aiming the boss for the second Marcomanni. Normally, we try to strike the torso or head of our foes with our shield, but I altered my aim slightly, turning the shield outward and pointing it to the spot where I hoped his right elbow would be. My purpose was both to block the oncoming blow from the Marcomanni's own sword; as is usual, his attack originated above his head, with his elbow sticking out parallel to the ground, and to ensure that his first attempt to split me was his last. His arm was just reaching full extension when the boss of my shield smashed into his elbow and, through the noise of the battle, I heard the crunching sound of his joint being shattered. He let out a scream, and the sword went flying off above our heads, tumbling end over end, and I was already moving.

Spinning on the ball of one foot, I turned my body so that I was quickly facing in the exactly opposite direction from where the warrior with the shattered arm had already staggered away. Inside me, I felt the molten core of my rage continuing to build, but unlike with Spartacus, I remember everything from that day.

Before I could set myself, my eye barely registered a brownish-gray blur hurtling toward me, and although I was able to move my shield across my body to partially deflect it with the outer edge, it felt as if an invisible giant punched me, well below my ribs and low on my right side. In almost the same instant that I felt the impact, I experienced what I say, only slightly tongue in cheek, was a stabbing pain in the same spot. Although I did not look down, I could see the brown shaft of the spear, looking as if it was sprouting out of my body, and I was just vaguely aware that right next to the *segmentata* was what looked like half the length of the blade of the spear, telling me that it was not terribly deep inside my body. I may have kept my eyes on my opponent, but that did not stop an explosive exhalation that was part gasp, part curse burst past my lips. The only way I can describe it is to ask you to imagine someone suddenly touching you with a burning oil lamp, but somehow they manage to push the flame of the lamp inside your body. However, I believe there were two factors at play that allowed me to keep my head, as my right arm moved upward with my blade, except instead of aiming at the warrior who even then was preparing to twist the spear in the exact same way we do, my target was the spear shaft. My fit of rage gave me the strength to slice through the wrist-thick ash shaft as if it were no more than a small branch on a shrub, thereby preventing him from causing me further damage, although the instant of contact sent a fresh jolt of agony through my vitals. Nevertheless, I am sure it was the fact that this was not the first time I had suffered a serious wound, even if it had been seven years before, which enabled me to keep my head and stay focused on the press of men trying to kill me. While it was true that the Marcomanni who stabbed me was essentially left holding a stick, he still posed a danger, as he quickly dropped it and then made as if to grab at the stub of the spear still protruding from my body, since I had not had time to try and withdraw it myself. Trying to keep his shield up to provide protection, his now-free hand snaked out suddenly, the hand open in a clear attempt to grasp the spear, but like every other Marcomanni around me at that moment, he seemed to moving much slower than I was doing. In less time than it takes to blink, he was suddenly left with a stump, his hand and about half of his forearm lying at his feet, while the remainder of his arm sprayed bright red fluid in an arc that I felt splatter across my face. Oddly enough, he did not scream, but just stood there, gaping down at his now-severed appendage, making no attempt to stem the gush of blood that, even in the remaining fraction of time I was paying attention to him, pulsed more weakly with every beat of his heart, losing distance and force with each one. The spectacle was just what I needed because it arrested the attention of every man around us long enough that, still holding my sword, I reached down and, with a tightly clenched jaw, pulled the spear free. Doing so created a brief flash of even greater pain, followed by a sensation of, if not relief, at least a duller, throbbing ache, but I do not believe the discarded spear had hit the ground before I was moving again.

Recalling the maxim that a great warrior never repeats the same maneuver twice, instead of spinning about again, I let out a bellow as I lunged, my sword now back to the first position, at a Marcomanni that I judged to be the biggest threat. He was not in the same league as a Vergorix in terms of dress, but he was clearly a member of their nobility, clad completely in armor, with a helmet that swept up into a cone, except with a protuberant knob that angled downward a bit, making the helmet look a little like a drooping flower. Instead of a blossom, the knob was decorated with a snarling wolf's head, while the armor covering his body was mail, but of a clearly high quality and, if not new, then extremely well cared-for because it gleamed in the dappled sunlight. His shield was one that, up to that point, I had seen but never had to face, a very elongated oval, but with two round notches, one on the bottom and one on the top. It was sheathed in what looked like copper, but like his mail, was polished to a high sheen, with the same snarling wolf's head etched in it in such a way that the boss appeared to be clutched by its jaws. Even more uncommonly, he was wearing greaves and matching manicae, leaving very little bare skin. As I mentioned, I had seen the shield before, but the men I had seen carrying it were all armed with spears, and used the notch to rest their spears in when they locked their shields together. This Marcomanni was using a sword, but unlike the long Gallic sword with the rounded tip, this one was shorter and slightly curved, coming to a double-edged point, telling me that it was both a slashing and a stabbing weapon. As I would come to learn, this is a sword more favored by men of Thrace and parts of Dacia, but this Marcomanni not only had adopted it as his own, he was clearly highly skilled with it. Meeting my charge, we crashed together, shield to shield and, for an instant, we were motionless, each testing the other. Then I lowered my hips and bent my knees a bit, paused for an eyeblink, then uncoiled myself. My hope was to throw him backward so violently that he stumbled, but while he did reel back a step, he recovered quickly, dropping his shield to block my thrust from the first position. While he caught my sword cleanly, I felt it penetrate the shield at least one or two inches, and he showed he was no mean foe when, instead of trying to withdraw his shield cleanly, he gave a hard downward shove angling across his body, trying to trap my blade by creating friction and thereby yank it out of my hand. It would have worked on someone else, but seeing his shield move downward, I instantly understood what he was trying to do and gave a mighty tug of my own, my grasp of the sword helped by the Vinician grip. This is the moment when that unusual grip, taught to my Avus, is superior to the conventional one because the Marcomanni's violent movement would have put extraordinary pressure on my thumb, which is the weakest part of the hand. But with my fingers wrapped over my thumb, my sword was not going anywhere, so when I resisted by jerking backward with my sword arm, he was not prepared for it, nor was he prepared for my own counter. Unfortunately for me, despite the fact that my move forced him to shift his feet to avoid falling forward right into the metal boss of my shield, he did so in a way that it did not give me the opening I sought. Worse yet, his own blade flashed forward, in the same kind of straightforward, stabbing attack that we Romans are famous for, but one I had never seen performed by a German. Striking like a serpent, the point jabbed directly for my throat, except I brought up my shield so that his blade skipped off the upper edge, making it flash by my left ear so closely that I felt the disturbed air, like an invisible woman softly blew a puff of breath on my cheek. Just as his blade shot by, I managed to recover my own, but it did not come back to its home for more than the time it took for me to aim another thrust, this time copying his own, yet coming from the high second position, hoping to come in above his shield. Once more, I was thwarted, but even before a feeling of frustration could blossom, I was forced on the defensive when my foe unleashed another thrusting attack, this time coming at my midsection.

I would make the argument that the task of trying to describe an action that is taking place within the span of a half-dozen heartbeats is one beyond even Cicero, who still ranks as the greatest of our time in his descriptive ability. Being frank, my fear, dear reader, is that I fail in conveying accurately events that, while I remember them move for move, happened in less time than it takes my pen to scribble the words. But because this battle proved to be a pivotal moment in my life, I will endeavor to explain what was taking place within the confines of my mind, even as this Marcomanni and I were trading blows with equivalent ineffectiveness. This fit of rage that I mentioned, which I had believed I could control and, more importantly, unleash like a dog, at my will, did enable me to see and experience all that was taking place in a way that made it seem as if I was moving at a speed just a bit faster than my enemies. And yet, in this moment, as both of us sought to gain advantage on the other, I was also aware that my time was running short. Perhaps a dozen heartbeats had occurred between the moment I began engaging with the nobleman and when I recognized that I had to do something to break the impasse I was experiencing with this man. Behind me, I could clearly hear my comrades fighting furiously, trying to cut their way through the press of Marcomanni to get to me, but while they were able to keep the other Marcomanni surrounding me occupied at that instant, all it was going to take was one of my comrades falling and giving whoever vanquished him the opportunity to attack me from either side, or, worst of all, directly from behind. Right then, the single line of enemy warriors that were essentially left between me and the rest of the Century had their hands full, but I knew that could not last.

The nobleman's thrust at my midsection was blocked by my shield, but as he recovered his blade, I punched out with it, so that it appeared as if my shield was a stalking beast tracking its prey back to its lair. I cannot say that this was ever a maneuver I had practiced, or even conceived of before that moment, but because of my longer reach and bulk, I essentially trapped his blade between my shield and his own body. And thankfully, like most barbarian tribes, this nobleman did not think to do essentially the same thing and use his shield offensively. Consequently, I had a fraction of time where he had no offensive capacity; the only way he could have extricated his sword was by twisting his body away from my shield, but if he did that his shield would not be wide enough to cover his right side completely. Taking full advantage, I made a hard feint, swinging my sword arm out wide, as if I was trying to get my point around and behind the left side of his shield, while at the same time suddenly recovering with my shield. As I hoped, he reacted to the feint, although it was not a total commitment on his part; I must say that his reflexes were quite good, but he did move his shield to his left perhaps three or four inches. Although I had unpinned his sword arm, it was still extended so that his sword was pointing downward, meaning that it had to travel a greater distance to offer a sweeping parry, which was his only defense against the point of my sword now that I had changed direction. My own blade point shot through the gap, yet even as I felt the sudden jolting impact of my weapon punching through his mail, his blade hit mine, his attempt to block my thrust just an instant too late. Because of the feint I had made, I had not twisted my wrist so that the blade entered into his body parallel to the ground as we are trained so that it would not get caught by the hard cartilage and bone of the ribs and breastbone. However, because my blade was perpendicular to the ground, the nobleman actually caused his wound to be much worse than it would have been when, clearly putting every ounce of his strength in sweeping his blade upward to try and block my thrust, his sword slammed into mine, causing my blade to rise upward, slicing him open from perhaps a hand's width above his navel, all the way up to his breastbone. He was a strong man, because without putting any pressure on it myself, I felt my sword slicing into his breastbone, cutting upward and parting the bone as if I were halving a chicken. Somewhat to my surprise, he did not make much noise; I suppose that he inadvertently severed his windpipe since by the time my sword stopped moving, the upper edge was just under his chin. For what seemed to be a long moment, but I am sure was not, he tottered there as I returned to a defensive position with not just my sword, but all the way up to my forearm covered in his blood, and burned into my mind is the image of his upper abdomen and chest slowly parting as his internal organs now had nothing holding them inside his body. There was a thought that suddenly came into my consciousness from some recess of my mind that remarked in a matter-of-fact way that he looked very much like an animal that was being field dressed, even as he remained upright. I know it could not have been long because I was beginning to turn and he was still standing when I felt a hard jerk on my harness from behind. Wheeling about, I shudder to think how close I came to running Bovinus through because he had been the one to grab me from his normal spot in the second file of the first rank. Frankly, I was surprised at the sight of his face;

not because it was spattered with blood, but normally, it would have been Asinius. That was when I remembered that I had been switched just a few moments before.

"Get back in your spot, you stupid bastard," he shouted, but I was relieved to see that essentially, I did not really have to move more than a step to the right and back to do as he demanded.

My Century had cut their way through the Marcomanni to reach me, but while I was still ready to continue fighting, Corvinus chose that moment to blow the whistle. Despite myself, knowing that I could not afford to disobey an order once more, I did not move immediately.

"Don't even think about it," Corvinus barked at me while, instead of stepping to his left as he was supposed to, Bovinus, I suppose on some signal from the Pilus Prior, moved to the right, then grabbed my arm.

"You're coming with me to the rear like you were ordered," he growled, but I did not argue, which turned out to be a good thing.

Together, we squeezed our way down the file and, by the time we got to the rear, the killing rage in me had subsided somewhat. At least, until I passed Maxentius, who had been relegated to my accustomed spot, glaring at me with a look that would have been a perfect match for the Marcomanni we were fighting just a couple dozen paces away. By the time we got back in place, however, the anger I felt at Maxentius soon gave way to larger concerns, namely the fact that it was not until then I remembered I was wounded. What reminded me was when Galens came trotting over from his spot, his mouth set in the kind of thin line that I had learned meant that there was some sort of eruption coming. Seeing him approach, I turned my head…and the next thing I remember was looking up at the sky with Galens and Bovinus peering down at me.

"Pluto's balls." The angry look that had been on Galens' face seemed to have gone elsewhere, and I noted with some curiosity that, for some reason, he looked relieved. "You scared the *cac* out of me, Pullus."

I remember frowning, trying to think why that might have been. Then, on reflex, I began to try and sit up; that was when I remembered, since it felt like whoever had shoved that hot poker into my side had come back.

"*Medici!*" Galens bellowed, while Bovinus bent down and examined me as best he could with the *segmentata* in the way.

Once more, I tried to sit up, but although I made it into a sitting position, the world around me began to spin so quickly that, without thinking, I reached down and clutched great handfuls of ground as if that would stop me from sliding off the earth.

"Lie back down, idiot," Galens muttered and, while I did as he said, I also watched him as he looked around, searching for a *medici*.

"Pullus, we're going to have to get you out of this thing, and I think we should do it now before the *medici* get here so they don't have to waste their time."

I was surprised, not because of what was said, but who said it, and I turned to see Asinius squatting next to me instead of Bovinus.

"When did you get here?" I asked, and I think the loss of blood was a cause of my confusion.

Asinius had remained in the last rank, which now that the first rank had been relieved, was the penultimate one from the rear, which meant that he was out of formation. For some reason, that worried me a great deal; it was one thing for me to get myself in trouble, but I wanted no part of one of my comrades falling afoul of regulations because of me.

"I told him to switch with Bovinus," Galens said, even as he was waving his arms at what I assumed was a *medici*.

Meanwhile, Asinius had not waited for me to get an explanation and, while I was very groggy, I did realize that Galens was not just doing me a favor by having one of my tent section stay with me; Asinius was one of those veterans with a *segmentata*, and his fingers were swift and sure as he undid the series of straps and buckles. Once the front was loosened, he looked down at me, his face impassive.

"Ready for this?"

He did not need to expand, but while a part of me wanted to scream that no, I was not ready for him to make me sit up so that he could undo the back straps, I merely nodded. Grunting with the effort, he pulled me upright and, despite my best intentions, I felt a groan escape from me as the invisible man started twisting the hot poker.

"I know it hurts," he said softly, "but we have to get it off."

Frankly, I was too dizzy and hurting too badly to make a comment one way or another, but finally the straps on both sides were undone. I am not sure what I was expecting, but it certainly was not the sudden spasm of agony that accompanied his quick but smooth movement in pulling off the *segmentata*. Suddenly, I was bathed in sweat, my tunic becoming soaked so quickly that if I had told someone that I had just jumped into a pool of water, I do not believe they would have doubted me. Determined not to make any more sound, I had begun clenching my teeth until I felt my jaw muscles seize up, actually going into spasms. Oddly enough, that actually helped take my mind off the pain in my side, but before I could dwell on my predicament any longer, the *medici* assigned to our Cohort showed up.

"About fucking time," Galens growled at him, but from the way he reacted, this was not the first time he had heard something like that.

"I apologize, Optio," he said with a tone that made it clear he was doing no such thing. "But as you can see, we have quite a bit of business today." He had already knelt down and gave me what I suppose was a smile. "Let's take a look."

Without waiting for my consent, or a comment, he lifted my tunic, and although I saw him do it slowly, it still caused me to stiffen from the sharp pain as the blood-soaked wool pulled away from the skin. I could tell just from how it felt that much of the blood had dried, except that when he pulled the tunic free, a fresh spate of it started. Although I did not really want to, I found myself craning my neck as I tried to look at my side. The moment I saw it, I wish I had not, and I dropped my head back. I distinctly recall that this was the first instant where I felt real fear, that I realized that this was not a trivial matter. The gash was perhaps five inches long, starting about midway between my front and back, then extending, still under the ribcage until it was more or less in line with my right nipple, albeit more than a foot below. I could feel the warmth of this fresh blood flowing down my side, but for a moment, the *medici* seemed content to watch me bleed to death, and I remember looking to Asinius in a mute appeal.

He caught my gaze, but gave me what I knew to be his smile. "It's all right, Pullus. He's just letting whatever blood is in there drain out. You don't want them to stitch you up without that blood getting out. That will end up killing you."

"He's right, Gregarius," the *medici* agreed and, even as he said this, I felt the flow come to almost a complete stop. "But even more important is what I need to do next." Then, he bent over, lowering his head so that for a brief, horrifying instant, I thought he was going to do something like lick the blood, or worse, kiss the wound, as all sorts of wild thoughts about pagan practices went through my mind. But, of course, he did no such thing. What he did do was to inhale deeply, not once but several times, as if smelling for something, which was exactly what he was doing.

"I don't smell *cac*," he said finally, and I had the queerest sensation of suddenly understanding what he was doing and being immensely relieved at the exact same time.

I saw Asinius visibly relax; Galens had left by this point, and I heard shouts that told me someone else had fallen, and he had resumed his duties. Thinking about it now, I suppose it is very strange to relate all this as if it was happening in the hospital tent in camp, rather than with a ferocious fight raging just a couple dozen paces away, but this is not unusual, and is, in fact, a very common scene.

"Still, you need to be seen by the doctor. I can stop the bleeding and bandage you up, but he needs to examine you," he finished.

He then proceeded to do that very thing and, in doing so, my body had finally had enough and I passed out.

Fortunately for not just my Century, or my Cohort, the other Pili Priores behind the baggage train did not tarry and, very quickly, what had been a thin line of just three Centuries was extended almost all the way to the base of the ridge. In perhaps a sixth of a watch, what had been an ambush that had a decent chance of success – it was learned that it was in fact their goal to cut through our lines to reach Drusus – turned into what I would imagine could be in one of the manuals that so many couch generals love to read. Slowly but inexorably, we pushed our way deeper into the left flank of the Marcomanni force, until the little end of our Century got within just a few paces of the far right end of the rest of the Legion. The best way to describe it is that, if looking from above, we would have formed the letter "L," with the Cohorts behind the baggage train forming the shorter part. All the Cohorts except for the Ninth, that is, whose men stood in exactly the same spot the whole battle, as if they were spectators at an arena watching one of the mock battles that are put on to entertain the people. Overall, the other two Legions suffered the brunt of the casualties, while the Cohorts in front of the baggage train; the First, Second, Fifth, Seventh, and Tenth took more losses than those Cohorts behind did. In my Century, we had two men killed and four wounded; one of those, of course, was me. The same cannot be said for the other two Legions, and the 14th, in particular, suffered heavy losses. From the accounts that I heard from other wounded men while I was in the hospital, the Cohort immediately behind Drusus and the command group in the column was bloodied particularly badly. Very quickly, in the aftermath, two things became apparent; the Marcomanni attack had as its aim the slaying of Drusus, and if it had not been for that Cohort – I believe it was the Sixth of the

14th – they would have succeeded. It probably comes as no surprise when I relate that we did not march any farther that day, actually making camp to the immediate north, or rear of where our column was when the attack started. I was too inexperienced to recognize that as a sign that our commander had been badly shaken, but when all things were considered, it is completely understandable. Perhaps the best news was that we had savaged the Marcomanni; they left almost three thousand dead behind, and my comrades were still looting the bodies well into the night, working by lamplight. I was unaware of this; by nightfall, I had passed out for the second time and would actually be unconscious until late into the next day. The reason for this was fairly straightforward; when the doctor came to examine me, he determined that a piece of my tunic had been thrust into my body by the point of the spear. This meant that he had to fish out the scrap of fabric, but before he could do so, he had to widen what was already, to me anyway, a gaping wound.

I had been awake when I was carried by a plank that is used as a stretcher by the *medici* to the makeshift field hospital, which was nothing more than a spot where some of the baggage train had been pulled out to form a rough semi-circular pocket, with the banks of the river on one side, and the wagons on the other.

There I joined what looked to be more than a hundred other men, although that number would climb, but honestly, I do not recall much after I had been set down on the ground, the bearers being as gentle as they could. Still, it was painful enough that I think I must have passed out yet again because my next memory is of being put back on a plank. This time, however, I was being carried into the actual hospital tent, which was close to full. I actually heard it before I saw the tent; when that many men are moaning in pain, or calling out for some relief for their suffering, usually in the form of poppy syrup, it is easy to locate. I was placed on a cot, where a clerk attached to the *medici* was waiting to take my name and who I belonged to, but while I gave him the information readily enough, it was difficult to concentrate, hearing so much suffering.

Despite my best efforts, whenever I was moved, a groan or gasp of pain invariably escaped me, but as long as I was motionless, it was bearable. It was impossible for me to fathom how much agony some of my comrades must have been in, judging by their cries. As I would come to learn, this is the normal after-battle scene in the hospital tent, but since it was my first experience, I was sure that what I was hearing was more horrific than normal. The bandage the *medici* had applied on the battlefield was now stained dark, which concerned me a bit, but none of the attendants in the tent seemed alarmed. Of course, they were also extremely busy, so it was hard not to be even more anxious than I already was. What I remember most vividly was the realization coming to me that I could actually die.

Finally, I was attended to by the physician, which was when I learned that, although my bowel had not been punctured; something he confirmed when he repeated the same process as the first *medici* had performed, that was where the good news ended. I freely admit that when he began examining my tunic, bringing the cloth back together from where it had been cut asunder by the spear as it entered my body, I was completely

253

flummoxed as to why he was doing so. But just a few heartbeats later, I wish I had remained ignorant.

"Gregarius, I believe there is part of your tunic that was driven into your body by the enemy weapon. What was it that cut you?" he asked, and nodded when I told him it was a spear. "As I thought. A fair number of these savages used barbed spear points and, when they do get lucky and stick one of our boys, it is very common that it takes with it some part of the clothing when it is thrust into your body."

"What does that mean?" I asked, but I knew the answer.

At least, I knew one possible answer. If the piece of fabric was not retrieved from my body, I would die one of the most agonizing deaths imaginable, as for reasons that I do not understand but know are true, your body rots from within. To that point, I had not seen death from putrefaction, but the gods know I had heard more than enough tales told by veterans about it.

"It means that in order for you to survive, I have to get it out," he replied, oblivious to my inner musings.

"You're positive that there's some part of my tunic in there?" I asked, but he hesitated for a moment before he answered.

"No," he admitted. "I don't know for sure, but I've seen enough wounds like this to know that the chances are very high that this is the case."

"So you don't know for sure," I pounced on this slender reed. "Which means you could kill me looking for something that's not there!"

For this was another kind of tale I had heard as well, of men who succumbed not to the wound, but to the attempted cure. I was, and am no physician, but I knew that rummaging around a man's insides is very likely to be bad for his health.

"Gregarius, I am well aware that there are risks in what I know I need to do. But, the alternative," he reminded me gently, "is worse."

Frankly, at that moment, I did not see it that way.

"Why can't you wait to see?" I suggested. "If I don't get sick, then there's no need to stick your hands inside my body, is there?"

He sighed, and I could tell that I was trying his patience; I did not care in the slightest.

"Because if we do wait, and the wound does corrupt, you will get very sick, very quickly," he explained. "So much so that you'll be too weak to survive what I would have to do. Which," he finished, "is why it needs to be done now."

Even in my weakened state, I tried to force myself to think quickly, but I could not come up with an argument that would defeat his, so I finally muttered, "Fine. Go ahead and cut away."

"You're making the right decision," he assured me, then stood and beckoned to an attendant.

I sank back and consoled myself with the idea that at least they could give me some of the poppy syrup that men were crying out for before he started carving me up.

That belief only lasted long enough for him to tell the attendant when the man reached him, "Get my tools. You'll need to assist me to hold him down."

"Should I get some poppy syrup first?" I asked, and even I could hear the anxiety, but I did not care.

He looked down at me, then shook his head gravely.

"I'm afraid that for the type of work I'm about to do, poppy syrup is likely to do more harm than good because it will alter your breathing."

I did not understand why this was so, and I said as much. The physician had turned away, arranging the tools that the attendant had brought on the tray, so it was the attendant who supplied the answer, but starting with a question of his own.

"Can you take a deep breath?" he asked me.

I started to, but before my lungs were half-filled, the agony became unbearable, so overwhelming that when my eyes filled with tears from the pain, I was not even ashamed.

"That's why we can't give you poppy syrup," he explained. "Something in the syrup retards your breathing, and you're having problems already. If we were to give you the syrup, it's true you wouldn't feel it, but that would be because you would be dead."

When it was explained to me in this manner, it made sense. Then, he produced a round, leather-wrapped piece of wood, motioning to me to open my mouth.

"This is the best I can do to help with the pain," he told me as I clamped down onto the wood, feeling the grooves and scars from gods only know how many teeth.

Despite my intentions, I still could not keep my eyes from the physician, and I felt my eyes go wide as he turned from the tray holding what was clearly a razor-sharp small knife, the edge of it picking up the light. He started to bend down over me, but just before he did, he stopped.

Seeming to notice for the first time my size and musculature, he stopped and looked about, finding someone out of my vision and calling out, "Come help us here!"

A new face appeared above me and, with a start, I recognized that it was Lysander, our clerk, who doubled duty as an attendant after battles. Seeing a familiar face was comforting, but he did not look down at me, so I do not think he knew who it was at first. I could not say anything because of the gag, but the first attendant had switched positions so that he was on one side, and Lysander the other. Fortunately, or at least so I thought, my vision was blocked from what the doctor was about to do.

An instant before I felt the knife cutting further into my flesh, Lysander looked down and I heard him gasp, "Pluto's cock! Titus!"

That is the last I remember until the next day.

Late the next afternoon, Asinius came to visit me, along with Tuditanus, who had emerged unscathed. Frankly, I was still in quite a bit of pain, partially due to the wound, but I also think in large part to how tightly the bandage was wrapped around my midsection. That gave me a good reason not to try to sit up when they arrived, the pair grabbing a couple of stools in the process.

Before Asinius could say anything, I asked him, "How angry are the Pilus Prior and Optio at me?"

"At first, very," Asinius admitted, then gave me a reassuring smile, "but I think they've decided you got your punishment by ending up in here."

"That's true enough," I said ruefully. "I suppose I just got carried away."

"Again," Asinius pointed out helpfully. "Except this time, you're not getting any gold arm rings or torq out of it."

"I only got one ring out of the last time," I protested. "I had to give the rest away."

"That's as it should be," Asinius replied, but before I could think of something to say to that, he moved on. "We're going to be here for at least two more days after this one."

That was a bit unusual; it is more customary for the army to pause one day after battle before moving on, at least if it is on the march somewhere. Before I could ask, Asinius supplied the answer.

"Drusus has ordered that we're to take the spoils of this last battle and make a monument on the banks of the river," he explained. "So the *praefecti* are out designing and making the framework that will be underneath it all."

I was not sure I understood, and said as much.

"Spoils? What spoils? All I saw were a bunch of dead bodies. And all their weapons and shields and such."

"That's what's going to be used," but I suppose he saw the look of horror on my face because he hurried on, "the weapons and shields, at least. Not the bodies."

"That's a relief." I almost laughed, but caught myself in time; even taking a deep breath was excruciating. "I'd hate to have to be on the work detail for that if it was going to be their corpses."

"What are you complaining about?" Tuditanus spoke up for the first time. "You're not going to be on any work details for, I don't know, but at least a month."

Truthfully, I had not thought that far ahead, but I will say that there is a side to every Gregarius, no matter who their ancestors are, that relish the thought of getting out of some of the more onerous or dull tasks.

"You know, you're right," I told him as I made a show of stretching out on my cot. If I could have lifted them, I would have put my hands under my head just to show how relaxing it was lying there. "But don't worry; I'll be sure and think of you as I lie here, catching up on my rest."

"Lucky bastard," Tuditanus muttered.

Then, the absurdity of what he had just said, the idea that my way of being lucky was to have a hole in my side hit him, then me, almost at the same moment. Before I could stop myself, I let out a chuckle that immediately turned into a groan. Tuditanus tried to look regretful, but from my point of view, he did a poor job of it.

"You won't think you're so lucky when you're bouncing around in that wagon," Asinius interjected. He always had a knack for that kind of thing, as he continued, "In fact, I bet you don't last a week before you're begging to get out of that damn thing and march with us."

Like all *Tiros*, Tuditanus and I had been given an earful from veterans about the horrors that awaited a wounded Legionary, not just in the hospital at the hands of the *medici*, but from the jolting one took when the army moved and you were consigned to the wagons.

"So did the butcher at least get whatever was in you out?" Tuditanus asked.

His question was completely understandable, but the truth was that, at that moment, I had no idea; I had been awake for perhaps a watch, but the orderlies and the *medici* had still been so busy with other patients that nobody had bothered to inform me.

"I don't know," I replied anxiously, suddenly bathed in a fresh spate of sweat as my thoughts went in a dark direction. "I mean, I *think* they did, just from the way I feel. He did tell me that if they didn't get it out, I'd get sick very quickly, but I don't feel feverish or anything."

Nevertheless, I began twisting my head about, looking for someone I could ask, hoping that Lysander was still pulling medical duties, but I did not see him. I asked Asinius, who informed me that the clerk was back with the Cohort.

Standing up, he said, "I'll go find someone."

As he went looking for a man who could tell me whether I was facing a lingering death, Tuditanus and I made desultory conversation about the fight, but the fact is my mind was elsewhere. Finally, Asinius returned, with the doctor who had cut me open and, as they approached, I must say that I had very mixed feelings at seeing him. While on the one hand I was thankful for what he had done; provided, of course, that he had actually accomplished what he set out to do, the fact remained that he had cut me open. But then, once he got close enough to see his face in the light provided by the drawn-up sides of the tent that allowed the daylight to come streaming into the interior, I saw that he looked exhausted, and it struck me that in all likelihood he had not gotten any sleep at all.

Consequently, I managed to keep a respectful tone as I asked, "Did you get everything out of me?"

I clearly heard the tremor in my own voice and, when he did not immediately answer, it suddenly felt as if my heart had dropped down to where my wound was.

Finally, he told me, "As far as I could tell, yes, we got not one, but two torn pieces of your tunic out of you."

I made no attempt to hide my relief, and it did me good to see that Asinius and Tuditanus looked almost as pleased as I felt.

"You're still not completely out of danger," he warned me, although I confess I was not really listening. "We're going to be changing bandages every day, but as long as the pus remains clear, or even just a bit milky, then you should be fine. Although," he thought to add, "you're going to have some stiffness in your side that you'll have to get accustomed to."

Sure that I would have no trouble with this, I thanked the doctor, but before he left, I did think to ask, "How long do I have to be in the wagons?"

He gave a laugh that, to my ears at least, did not seem to hold much humor.

"Ah," he replied lightly, "another Gregarius who doesn't want to ride in the wagons. Well, I can't say that I blame you. It does get quite bumpy. That's one reason we bind your wounds so tightly, so that everything we've sewn together holds up from the bouncing around." He considered for a moment, looking me up and down before finishing. "You're certainly one of the biggest and strongest patients I've had, so you'll probably heal more quickly than most men. I'd say only two weeks."

"Two *weeks*?" I gasped. "I can't stay in the wagons for two weeks."

"You can and you will if that is what I order," he shot back sternly, all friendliness gone from his tone or face. "Or do I have to get your Centurion involved?"

Oh, he knew what to say, and I hastily assured him that it was not necessary. Once he departed, I lay there, as Asinius and Tuditanus joined my glum silence.

At last, Asinius stood and told me, "I better get back to the section. Is there anything from your pack that you want?"

"You mean, other than keeping someone from stealing what's inside it?" I asked, and I was only half-joking. I had to think for a moment before I shook my head. "No, thank you, though. Just please make sure nothing of mine gets up and walks off."

"It's already locked up in the Cohort wagon," he assured me. "So your gear will be waiting for you to start carrying it again."

Mention of my gear made me think of something else, and I stopped him.

"There is one thing," I told him.

"Oh? What's that?"

"Can you take my *segmentata* to get repaired so that it will be ready when I'm put back on regular duty? Remember they…"

"…Yes, I remember," he reassured me. "They have to match that plate and not just stick you with a standard one or it'll be too small. Believe me, I haven't forgotten."

"Thank you," was all I could think to say, and they left me mulling over the idea of two weeks consigned to a wagon.

The construction of the monument to our victory over the Marcomanni actually took three days longer than had been planned, but only because the weather turned. We had experienced rainstorms before, but this was the first time on this campaign where we had three days of nonstop downpour, turning the entire camp into a river of mud. The water even came flowing into the hospital tent, so that whenever I put my feet down to stand up and relieve myself, which was an ordeal all its own, I was in ankle-deep water. And while I do not know why, the weather took an even greater toll on some of the wounded, although most of those who succumbed were already waging a battle against a corruption of their wound. Still, the section of the tent that Legionaries refer to as Charon's Boat, where those in the last watches or moments of their life are consigned, remained full, instead of emptying out as it normally does in the aftermath of a battle. The only bright spot, at least as far as I was concerned was that I got to eat better than I had all campaign. I remember that at several points of my Avus' account, he would give an example of some of the seemingly small things the Legions of Rome do differently than the armies of other nations, but I do not recall him ever mentioning this one, which I think is extremely important. Men who are wounded, or even are ill, are given extra rations and, much to my surprise, there was more meat in our diet than we got normally. My Avus was one of the few Romans who actually preferred meat over bread, but while I cannot say I go that far, I do like it more than most of my comrades. Add to that my normal prodigious appetite, especially then at seventeen, since I was still growing, and it meant that this was one aspect of hospital life I enjoyed a great deal. By my rough estimate, about a tenth part of those wounded in battle are able to be treated, then sent back to their Centuries the same day. About a quarter of the remainder have to stay in the hospital for two to three days. More than half of the men were gone by the end of the week to the day after the battle, leaving the rest of us behind. During my recovery, I actually became friendly with men, not just from other Centuries or Cohorts, but from other Legions as well. The man on the cot to my right was from the 14th, and was in the Third Century of the Sixth, which was the Cohort that had saved Drusus' bacon. It was from him – I believe his name was Marcellus – that I learned how desperate and bitter a fight it was, and how close the Marcomanni had come to getting to Drusus.

"There wasn't nothing left between him and them but the boys of the third section and the ones from mine," he told me. "Those *cunni* just hacked and chopped their way through the rest of my Century until it was just us left. And then I went down."

He did not have to explain why he did so; he had suffered a really nasty wound that started just above his knee and ran down the side of his leg. Although it was heavily bandaged, I could clearly see the line of blood that had soaked through, all the way to about mid-calf.

"What did you do?" I asked, curious about what a man did when the circumstances were so dire.

"I did the only thing I could do," he replied honestly. "I pulled myself up as tight as a bedbug and got under my shield. I didn't dare peek out, so I had to lay there listening to those bastards as they...."

He had suddenly stopped and, when I glanced over, I saw that there were two shiny trails down his cheeks from where he had been crying at the memory of lying helplessly under his shield and listening to his friends being killed.

Not wanting to shame the man, or to make him go through reliving it just for my sake, I hurriedly asked, "What about Drusus' bodyguards? Weren't they there?"

His first response was to spit onto the ground next to his cot.

"Oh, they were there all right," he agreed. "But as to what they were actually *doing*, well..." he stopped there and just gave a shrug. I don't believe he meant for me to hear as he muttered, "It was almost like somebody had ordered them to stay out of the fight."

Needless to say, I found that extremely unsettling. It seemed that the omens involving this campaign were getting worse every day. Now even the elements were against us, I thought; what hope do we have now?

Chapter 5

Thanks to the bad weather, my time in the wagons as they were moving was actually a week and, even then, because the days of rain had softened the ground, the ride was not as jolting as it could have been. The only time where it was almost unbearable was when the wagon got stuck and had to be rocked out of the mud with the help of whoever happened to be marching behind the baggage train that day. Fortunately, that only happened twice, but it was not only painful, it was difficult to listen to my comrades, even if I did not really know them, shouting in agony at the jolting movement. Speaking frankly, while the ride was rough, that is not what the worst about the wagon was as far as I was concerned. The worst part was the combination of the cramped conditions, accompanied by the smell of sickness, which is a combination of puke, piss, *cac*, and corrupting flesh. However, almost as bad was the knowledge of where we were now headed, which was not along the Albis any longer. The only way I knew that our destination had changed was when I overheard the *medici* talking outside my wagon.

"We're going back to Mogontiacum?"

"Those are the new orders. At least, that's what I heard from Andris."

"Andris?"

"He works in the *praetorium*. He said that we're going back the shortest way possible."

Whoever was talking lowered his voice, making it hard to hear, and I found myself straining to catch what he said next.

"Andris says that the entire *praetorium* is in a panic. He swears he's never seen things this bad before."

"And what is Drusus doing about it?" The other man matched the first one's tone, but I could hear the hope in his voice.

"Nothing," the first *medici* scoffed. "Andris says that he goes into his private quarters as soon as the tent is put up, stays there until the next morning." The first man's tone changed, and it was clear that he was worried. "Have you seen him lately? He looks like he's wasting away and he walks about all hunched over. I don't know what's happened to him, but I don't like the signs I'm seeing."

The pair moved off then, and I heard the buzzing of their conversation continuing, but I could not make out anything else. However, what I had heard was more than enough, although I will say that it gave me much to think about as I bounced along in the wagon.

One thing that the conversation helped explain was why we had resumed our slower progress, although in the moment, I assumed that it was simply because, for whatever reason, the vegetation had thickened along the riverbank. But the truth was that we had turned from the Albis, heading on a southwesterly course that was the shortest route back to the safety of the Rhenus. In doing so, it meant that the column spent a fair amount of time stopped, while the leading Cohorts once more chopped a path through the Black Forest, this time skirting to the south of the mountains we had bypassed from the north side on the way to the Albis. Speaking personally, I did not mind the slower movement, thinking that every moment I spent motionless gave my body time to heal without having to combat the jostling and jolting of the wagon. Perhaps the only positive thing that came from my time were the friendships that I made with the other wounded men; when one spends literally every moment, waking and asleep, with other men, without the distractions of the march and the freedom to move about at the end of the day, the choices for spending that time are limited. The way we were arranged in the wagon was in tiers, slung from the kind of hammock that sailors use to limit the motion from the waves that are inevitable when sailing. There are four tiers, with two rows that leave only a narrow space between us where the *medici* assigned to our wagon moved and operated. I was on the top tier, I suppose because of my size, but although it is the most comfortable, it is also the hardest to get to, and those men with the less serious wounds are consigned there. Being on the bottom tier is the worst spot, in more than one way; this is where the most seriously injured men are put, but it is also the least comfortable.

The man directly across from me was a Gregarius from the Second Cohort of my Legion, a veteran named Glabrio, who was about ten years older than I was. Despite the age difference, I found that he and I shared a similar outlook on things, mainly in the way we tried to find something to laugh about, even under our current circumstances. He had taken a serious wound to the thigh that compromised his ability to walk, let alone march with a load on his back. The man immediately below him I did not care for so much, perhaps because he was from the 14th, but I believe it was more to his constant moaning and groaning and his overall gloomy disposition. Naturally, I had not been the only one to hear the conversation outside the wagon, and this man in particular reminded me of Tubero in his outlook, particularly in what I considered an unseemly desire to see his dire predictions come true.

"Drusus is fucked, and if Drusus is fucked, we're all fucked," he would intone at least once every watch.

I cannot deny that one of the reasons it was so grating, besides the repetition, is that I could not deny that there was a part of me that agreed with the overall sentiment, but hearing it over and over made it even worse.

Finally, I could not take it any longer; while others had importuned him to shut his mouth, it was not until I finally, despite the pain it caused, rolled out of my hammock to stand in the middle of the wagon, holding onto one of the posts to counter the bouncing, and snarled at the man, "If you say that one more fucking time, I am going to make sure that you never get out of this fucking wagon!"

I was gratified to see that, even in my weakened state, he visibly went even paler, recoiling and shrinking back away from me.

"I...I didn't mean nothing by it," he protested. "I was just talking!" The sound of his own voice seemed to give him a moment of courage because he continued, "Besides, I'm just speaking the truth! There's no law against that, even if it's not something you want to hear!"

With my free hand, I reached out and placed it on the bandage that covered the wound high on his left shoulder and, while I did not put any pressure or squeeze in any way, he understandably flinched.

"I've already told you what's going to happen if you keep talking," I told him quietly. "And I don't give a fuck if you think you're just 'speaking the truth'," I mimicked what I thought was the whiny quality to the man's voice, "or not. I'm not going to tell you again."

Without waiting for an answer, I struggled to climb back into my hammock and, by the time I was through, my tunic was damp from the perspiration from the effort. By the time I was settled back in, I felt much like I did after a long, hard march. As I lay back down, I heard a couple of whispers from the other men in the wagon who were conscious, but I ignored them. Once I was back in the most comfortable position, I felt a pair of eyes on me and I turned my head to see Glabrio regarding me, and although he was smiling, there was a nervousness that I believe I saw in his features.

"Remind me," he said this in a joking manner, but I think he was also being at least somewhat serious, "to never make you angry."

Outside of our wagon, the world of the Legions continued apace, back into the rhythm of what had become the standard day's march in this campaign. Actually, that rhythm was even slower than it had been when we were marching to the Albis because, as we discovered, the region to the south of the mountains was riddled with even more bogs and marshes, so that I imagine the line of our march on a map would look like a series of zigs and zags. I will freely admit that there was a part of me that, once I heard from Asinius or Figulus, both of whom came to visit every couple of days at the end of the day's march, was fairly happy that I was missing out on all the filthy mud. More than once they showed up before getting cleaned up, and if the sight of them covered in mud up to the knees was not enough, the smell of that stinking mud was sufficient to not only tell me what I was missing, but to draw the complaints of the other men in the wagon, at least those who were awake when they showed up. By the middle of the second week after the battle, the wagon had lost about half of the original occupants; one man died, but the others had been allowed to return to duty. Obviously I was not one of them, but I had been informed by the doctor that I would be discharged from the wagon three days after the stitches were removed.

"We need to make sure that the stitches did their job and that you don't come bursting apart like a ripe melon," one the *medici* had joked.

I like to think I have a good sense of humor, but frankly, I did not find anything funny about that thought. I had gotten a view of the wound every day when the bandage was changed, and it had taken some getting used to, seeing what had been a gaping hole stitched closed, creating a scar that ran from the middle of my right side, then curving up slightly across my body. Although the original wound had sliced me open to the point that it ended roughly even with my right nipple, the subsequent surgery, as the doctor fished out the scraps of my tunic, had widened it so that it was almost to a spot about three inches above my navel. Despite knowing that it was necessary,

269

I cannot deny that a part of me was reminded me of the Gregarii's belief that a man went into the hospital and came out worse for wear. Once the sutures were removed, I found myself checking the wound frequently, suspiciously staring at it for any sign that it was about to do what the *medici* had joked about. But, while it did stretch, I suppose from the pressure of my insides pushing against the muscles and flesh, it obviously did not happen. However, one thing that I find curious is that, of all the scars I now carry on my body, while most of them slowly turn from an angry pink to a duller shade before finally becoming a white line, this scar, now fourteen years old, is still pink. Nevertheless, those remaining days in the wagon I was so insistent on checking myself by pulling up my tunic that Glabrio could not resist poking fun at me about it.

"Oh-oh, Pullus is checking his scratch; it must be the start of second watch," he would announce, and those men who were able would join in his laughing at me.

Again, normally I did not, nor do I now like being the butt of a joke, but for some reason, I did not mind this very much and I would probably have joined in more if it was still not so painful. While our wagon lost several of the original occupants, it remained filled, as men from other wagons were shifted into ours and a handful of others were consolidated. Finally, the day came when I was allowed to leave the wagon and return to my Century, although I was still exempt from full duty for the next two weeks.

"I'm not going to order this, but I don't think it's a good idea for you to wear your armor for at least another week," the physician told me.

I stared at him with an expression that I suppose might have suggested that he had suddenly sprouted a third eye.

"Not wear my armor?" I asked incredulously. "We're still in the middle of the Black Forest! And you expect me to just march along wearing just my tunic?" I shook my head and finished adamantly, "I might as well stay in the wagon because I'll be coming back to one anyway! If I'm lucky."

"That's why I'm not making it an order," he replied, but suddenly, he did not seem so anxious to look me in the eye. "Besides, I have orders of my own that I must obey, just like you do, Gregarius."

I did not understand the comment, but no matter how hard I tried, he said no more, leaving me both confused and a little apprehensive. Despite this, the overwhelming feelings I experienced were relief and the desire to get back to my comrades in the Century.

Men being sent back to their Centuries from the wagons are released not at the beginning of the day's march, but at the completion of it. This makes sense; it gives the returning man time to rejoin his Century, draw his pack from the Cohort wagon, which is where all wounded and dead men's gear is stored when they are unable to carry it. It also gives the returning man the chance to ease back into the daily routine of his section. Although it might not seem this way, it is a truth that when a man leaves his section and Century, for whatever reason, life goes on. There are incidents that are both funny and sobering, conversations, even jokes that have taken place while he is gone. I do not know why, but a returning man has to accept and endure a period of awkwardness, as both he and his comrades adjust to his presence once again. While I do not know why this is so, what I do know is that the shorter the absence, the less awkward it is and, while I had been gone two weeks, there were men who were gone much longer and consequently had to endure a fair amount of strain.

By the time I had done all the necessary things for a man returning – it seems that there are at least a half-dozen wax tablets that must be signed – my comrades were already arrayed around the fire, finishing the last of the evening meal.

"Pullus!" Metellus was the first to see me approaching. "You lucky bastard! Did you finally feel guilty that you were missing out on all the fun?"

"Something like that," I replied, and I was surprised that the rest of the section had come to their feet, each of them greeting me with varying degrees of warmth.

I believe it was Bassus who, without thinking, gave me a playful shove, wrenching a gasp from me as the sudden movement sent a sharp stab of pain across my midsection.

"Pluto's cock," he exclaimed, his face showing his concern as he reached out to give me an awkward pat. "I didn't mean to hurt you!"

"It's all right." I mumbled this because my jaws were still clenched tightly as I waited for the pain to subside, which it did after a moment.

I saw, out of the corner of my eye, Asinius eyeing me closely, and he was the one who asked, "Are you sure that you're all right to come back?" His tone turned suspicious. "Did you get released by the *medici*? Or is this one of your bright ideas?"

"No," I assured him. "They released me. I'm fine," I insisted. "Just sore."

"Well, let's see it," Dento demanded, and they all crowded around me as I lifted my tunic, even Tubero, who had given the coolest reception to my return.

I admit I felt quite proud when one of my comrades gave a whistle, and the rest competed with each other as they remarked on the livid, pink gash across my stomach.

"I'll say this for you," Bassus laughed, "when you get wounded, you don't fuck about, do you?"

"How did your guts not fall out?" Metellus asked. "And how is it possible your bowels weren't sliced open?"

"I don't really know," I replied honestly, although I had thought about this at length. "The best I can figure out is that it came at an angle," I demonstrated with my hand, trying not to wince again, "like this." I placed my hand flat against my stomach, starting from my right side. "I think it just slid between my skin and my guts, but somehow didn't puncture them."

"I hope you plan to offer a pretty big sacrifice to Fortuna," Asinius said, and I assured him I intended to do that very thing.

"Let's go find Galens to unlock the Cohort wagon," he told me and, without waiting, turned away.

"Wait," I objected. "I haven't eaten yet!"

"You're too late, you big bastard," Bassus told me cheerfully, then laughed as he rubbed his stomach. "And I have to tell you, we've gotten used to not having you around. We haven't eaten this well since before you showed up."

This brought a round of laughing agreement, to which I answered with an obscene gesture of my own and declared, "Well, that's over now. You know that men who are healing from wounds need more food, so you better enjoy this last meal!"

Turning to follow Asinius, I left my comrades shouting insults at my retreating back, while I had the broadest smile on my face that I had worn for some time. It was good to be back.

I retrieved my gear, trying not to show the strain I felt hefting my *furca* on my shoulder, then we went to the *quaestorium* to pick up my *segmentata*, which had been repaired. However, as Asinius had warned me, the *Immunes* in charge of the armory was not willing to let me just have it, not without me handing over some coin.

"We have to keep a set of plates in stock just for you," he told us when we showed up.

"That's a load of *cac*," Asinius retorted. "You specifically told me that as long as you had a plate from his original that it wasn't going to be a problem fixing it!"

"It's not a problem to *fix* it," the *Immunes*, a grizzled, leathery piece of gristle whose head barely reached my shoulder, although he did not seem the least bit intimidated. "But it *is* a problem when one of the plates has to be replaced. We had to start from scratch and forge a whole new plate for this big bast..." Fortunately, he cut himself off, perhaps because I had balled one fist up. "...Gregarius. That means almost one whole ingot, just for him!"

Asinius looked disposed to continue arguing, but I put a hand on his shoulder, telling him wearily, "It's fine. I'll pay." I turned to the *Immunes*. "How much?"

He pursed his lips as if thinking about it, but I was sure that if he was thinking, it was only trying to calculate how much he could get away with, without me beating him to a pulp.

"No more than ten sesterces should cover it," he said.

"Ten!" Asinius and I exclaimed together. Before I could say anything more, Asinius leaned towards the man, and I admit I was somewhat chagrined to see that the *Immunes* seemed to be more intimidated by my Sergeant than me. "You're a fucking thief, Manius! There's no way an ingot of iron costs ten sesterces!"

"What about the extra labor involved?" Manius retorted.

"That's what you get paid extra for," Asinius shot back.

"For normal work," Manius argued, but I saw his eyes dart over to where some of his comrades were standing.

I leaned over and whispered to Asinius, "He plans to keep whatever he gets from us for himself. Did you see him looking over his shoulder at the others to see if they heard?"

Asinius gave no overt sign that he had heard, but I realized he had when his voice raised. "So who actually did the work, Manius? I think that if we're going to have to pay, it should at least go to the man who actually did the job."

We were rewarded by a look of panic on the face of the *Immunes* who, shooting one last glance over at the other armorers, said quickly, "Let's make it five sesterces, and that just covers the cost of the ingot."

"Which you aren't going to report," Asinius pointed out, and I saw Manius flush. Turning to me with a questioning look, I just gave him a nod. "But we'll pay up."

Then he turned to me and told me to pay Manius; that was when I flushed with embarrassment because I did not have the coin on me.

"Then you're not getting that *segmentata*," Manius retorted, pulling it back across the table that served as a counter for the armorers.

I opened my mouth to protest, but Asinius beat me to it, although I was not prepared at all for what he told Manius.

"Do you know who this is?" he asked Manius, but quietly enough that the others could not hear.

"I know he's about the biggest Gregarius we have in the Legion," Manius replied.

"This is Titus Porcinianus Pullus," Asinius told him.

I am not sure exactly what reaction I was expecting; I imagine that I thought it would be from my Avus' name, but that was not the part that triggered his reaction.

"Wait." He suddenly turned to examine me more closely. "This is Pilus Prior Porcinus' son? The one who...."

"That's the one," Asinius cut him off, but I was curious what he was going to say.

The change in Manius' behavior could not have been more dramatic, and he handed me the *segmentata*, then waved his hand.

"You don't owe a brass *obol*, Pullus," he assured me. "Now that I know who you are, if you ever need anything," he stared hard at me, "and I mean *anything*, you come see old Manius."

Confused and pleased in equal measure, I thanked him, but when I reached to take the armor, I could not stop a gasp escaping from my lips. Between my *furca* and the *segmentata*, it felt as if the scar was tearing apart, although it was not. This was a feeling to which I had to become accustomed, as the tissue that had formed to close the wound, having lost the normal elasticity of skin, had to be pulled and stretched apart. Even as it happened, I recalled reading in my Avus' account of this very phenomenon, but in that moment, I was sure that my scar had torn open. Not wanting to drop my load and show weakness, I grit my teeth, mumbled a thank you, then turned to walk, or stagger, away. Asinius was beside me, and I felt his eyes on me, then he reached over and grabbed my armor.

"Don't be an idiot," he muttered. "It's going to be a while before you're back to normal."

Relieved of the burden, we continued back to our tent, but it was not long before I blurted out, "So what was that all about?"

"What was what?" Asinius asked, but I was in no mood for his evasions, and I said as much.

"Manius was in the Fourth," he told me. "If I remember, the Fifth Century."

"He's not anymore?" I asked, and he shook his head. "Did he get promoted to the First?"

That was the most likely explanation; the most experienced, and men who proved to be the best fighters were often moved up to the First Cohort, but Manius did not strike me as a formidable warrior.

"No," Asinius' reply was terse, and I had learned that this was the sign that he did not wish to continue a discussion.

However, as I had learned, simply continuing to stare at him generally worked on loosening his tongue.

"Fine," he sighed, then paused for so long, I thought he had changed his mind, and I was about to say something when he continued, "Like I said, he was in the Fifth Century."

The way he said it told me that he had remembered all along, but I did not comment on it.

"Anyway, there was a...difficulty that Manius had with a couple other men of his tent section." He shot me a glance and finished, "About a woman."

That in itself was not surprising; even in my short time in the Legion, I had seen at least a half-dozen disagreements over the favors of a particular woman boil over into a brawl, but there was something that did not make sense to me.

"A couple men?" I asked. "Isn't that unusual that there are three men fighting over the same woman?"

"At least you can add," Asinius replied dryly. "But yes, it was a bit unusual, but not as much as you think. Except that in this case, it was only one of the men who was actually involved with the woman. The other man who backed him up was the man's brother."

"Ah." That made sense. "So why was this enough to get Manius out of the Fourth?"

"If you would stop asking questions, I'll tell you," Asinius shot back tartly. "As I was saying, there was a dispute, and the brothers came after Manius one night. This was when we were in Siscia, back when your father was still Pilus Prior."

"Thank you." I could not resist replying in the same manner in which he had just addressed me. "I gathered as much since you mentioned him to Manius."

I will admit I was a bit surprised when Asinius, instead of getting more irritated, gave a chuckle and said, "I suppose I deserved that." He paused again, then continued, "Anyway, they jumped him in the baths. You know, the usual place."

I nodded, but did not say anything; as a child of the Legions, I had long since learned that the bathhouse was the favorite spot for settling quarrels in an other than official manner, although it is just as common that it is a Centurion handling the problem as it is rankers.

"Manius may not look like much, but he's a tough old bastard." Asinius chuckled. "And while nobody knows exactly what happened, at least other than what little Manius and the other man said, what was obvious was that the man who had the problem with Manius wasn't going to be under the standard anymore."

This caused me to regard Asinius for a moment, trying to determine the exact meaning. By unspoken consent, we had slowed our pace in order to finish this conversation before we reached our tent.

"Manius killed the man?" I asked cautiously, but Asinius shook his head.

"Worse," he told me. "Manius gelded the man. And beat the man's brother half to death."

Despite thinking I had prepared myself, I let out a gasp. That, in all truth, was absolutely worse than being killed, at least to any man I know.

"Was Manius flogged for it?" I asked, but again Asinius shook his head.

"No," Asinius said. "Because the brother who didn't get his balls cut off refused to give the Centurions any information about what happened. But," he continued, "it probably won't surprise you to know that the brother swore that he would have his revenge. Which, of course, meant that Manius would never be able to sleep a wink. So your father decided it would be best to get him not just out of the Cohort, but out of the Legion."

That made sense on a number of levels, and we were silent as I absorbed this. Not only would Manius be safe, there would be an enormous source of tension removed from not just the Century but the Cohort. Transfers from one Legion to another are not uncommon, as I would learn myself, although the reasons behind this one were unusual, but it is always initiated by a Centurion and, depending on the circumstances, it could require the passing of money from one hand to another when the Legionary being transferred is considered a problem case of some sort. I was thinking about this, while Asinius had fallen silent, and I thought that was all there was to the story. Then I became aware that I was suddenly by myself, about fifty paces away from the tent, where I could see my comrades still gathered, but not having spotted us coming. I turned to see Asinius standing there a couple paces away, with what I would call a pensive expression on his face, as if he were considering something.

I suppose that was what prompted me to say, "There's more to this, isn't there?"

Asinius did not reply, but then gave a slow nod.

"Yes." He exhaled a breath. "There is one thing you should probably know."

Even as my mind raced over what he had told me, I could not see what, other than the identity of the Centurion who had been responsible for getting Manius out of danger, this had to do with me.

"The brother of the man who was gelded is still in this Cohort," Asinius explained quietly.

That was not necessarily a surprise, but I also understood why it could be bad news for me, considering the fact that it was my father who removed Manius from this man's reach. But as I was about to discover, things were about to become much worse.

"He's also in this Century," Asinius continued, and I will say that an instant before he uttered the name, I had a sudden intuition so that it was not a complete shock when he finished, "in the first section. The man's brother was Maxentius."

The only positive thing I can say that came about from this revelation was the fact that suddenly my side did not seem to bother me nearly as much.

The next few days on the march were some of the most agonizing, physically and mentally, of my young life to that point. In fact, I was experiencing a feeling that closely resembled those that I experienced seven years before when I was sitting, huddled in a cave, nursing a wound and worried about men coming to finish what they had started. Any thought of not wearing my *segmentata* had fled with what Asinius had told me about the identity of the survivor of the disagreement with Manius. Suddenly, I was aware of glances in my direction that were cast my way, not just by Maxentius, but by the members of his section and those other men with whom I knew he was friendly. Before, I had ascribed those quick looks as nothing new; I have been stared at much of my life because of my size, and I suppose because of to whom I am related. But in those days after I returned, those looks took on a new, much more sinister meaning, and I began watching everyone around me for signs that there might be something afoot. I cannot say that this was not without some cause; after all, Maxentius had more or less sworn that he would exact some sort of retribution on me. However, whereas before I had assumed that it was a result of our own interactions, now that I knew there was a larger cause for his hatred, I think I can be forgiven for seeing threats lurking everywhere. What better way to avenge his brother than by exacting vengeance on the son of the man who removed Manius from his reach? That much I understood and, in fact, if it had just been Maxentius, I would have been concerned, but not consumed with worry. What did concern me a great deal, and caused me watches of sleep lost despite my almost overwhelming fatigue, was whether or not he had any allies in his cause. Suddenly, the little comments and snide jokes that I had assumed just to be part of the initiation that all *Tiros* must endure took on more sinister meanings. Even in my own section I was unsure of who I could trust; Asinius was the one man I was sure about, along with Bassus, and probably Metellus. Dento was a question in my mind, as was Scrofa, but I was sure that I could not trust Tubero, although as an immediate threat I will say that, even in my weakened state, I did not worry about him at all. Outside of my section was a different matter altogether, and I realized that, despite my intentions, it was entirely possible that there were men who would have loved to see me taken down at least one peg. I am somewhat ashamed to say that, in my state of mind at the time, it never occurred to me that, even if a good number of the men in my Century did not care for me personally, there were more men who held my father in such high regard that they would not allow his son to fall victim to whatever Maxentius and those of a like mind had in store for me. As far as I was concerned, I was as alone as I had been in that dank cave when I was ten years old, and I found myself lying on my cot at night, my eyes filling with tears as I longed for the security of my longest companion, my wonderful champion Ocelus. He had been what got me through that night those seven years earlier, and I would have offered all of my fortune, or my father's fortune, if he had been nearby during that march. But although he was still alive at that point, he was in his dotage and far away in Arelate.

I offer this only as an explanation for the feeling of isolation that I experienced during this, the march that for all intents and purposes was a retreat back to Mogontiacum. My preoccupation with my own predicament was such that I was barely aware of the larger events taking place. However, what I did know was that the pall of gloom and despair that had been lingering about this army like a bad odor, despite our continued success on the battlefield, now was draped over all of us like a sodden cloak, reeking of hopelessness. And I will go to the afterlife convinced that because of men like Tubero, who I must say was far from alone, whatever problems were dogging this campaign were exacerbated.

"All I hope is that we make it back to Mogontiacum." He would say this, or some variation thereof, at least three or four times a day. "And with all the signs, that's not very likely. Especially now, because I heard…" Whereupon he would go on to relate, in lurid detail, the latest portents and signs of catastrophe that had occurred.

And not surprisingly, at least to me, was that the name of Drusus was being attached to most of these in some way. Not helping matters in the slightest was the weather, as it started to rain every day for varying lengths of time. My own lot was one of sheer misery; despite my best attempts to pad the area around my wound, the weight and friction of the *segmentata* was such that, while it did not rupture and spill my guts out onto the ground, it was extraordinarily painful, causing the skin around it to remain an angry pink long after the time the *medici* had assured me that the worst was over. Even less of a surprise was the fact that the constant irritation, both from my wound and from having to endure the dire talk of men like Tubero, put me in a truly foul state of mind. Unfortunately, at least for my mood, the army of Drusus marched in a southwesterly direction without anything other than a few sudden surprise attacks, and none of them involved my Century, let alone my Cohort. Once every two or three days, the column would suddenly erupt in sound as the *corniceni* sounded the alarm that an attack was occurring, but it was never anywhere even within my line of vision, always taking place farther up or down the column. I am not sure why, but at the time I was sorely disappointed; despite my lack of mobility, I was desperate for the outlet that came with combat. Much like my Avus and my father, I had been infected by the illness of battle, where I craved the fury and confusion of combat in much the same way that a drunkard needs his wine. More than any other reason, the tension caused by the uncertainty of my own personal situation, along with the overall mood of the army, caused me to crave the release of a fight, where I could purge my soul of all the burdens and hatred that I was feeling. However, the gods were not particularly concerned with the desires of a lowly Gregarius like me, busy as they were toying with men like Drusus as they were. At least, that was what most men believed when the very thing that so many of them had been predicting finally occurred.

I will not pretend that I knew Drusus that well, but I would like to think that by virtue of the two conversations that I had with the man, I am not speaking falsely when I say that the bitterest disappointment he experienced was not from his death, but from the manner in which it happened. After several campaigns and numerous close calls because of his insistence on leading from the front in the manner of Divus Julius, what ultimately killed Nero Claudius Drusus was a rearing horse. More specifically, the fact that his horse, after suddenly shying, lost its footing and came down on his leg, snapping the long bone in his thigh, is no way for a Roman Legate to die. Oh, he did not die right away; in fact, immediately after his accident, the word around the fires was that he would be up and around in a few days, albeit on crutches, and back to normal in a few weeks. I cannot recall exactly when that changed; my recollection is that it was no more than a week after the fall, but it might have been longer. However much time passed, the moment his condition worsened, the news shot through the army. What I do remember is that, when I first heard of this development, I mentally counted the heartbeats before Tubero spoke up, and made a mental wager with myself about what it would be; I do not believe I made it to twenty, and I won a tremendous fortune in my imagination.

"This is the work of that witch," he declared.

Although this was far from the first time he had mentioned the Suebi woman since our encounter, it was the first time I could recall where nobody, not even Asinius, immediately objected. Instead, this was met by a somber silence, but while I was still trying to maintain my self-imposed policy of silence around the fire, once it became clear that nobody was going to say anything, I could not keep quiet.

"How in Hades could that Suebi woman have anything to do with Drusus falling off his horse?" I asked incredulously. "She's miles and miles away! We're not in Suebi lands anymore anyway."

"How else do you explain it?" Tubero shot back.

"It was an accident," I replied with what I thought of as the obvious answer.

"To a horseman like Drusus? You've seen him; he rides, or did ride as if he was born on a horse," someone said.

There was a silence, but only because of the shock I felt, not at the words, but who had uttered them, because they came from Asinius.

I will say that he did look a bit uncomfortable, shooting me a sidelong glance as he continued, "As much as I hate to admit it, I think there's something to what Tubero is saying. It's just too…convenient that this happened after that bitch showed up."

"But that was weeks ago," I protested.

"And you know as well as anyone that things have been going to *cac* since then," Tubero shot back and, for once, I was unable to think of anything to say to him.

The truth was, as I saw it then anyway, that he was right, at least as far as the mood of the army and campaign changing from that moment. Although it was equally true that there had been other disturbing signs – the appearance of the mysterious twin boys riding through camp was one – these had been laughed off, or explained away by most of the men, those like Tubero being the exception, of course. Then the Suebi woman had shown up and, despite not wanting to, I had to admit that not only had the army's mood changed, so had that of our commander. Like everyone else, I had seen how preoccupied Drusus had become, how withdrawn, for him, at least. Oh, he still would trot up and down the column on the march, making jokes and swapping tales with we rankers, but even from a distance, I could see that it was forced and, if I could, there is no doubt more experienced men could as well.

"Does anyone know exactly what happened?" I finally asked.

"All I heard was that it was after we made camp the night we marched vanguard," Asinius said, then shot me a grin. "You remember, when you got to stand and watch us work like slaves."

Despite knowing it would hurt, I could not help laughing, as did the others. He was speaking the truth; the one thing I did enjoy about being on light duty was on days like that one, when we had ostensibly been chopping a path but, like almost every other day, ended up marching into a section of boggy ground. My comrades had emerged from it filthy, tired, and in a foul mood; I just had the mood, although I did have to clean up my *caligae* and legs up to mid-calf from the stinking mud.

"Anyway, we had already made camp, and he decided to ride the line," Asinius continued, using the term we use for a commander who makes a circuit of the inside of the camp walls.

"He always walks," Bassus pointed out, "except this time."

285

"And this time was enough," Asinius agreed grimly. "But supposedly, something spooked his horse when he was over in the 14th's part of the camp. It reared, but while he stayed in the saddle, the horse lost its footing because of the mud and rolled on him."

I did recall that the camp for that day was on ground that was softer than usual, which was something of a statement itself, given the terrain and the fact that it had rained so much. Still, I did not see how Drusus could have been caught out that way because, just like the others, and perhaps with more appreciation, I recognized in him a fine horseman. In fact, the only man I had ever witnessed who was more at home in the saddle was our slave Simeon, an Armenian who belonged to my Avus and, next to me, loved Ocelus more than any other creature on the earth. I had learned a great deal from Simeon, but even when I was a regular rider, I was not a shade of what he was, and Drusus was just a fraction less than Simeon. That was why I found it hard to believe, but even as that thought went through my mind, a part of me recognized that I was, in fact, making a case for what Tubero was saying as a possible explanation.

"Did anyone ever find out what spooked the horse?" I asked, but there were shakes of the head all around, save one.

Then Tubero spoke up. "It was a *numen*, conjured up by that witch, and it was waiting for the right time and place to strike."

Once more, I opened my mouth to argue, but then I saw the expressions on the faces of my comrades and thought better of it. In truth, it was as good an explanation as any, and we spent the rest of that evening talking about what it might mean.

We continued on towards Mogontiacum, but with every mile that passed under our boots, hooves, and wheels, Drusus' condition worsened. Just a matter of one or two days after our conversation, we learned that he had come down with a fever; that was when we all realized how seriously and gravely ill our commander was, and I was not alone in rushing to the army priests to make offerings for his recovery. I suppose it is always the case with a Legionary's first Legate that there is a bond there, particularly when it is a man like Drusus; the fact that he had decorated me made me even more attached to him, and I recalled my Avus describing what were my own feelings towards his first general, Divus Julius. In the case of my Avus, he marched for Caesar for something like eighteen years, longer than I had been alive at the point of my first campaign, so it was hard for me to imagine how worried I would have been if such had been the case with Drusus. And, looking back, perhaps it was better for me in the long run that I was destined to march for the man only one campaign. It certainly did not feel that way then and, even now, I have mixed feelings about this sentiment, but my feelings today have no bearing on my mind in those last days of the campaign. Frankly, I was almost beside myself with worry; the one slight positive that came about was that my preoccupation with Drusus' condition meant that I did not pay much attention to mine.

Gradually, the skin around my scar toughened up, although it is still a bit more tender than the surrounding area, despite it happening so many years ago, and the gods know I have more wounds with which to compare it. Nevertheless, I slowly returned to normal, wearing my armor and marching with my *furca* alongside Asinius, both of us pretending that nothing had changed. But that was not true, and I think he knew that as well as I did. Not between us, or among our own section, but overall, throughout the entire army. It was as if all the men were holding their collective breaths, waiting for the next catastrophe to befall us, and I would be lying if I said that none of us thought it would happen to anyone but Drusus. Finally, we reached a point perhaps three days' march from Mogontiacum, where we were forced to stop because carrying our Legate any further would have killed him, and we ended up staying there for a week as Drusus lingered, but never got better. Despite the fact that we had never been defeated on the field, the pall hanging over the army was such that, to a casual observer, they would have been likely to swear that we were returning from a stunning loss. Among us rankers, I think the best way to sum up the collective mood was one of relief that the campaign was over, despite the fact that most of us had little to show for it. Aside from the gold torq appropriated by Urso, of course, although none of my Century, nor Corvinus and Galens, received a brass *obol* from the proceeds of its supposed sale. I suppose it was fortunate that I did not need the money, and that I had been warned by those who knew better that we would never see the torq or any money associated with it, so that my reaction was more of resignation than anger. Still, it told me a great deal about Urso. However, I was to learn even more.

It was only because my Century happened to be on guard the evening that I witnessed when Drusus' older brother Tiberius came pounding up to the camp, his horse lathered and foaming at the bit, yanking the poor animal's head with a savage jerk to bring it skidding to a stop.

Luckily, it was Corvinus who was actually standing at the gate, and he recognized the Legate who, as might be expected, did not know the proper password and countersign. Consequently, he was only delayed for as long as it took to open the gates, but when he kicked his horse forward, it took only one more step on trembling legs before its front legs buckled. Tiberius barely managed to keep from being pitched headlong into the mud, and I must admit he showed impressive agility in kicking free of the poor, doomed beast to land on his feet. In fact, it almost looked as if he planned on this maneuver, barely breaking stride without so much as a backward glance at the horse he had just killed. Still, I vividly remember thinking of the tragic irony it would be if he was injured or killed in the same way as his brother, who he was coming to see before he died. It was probably because of my affinity for horses that I barely noticed Tiberius running down the Via Praetoria, my eyes fixed on the horse who, by this point, had rolled over to lie on its side, huge chest heaving as its lungs struggled to work. Even from where I was standing, I could see from the frothy blood coming from not just the horse's mouth, which could have been from Tiberius' heavy hand on the bit, but from its dilated nostrils, that the animal was dying.

I suppose that was what prompted me to ask Corvinus, "Pilus Prior? Can I go put the horse out of its misery?"

Corvinus had been staring back into the camp, watching Tiberius disappear into the gloom of the deepening dusk; he had arrived just as we were lighting the torches for the night. Clearly not hearing me, I repeated the question, and only then did he turn to look at me and, even in the poor light, I saw the sadness in his eyes, but I knew that, unlike in my case, it had nothing to do with the horse.

He hesitated for a moment, then shrugged and said, "Go ahead. I doubt Tiberius is very worried about his horse when his brother is dying."

I was not sure if there was a rebuke in his words, but I felt myself flush nonetheless, although I did not reply. Climbing down from the rampart, I motioned to Asinius, asking him to come help me. He did so readily enough, but I could see he was not happy about it. I do not know why, but like me, many of my comrades seemed to have a harder time killing animals like horses and dogs than they did other men. I suppose it has to do with the idea that neither species of animal has any say in their destiny and, for the most part, serve us humans faithfully and well, without complaint. At least, without any that we can understand. Reaching the beast, I saw the whites of the eye facing upward as it rolled in fear at our approach. Now that I was by its side, I clearly could hear the gurgling wheeze that told me the poor thing's lungs had ruptured; Tiberius had ridden this horse to death, but as I was to learn, this one was merely the last that he had treated thusly in his haste to reach his brother's side. I motioned to Asinius to kneel and place one knee on the horse's neck, while I stroked the animal along its broad forehead, knowing that this helped to soothe Ocelus.

"I'm sorry, boy," I told the horse softly. "You didn't deserve this, but I'm going to end your pain for you now."

And I did exactly that, using my *pugio* to put the horse out of its misery. When we walked back into the camp, there were already slaves there to haul away the carcass.

"Looks like someone's going to be getting horse meat tonight," I heard one of them mutter, and this angered me a great deal.

"You're not going to butcher that animal," I said loudly and harshly.

Stopping their exertions of dragging the dead horse onto a sled they had brought with them, the leader of the half-dozen men looked at me and, while at first he seemed disposed to argue, when I stepped closer so that the difference in our relative sizes became more apparent, he apparently changed his mind.

"As you say...*Gregarius*," he said sullenly. "But it's a sin to let the amount of meat this horse will offer up to feed us go to waste."

Deciding on the fly, I changed my tactic and, instead of continuing to argue, I gave him an elaborate shrug.

"Suit yourself." I gave a wave of my hand. "Of course, you're right. If you want to butcher Tiberius' favorite horse, then by all means go ahead."

I turned away as if to return to my post. I could feel the eyes of my comrades on me, and I am sure that most of them were curious as to why I seemed to care so much.

"How do you know this is his favorite horse?" the apparent gang leader demanded. "He just got here!"

"I grew up in Siscia," I replied, "when Tiberius was in command there. I had a horse of my own, so I tend to notice when other men favor one particular mount." That was all true. "And I remember him coming down to the stables every day to feed that horse," I pointed to the carcass, which had been lashed to a sled, the blood from where I cut its throat still dripping over the side of it. "He was very fond of it. But," I shrugged again, "if you want to eat Tiberius' favorite horse, don't say I didn't warn you."

I did not wait for a reply, but I heard them talking among themselves, then their leader spoke loudly enough so that I could hear. "As you say, Gregarius. We mean no disrespect. We'll take the horse off to be disposed of as the Legate wants."

By the time I had resumed my post on the rampart, the sled was being dragged in the direction of the Porta Decumana, the back gate by which all our dead, two- and four-legged, are taken to be dealt with as is appropriate. Asinius was grinning at me, as were some of the others who had heard the exchange. Corvinus just regarded me thoughtfully, although I thought I saw a small smile.

"So," Asinius asked, "*was* that Tiberius' favorite horse?"

I laughed.

"I highly doubt it," I admitted. "I've never seen it before in my life."

I was joined by the others in laughing, but it would not be long before all cause for mirth died.

We were still on guard, albeit about a third of a watch before we were relieved, when there came a sound that, had we still been deep in the Black Forest, would have caused every man to jump from his cot and rush to the ramparts, sure that the Suebi witch had summoned some demon to lead an assault. And perhaps she did; what I was once so quick to dismiss, I am no longer quite so sure about. But this sound, or shriek to be more accurate, did not come from outside the walls, but from within the camp and, while it did not last long, it is a sound I will never forget. Because in it was expressed so much grief and loss that there are no words that would ever adequately convey the same depth of those feelings, and all of us knew what it meant.

"He's dead." I jerked at the sound of Asinius' voice as he stood next to me and, like me, was staring back toward the *praetorium*, the source of the noise.

Immediately after uttering those words, I heard Asinius begin whispering, and it took a moment for me to recognize that he was reciting our prayer for the dead, pleading with the gods that their passage to the afterlife be smooth, and that they be accepted. He was quickly joined by the others, as each member of my section slowly moved from his spot along the wall to come and stand together, as if seeking the company of each other in a moment of need. This was bad enough, but when I glanced over at Corvinus, who was standing next to Galens, I was shocked to my core to see his lips moving in the same way. In all the years I had known him, when I was a boy and then as a man, I had never once seen Corvinus display any sign that he was religious; in fact, it had been a source of exasperation to my father because he believed that by refusing to acknowledge their existence, his friend was practically daring the gods to strike him down. Many an evening had been passed in my boyhood home of Siscia before we moved to Arelate with my father and Corvinus arguing about this subject. Seeing Corvinus moved to do as he was doing that night on the parapet had more of an effect on me about the import of what had happened than anything that was said in the coming days.

The sound did not last long; at least, it was not of a volume that it reached our ears on the rampart of the camp, but when we were relieved, we were marched directly past the *praetorium*, and all of us could hear the unrelenting sobbing of at least one man. I am sure that it was Tiberius, but as I was to learn, there was more to his grief than the passing of his brother. In fact, I suspect that Tiberius had worked out for himself that he might have been the unwitting cause of his brother's demise.

In the cesspit that is Roman politics, it was no secret that of the two brothers Tiberius and Drusus, Augustus favored the latter as being made of the right mettle to step into his boots whenever the Princeps decides to lay down his imperium, either voluntarily or when he ascends to the heavens to take his place beside Divus Julius, which is a virtual certainty. Despite their feelings for each other and the mutual devotion they shared as brothers, to those for whom such things matter, it made the pair rivals. And whenever there is a rivalry among the upper classes, especially when it comes to who would rule Rome, there are men on every single rung of our ladder lower than the two contenders who then decide which rival to back. While it is true that most men will try and steer a middle course, doing nothing overt that might antagonize either of them, there are some for whom this moderate approach is not enough. Whether it is ambition or cupidity that moves them does not matter overmuch; what does is that they are not willing to act in a passive way, but do what they can to influence the outcome of the contest. That is why it should come as no surprise that, within a watch of Drusus' death, the talk about the Suebi witch changed. It was subtle at first; the topic of the witch would come up, then a man sitting at a fire would wonder aloud if there was more to what had happened than met the eye, that perhaps there was an even larger and darker reason for Drusus' downfall than the incantations of a Suebi witch.

"It makes matters a lot less complicated," Tubero declared the next morning, seemingly out of nowhere.

But I was not fooled; Tubero never talked without having a point to go to with his words, and I glanced and saw that the others were of a similar mind.

"No doubt you've been thinking about this," Asinius sighed. "And I also know there's no way to shut you up. So, let's hear what this all means."

His tone was sardonic, but I sensed that he was also truly interested. As was I, no matter how much I did not want to admit it.

"Before, there were two choices for Augustus." Tubero did at least have the sense to glance about as he said this, keeping his voice low to keep from being overheard. "Now there's just one."

"That's not true." I was surprised only in the sense that it was Scrofa, who had beaten me to it. "There's his grandsons. They have closer blood ties to him than Tiberius does. Or Drusus did."

If that was meant to impress Tubero, it clearly did not.

"Bah." He dismissed the pair of boys with a wave of his hand. "They're children! What chance do you think they have of staying alive and growing up? Not with *her* around."

Tubero did not mention a name, but he did not need to; we all knew to whom he was referring. Livia Drusilla had been at the right hand of Augustus for many years, and there was no disputing the enormous amount of influence she had with the Princeps. But if that was as far as it went, it still would not mean much. But there were far too many rumors about Livia and her ambition for them all to be untrue, and Tiberius and Drusus were, in fact, of her blood, not that of the Princeps, despite their adopted status. Even considering my overall opinion of Tubero as a Legionary, I could not deny that he had a keen insight into the more devious matters of Rome, and I have since met men like him. They look at any situation in the most cynical, self-serving light, searching for the hidden reasons behind another's deeds that will align with their own particular view of the world. If a man performs a noble act, these men will examine it and insist that behind it there is a darker motive, one that fulfills their vision of the world and how men operate. In short, there is no such thing as a good deed to these men, and such was the case with Tubero.

"But Tiberius is almost out of his mind with grief," Asinius pointed out to Tubero, and I was pleased to see the other man's thin face flush.

"I'm not saying Tiberius had anything to do with it," he protested. "But that doesn't mean that someone didn't do something without him knowing about it."

Looking back, I believe that was the moment when things started to fall into place in my mind, and I remember feeling a distinct twinge in my gut as all the seemingly random and disparate facts came together. Such were my thoughts that I worried it might show on my face, and I shot a glance over at Asinius sitting next to me, then across the fire to Bassus and Scrofa, but they were all too absorbed in their own thoughts to notice me; at least so I hoped.

"And who do you think is behind it?" I tried to keep my tone such that I sounded almost bored, as if I had little interest in his answer.

Tubero, on the other hand, suddenly looked extremely uncomfortable, and there was no missing the glance he gave over to Asinius. Because of where our Sergeant was sitting, right next to me, I could not see his expression, but even from where I sat, I sensed him stiffen and, out of the corner of my eye, I saw his head shake, very slightly but definitely noticeably.

"I have no idea," Tubero replied at last, accompanying the words with a shrug. "But that doesn't mean it's not possible."

"Oh, I agree that it's possible, but it's something none of us have any way of knowing." This came from Asinius, who suddenly stood and stretched, announcing, "And it's time we get on about our business for the day."

The rest of the section, including me, followed suit, but when Asinius walked in the direction of the latrines, I decided to follow along. We did not have long before the morning formation, and I for one was not looking forward to being informed officially of something we had known about for a couple of watches. Catching up to him, we walked in silence for a few paces, and then I could take it no longer.

"What do you think about what Tubero said?"

"What do I think?" he echoed, then gave a disgusted snort. "I think he talks too much."

"You know what I mean," I insisted. "And I *think* I know who he's talking about."

That brought him up short, and he turned to stare into my eyes.

"You *think* you know?" he asked harshly, then gave a mocking laugh. "You have no idea what you know or don't know."

Normally, that would have been enough, but this time, I was not cowed by Asinius' words or attitude; too much had happened and, as I saw it, I was no longer a raw *Tirone*.

"I know that Urso rescued my father from certain death, and I'm positive he did it on orders from Tiberius. And like Tubero said, I think that someone might have decided to act in what they thought was Tiberius' interests because it would benefit them by extension." I paused for a moment, and it was not lost on me that for the first time since I had known him, Asinius refused to meet my gaze. Deciding to press my advantage, I asked him, "Are you saying that you don't think Urso would be capable of doing something that might help himself by helping Tiberius?"

Only then did he look up at me sharply, his face searching mine as if trying to decide what hidden motive I could have for pursuing this dangerous line of thought.

At last, he expelled a harsh breath and answered, "I think Urso is capable of anything. And I mean *anything*," he emphasized, adding to that with a poke in my chest with a finger, "and that means making sure that some Gregarius who's asking the wrong kind of questions disappears."

That, I was forced to acknowledge, was well within the power of any Primus Pilus, let alone a man like Urso, and I realized that Asinius' hesitance was based more on my welfare than for any other reason, so I softened my tone.

"I understand," I assured him quietly, "which is why I decided to follow you away from the tent. But don't you think someone should know?"

I admit that when I look back on that moment, I have to chuckle at my naivety and how unbearably earnest I was in pursuing some sort of justice, as if there is some such thing available to men of our status. But at that time, I had come to realize that, along with the sadness, there was a sense of outrage about what happened to Drusus buried within me, which I suppose can be attributed to the fact that he was my first Legate. Even without the fact that he had personally decorated me, and remembering our brief conversation outside the *praetorium*, I would have a bond of loyalty to the man, but adding those together meant that I deeply wanted to see his death avenged. Oh, I was aware that it could have been an accident, but this was the one thing I shared with Tubero and men like him, a conviction that there were sinister forces at work. And I was not referring to the Suebi witch.

"Know what?" Asinius asked me. "Know that you have a suspicious mind? That you're sure there's more to it than meets the eye?" He gave a snort. "Well, you go right ahead with that and see how far you get." Grasping me by the arm, he squeezed it hard enough that I winced, despite not wanting to, as he admonished me, "Not to mention that you'd be a dead man before more than a day or two had passed."

"So you believe it was an accident and that Urso had nothing to do with it?"

The silence hung between us for a long time before Asinius finally heaved a sigh and said, "No. That's not what I believe. But what does it matter what I believe? Or you? But here is what I know; if you don't keep your mouth shut, you're very likely to have a fall in the night."

"I'd like to see someone try," I retorted.

Such is the hubris of youth, and add to that the confidence that comes from being bigger and stronger than most men, yet Asinius was not impressed, knowing that I was indulging in the bluster of a teenage boy.

"Not even you have eyes in the back of your head. And there are more men who would love to be part of taking you down a notch than you'd care to admit. I can think of one man in particular."

"Maxentius," I muttered.

"And you know that he wouldn't even need to be paid," Asinius chose to point out, which, in my mind, was not necessary.

Heaving my own sigh, I finally said, "Fine. I'll keep my mouth shut." I glared at him. "But I don't like it."

"I would be worried about you if you did," he assured me quietly.

Then there was nothing left to be said, and we both returned to what we were doing, making ready to face what would be a trying day.

The announcement that Drusus had died came from the lips of Tiberius himself and, even from the distance I was from him in formation, I could see how white his face was and how he seemed as if all the energy had been sucked from his body. Acting as if every word and gesture required tremendous effort, he informed us about what we already knew. However, I do not believe he was prepared for the reaction he got from us.

"Give his body to us! We want to give him a sendoff worthy of his status as our general!"

As it turned out, that was just the first call, but it was immediately drowned out by a chorus of other voices, all of them shouting essentially the same thing. It reminded me of what I had read in my Avus' account of his time with Divus Julius, and how his men loved Caesar as fiercely as any army of Rome has loved its general. Since I only had his written word with which to compare, I cannot say whether or not the men of Caesar's army loved their general any more or less than we loved Drusus. But what I can emphatically declare is that the army of Nero Claudius Drusus was adamant that we be allowed to mourn our general in a manner that would have men talking about it for years to come. Tiberius stood, silent and unsmiling, surveying each Legion one at a time, but I saw that he was weaving about as if he had drunk an amphora of wine. I am sure that it was a potent combination of exhaustion and grief, but one thing I will say of our upper classes is that in moments of great duress such as this, they conduct themselves in a manner with which none of us could find fault, behaving as a true Roman. Erect, and as formidable looking as one of the statues of our great men, Tiberius allowed the men to carry on in this manner for a bit before he raised his arms, hands outward in a sign that he was asking for us to fall silent. We did, but it was not very quickly.

"Men of the Legions," Tiberius' voice had started out hoarse, but now it was even more difficult to hear him clearly, "I understand and I thank you for this show of devotion to my brother, whom I loved well." He paused for a moment before continuing, "But this is not just a loss for the Legions; it is a loss for all of Rome, the entire Republic! And I would be remiss if I did not bring my beloved brother's body back to Rome, where he can then be interred with the honor that he so richly deserves!"

299

If Tiberius thought that this would put an end to the pleading of the men, he was gravely mistaken. In fact, if I am any judge, men got angrier at what I suppose they perceived to be a slight against them, although I am sure this was not at all what Tiberius intended. In fact, the tumult grew so loud and boisterous, as men continued shouting their protest at being deprived of honoring their general, that finally Tiberius turned and tottered away, heading back to the *praetorium*. Only then did we fall silent, more because we were stunned at this action than for any other reason. For the first, but would not be the last time, I witnessed an army perilously close to refusing the orders of their Centurions to disperse back to our respective areas in the camp. Finally, the habit of obedience held sway and we all returned to our tents, and the contrast between the roaring tumult and the sullen silence that now blanketed the camp was perhaps the most unsettling part of the whole affair, at least to me.

Luckily, the Primi Pili were neither deaf nor blind to our mood, and Urso, along with the other Primi Pili, immediately went to the *praetorium* to confer with Tiberius. This we knew; what we had no way of knowing was the astonishing sequence of events that was about to take place, and of all the momentous moments in my career to this point, I am proud to say I was part of this one. In fact, I am hard-pressed to imagine a greater honor occurring in whatever time I have left under the eagle. Our first warning was in the *bucina* call summoning the Pili Priores, followed about a third of a watch by Corvinus' *cornicen* sounding the call for our Centurions. The buzzing of our talk as each of us sat in front of our tents could be heard the length of our Cohort street, and I am sure it was the same around the camp. However, I feel confident that none of us, no matter how prescient we may have been, came close to guessing what was in store for the army. Our first hint that there was a new development came when one of the men in the third section of our Cohort, answering a call of nature, saw on his return to our area a group of horsemen gathered outside the *praetorium*. Since none of them were part of the bodyguard, this drew his attention, and he paused to watch as they departed the forum. What was puzzling to him, and then to us, once he relayed what he had seen, was that they did not exit the camp as a group; instead, they used all four gates, with what were clearly pairs of riders heading in four different directions. Naturally, this served to freshen the speculation, which had begun to flag as men ran out of ideas about the cause of all the disturbance. Then, about a third of a watch before dusk, our *cornicen* blew the series of notes that called us to assemble at our normal Cohort meeting place, the intersection of our Cohort street and the Via Praetoria. It was cramped, but I could not help noticing how much more space we had in which to gather than we did before departing for Siscia. That was when it came home to me the losses we had incurred during this campaign. It was true that many of the missing faces would be back at some point after they recovered from their wounds, but there was still a fair number that would never be seen again. Moments like this always served to remind me that this life I chose for myself is a dangerous business and, even if I did not know any of the missing men by more than sight, or, at most, a name, I still missed seeing their faces. Corvinus strode up, the other Centurions with him and, without any formalities, began talking.

"All right," he began. "I'm not going to bore you, since I know everyone here understands what this is about. The Primi Pili have gone to Tiberius and gotten his permission for something that, as far as I know, has never been done before."

The silence was total, and I felt myself leaning forward, so intent on hearing about whatever this thing was that had never been done, but I had to suppress a sudden chuckle when I noticed my comrades doing exactly the same thing.

"As you all know, Tiberius is determined to take Drusus back to Rome. On this, he won't change his mind. However." He took a breath, then continued. "He understands our desire to honor his brother. That's why we're going to be marching." I was confused, and I could see that I was not the only one, but nobody pressed Corvinus, allowing him to finish, "We're going to be part of the procession as we carry Drusus back to Mogontiacum. After that I don't know, but it's possible that we'll escort him all the way back to Rome."

Silence continued for a moment as each of us digested this, then the babbling began.

"What does that mean, exactly?"

"How are we supposed to do this surrounded by these savages?"

That is just a sample of the questions, but they were far from the only ones. For whatever reason, Corvinus seemed content to allow the uproar to continue for several moments before he finally raised a hand for silence.

"If you all would shut your mouths, you'd learn the answers to all these questions," he scolded. "Some of you may have noticed the riders leaving camp." Seeing most, if not all, of us nodding our heads, he continued, "They've been sent to the various branches of the tribes in the area, under a flag of truce. They're going to explain what's happening, and that we're asking to be allowed to carry our general back to Mogontiacum without having to march in *quadratum* with uncovered shields the whole way."

When combined with the events of the previous day, this was almost too much for many of us to comprehend.

"Why would they agree to that?" someone asked. "We've just finished killing them by the basketful, along with their cousins."

"Because of Drusus," Corvinus answered quietly. "They may be barbarians, but they respect great warriors, and Drusus was one." He paused for a moment, then added, "You need to remember that this might be our first campaign under him, but

302

this wasn't his first campaign. He's been up here fighting these bastards for years now, so they know him and what he's about."

Although I understood this, I freely acknowledge that I was among those men who were skeptical. It just shows that, as much as a teenager may think he knows, the reality is far different.

Within two days, all the riders had returned with the assurance of the German tribes, namely the Alamanni, the Hermunduri and the Burgundiones, through whose lands we would be passing, that we would be allowed to convey Drusus back to Mogontiacum with all the honor due him. If they had returned with just the word of these Germans, I doubt the men would have been willing to trust that, but each contingent did not come back empty-handed. Accompanying them were highborn hostages from each of the bands through whose territory we would pass, as a sign of their good faith. More than anything they could have said, this sign of their intentions was what convinced us that they could be trusted, at least with this. Orders were given to strike this camp, which had been given a name, something I have not seen since for a marching camp. From then on, any man who uttered the words Camp Cursed was instantly understood, at least by those who had been there as well. At dawn the next day, a procession the likes of which had never been seen before marched away from the camp, which, as custom and regulation decreed, was destroyed, the ditches filled in, the stakes pulled up, and all the wooden towers and structures put to the torch, sending a greasy black stream of smoke into the sky, which I thought was appropriate. Leading the procession was a vanguard composed of the First Cohort of the 14th Legion, their shields covered and with a drape of black cloth wrapped around their helmets as a sign of mourning. The standards were similarly covered, which I believe had to do as much with assuring those men we had been fighting just weeks before that our intentions were peaceful as anything. By the standard of a normal day's march, especially considering that we were marching back along the same road we had cleared at the beginning of the campaign, we would have reached Mogontiacum in no more than three days. But not only was our pace slower, something so extraordinary happened that, even now, I am hard-pressed to describe it adequately.

It began about midday of our first day's march and, because we were marching in the rearmost position, it took some time for the word to filter back to us the reason for coming to a halt. As I said, the First Cohort of the 14th was in the vanguard, but unlike a normal march, the First was immediately followed by Tiberius and the other highborn Romans attached to the army, all of them wearing black cloaks over their armor. Immediately behind them came the *lictors* that had been assigned to Drusus for the year by virtue of his status as Consul, except that the rods they carried had all been broken, and the axes were turned backward, the traditional sign of mourning. Then came the wagon bearing the body of Drusus, but instead of being inside the wagon, he had been placed on the top of it, on a bier specially designed and fitted to withstand the jolting ride back to Mogontiacum. Naturally, he was dressed in his ceremonial armor, but only after his body had been washed and cleaned in an attempt to erase the signs of the sickness that had ravaged his last days. Just before we departed the camp that first day, we had been allowed to march past his body, rendering a salute as we passed by and, because of my position on the outside and my height, I got a good look at him. In some ways, I wish I had not; while he looked as if he was asleep, there was no hiding how gaunt he was, the skin over his cheekbones stretched so tightly that it amazed me they did not poke through. He was still handsome, and I cannot deny that my vision clouded as we marched past him for the last time, but thankfully, I was not alone. But now we had come to a halt, not long after our customary rest stop, and we stood there muttering to each other about the possible cause. Frankly, I believe a majority of my comrades were expecting some native trick, but such was not the case. It was only after we resumed the march and reached the spot the vanguard had halted that we determined the cause. Lining the rough road in front of us, just a few paces off the makeshift roadway, were two rows of German warriors, standing in what I believe was their version of an honor guard. Speaking for the men of my Century and, from what I heard the rest of the army, we were too shocked to speak, marching by the twin rows of men and, I must say, a fair number of women, with only the sound of our boots tramping the packed earth. I cannot say that there were not some hostile gazes thrown in our direction, but for the most part, they looked at us impassively, but what I noticed the most was how every warrior carrying a spear held it vertically, but with the point down, while all the swordsmen had their blades sheathed. By my estimate, the line was a mile long before we reached the last man, but nothing was said, no sign was given. Despite myself, I could not help casting a glance over my shoulder, still suspicious of some sort of trickery, but although that was the first such display, it would not be the last. Every day of our march, the same sort of thing occurred, and the day before we reached Mogontiacum, it happened twice, and our journey lasted one day short of a full week. Only the day before we arrived was the 8th allowed the vanguard spot which, despite knowing why, still did not sit well with us. But on the day we marched into Mogontiacum, there was a surprise waiting for one of us, and I have often wondered the true reason why I was suddenly summoned to meet with Urso.

"You've been chosen by Tiberius to walk beside Drusus' bier when we march into Mogontiacum," Urso's tone was abrupt, giving me the distinct impression he was not happy.

I was standing at *intente*, but while my body remained perfectly rigid, my mind was reeling.

"Sir?" I finally managed. "I don't understand…"

"Neither do I, but those are his orders," Urso said sourly, his expression akin to someone who has bitten into the sourest lemon they have ever tasted. Shrugging, he continued, "Oh, I suppose it has to do with the day Drusus decorated you. Undoubtedly, someone told Tiberius about it. And," he glared up at me as if I had somehow been involved, "who you're related to. Which is probably the biggest reason."

Despite knowing that he did not mean this as a compliment, I maintained my composure, even with the flicker of anger I felt.

"Anyway," he seemed disappointed, probably because I did not take the bait, "you're ordered to be there in full uniform a third of a watch before dawn. Apparently, he has some special instructions for you."

He gave a disgusted wave of his hand in dismissal, and I executed the proper turnabout to exit, but just as I reached the flap that separated his private quarters from the outer officer, he called out to me.

"And Pullus, get those arm rings from whoever you gave them to. I want you wearing all five of them."

For an instant, I opened my mouth to ask him about the torq, but fortunately, I saw by his expression that he was expecting me to ask, and I guessed that I would not really like the answer that he had prepared for me. Somehow, it just seemed like a trap, so my only act of defiance was simply to nod my head, then step through before he could make an issue of it. I walked two or three steps with my shoulders hunched, waiting for him to call me back to exact some sort of punishment, but I suppose he was distracted enough worrying about what was truly behind my summons.

I presented myself to the *praetorium* at the appointed time with a case of nerves very close to those I experienced before battle, thankful that my comrades had pitched in to help get me ready. My *segmentata* gleamed like it never had before, and the arm rings looked like they were touched with fire. I was slightly worried about my plume because there had been no time to redye it with the madder that we use for both plumes and tunics, although I was wearing my parade tunic. When I got to the forum, I experienced relief and disappointment in almost equal proportions; I was not the only one summoned by Tiberius. Standing in a small knot were other Gregarii and, as I drew near, I understood why I had been chosen because we were all roughly the same size. However, I must admit to feeling a bit of satisfaction that not only was I the largest, at least across the shoulders and chest, I was the only one wearing decorations given to me personally by Drusus. That, however, was about to cause me a moment of discomfort.

"Who told you to wear decorations?"

The question came from behind me, and I whirled around to see none other than Tiberius staring at me, his features made even harsher by the deep shadows cast by the flickering torches. Drawing up to the most rigid position of *intente* I could manage, I opened my mouth to tell him, but I was saved from an unexpected ally. From behind Tiberius came the same Legate with the short-cropped gray hair who had been present with Drusus; evidently, he had been detained, or Tiberius walked faster than he did. Whatever the case, he reached out and touched Tiberius on the shoulder, and Drusus' brother turned about to listen as the other man whispered in his ear. He listened intently, but even in the dim light I saw one eyebrow lift in what I took to be some surprise. After a moment of conversation that I could not hear, he turned back towards me, and I fixed my eyes above his head as he approached me. Stopping in front of me, he reached out to touch one of the arm rings gently, and I felt his fingertips on my bicep, hot against my own skin and making me wonder if he had a fever himself. Despite keeping my gaze straight ahead, I could tell he was staring at the armbands, and the fleeting thought came to me where I wondered what his reaction would have been if I had been wearing the torq.

"My brother gave you these?" He asked it as a question, but there was such a tone of wistfulness that I dared to look down at him.

"Yes, sir," I answered quietly, then, without thinking, I added, "It was the greatest honor of my life so far."

If he was surprised, he hid it well, just nodding his head, but keeping his eyes on the rings.

"I also understand that you come from a distinguished line of men of the Legions yourself," he said in a monotone, giving me no hint how he viewed this news.

"Yes, sir," I answered, but said nothing more.

"I never met Titus Pullus, but your father served under me," he continued, then gave a short bark that I took to be a laugh. "But I suppose you know that already."

"Yes, sir."

Only then did he look up at me, and I became uncomfortable as he examined my face as if he could see something there. Which, I suppose he was doing, considering what he said next.

"You're in the 8th, under Canidius," he began. "I'm the one who promoted him to the post of Primus Pilus, after that…" his mouth twisted into a bitter grimace, "…creature Barbatus had the good fortune to die. But," now there was no way I could pretend I did not see him staring up at me, "I suppose you knew that as well. Correct?"

"Yes, sir," I said yet again, but this time, felt compelled to add, "Primus Pilus Canidius saved my father's life, sir. I'll always be grateful to him for that."

"As you should be," Tiberius agreed.

Suddenly, he reached out again to touch my armbands and, this time, it made me acutely uncomfortable because it felt more like a caress than anything.

"But do you know who ordered Primus Pilus Canidius to do so?" he asked me abruptly.

I suspect that he did this to catch me off guard and, while he did to a degree, I somehow managed to be cautious in my reply.

"Only rumors, sir," I told him. "I've never been told exactly what happened. By anyone," I added in emphasis, trying to reassure this man that nothing I did know had come from my father.

His response was a non-committal grunt that gave me no hint as to his thoughts, but then he said, "Well, if and when you find out, I suspect that you will want to reward that man with the same kind of loyalty that your Primus Pilus has shown…to Rome, of course," he added.

Without another word, he turned and moved to the next man, leaving me with a pounding heart and a sense of dread. Was he giving me a veiled order? I wondered. That I was to obey Urso, no matter what? Or was he referring to himself?

The task given the other Legionaries besides me who had been selected was to carry Drusus' bier, on our shoulders, across the Rhenus, and into the permanent camp at Mogontiacum. Naturally, the people who lived in the town had been alerted and they lined the road in much the same manner as the Germans on the opposite side of the Rhenus, except these people were not circumspect at showing their grief. The distance we had to cover, first starting at a spot just around a slight bend in the road about a quarter mile from the bridge, then across the Rhenus and the rest of the way into the camp was perhaps a mile and a half. Not a huge distance, but when you are responsible for carrying a heavy wooden platform, even when the load is shared, it is extremely tiresome and trying. Yet, I barely noticed, and I suspect that the other men of this detail felt the same way. We were no more than fifty paces across the bridge before the crowds started, lining the road the rest of the way. That was impressive enough, considering that up until just three or four years before, Mogontiacum did not even exist, at least as a Roman town, but the noise created by the common people expressing their grief was positively deafening. Particularly piercing were the shrill cries of the women, many of whom were down on their knees, their arms upstretched towards Drusus and the heavens as we marched past in total silence. No horns, no drums; just the sound of our boots competed with the wailing of people whom I am hard pressed to believe were being completely sincere. Perhaps it is cynical, yet from my point of view, these people were not behaving in this manner for Drusus, but for Tiberius, trying to show their loyalty and patriotism towards Rome. Oh, I suppose that there were some real tears shed; Drusus was much loved by the people of my class whether they were in uniform or not, particularly in Mogontiacum. Whatever the case, by the time we arrived at the camp forum and were given the command to lower Drusus' bier gently to the ground in the exact middle of the forum, I was soaked in sweat and as tired as if I had marched thirty miles instead of the seven that we covered that day. Thankfully, we were immediately dismissed, to be replaced by an honor guard, but not before Tiberius did dismount and, in a move that surprised me a great deal, offered each of us his hand in thanks.

"Each of you was chosen because you meant something to my brother, and I thank you for rendering him such faithful service, no matter how much he may have deserved it just because of the kind of man he was. All I ask of you is that, should the opportunity arise, you give me the chance to show you that I am worthy of the same kind of loyalty and devotion."

With that, he spun about and walked to the brick *praetorium*, his back straight and head erect, and I could only imagine the amount of self-control it took for him to continue behaving in the manner expected of him, not just by the people of Rome, but by Augustus himself. In fact, I kept reminding myself that this entire display, from the moment Tiberius arrived until we reached Mogontiacum, was meant just as much for a man who still lived as it was for the one who had died. I had no doubt that within no more than a matter of a week, Augustus would hear of everything that had taken place here, and I wondered what it would mean for all of us.

Chapter Six

With our campaign more or less completed, we were allowed to leave the camp while we waited to receive orders for what we were about to do next. The big question was whether or not we would spend the winter in Mogontiacum, or return to Siscia. Naturally, this meant that the betting was brisk and, as far as I could tell, the money was evenly split between the two alternatives. Those who argued against Mogontiacum pointed out that this camp had not been made to accommodate an army of four Legions, which the men betting on Mogontiacum immediately dismissed, in turn pointing to the fact that there was more than enough labor, and time, in which to enlarge the camp. Personally, I barely noticed the debate; I had more things on my mind than where we would spend the winter. This was especially true, since I no longer had family in Siscia and no kind of romantic entanglement that so many of my comrades did. With my long association with the Legions, I understood that their anxiety to get back to Siscia had as much to do with the fear that their women would succumb to the blandishments of the men left behind as they wanted to be back in familiar surroundings. As I had long since observed, this was a fear that was extremely well-grounded. This was part of the reason that I had promised myself that I would not fall victim to such entanglements. The other was perhaps even deeper; after reading my Avus' account of his life, even as young as I was when I read it, I could feel the raging sense of loss and sorrow that came as a direct result of his loving two women in his life, both of whom he lost. One was to a plague that claimed his two children as well, and the other in childbirth, victim of the same problem that claimed his own mother when the baby was too large. Of all the reasons I gave myself for avoiding putting myself in a position where I could have a family, this last is the most powerful one, especially because, as I was told so often, I am at least as tall and, if anything, broader through the shoulders than my Avus. Although I can point to my own birth, my mother being as small as she is that I could have children of my own I am, in this matter at least, naturally cautious. Consequently, even now that I am a fully grown adult in my thirtieth year, I find it impossible to fathom this as even a possibility, but I have decided that this is due as much to my Avus' personality and the path he blazed for first my father, then me. I will not lie and say that meant I avoided all contact with women, but my liaisons are only measured by the watch and amount of coin I am willing to spend and, I am somewhat ashamed to admit, the occasional liaison with a woman who belongs to another Legionary. Even with the gloomy occasion for our return, when my comrades of my tent section insisted that I go into town with them that first night, I did not have to be persuaded, since I had an itch that only a woman can scratch.

Tiberius, and his brother, only spent a night in Mogontiacum before continuing their march to Rome, but ended up leaving most of the army behind. Accompanied by a hand-picked honor guard composed of the other Legions, along with Drusus' *lictors* and bodyguards, the cortege continued on its way, while the fate of the 8th and where it would spend the winter remained undecided. At least, as far as we knew; I found it hard to believe that Tiberius would have continued on without leaving some sort of orders behind, but it appeared that was, in fact, the case. Consequently, once we attended to the various tasks needed to be done when we were back in any camp where we would be spending a stretch of time, we did not have much to do, and although the mood was definitely subdued for the first few days after Tiberius continued on his journey with Drusus, it did not last. This was another lesson I learned during my first campaign; as human beings, we cannot seem to grieve for a long period of time, at least collectively. Before too much time passes, we seek a way to laugh again, and this is especially true in the Legions. Considering the fact that sudden death is always with us, especially on campaign, I suppose it makes sense that none of us linger too long over the death of someone close to us. Consequently, it was not long before the men of the Legions were back to what passes for normal for us, meaning that there were brawls occurring on a nightly basis in the various squalid wineshops and whorehouses, most of the time between men of different Legions. Not always, however, and I suppose that, at least looking back, I should have expected that this interlude would be viewed as an opportunity by Maxentius and some of his friends.

It started out innocently enough, in the second week we were at Mogontiacum. The speculation about our future had become more intense with every passing day, and the rumors that were flying about seemed to change by the watch. I was nursing a raging hangover from the night before, yet when my comrades began teasing me about how I had a weak head for wine, I felt compelled to answer the challenge. There was a spot, I believe Bassus knew of it from his time in the 14th, which had become our favorite spot. Part of the appeal was that, besides wine, they also served a drink favored by the tribes across the Rhenus that is made of fermented honey. It is extremely potent, at least in how quickly it can render a man insensible, which makes it a popular drink for those men who are seeking to render themselves unconscious. That night, after enduring the jeers and taunts of my comrades, the most vocal being Tubero, I finally acquiesced and drank my first cup of what the Germans call mead. Being honest, I should say I attempted to drink my first cup; it was so thick and foul-tasting that I almost gagged it back up. Fortunately, by the end of the second cup, it did not taste nearly as bad. Also, I began noticing something; although my tongue grew thick as it did with wine, for some reason, I found that my comrades, even men like Tubero, suddenly did not seem to irritate me as much as they had in the past. Only now, with a clear head can I look back and recall that it was, in fact, Tubero who insisted that as soon as I emptied my cup, it was immediately refilled. I can only plead the ignorance of youth and inebriation, that meant I was not immediately suspicious about this man, who I loathed so deeply, was the one who seemed the most intent on getting me the drunkest I have ever been, then and now. I believe it was by my third cup that I realized with some surprise that I was drunk, and not just mildly. In a relatively short period of time, I had achieved a level of inebriation whereby my already healthy ego and belief in myself was given free rein.

"I can take any man in here and tear them to pieces!" I remember roaring at one point.

Fortunately for everyone involved, none of the other patrons felt the need to test my assertion. At least, there in the tavern. As I was about to discover, not even the strongest man is immune to a beating.

Along with the reason for me becoming so drunk, my only defense for what happened afterward is inexperience and inebriation. Otherwise, I highly doubt I would have fallen for the ruse that was used to lure me into what still ranks as the worst beating I have ever endured. As usual, it was Asinius who stood, the signal that it was time for us to leave and return to camp. However, when I made to follow, although it took me two tries to gain my feet, I was restrained by a hand on my arm. I stared down in bleary surprise at the hand, then it seemed to take a great deal of time for my head to follow the arm it was attached to, all the way up to its owner. It was Tubero, and again, I should have been instantly suspicious.

"Oy, Pullus," he said to me, favoring me with a smile that, at the time at least, seemed friendlier than I had ever seen. "Why don't you hang back with me and have another?"

"What are you up to?" Asinius' voice came from behind me and, once more, I took great care to turn my head slowly enough that it did not cause more dizziness than I was already experiencing.

He was standing at the door and, as inebriated as I was, I could see that even if I was not, he was suspicious.

"Nothing," Tubero protested, and I saw him holding his hands up out of the corner of my eye, making a placating gesture towards our Sergeant.

Asinius was clearly unconvinced, and Tubero got to his feet and tottered over to Asinius, where they held a whispered conversation, the content of which I was only told about later. Essentially, Tubero told Asinius that, after reflection, he realized he had been treating me unfairly, and wanted some time alone with me to clear the air and make peace. Even through my haze, I could see that whatever Tubero was saying to Asinius, my Sergeant did not like, and there was a quiet argument. Finally, Asinius looked over Tubero's shoulder at me; unfortunately for me, I did not appreciate the concern I was being shown, convinced as I was that if Tubero, in fact, wanted to start something with me, even in my state of inebriation, I was more than capable of handling it. So I gave a dismissive wave in his direction, and although he opened his mouth to argue, he then gave a shrug and after another whispered exchange with Tubero, turned and exited the tavern.

When Tubero returned to our table, I demanded, "What did he want?"

"He was just looking out for you, is all," he said, and then, in what I imagine was an unconscious imitation of Asinius, gave me a shrug and finished, "I can't blame him. I haven't been fair to you, and everyone knows it. That's why I wanted to clear the air between us."

I should have known better. It was only later that I recalled something that my Avus had written, about how unlikely it is for a man to change his true nature and, while he might disguise it, sooner or later, the true, the base metal a man is made of will expose itself. Again, I can only plead ignorance at that moment not only because of my youth, but aided by two more cups of mead with which Tubero plied me. Frankly, I do not remember much of what he said to me while we were in the tavern; something about how sorry he was for always giving me such a hard time, and how he had been unfair in his treatment of me. I do remember him offering his hand, which I accepted, clasping his forearm in our manner, although I could not resist giving him an extra squeeze that made him wince and rub it afterward. Then I toasted him, draining what was my last cup of the stuff that I have never touched since that night. Finally, he got up and weaved his way to the bar, dropping coins on it to settle up, then came back and, with some huffing and heaving, helped me to my feet. We staggered to the door, which I was sure was twisting sideways to keep me from grasping the latch, while I had one arm draped over his shoulder, making him struggle under my weight. Somehow, we managed to make it outside, but when I turned to go back to camp along our usual route, he stopped me.

"This way's shorter," he assured me. "We just have to cut through that alley over there, then we're almost home."

I allowed myself to be guided in the direction that Tubero had indicated, and we continued staggering on our way back to camp, or so I believed. Then Tubero began singing one of our marching songs and I joined in which, as I know now, was his way of covering the noise of rushing feet that closed in on us as soon as we were a few paces into the alley. My memory of what happened next is just a piecemeal collection of fragments of the event, but what I do recall clearly was a sudden flurry of motion that disturbed the air. I was just turning my head when I saw and heard simultaneously some object striking Tubero on the back of the head, and he went down immediately. It might have been the same moment, but I believe it was a fraction later when something slammed into my back with tremendous force, although I do not remember that much pain. At least, at first. Regardless of what I felt, the force of the blow sent me staggering forward a couple of steps, which helped give the next blow even more momentum as I walked right into the punch that smashed into my face. After that, it seemed like it was raining blows, with fists and what I assume from the bruises afterward were cudgels, although I will say that they did not strike me in the head with them, or I would not be writing this, using only fists for my face and head. I cannot say exactly when I finally fell, first to my knees, then finally face down in the filthy muck of the alley, but what I vividly remember is the rank smell of piss, and worse, since when a man or woman needs to relieve themselves while they are out and about in a frontier town like Mogontiacum, they do so in alleys exactly like the one I was currently in. Between the smell, the pain, and what I had ingested in the tavern, I suppose it was inevitable that my stomach expelled the contents of what I had forced it to take on, which only added to the stench. I do remember feeling the slimy, warm mead that I had not yet digested puddle around my face, but that only lasted a moment before a pair or pairs of hands grabbed my tunic and roughly jerked me over onto my back. Someone groaned, I assume it was me, and I lay there helplessly as I felt one set of hands searching through the folds of my tunic around my belt. Inevitably, they found my coin purse, except their initial shout of triumph turned into curses, and I heard voices for the first time.

"I thought you said this bastard carried a lot of money, that he was rich!"

"I said he was rich," another voice replied, and the sound of the voice was so familiar that I almost opened my eyes in surprise. "You assumed that because he's rich, he carried it with him."

As groggy as I was, as scrambled as my thoughts seemed to be, I can only ascribe the fact that I maintained my presence of mind enough to keep from opening my eyes to the favor of the gods. Even in the darkness, I have no doubt they would have noticed that I was awake, and I am almost positive they would have cut my throat, whether that was the original plan or not.

Because the voice of the second man was clearly Maxentius and, once I realized this, the identity of the other voice came to me as well.

"This is hardly worth our time." This came from a third voice, and it was accompanied by the small clinking sound of the few coins I carried in my purse, and I recognized this one as well.

"I said," Maxentius tried to sound patient, "it's supposed to *look* like a robbery. But you both know that's not what it's about."

"We do," the man who had ripped my purse off my belt said, his tone resentful. "But that doesn't mean we should take a risk like this without something to show for it."

"I do," Maxentius shot back, then there was an instant's silence.

WHAM! The kick he aimed at me struck me in the side, but thankfully, because of the dark, it was not a solid blow. Even so, another groan escaped me, but I somehow managed not to move and keep my eyes shut.

"This bastard has had this coming for a long time," Maxentius went on. "He thinks because of who his father is his *cac* doesn't stink. Well, he knows differently now, doesn't he?"

"What about him?" This came from the third man, and I assumed he was referring to Tubero.

"What about me? You didn't have to hit me that hard, you *cunnus*!"

"I did if you want it to look good," Maxentius said coolly.

There was another pause, but I felt the ground vibrate as Maxentius walked over to Tubero.

"Give me your purse," he told Tubero.

"My purse?" Tubero protested. "Why do you need mine?"

"To make it look like a robbery, you idiot," Maxentius snapped. "If they find this *cunnus* lying here without his purse, but you still have yours, how do you think it's going to look? That's why you're staying here."

"Stay here? Why would I stay here?" Tubero's voice was bewildered.

"Because," just from his tone, I knew Maxentius was struggling to remain patient, "you were seen with him last. You need to be here when he comes to. Or," he added, "you get found, whichever happens first. Now, hand it over."

Tubero sighed, but then I heard a clinking sound as he handed his purse to Maxentius.

"Now lie down and catch up on your sleep," Maxentius ordered.

Grumbling, I suppose Tubero obeyed because there was a thud that carried through the ground under my body and, a heartbeat or two later, I could sense that Maxentius was standing next to me again. The blood had been pouring out of my nose, but it was beginning to clot, making breathing difficult, and I was afraid that I would be forced to betray that I was at least semi-conscious.

"Let's get back to camp," Maxentius ordered.

Because my eyes were closed, I did not anticipate the last kick he gave to my head, but this time, it was unfeigned. I remember lights of a thousand colors exploding in my head, then...nothing.

I awoke to the sight of the rafters of a wooden roof and a feeling that there was not an inch of my body that was not in pain. Trying to lift my head, I was stopped by a combination of a sudden pounding inside my skull and a dizziness that was only slightly less than what I remembered from the night before. Or at least what I thought of as the night before. The movement of my head must have attracted attention because my view was suddenly filled with the sight of a face peering down at me, one that I did not recognize.

"At last you're awake, Gregarius." The man, who did not look much older than me, spoke with an accent that sounded Thracian.

"Where am I?" I did not even recognize the voice as my own.

"Why, in the hospital, of course," he said with a cheerfulness that, frankly, I found a bit obscene.

Moving carefully, I lifted my arm so that I could reach up and touch where the most excruciating pain was coming from, the side of my head. But then my fingers touched not my hair or scalp, but fabric, and just the slightest contact made me wince.

"You had a nasty laceration on your scalp that we had to sew up," he told me. "The skin on your head was hanging off like a flap."

My stomach lurched at this graphic explanation, and the result was another paroxysm of agony as the muscles of my stomach contracted, then immediately protested. Despite not wanting to, I flinched, which in turn caused my lower back to react with an agony that I had never experienced either time I had been wounded. If I had had my wits about me, I would have been struck by the irony that I had just recovered from a wound, only to find myself back on the sick and injured list.

"What else?" I asked.

He pursed his lips as he thought about how to sum up my injuries.

"You have at least two ribs cracked, close to your spine," he began, using his fingers to enumerate all that was wrong. "You have massive bruising all up and down your torso, and I've already mentioned your head. Although," he added with a smile, as if he was imparting joyous news, "your skull doesn't appear to be fractured." He snapped his fingers, "Oh, and your nose is broken. The doctor tried to reset it, but until the swelling goes down, it will be impossible to tell if you'll look the same."

That at least explained why I was breathing through my mouth, and I suppose it was a blessing that the other parts of my body hurt so badly that I had not noticed my nose. At least, until he mentioned it, after which I became acutely aware that there appeared to be something stuffed up both nostrils. But when I reached up and brushed my nostrils with my fingertips, I was stopped by the *medici*.

"I wouldn't do that just yet, if I were you," he said gently. "Because you'll not only start bleeding again, but any chance of your nose resuming its former shape will be lost."

I did not say anything in reply, but I sighed and dropped my hands.

"Now," he continued and, even in my addled state, I noticed the change in demeanor and tone as he asked, "maybe you can tell me what happened to you?"

When I opened my mouth to answer, in that moment, I had every intention of telling him the truth, and I honestly do not know what stopped me; maybe another intervention by the gods who spared me.

Swallowing instead, I felt the coppery taste of the blood that was still leaking into my mouth from my nose, then I said, "I was robbed."

"Yes, so I gathered," he said wryly. "But do you remember anything about who attacked you?"

I started to shake my head, but it hurt too much, so instead, I answered him verbally.

"Well, you need to think about it because the provosts will be here shortly to ask you that very thing."

He turned to go, but before he did, I stopped him, asking, "Did I come in alone?"

"No," he answered. "Your friend was brought in like you, although his injuries aren't nearly as severe. From what he remembered, he was the first one to be knocked unconscious."

I kept my expression the same, although it was a struggle. Despite knowing how much it would hurt, I forced myself to turn my head to examine first the cot to my left, then to my right, but they were both empty.

"Where is he now?" I asked the *medici*.

"Oh, he's already back with your section," he said. "He left the hospital yesterday."

Now I was completely confused.

"Yesterday?" I asked. "How is that possible? We were…attacked last night."

Now the *medici* laughed, but it was not a cruel one, and he actually reached out to pat me on the foot.

"No, you were attacked three days ago," he told me. "You've been out for two full days."

That was when he went to attend to his other duties, leaving me in a very confused and thoughtful condition.

Not long after I regained consciousness, Asinius, Bassus, Scrofa, and Galens showed up, the latter acting officially.

"Looks like you found another way to get out of duty," Galens joked, but I sensed that there was real worry beneath the bantering tone.

Bassus leaned over my bed, examining me before letting out a low whistle.

"Whoever did you was serious," he said, then pointed at the bandage around my head. "That alone is bad enough."

"What do you remember?" Galens asked me.

I described the sequence of events truthfully, at least up until the moment where I regained consciousness the first time in the alley. That part I left out completely, and I could tell Galens was unconvinced, but I said nothing more. Finally, he finished incising the report in his tablet, then gave a grunt as he snapped it shut.

"That's more or less what Tubero said." He eyed me for a moment as if waiting for me to say something more.

I did, but probably not what he was expecting.

"How is Tubero?" I asked. "I saw him get hit and go down, but that's all I remember."

"He'll be all right," Galens assured me, but there was no missing the glance he exchanged with Asinius. Finally accepting I was not going to give anything more, he gave me an awkward pat on the shoulder and said, "I'll leave you to get your rest. The doctor says you'll be in here a few days. Oh." He snapped his fingers. "I forgot to tell you. We're marching back to Siscia next week."

Despite this being good news for everyone else, I could not stifle a groan.

"Which means I'm going to feel like *cac* the entire way back," I complained.

Galens chuckled and acknowledged that this was indeed so.

"But," he pointed out, "at least you'll still be with us, neh?"

"True," I granted.

Then he left, Bassus and Scrofa going with him, leaving Asinius who, up until that moment, had not said a word after his initial greeting. He watched the others file out of the room, then turned back to me.

"Well?" he demanded, a scowl on his face.

"Well what?" I asked.

Sighing, he said, "Are you going to tell me what really happened?"

"I told you," I protested, but he cut me off.

"Not that load you gave Galens. Which," he thought to add, "I can tell you he doesn't believe any more than I do." He leaned over close to my face and whispered, "I saw Tubero, remember. Yes, he has a bump on his head, but nothing near big enough to knock him out. I've seen enough things like this to know."

"Maybe his skull isn't as tough as mine," I pointed out, but he snorted in clear disbelief.

"It has nothing to do with the thickness of his skull." He glanced over his shoulder, then asked me in a whisper, "It was Maxentius, wasn't it? At least, he was the leader of them."

Part of me wanted to acknowledge the truth, but I am afraid that between my state of mind and all that had happened in my short career in the Legions to this point, I was not willing to admit anything.

"I don't know who it was," I insisted. "But I'm sure it wasn't Maxentius."

"If you don't know, how can you be sure it wasn't him?" he pounced immediately, and I cursed myself for allowing this lapse.

"W-well," I stammered, "because I remember hearing voices, but I didn't recognize any of them. If Maxentius had been there, I surely would have heard him."

The amount of time Asinius' eyes bored into mine lasted for a dozen heartbeats at least, but I managed to keep my gaze from wavering. Finally, he relented, sighing again.

"Suit yourself," he muttered. "If you're not willing to admit it was Maxentius, I can't be expected to help watch your back."

He almost had me then, and I opened my mouth for a moment…but nothing came out. I was and, to some extent, still am mulishly stubborn, and at some point in the period of darkness between the time Maxentius kicked me in the head and waking up in the hospital, I had decided I was going to handle this problem on my own, and in a way where he would never bother me again.

Thankfully, we were not required to wear helmets when we marched out of Mogontiacum because the bandage around my head was still too thick. The stitches were still in place; I would have them removed on the second day of our return to Siscia, leaving a vivid pink scar in a roughly half-moon shape, ranging from just in front of my right ear to the back of my skull. Even now, while the scar has faded, no hair grows there, reminding me of what happened. The marching itself was only slightly less painful than after I had been wounded in battle, although my back ached a great deal by the end of the day. For one of the few times during my time as a Gregarius, Galens and Corvinus looked the other way when I did more leaning on my shovel than using it at the end of the day, but it was not the physical part of the march that put me into the most difficulty. Being forced to pretend that I did not know who was behind the attack, despite the fact that I would catch Maxentius smirking at me whenever he thought I was looking was bad enough, but it was being cordial to Tubero that was the hardest. He made a great show of concern over my condition and, more times than I could easily count, I would hear him declaring to anyone who would listen how he was also a victim of what had happened. My jaws became sore from clenching them together so tightly, but the physical pain had little to do with it. Compounding matters, Asinius was decidedly cool towards me, sending me the clear message that he took my silence personally, and I did have some regret about not confiding in him. Yet, I had made up my mind what to do about it and, once my course was set, I would not be deterred. Galens, who had counted Maxentius as a friend, suddenly stopped being so friendly towards him.

Before a week on the march had passed, it was clear that our Century was split into two camps, all without a word being said. I will say that this gave me even more pause; despite the fact that the men of the First seemed to be heavily weighted in my favor, there were at least a dozen men who showed their allegiance to Maxentius. And through it all, Corvinus and Galens seemed content to remain silent and not dispense what we call bathhouse justice. This puzzled me a great deal; at least it did then, although now that I am a Centurion, I understand it better. If we had been marching to a campaign, I am sure that Corvinus and Galens would have acted in a way that sent a message that such a breach would not be tolerated. But given that we were marching to winter quarters, both men were experienced enough to know that these kinds of disagreements have a way of working themselves out over the winter months. On the other hand, I did not, at least back then, and I regret to say that I began to view both my Optio and Centurion as possible enemies. Now that time has passed, I would not be a bit surprised if both of them did not guess what my intentions were, and had decided to let me handle this issue on my own. That, however, is just speculation; we never spoke about any of this, even after everything was settled. Meanwhile, my body healed fairly quickly, but there was still a darkness in my mind that caused me to spend many watches on the march brooding. It should not have surprised me that the distance between Asinius and me grew as a result, and the only reason it did was because I was still in so many ways just a boy.

Not long into our march, I began excusing myself from our fire and went wandering about, often ending up at the fire of either Tuditanus, or more often, my older friend Figulus. Although they both knew that I had been attacked, because they were in different Centuries, they did not know many details, other than what was whispered from one fire to the next. Fortunately, very quickly, the both of them recognized that asking me about it would not yield anything and, if the truth were known, one of the reasons I sought their company was it allowed me to escape the tension that permeated not just my section, but the entire Century. Mostly, we talked about the campaign we had just finished, although I will say that not all the conversations were lighthearted in nature. Inevitably, we talked about Drusus and the tragedy that had befallen him, and I learned that, just like around our fire, there was a feeling there was more to what happened than just an accident. Like every exchange where the subject of Drusus came up, the talk was in whispers, with furtive glances over shoulders as we discussed the happenings of this campaign. Even for someone like Figulus, who had been in the Legion for three years, nothing like what happened under Drusus had ever occurred before, and for Tuditanus and me, it was even more unsettling. Were all campaigns like this, we wondered, despite the veterans assuring us that they were not? As we got nearer to Siscia, gradually the topic of conversation changed, as men became more excited about returning to the place they called home. Men with families were the most anxious, but even younger rankers like I was savored the idea of returning to the familiarity of Siscia, where each of us had our favorite spots in the form of wineshops or whorehouses. I was looking forward to getting back to Siscia as well, but for completely different reasons, as a plan had come together in my mind.

We arrived in Siscia the last week of the month named for Augustus, earlier than expected because the campaign had been cut short. Still, there was quite a crowd gathered on each side of the road from town that led to the camp, composed of the families that the men are not supposed to have. Of the men in my section, Bassus, Scrofa, and Dento all had families with at least one child; Bassus, being the oldest, had four, and his woman and children were at the front of the crowd, calling to him as we marched by. Asinius had a woman, I knew, but no children, although she had been pressing him that it was time to start one, which he was clearly reluctant to do. On the other hand, there was nobody there to greet me, and I think this was the first time I actually felt that lack keenly, although I quickly dismissed it. There was still too much I wanted to accomplish and, as much as I appreciated all that my father had given to his family, I was also aware that his devotion to us had been viewed as a detriment to his career in the army. But while my father is a devoted family man, I felt more connected to my Avus and his ambition in this than I did with my father, at least when it comes to the Legions. Over the years, I have pondered on this a great deal, and I have come to the conclusion that I think our similarity in size and strength had as much to do with shaping my view of the world and my conviction that I was best served trying to follow in the footsteps of Titus Pullus than Gaius Porcinianus Pullus. As much as I love and respect my father, who was one of the best Centurions of his Legion, I wanted more than that; like my Avus, I wanted, and still do now even more than I did in those days, to be considered a legend in the Legions. This ambition has never been something I have uttered aloud and am somewhat reluctant to commit to this record I am writing, but if I cannot be honest here, there is not much point in creating it. At the same time, even at my young age during that first campaign, I understood that what I had in mind was a terrible risk that could see my career effectively ended before it ever took flight. Yet, I also knew myself well enough to understand that I would never be able to live with myself after what Maxentius and his friends had done. In this matter, I recalled my Avus' account, and his revenge on a man named Prixus, who had been a bodyguard of the Legate in command of this very Army of Pannonia, when my grandfather first assumed the post of Camp Prefect. It was not without some cost to himself; I clearly remember, as a child, the leather harness he wore to cover the stump of the little finger of his left hand. Yet, when I had asked him about what happened, no matter how much I pestered him on our daily walk down to the stable to feed Ocelus his apple, he never once gave me a hint, other than to give a vague answer about losing it in a fight. Not until I donned the *toga virilis*, and my father allowed me to read his account, did I learn the whole story. When I asked my father what he knew, he informed me that he was as surprised as I had been on learning the truth, because his then-uncle had never divulged any details. That finger had not been chopped off, as I had assumed when I was a child; it had been bitten off in his fight with Prixus, in a dark room in the town of Naissus. I suppose it is likely that the example set by Titus Pullus was what drove me to concoct the plan I did concerning Maxentius, although I think it may be just as likely that I would have gotten there on my own, without any knowledge of Prixus. However, my Avus killed Prixus; this was not something I was willing to do, mainly because of our respective statuses. While Prixus may have been a bodyguard to a nobleman, he was also a gladiator and had been a slave who won his freedom. Maxentius was a citizen, and he was a veteran of the 8th Legion, so I understood that killing him, no matter how I did it, would raise too many questions, and would likely spell the end of my career and probably my life. Consequently, I concocted a course of action that required me to strengthen an attribute that, to that point especially, was probably my weakest character trait, the quality of patience.

When an army returns from campaign to their winter quarters, there is a flurry of activity that is almost the exact duplicate of what takes place before marching out of the gate, except in reverse. Our artillery is broken down and placed in storage, the torsion ropes given to the armory *Immunes* for inspection; our javelins are also returned to the armory, although we keep our swords and daggers. Shields are also checked in, and the woodworking *Immunes* immediately go to work, repairing or replacing them. In particular, shields are expected to be turned around more quickly than any other piece of gear, especially in Siscia, since some sort of uprising or rebellion in the winter months was commonplace. Although we would not be the first Legion called out in such an event since we had just returned, as I knew very well growing up in the region, the Pannonian tribes are a fractious bunch and, even now, have only accepted our rule very grudgingly. That meant it was a definite possibility that we would find ourselves marching out to support the other Legions if matters became too serious, and I for one would not have been a bit surprised if that occurred. Consequently, we were kept busy for almost a week before we were informed during our morning formation that we would be going into our normal garrison routine. Naturally, this raised a resounding cheer from the men, both those with families who would now be allowed to spend their nights in the town with their loved ones, and the single men like me, who would be set loose to pursue the various leisure pursuits that make up the pastime of a Gregarius. Almost all of those pursuits involved wine, women, and gambling in some form or another, yet when Asinius asked me to go with him into town, I declined. I told him that I was still not completely recovered from my beating, and that I was going to take advantage of an opportunity to rest, and although there was some truth to this, it was not my main motivation. In fact, I was unwilling to run the risk of an encounter with Maxentius, or Tubero, for that matter, when we were not under the standard, and when Bacchus did not have at least a partial grip on my senses. As callow as I may have been in those days, I knew myself well enough to recognize that I did not possess enough self-discipline to avoid confronting either of them out in town when we would inevitably run into each other. Nevertheless, it was true that I was not in perfect condition, and I understood I would have to be at my very best to accomplish the task I had set for myself.

This began a period where the bonds I had formed with the men of my section over the course of the campaign were put to the test because, from their viewpoint, I became almost a recluse. Of course, I performed my duties alongside my comrades; whenever we trained or had some sort of work to do, and when Basso, Dento, Metellus, Asinius, or Scrofa talked to me, I carried on a normal conversation. But the moment we were secured from duty, I disappeared, making myself scarce until I was sure that they had given up searching for me to go into Siscia with them. Sometimes, I would spend my time hiding with

Figulus or Tuditanus, but fairly quickly, they became aware that I was up to something and, when I refused to share my plans, they made it clear my presence made them uncomfortable. Only when I was sure that I would not be observed did I slip out of camp, except instead of town, I headed in the opposite direction, although it was not far at all to reach my destination. Then, I would work, even in the dark, until I was soaked in sweat, before I returned to the camp. Gradually, all the soreness left my body, and I felt confident that I was back to full strength, but even then, I did not stop what I was doing. All of this I did unobserved; at least, so I believed.

The weather changed, the leaves turning colors as they do every year, and the older men claimed that the coming winter would arrive early and be hard. Meanwhile, in Rome, Drusus had been interred in the mausoleum where all members of the family of Augustus reside, or will when their respective time comes. Tiberius' name was being whispered as the most likely successor to Augustus, although there was no sign that the Princeps had any intention of dying anytime soon. The tribes in Germania, after their momentary cessation of hostilities, quickly resumed their normal activities, raiding across the Rhenus and fighting with each other. On the surface of things, all seemed normal; we were preparing for the long, cold months of winter, and the rhythm of life in the Legion that had been a part of my life in one way or another for as long as I could remember continued apace. Perhaps a month after our return, I had become acutely aware that I was under heavy scrutiny, mostly by Galens, but by the Pilus Prior as well, and I would feel their eyes on me as I went about my tasks. Following the example of both my father and my Avus, I made sure to avoid running afoul of the many regulations that govern our lives, not wanting to have any official cause to come to the attention of my Optio and Centurion. Only once was I worried that they had somehow divined what I was up to, when I was summoned to the Cohort office. Waiting for me there was both Galens and Corvinus, the latter sitting behind his desk, while my Optio was in his accustomed spot in a chair against the wall. Coming to *intente*, I rendered my salute, but while Corvinus returned it, that was all he did at first, just leaning back in his chair and studying me with eyes that I was sure could divine my secret.

"So, Pullus," he finally broke the silence. "We haven't spoken in a while, especially after your...incident in Mogontiacum. Are you healed? Everything all right?"

I assured him that I was suffering no lingering effects from my beating. Even so, just the mention of what happened brought a flush to my face, something Corvinus did not miss.

"I can see that you might be physically fine, but it still bothers you."

My mind raced, but I could see no hidden trap, and I admitted, albeit grudgingly that, yes, in fact, it did occupy my thoughts.

"Still don't have any idea who did it?"

This came from Galens, and I was sure that they were acting in concert, and the Optio was launching a surprise flank attack, as it were.

I turned to face him and made sure I met his gaze when I lied, "No, still no idea. I've been listening to men talk to each other because that's the only way I'll recognize them." Suddenly inspired, I added, "Which is what I've been doing. On my off-duty time, of course," I added hastily. "I've been wandering around the other Cohort areas, just listening."

It was an extremely thin gruel of an excuse for my disappearances I knew, but I reasoned that it was better than making no attempt at all, and I was rewarded with the sight of them shooting a glance at each other. Out of the corner of my eye, I saw one of Corvinus' shoulders rise in a half-shrug, as if he was saying that he supposed it was possible, however unlikely.

"And if you do hear the voice of one of the men who attacked you, what do you intend to do?" Corvinus resumed his questioning.

"Come to you," I tried to assure him, being as sincere as I thought I could get away with and not making it obvious I was lying. "Then let the army handle it."

"That's a...commendable attitude," Corvinus replied evenly. "But, I don't know that I believe it."

I was about to open my mouth to protest that he, in fact, could believe me, but a small voice somewhere inside me warned me that this was, in fact, what he wanted me to say, that he had some sort of trap laid.

"I don't know that I believe it myself," I finally said, which was at least a half-truth. "But I'm still in my first year and I'm just a Gregarius. If I were to do something outside of regulations, whatever satisfaction I might gain would be outweighed by what would happen to me at the hands of the army."

Silence hung between us for several heartbeats as he considered what I said. Finally, he gave a shrug.

"That makes sense, I suppose. And I'm happy that you see matters so clearly, because you're right. Anything you would gain by taking revenge would be pretty puny compared to what would happen when the Primus Pilus found out about it."

I cannot say exactly how I knew, but I sensed that there was more to this statement than just the words Corvinus had uttered, that under the surface there was an even deeper warning. Regardless, I was not about to probe to find out if my suspicions were correct, just assuring Corvinus that I understood. We chatted for a short while longer, then I was dismissed. Returning to my hut, I walked slowly as I tried to think through the conversation, worrying that I had somehow betrayed my true intentions. Finally, I decided that there would only be one way to find out, and that was when I went through with what I had planned.

It was not until the Ides of the month of October, when we arose one morning to a thin coating of snow on the ground, that I finally decided it was time to act. Being honest, I cannot say that the weather had anything to do with it; I think it was as good a reason as any, and I was not only completely healed, but I felt confident that between the experience I had gained during the campaign and the work I had been doing on my own, that this was as good a time as any. When we are in garrison, at least when we are at a permanent camp like the one at Siscia, where everyone has a hut, the meals are prepared on the small stove in each section hut. It is very common that men who are friends, but in different sections, will actually have their meals together, so that it is not always the case where, for example, if one were to go looking for a man in the Third Section at mealtime, he would be in their hut. Such was not the case when it came time for me to find Maxentius, because I made sure that he was one of those men who was always in his section hut. Approaching the building, I could hear the normal chatter through the door, as men sat at the communal table that is the dominant feature of the section hut, placed in the middle of the room, while our bunks line two walls. Standing outside, I did hesitate and thought about knocking, but then decided against it, wanting what I was about to do to have the maximum effect. Aside from my main goal, I wanted what I was going to do to have the largest audience possible, and I knew the more dramatic my entrance, the more men would talk about it. Taking a breath, I flung open the door, except that I did it with so much force that it not only slammed against the wall, but bounced back with considerable speed; if I had not stopped it with my hand, I would have suffered the indignity of having it slam in my face. Fortunately for what I was trying to accomplish, that did not happen. I was rewarded by shouts of alarm, as the men of the First Section leapt to their feet, or at least tried to, although one man actually stumbled and landed, hard, on his rear end. Maxentius had been seated on the bench facing the door, at the far end, which I expected, but like the rest of the men, he wore a look of alarm on his face at my sudden appearance. I stood there for a moment, temporarily forgetting why I was there, discomfited at the eight pairs of eyes staring back at me. I opened my mouth, but before I could say anything, Maxentius' face split into a smile of such malice and hatred that it caught me short, and I realized that as much as I hated him, he felt at least as much the same way.

"Well, well." He gave a harsh, barking laugh. "Look who's here? The rich boy who thinks he's as good as me with a sword."

The moment he uttered those words, I felt better because, behind the bluster, I could sense that he really feared me. Suddenly, my nerves disappeared and I was calm, or at least as calm as I could be under the circumstances.

"That's why I'm here," I replied. "Because I think it's time for us to settle that question."

"Question?" he sneered. "There is no question! Just because you're big and you were one of those *Tiros* who knew which end of the sword to hold doesn't mean *cac, boy*."

"Then it shouldn't take you long to prove it," I shot back.

Now that the others understood what was happening, their expressions were akin to men attending at the games, avidly watching our exchange.

"And why would I waste my time?" Maxentius countered. "I doubt I'd work up a sweat."

"Then you'll have even more to brag about, since it'll be so easy."

Maxentius did not seem to know how to respond to this and, for the first time, despite the lower level of lighting because of the lamps, I saw the sheen of sweat on his upper lip, encouraging me to keep up the pressure.

"I'm not sure why you're hesitating," I told him. "After all, you've been telling me since I joined the Legion you were going to teach me a lesson. Now's your chance. Or," I shrugged, "maybe you're just talk. Maybe you need to have your friends to attack someone when they're drunk, in a dark alley, because you know that I'll destroy you if you dared to face me with a *rudis*. Maybe you're just a coward."

Maxentius' face suddenly turned deep red and he stood up, his fists balled up, one of which he shook at me.

"You're a fucking liar," he roared. "And I don't need any help to cut you down to size!"

"Prove it," I shot back. "Tomorrow, at the beginning of second watch, outside the camp at the stakes."

There was no way that he could refuse, and I saw by his expression that he understood this.

"You're going to wish you hadn't walked in here," he said. "But I'll be there. You can count on it."

"That's all you had to say in the first place." I backed to the door, then exited.

I had achieved the first part of my plan, but in doing so, I had learned even more than I originally hoped. When I had mentioned the incident in the alley, while my eyes had been on Maxentius, I had caught two of his section mates whose faces had turned a color very similar to that of Maxentius. There was no way to prove it, but I was sure that I had his two accomplices.

I returned to my own hut, where the meal was waiting, but I acted as if nothing was amiss, taking my accustomed spot next to Asinius. Nevertheless, we were not through our meal when there was a banging on the door and, while I was expecting it, I could not help jumping a bit, although it was not as much as the others. Bassus got up from his spot to open the door, but despite his body blocking my view, I got a glimpse of who had disturbed our meal. There was an exchange of whispers, then I heard Bassus gasp and shoot a glance over his shoulder at me, which I pretended I did not see.

"Asinius," he called. "You need to come hear this."

Holding a piece of bread, he got up and joined Bassus, and there was another bout of hushed conversation, at least at first.

"What??"

Asinius' tone was not quite that of a shout, but it was close, and he whirled about to face me angrily.

Pointing his finger at me, he demanded, "Is this true?"

"Is what true?" I asked blandly, then stuffed a piece of bread in my mouth.

"Juno's *cunnus*, you know exactly what I'm talking about, boy!"

I had prepared myself for some sort of outburst, but I bristled at being called a boy, so despite my resolve to remain cool, I snapped, "You're fucking right it's true."

Out of the corner of my eye, I could see the bewildered expressions of my comrades as they exchanged confused glances.

"What is this about?" Dento broke the silence as Asinius and I glared at each other.

"Ask him." Asinius pointed at me.

Feeling all eyes on me, I gave what I thought was a casual shrug, then replied, "I challenged Maxentius to spar with me tomorrow."

Immediately, the hut was in an uproar, but I had turned my gaze on Tubero, who looked as if somehow every drop of blood had suddenly been drained from his body, his jaw hanging open so widely that I saw his partially chewed meal.

"Are you mad? He's going to hurt you, and hurt you badly!"

"Maxentius hates you! He's not going to stop until he's broken every bone in your body!"

I looked over at Dento, one of my comrades who had just expressed that opinion, and regarded him coldly.

"You don't have much faith in me, Dento," I said quietly, and he did flush, but he shook his head.

"Pullus, you're good; there's no denying that. You're very, very good. But Maxentius has been doing this a lot longer than you, and he's still the best man with a sword in the whole Cohort. Maybe in the Legion."

"Not after tomorrow," I replied with more assurance than I actually felt.

"And you think there aren't going to be consequences, even if you win?" Asinius spoke up from his spot, still standing at the door.

I turned to address him and saw that the man from the first section who had brought the news was already gone, no doubt to spread the word throughout the Century. Then it would be no more than a third of a watch after that before the entire Cohort knew. By the time morning came, the whole Legion would know, and then it would be in the hands of the gods, or the Primus Pilus, on whether or not to allow the bout to continue. This was the part of the plan that I did not have any control over, although I did have one throw of the dice in the event that I was forbidden from going through with it. I just hoped it would not come to that.

"There may be," I agreed with Asinius, which he was clearly not expecting. "But they're mine to deal with, nobody else's."

Our Sergeant opened his mouth to argue, but instead expelled a breath, then just shook his head.

"That's true. I just hope you know what you're doing."

"I do," I said, then turned back to finish eating.

It took a few moments before Asinius came back to the table, and we resumed our meal.

It surprised me that we had no other visitors that night; I expected Galens at the very least, and perhaps even the Pilus Prior himself, but neither one showed up. Retiring for the night, I was surprised that I actually had no trouble falling asleep, even when I could hear the muttered conversations taking place around me, as my comrades debated the folly of what I was doing. Tubero had excused himself immediately after the meal, yet if anything, he was more shaken when he returned than he had been when he left, something in which I took great satisfaction. I had taken great care not to utter a word to, or about Tubero, for that matter, that would indicate I had any knowledge of his role in the ambush, appearing to take at face value his claim that he had been attacked as well. He returned shortly before the *bucina* call came that announced we had to be in our own huts for the rest of the night, but went immediately to his bunk, not saying anything. When the call sounded to start the next day, I arose and began my preparations for the coming trial with a hearty break of my fast, scooping up the porridge from the night before that we reheat in the morning. Not until I emerged from my hut to make my way for the morning formation was I stopped by Galens.

"Are you mad?" he asked abruptly, in an unconscious echo of Dento.

"Not that I know of," I tried to joke, but he was not impressed at my attempt at levity.

"You're going to call this off, immediately," he ordered.

Taking a deep breath, I said simply, "No."

For a moment, he said nothing, just stared at me if a third eye had suddenly sprouted in my forehead.

"That wasn't a suggestion," he finally managed, his words somewhat difficult to understand because his jaws were so tightly clenched. "That was an order, and it comes from the Pilus Prior."

"I understand," I shrugged. "But I'm not calling it off."

His hand snaked out with surprising speed, but I took it as a good omen that as fast as his hand moved, I was able to dodge the slap he had aimed at the side of my head.

Before he could hit me again, I held up my hands in a gesture that requested his silence for the moment. He relented, but his hand still hovered in the air.

"As I remember, there's been a tradition in the Army of Pannonia that any man can challenge another man to a sparring session to determine who's the best with a sword."

As I had hoped, Galens' face took on a nonplussed expression, reminded now that this was in fact the case.

"But that was for your grandfather when he was Camp Prefect," he finally said. "It wasn't meant to extend to every rank!"

"Can you show me that in the regulations?" I asked pleasantly, although I knew the answer already. Pressing my momentary advantage, I pointed out, "And remember, I grew up here. I watched more sparring sessions than I can count where one man challenged another, and it wasn't between my Av...Prefect Pullus and someone else. It was between rankers."

For a moment, I thought he was going to try to hit me again because his face got even darker, but then he dropped his hand.

"You're too fucking smart for your own good," he finally grumbled. If I thought he would relent without any more fuss, I was wrong. "But even if you can't be stopped from this madness, how do you think the Primus Pilus is going to take it?"

"I think," I said carefully, "that he's going to remember what I just told you, that this is a custom that's been around for a long time now." I shrugged. "Outside of that, I'll just have to deal with whatever comes." Understanding that I needed Galens to, at the very least, accept this, I finished by pleading, "Galens, you know why I need to do this. How will I ever be out from under what happened to me if I don't take some sort of action? Even if I do lose, at least the rest of the Century is going to know that I won't just lie down and take a beating, no matter who it comes from."

"I suppose," he said grudgingly, "when you put it like that, it makes sense. But," he at least used his hand to point it in my face instead of hit me with it, wagging his finger as he said, "this better not start a whole bunch of nonsense, with you trying to get even if Maxentius beats you, or him doing the same if you beat him. We can't afford to have that kind of *cac* going on because it will tear the Century apart."

"If Maxentius beats me," I assured him, "you have my word that this will be the end of it. But," I could not help adding with a grin, "that's not going to happen. As far as Maxentius trying to get even after I beat him…" I shrugged, and finished by lying, "I know you and the Pilus Prior will handle it."

With a sigh, he made a jerk of his head towards the forum where we were forming up for the morning formation and, without saying anything more, I trotted off after the rest of my comrades. What I did not tell Galens was that, if everything went as I hoped, Maxentius would not be in any condition to exact vengeance.

Asinius silently helped me with my *segmentata*, checking each buckle and strap. Otherwise, the hut was deserted; everyone else was already outside the camp, wanting to get there early to have a good vantage spot.

Finally, he broke the silence. "There; I think that's good."

342

I twisted back and forth, then had him pull one strap just a bit tighter.

"Titus," he said, and I believe this was the first time he used my *praenomen*, "I know why you're doing this. And I don't blame you. But as good as you are, Maxentius *is* very good with a sword. And," he added ominously, "he'll do whatever he needs to do in order to beat you. In fact, I think he'll do his best to try and kill you."

"Then he'd be in just as much trouble as if I killed him," I pointed out.

But despite hoping he would reassure me this was the case, Asinius gave a slow shake of his head.

"That may be, but I wouldn't bet on it," he finally muttered. "Maxentius has been in this Legion a long time and he's got some powerful friends. And he's done…favors for the Primus Pilus that may weigh in his favor."

Although this did not surprise me, it was still daunting to hear it put so plainly. But I was committed, and I reached out and patted him on the shoulder.

"Thanks." I know I sounded awkward, but expressing gratitude was, and is not something that comes easily to me. "I appreciate what you're saying. But I couldn't live with myself if I let what he did go unchallenged."

"I know," Asinius said. "I just wish none of this had ever happened."

"So do I," I agreed fervently and, in this, I was being completely honest.

Finally, there was no more cause for delay, and he said simply, "Let's go. Don't want to keep all the bettors waiting."

Even with the knot in my stomach, I had to laugh, knowing he was being accurate.

343

Galens and Pilus Prior Corvinus were still in the camp, actually waiting for me at the intersection.

"Are you sure you want to do this?" Corvinus was the one to ask me this.

"Yes, sir," I replied, surprising myself that my voice sounded so calm, even with my stomach doing the kinds of twists and flips that were close to what happened when I drank too much.

Instead of arguing, Corvinus just nodded his head.

"I understand," he told me, but then he raised his *vitus* and pushed the end against my chest. "But just because I understand, that doesn't mean I approve. However, as Galens reminded me, you're quite the historian of the Legion, so I don't feel right locking you up. It would be bad for morale at this point."

Heaving a silent sigh of relief, in my mind, I offered a prayer of thanks to the gods for confirming what I had been gambling on all along, that the weight of tradition, and the makeup of Corvinus as a fighting man, would prevail.

Spinning about, he started to walk away, then stopped and faced back to look me in the eye.

"I can't officially take sides in this dispute," he said quietly, "and if you ever repeat this, I'll call you a liar. But you beating Maxentius wouldn't be the worst thing, not just for you, but for this Century. He's become a bit...much to handle."

Without waiting for a reply, he resumed his progress out of the camp, but Galens paused.

"He used to be a friend of mine," Galens told me. "But not anymore. Not after, well, you know. So, beat him, Pullus. Beat him bad."

Then he turned and trotted to catch up with Corvinus.

"At least I have those two on my side," I commented.

"Maybe," Asinius replied, his tone doubtful. "But like the Pilus Prior said, he can't be seen to take sides. I, on the other hand," he favored me with a grin, "will make no secret. I hope you beat that bastard bloody."

I did not answer, but I thought grimly, you have no idea.

If it was not the entire Legion turned out for the spectacle, it was at the very least all those Gregarii who were not *Immunes* and working on something. But I was most worried about the presence of one man, and one only, and it was not Maxentius. Although I had swayed Galens and Corvinus, Urso could still have stopped this from happening. Then, I saw him, standing with Corvinus and a couple of the other Pili Priores and, while he was not in full uniform, he wore his belt and *vitus*, the symbol that he was there in at least a semi-official capacity. He did not look happy, yet when I approached him to render a salute, he returned it readily enough, then just regarded me for a moment.

Finally, he said, "Pullus. Are you sure you want to do this?"

"Yes, sir," I repeated what I had said to Corvinus.

Unlike Corvinus, Urso made no attempt to talk me out of it, or admonish me in any way.

Instead, he turned slightly and raised his voice so that all the men in the area could hear, "Then so be it. Whatever happens in this sparring match, happens. The outcome is up to the gods, and you're going to have to take your lumps because I won't intervene." Only then did he look over at Maxentius, and finished, "No matter what happens."

Maxentius gave Urso a salute, as did I, but he was smiling broadly as he did so. Urso had worded his pronouncement in such an ambiguous way that Maxentius could argue that he had been given permission to hurt, cripple, or kill me. However, what I found interesting was that none of the onlookers cheered this signal of the possibility of real bloodshed; if anything, there was an air of uneasy puzzlement, and I saw Corvinus and Galens look at each other, standing just behind Urso. Not lost on me was the chance that Urso was hoping that the outcome of my bout would end in my death, but this was something I could not help. Asinius guided me by the arm to the opposite side of the open space from where Maxentius and one of his comrades from his section was with him, acting as his second, and not lost on me was that it was one of his accomplices from my beating. We were in the spot just on the side opposite from the fort, using a cleared area on the far side of the stakes that is used for official sparring sessions and mock battles. The boundaries were set by the men of the 8th, forming a rough square of flesh and bone that was becoming noisier and more boisterous by the moment. Asinius handed me the padded sleeves we use for sparring, but I shook my head.

"What?" he asked incredulously. "You need to wear these!"

Again, I shook my head, but I refused to say any more, until he finally dropped them in disgust. For a moment, I considered telling him why, then decided against it, although it was all part of my plan. But when he tried to strap the wicker guard over my face and I demurred at that, he lost his temper.

"You're going to at least wear that, or I'm going to the Pilus Prior and ask him to stop the bout," he snapped.

I saw that he was serious, so I lowered my head so that he could reach up and tighten the thongs that hold it in place. In all honesty, I have always hated these things because, while there is an opening around our eyes so our view is not obscured, you can still see it at the corner of your vision, which I find distracting. Once finished, Asinius stepped aside and I saw that Maxentius, unlike me, had put on the arm guards. I came very close to panicking at that moment, except before I could make an issue of it, Pilus Prior Corvinus entered into the makeshift arena. Walking over to Maxentius first, he demanded to see the *rudis* that Maxentius was going to use, inspecting it carefully, whereupon he did the same to the wicker shield. When he was

346

satisfied, he turned about and walked in my direction, and I expected him to come inspect mine. However, he did not; instead, he stopped in the middle, and raised his hands for silence. But rather than quieting down, there were shouts by some of the spectators, all of them clamoring to be heard.

"Why aren't you checking his weapons?"

Whoever shouted this was drowned out by the cries of other men, but they were supporting the first man's question, not trying to shout it down. If Corvinus was upset at this, he did not show it and, finally, he managed to get men quieted down.

"Because I know both of these men," he called out. "And I inspected Pullus' weapons before we got here. You saw me do it in camp!" He turned to gesture to Maxentius and he finished, "He was already here."

This seemed to satisfy the crowd, but I exchanged a glance with Asinius, who shrugged. It was true we had held a brief conversation, except that he had not checked my *rudis* nor my shield, and I wondered why he would act in this manner. Did he know something in particular, or was it just Maxentius and his character that prompted his behavior? Urso looked anything but pleased, but he did not object; I supposed that calling his own Pilus Prior into question would create a whole new set of problems. Finished with his explanation, Corvinus turned and motioned us to approach. On the walk to meet him, my mind raced, because if Maxentius wore his arm guards, that was likely to be a fatal blow to what I had in mind. Conversely, I would then be forced to choose whether or not to don my own, yet the thought of doing so and how it would be viewed by the assembled men was such that I could not bear the thought. Then, just before I reached Corvinus, I had an idea.

"That's a good idea, Maxentius," I called out in a loud voice.

He had been approaching and was about equidistant to Corvinus as I, but he slowed, his face screwed up in clear suspicion.

"What's a good idea?" his voice was raspier than normal, another sign that he had a case of nerves. "What are you talking about, you *cunnus*?"

Pointing with my *rudis*, I replied, "Wearing those things. I don't want to leave you too bruised. I know your delicate skin takes a long time to heal."

Just as I had hoped, my jibe brought a roar of laughter by those who had heard it, but more importantly, it clearly infuriated Maxentius.

"Fuck you, *Tiro*," he shot back, but he was clearly rattled. "I don't need these things because you won't touch me!"

"Then why are you wearing them?"

I am not sure who shouted this, but it sounded like Bassus; for my part, I just grinned at him and moved my head in the direction from where the shout had come.

"What he said." I forced myself to laugh. "If that's so, why are you wearing them?"

Glaring at me, Maxentius tried to shake the guards off his arms, but was unsuccessful, so they ended up only being halfway down, and he had to endure the ignominy of turning to his second, who came scampering out to help him shed them.

Seeing that we were both equally equipped, Corvinus said, again loudly enough for most men to hear, "You know the rules of sparring. There will be *no* thrusts or slashes to the head or face!" He glared first at me, then turned to Maxentius, holding his stare until the other man gave a grudging nod. Continuing, "When one of you is in danger of being seriously injured, I am going to stop this immediately! And anyone who doesn't obey, INSTANTLY, will be scourged! Do both of you understand?"

I felt my head nodding, but inwardly, I was reeling, wondering if my carefully laid plans had been brought low in the space of time it had taken Corvinus to instruct us.

"Go back to your seconds," Corvinus instructed, and both of us turned and walked away from the center of the ring.

That walk seemed to take forever as my mind raced, trying to think of a way I could prevail in the event that Corvinus did as he promised. Deciding I would just have to take advantage of the first opportunity instead of what I had planned originally, I paused for a moment, then turned about, and immediately began summoning what I hoped would be my most potent weapon.

Looking back, I realize there were a number of factors that worked in my favor and, oddly enough, the first was the crowd of faces peering back at me. Outside of my Century and Cohort, I was still largely unknown, while Maxentius had been marching for years, which meant that the men acting as spectators were largely cheering for him. I suppose I had vaguely assumed that this might be the case, yet hearing Maxentius' name being shouted as much as it was served as a slap in the face that woke me up. More importantly, it also transported me back in time, to another moment very similar in nature, when I had convinced Vulso to allow me to face the dwarf Spartacus again. Much like that time, the fact there were men actively cheering for me to fail caught me by surprise at first, before it ignited the anger at the injustice of it. Did these men not know what Maxentius was truly about? Had they not heard of what he did to me in Mogontiacum? From there, it did not take much for my mind to turn to Maxentius himself, remembering all the insults and slights he had hurled at me from the first moment of my joining the Century, even before he had beaten me. I do not know how much time elapsed between turning about to face Maxentius and the moment Corvinus made the signal to start the bout with a sharp chopping downward motion with his arm; my guess is no more than fifty heartbeats. Nevertheless, it was long enough that the ball of molten lava in my belly burst, shooting through my body with a heat that made me instantly erupt in sweat as, with a roar, I rushed forward towards Maxentius. Crossing the ground, I moved much faster than he expected, thanks to my longer legs, and I saw his eyes widen in surprise and he had barely gotten started on his own countermove when I went smashing into him, my shield hard up against my shoulder. The breath exploded from him, washing me in a sour smell of wine, telling me that he had fortified himself for this contest. Still, he was no *Tiro* and, while my superior weight knocked him back a step, instead of shifting his shield away from his body to keep his balance as a less experienced man would, he kept it in front of him as he broke contact with the dirt for an instant and made a small hop that brought his feet off the ground. This enabled him to keep his balance and, in fact, land just a pace backward than where he had started, essentially bouncing off of me. Before I could try to follow up with an offensive move of my own, his wooden blade shot over the top of his shield. If I had been an average size, the tip of his *rudis* would have been perilously close to the vicinity of my face and might have caused Corvinus to stop the bout. But I am sure he had calculated that in doing so, because of our size difference, the point of his blade instead hit me a few inches lower in the center of my chest. Despite managing to lean backward to rob the thrust of most of its force, the impact still caused my breath to leave in an explosive gasp, which he heard.

"This will be too easy," he sneered, already moving even as he said this.

Recovering his blade, he pulled it back so that it was out of sight behind his shield, then he shot his shield out to crash into mine. Despite his smaller size, I felt the power there, causing my rearmost foot to slip backward just a matter of an inch or two, but enough that it drew a shout from the crowd, who sensed that I was in trouble.

Thanks to those cheers, that divine madness quickly reached its full potency and, suddenly, Maxentius slowed down, or at least so it seemed. Following up his punch with the shield, his *rudis* came out from behind it, except this time at an angle, with his arm held out so the point would get in behind the edge of my shield to hit me in the ribs. Countering, I swept my shield outward, not much, but just enough to catch his thrust and send the point sliding by the outside of my left arm. Even as I did this, my own *rudis* was moving, except I was not aiming at his torso, choosing instead to land a blow with the flat of my blade against his left shoulder. I was able to do this thanks to what I had observed that day in battle, when Corvinus had reversed our formation so that for the only time, instead of Maxentius being behind me in the relief line, I was behind him. During that fight, I had noticed that when he made a thrust, he had a tendency to drop his shield just a bit. It is a common thing because it helps to counterbalance a man when he extends his right arm; it is also a habit my father had beaten out of me long before. Being fair, the reason Maxentius had gotten away with it for these years was due both to the quality of our enemies and because he was faster than almost everyone I had faced. That day, however, his fastest was nowhere near quick enough, as once more things seemed to slow down for me. Now he was the one who hissed in pain, but again, he recovered quickly, bringing his shield back up.

"That looks like it hurt," I taunted him, to which he responded with a growl.

Regardless of my provocation, he was too wily to try and lash out immediately, so that for the next few moments, we shuffled about, feinting and trying to maneuver ourselves into our favored position for offense. I was only vaguely aware that the men around us were shouting; instead, I was listening to his breathing, and I was heartened to hear it already coming in shorter gasps than my own. For his part, he tried to move me around so that the sun would be over his shoulder, but every time he tried, I sent him back behind his shield with a quick thrust. Dust was starting to drift upward from our shuffling feet; I believe that was what gave me the instant's warning of what he was about to do because, with a quick, sliding step with his right foot, he kicked up a handful of dirt, trying to get it into my face. My height also helped me, so that not only did I see it coming, it did not obscure my vision at all, allowing me to see and anticipate what he was about to try. Pivoting on his left foot, aided by the fact he had just lifted his other one when he kicked dirt at me, he spun around with a speed that would have been impressive against anyone else but me in my current state, in an attempt to bring his blade around in a backhand that originated from my right side. In doing this, for an instant, his back was turned to me, a move that is either extremely foolhardy, or performed by a man who is supremely confident in his skill. I must admit, against someone else, it probably would have worked; instead, it gave me the opportunity I needed. Aided by the momentum of not just his arm, but his entire body as it spun towards me, I added to my own force by twisting not just my hips, but my entire body in a manner very similar to when we hurl the javelin. Just as his right arm began to swing at the elbow, the point of my *rudis* struck with pinpoint accuracy, directly on the elbow joint and, even above the shouts of the crowd, they could hear the snapping sound of his breaking arm. However, I was not through. Making it look as if it was simply a matter of my own momentum, I continued whipping my body around so that the large boss, despite our practice shields being made of wood and not iron, still smashed into roughly the same spot on his arm. Hitting the exact same spot I had with my *rudis*, I felt the joint shatter, making a crunching, crackling sound that was drowned out by a scream that was so shrill it temporarily deafened me. I was dimly aware of Maxentius' *rudis* flying from his grasp, tumbling with great speed, and there was a shout of pain as it struck one of the spectators. Before Maxentius could fall, my momentum carried me so that the bulk of my body slammed into his, as he had taken a staggering step forward with his forearm suddenly dangling at an angle that it was not meant to go. Our feet got tangled up, sending Maxentius flying, while I took several stumbling steps before I managed to get my feet back from under me. Out of habit more than any other reason, I spun about to face Maxentius, my shield back up into position and my *rudis* ready to strike again. Except there was no need; Maxentius was sprawled in the dirt, his arm bent backward at a grotesque angle and, from appearances, he was unconscious. Only then did I become aware of the complete silence. For a moment, I stood, staring down at his body, which was twitching as he began coming back to an awareness that his life was essentially ruined. Then, I spat on the ground in his direction, threw down my *rudis* and shield next to his body, and turned to walk away, back to Asinius and the stunned crowd.

"I should have you scourged."

The words were troubling enough, but the fact that Urso uttered them so quietly was even more unsettling. My legs started trembling, but I remained at *intente*, and did not say a word in response.

"With all due respect, Primus Pilus, if you do, there will be trouble."

Corvinus' tone was mild, but it angered Urso nevertheless, and he turned away from me to glare at my Pilus Prior.

"Is that a threat, Pilus Prior?" he asked, again in a quiet voice.

"Not at all," Corvinus responded, and only he knew whether he was as scared as I was at that moment. "But you did make a public announcement, in front of almost the entire Legion, that you wouldn't retaliate against the winner."

"I know what I said," Urso snapped. "And that's not what I said." He suddenly looked away. "Not exactly," he amended.

"True," Corvinus agreed. "Not exactly. But do you think the rankers will see it that way?"

Urso took a deep breath and, for a moment, I thought it presaged an explosion, but he exhaled and his tone was tired as he admitted, "No, I don't think they will." He turned his attention back to me and pointed an accusing finger. "But you," he fumed. "You knew exactly what you were going to do to Maxentius, didn't you?" He gave a disgusted snort. "You probably planned this whole thing, and this is what you had in mind all along."

He was exactly right; this was, in fact, what I had planned and hoped would be the outcome. I knew that I could not kill Maxentius without running a huge risk to myself, but neither did I want to look over my shoulder the rest of my time under the standard. Frankly, I had planned on crippling him by smashing his left elbow joint, but then he presented me with an opportunity that I could not pass up. Now, he was in the hospital and missing an arm from just above the elbow, the doctors saying that there was no way to save the arm. And I was in the office of the Primus Pilus, waiting as he decided my fate.

Seeing that he was expecting some sort of response, I said, "That's not true, Primus Pilus. Maxentius is...or *was*," I could not resist adding this, and I saw Corvinus' head suddenly drop as he looked away, "the best man with a sword in the Cohort. How could I have possibly planned what happened? I just wanted to prove to him that, if not as good as he was, I'm at least good enough that he'd leave me alone."

Urso made no response, but I could see that I had scored a point with this argument, even if it was a lie.

Finally, he sighed, "Be that as it may, you still have crippled a veteran Legionary, and that's not just a loss to your Cohort, or to the Legion. It's a loss to Rome. Which means that Augustus will undoubtedly hear about it."

My blood froze; this had not even occurred to me. Now Urso smiled, but it was not a pleasant one.

"And, given your family's history with the Princeps, I can see where this might be…problematic for you. And your father."

It took all of my self-control not to stagger backward, yet somehow, I managed to maintain my composure, and I was forced to offer a bitter but silent salute to Urso for knowing my weak spot and exploiting my fear in this way. He did not say anything more at that moment, just sat looking up at me, regarding me.

Finally, he said, "I have a lot to think about. You're dismissed, for now. But," he pointed at me again, "you're confined to your hut until I decide. Is that understood?"

I gave my answer, then rendered my salute and turned to exit. Corvinus started to get up out of his chair, but I assume Urso stopped him with a gesture.

"No, you stay here," he commanded my Pilus Prior. "We have a lot to talk about."

Returning to my section hut, I was somewhat relieved to see that it was empty, and I vaguely remembered that our Century had been scheduled for a work detail of some sort in town. Stripping off my *segmentata*, I found that my tunic was plastered to me, and I automatically started to head to the baths, then stopped. I was not sure if Urso meant I could not bathe, but I was not going to chance it. Calls of nature I had to assume were allowed; I could not imagine him wanting me to urinate or defecate in our hut, and I knew my comrades would certainly not stand for it. Rubbing myself down as best I could, I changed my tunic, then lay down on my bunk, sure that my mind would be much too busy for any sleep. I was wrong, and my next memory is a hand shaking my foot.

"Pullus! For fuck's sake, wake up!"

I jerked awake, chagrined that I had actually fallen asleep, seeing Asinius standing at the foot of my bunk. I sat up, but before I could say anything, he thrust a huge hunk of bread, a small stopper of oil, and a ball of cheese at me.

"Here, I bet you're hungry."

In fact, I was, and I got up and sat down at the table, consuming what he had given me in silence as he sat on the bench next to me. Finally finished, I turned on the bench to face him.

"Well?" I asked.

"Well what?"

I was in no mood for being teased, and I said as much.

"Actually, there's so much going on with you that I'm not sure where to begin."

"If you're trying to make me feel better, you're not doing very well." I was only partially joking.

"Nor was that my intention," he retorted. Then, "Which part do you want to hear about first?"

I considered, then asked, "How's the Century taking it?"

"Actually, not badly," he admitted, which relieved me a great deal. "I always knew a lot of men didn't like Maxentius. I had no idea how much a lot of them hated him."

That was heartening, and I said as much.

"Oh, a couple of the men of his section were making trouble," he told me. "But they got straightened out pretty quickly. They know that more of the men see you as a hero than someone who needs to be punished."

"Which ones?" I asked, although I was sure I knew their identities.

Asinius was adamant in his response, poking me with a finger as he said, "You don't need to worry about who. You just need to know that they won't make any trouble."

"That's good," I acknowledged. "Gods know I don't need more trouble than I already have."

"Urso?" he asked me.

I nodded, then added grimly, "He made mention of my father, and telling Augustus."

Asinius whistled.

"I can see why you're worried." He thought for a moment, then shook his head. "But unfortunately, I think it's a possibility."

"Thanks," I said sourly. "You're very encouraging."

"Do you want me to lie to you?"

"Actually," I replied. "Yes, in this case. I would love it if you lied to me."

"Oh, well then." He turned cheerful, then slapped me on the back. "You're going to be fine. There's nothing to worry about!"

I glared at him, and was just about to open my mouth when we both heard movement outside the hut, then the door opened without anyone knocking. Galens was standing there, his face impassive.

"Pullus, come with me," he ordered. "The Pilus Prior needs to talk to you."

"What?? When?"

I stared at Corvinus in disbelief and a fair amount of anxiety, but I found nothing comforting in his face.

"Immediately," he answered the last question first. "In fact, as soon as we're done, you're going to pack your gear and report there."

"But...why?" I was completely bewildered, but there was nothing in the face of the Pilus Prior that brought me any answers, or comfort.

"I don't know why, and I didn't ask," he said, except I could not help noticing that he would not meet my gaze. "All I know is what I was told. You're being transferred to the First Century of the First Cohort." That was when he did look up, and I suppose he was doing what he could to soften the blow. "You know, Pullus, that when a man is transferred into the First Cohort, let alone the First Century, that's usually a compliment. It means that you're considered one of the best fighters in the Legion."

While I appreciated his attempt to cheer me up, I could not resist asking him, "Is that what you think is going on here?"

He looked away again and just shrugged. When I saw he was done, I requested permission to be excused.

I reported to the Primus Pilus, depositing all of my gear outside the Legion office. While I knew that I was going to the First of the First, it would be up to the Primus Pilus which section I was going to be in, and which hut I would occupy. I cannot say I was all that surprised when I was kept outside his private quarters for at least a third of a watch, yet somehow, I managed to remain upright and at *intente*, despite the fact that I was getting more and more fatigued by the moment. In the aftermath of my fight with Maxentius, all the energy that I had felt flowing through me had dissipated quickly. Finally, I heard him call my name and I pounded on the door to his private quarters. Again, I waited for several heartbeats before I heard him bark that I should enter. Once more, I stood in front of his desk and saluted. He was writing in a wax tablet and did not look up for a bit, until he was finished, then closed the tablet shut.

"You have all your gear?" he asked abruptly.

I assured him that I did, but he did not seem impressed.

"Fronto will be the judge of that," he said.

Fronto was his Optio and, while not feared as deeply as the men feared Urso, it was close.

"In fact, Fronto is going to be spending quite a bit of time with you. Just to make sure that you're worthy of marching in the First Cohort, you understand."

He watched my face intently, but I managed to suppress my natural inclination to anger at what I saw as a slur on my abilities, understanding that he was waiting for such a thing. Seeing that I was not rising to the bait, he seemed disappointed.

"Anyway," he finally said, "you're going to be here in my Cohort, and in my Century, where I can keep an eye on you. Because you seem to have an insubordinate streak in you. But we'll fix that." He chuckled; I was not inclined to join in.

Staring at me for another stretch of time, he finally waved a dismissal at me, but I did not move.

"Well?" He glowered at me. "What now?"

"Sir." I tried not to stammer. "What section am I supposed to be in?"

I will say that he had the grace to look embarrassed at his oversight, and he muttered, "Ah, yes. That. You're going to be in the First Section."

For a moment, I was sure I had misheard him.

"First Section, sir?" I managed.

"Yes, First Section," he snapped. "I don't stutter."

"No, sir," I assured him. "It's just that…isn't that where the most experienced men should be?"

"No," he shot back. "Whoever I say is in the front line is in the front line. Besides," he finally smiled, but it was without any humor, "you just proved you were the best man in the Legion with a sword. Or have you forgotten already?"

Realizing there was no real right answer, I replied, "No, sir. I mean, yes, sir. I mean, no, I haven't forgotten, sir."

"That's all. Go to the first section hut and report to Gnaeus Philo. He's the Sergeant of the section."

Saluting, I turned to go, but just as I reached the door, he stopped me, and I realized this was a favorite trick of his.

"You want to know why you're really here, Pullus?" he asked so softly I was not sure I heard correctly.

The truth is, I was not at all sure I wanted to know, but I told him that I did.

"I suppose I should tell you at least that much, given who your father is," he began and, for the first time, he actually looked somewhat uncomfortable, and I wondered if mention of my father prompted it. But then he looked up, his expression back to the hard look I had come to expect. "You're mine now, Pullus."

"Sir?" I tried to sound confused, but the sudden lead ball in my stomach said I understood him perfectly well.

"You're going to work for me," he said reasonably. "After all, I have to replace Maxentius with someone and, given how easily you handled him, it might as well be you. So, as of now, you're one of the men who I use for…various purposes." He smiled at this, I suppose, because of the vague way he put that I was now one of those men he used for muscle.

"And if I refuse?" I asked quietly.

The smile froze, and suddenly there was a glitter to his eyes that I will remember for the rest of my life because, in them, I saw that he was truly one of the most dangerous men I had ever met.

"If you refuse, your life will be measured in watches." His tone was matter-of-fact, as if he was merely relaying the count of chickpeas in the Legion stores instead of the end of my life.

"But, if that's not enough incentive, then consider this." He leaned forward, and his gaze was so piercing that I do not think I could have looked away from him, even though I desperately wanted to do so. "I wasn't joking about how Augustus would react if he were to learn the identity of the Gregarius who crippled one of my best men. You of all people should know that he has a very, very long memory and, while he may have overlooked the fact that your adoptive grandfather had a lot more money than he originally thought when he first confiscated it, he never makes the same mistake twice. What do you think he would do to your entire family if he were to learn about that?"

Two things happened in the next moment. The first was my realization that, as strong and skilled as I might have been, I lived at the whim of the man sitting before me. Worse, so did my family, and anything I did to cross him would mean the cost would be borne not just by me, but my entire family. The second, following instantly on the heels of the first was that, as much as I hated Maxentius, it was a shade compared to how I felt about Primus Pilus Canidius, yet as dangerous as Maxentius was, he was a shade compared to Urso. Consequently, before I left his office, I assured him that I would do his bidding, in whatever manner he saw fit.

This was how I ended up in the First Century, First Cohort of the 8th Legion, under the command of a man who controlled my destiny even more thoroughly than a Primus Pilus does normally. My reception into the First Section was, as one might expect, guarded, but as I quickly found out, it was more than fighting ability that got my comrades into the First Century. And the First Section consisted of men selected for more than just their handiness with a sword, but for their total loyalty to Urso. Consequently, I felt more like I was under guard and under watch than serving under the standard. At least, at first. I did manage to slip away the day after I was officially transferred, seeking out Corvinus, who was understandably reluctant to meet with me, but to his credit, he did.

"Isn't there anything you can do?"

Even I could hear the begging tone of my voice, but I had never been this desperate.

"It's too late, Pullus." He shook his head, and if his distress was feigned, it fooled me. "There's no way that I can get you back into the Fourth Cohort. You made Urso too angry."

"So I'm going to be dead soon," I said bitterly, but to my surprise, he shook his head again.

"No," he replied emphatically. "He's not going to kill you. As bad as he may be, I do think he respects your father. But," he warned, "that's only if you show him you're loyal."

"To him," I retorted. "Not to the Legion."

"To Urso, they're one and the same thing." Corvinus shrugged. "And maybe he's right. The truth is, I don't know anymore. Things just aren't the way they used to be."

"And this means that if I work for Urso, I work for Tiberius," I mused, not aware I had said it aloud.

At least, until he agreed, "More or less, that's true. But there are worse men to follow."

I stared at Corvinus, not sure what meaning his words held.

"Not you too," I protested, but he waved it away.

"That's the way things are, Pullus. Especially in the Legions. We're the power that makes the First Man, and we choose who wins and who loses." Sighing, he took a sip of his wine before he continued, "It's been that way since your grandfather and the 10th switched sides at Actium."

"They didn't switch sides," I retorted angrily. "They were never given the choice! My grandfather didn't want to march for Antonius in the first place!"

"That's not how Augustus sees it," he replied quietly.

That was when I realized it had not been a random thing when Corvinus mentioned the 10th Equestris and its role in the second civil war. I also recognized the point he was making.

"Fair enough," I finally said. All I could do was give my own shrug and finish, "I suppose I have to make the best of it, then."

"That's all any of us can do, Pullus. We have to deal with the roll of the dice the gods give us, and make do with it the best way we can. And that's especially true for you." He pointed at me. "Now, get out of here before your absence is noticed."

When I had the chance, I sent my father a letter, telling him about the campaign, and the fact that I had been decorated by Drusus. But when I came to the part about my "promotion" into the First of the First, I thought long and hard before deciding that I would have to bring it up, but give him the impression that it had been done for the best possible reason, and not for the real one. Our mail is delivered regularly, and it is of such a quantity that I supposed it was possible that it would arrive unnoticed in Arelate. Regardless, I was not willing to take that risk. Maxentius was in the hospital for two weeks, then was discharged; one-armed Legionaries are of no use to Rome. According to those few men who went to visit him afterward, he was a broken man, barely able to summon the energy to talk to them, let alone learn how to do for himself with one hand. Perhaps three months later, around the beginning of the next year, which was of the Consulships of Gaius Marcus Censorinus and Gaius Asinius Gallus, word came that Maxentius had managed to learn how to use his left hand well enough to slice open his veins. Even now, I have no regrets for what I did to him, and I certainly did not lose any sleep when word came of his suicide. He had been an enemy of mine and, while I had not sought it out, when the time came, I made sure I prevailed in our battle. I never retaliated against the two comrades of Maxentius who helped him in the attack on me in Mogontiacum, considering them as little more than the tools of Maxentius in the same way as his sword was. As far as Tubero, his luck ran out not long after Maxentius. He did not show up for morning formation after a night out in Siscia and he was not found for two days, when his corpse was discovered in a pig sty that has served as a good disposal spot for bodies for many years, going back even to when I was a child living in Siscia. His throat was cut and, in addition, his tongue had been cut out, but that was never found. His killer has never been found either, and I doubt that he will be. The fact that it was perhaps a week after I finally had earned the trust of the Primus Pilus to be allowed to go into town without being accompanied is just a coincidence.

And that is all I have time to relate at this moment. We are about to go back out on campaign and, as a Centurion, I have much to do and make sure is done before we march. There is a revolt in Illyricum, and the natives there are going to taste the iron, as we like to say. I will do my duty to Rome, as my father and grandfather before me, and if the gods will it and I survive, I will continue the tradition started by Titus Pullus in leaving a record behind of the men of the Legions of Rome, and tell my story.

52436257R00219

Made in the USA
Lexington, KY
29 May 2016